In the Service of Their Country

In the Service
of Their Country

WAR RESISTERS IN PRISON

Willard Gaylin, M.D.

THE VIKING PRESS

NEW YORK

To the women in my life:
Betty, Jody, Ellen, Fay, and Anne

First published in 1970 by The Viking Press, Inc.
625 Madison Avenue, New York, N.Y. 10022

Published simultaneously in Canada by
The Macmillan Company of Canada Limited

SBN 670-39699-0

Library of Congress catalog card number: 70-104155

Printed in U.S.A. by The Colonial Press Inc.

AUTHOR'S NOTE

To protect the anonymity of the prisoners I have changed the proper names, places, locales, occupations of parents, details of family structure, physical descriptions of home, physical descriptions of the men themselves, etc. Any changes offend the scientific observer in me, and I have tried to retain the flavor and the spirit of the original. By making these minor changes I have been freed to quote the interviews at their most personal and in their exact words. The narrations, therefore, will be readily identifiable by the narrators themselves, and it is typical of the trust and courage of this group that I was granted by all—indeed, encouraged by all—to use their stories in any way I might find useful.

ACKNOWLEDGMENTS

I owe more than this book to the men in prison. Had they not demonstrated the courage, honesty, and simple generosity to talk so fully, so freely, and so trustingly to a once stranger, there would, of course, be no book. But the greater loss for me would have been the deprivation of the privilege and joy that have come from knowing these gentle felons.

That I was capable of seeing them at all was a reflection of the respect for inquiry and the willingness to be exposed to criticism that have characterized the Federal Bureau of Prisons and its Director, Myrl E. Alexander. John Conrad, then Director of Research, shattered all my stereotypes about "bureaucrats."

A man of great charm and knowledge, he and his entire staff were cooperative beyond any real obligation.

My interests in the area of psychiatry and the law have been sustained over the years by the encouragement of Dr. Lawrence C. Kolb, Chairman of the Department of Psychiatry, Columbia University. The specific research from which this book was drawn was facilitated by the generosity of Mrs. Elizabeth K. Dollard, whose enthusiasm for the project, early a matter of faith, was deeply appreciated.

I would like to give private thanks to all those (the Rev. E's and Dr. B's) who, for purposes of anonymity, I cannot publicly acknowledge, but who must know my gratitude.

To my colleagues at the Institute for Society, Ethics, and the Life Sciences, my thanks for those opportunities for informal consultation which characterize such a group.

In the serendipitous fashion that has characterized my life, I managed to find (be found by, is more accurate) a combination critic-champion-coach-comforter, a cream puff disguised as an editor—Beatrice Rosenfeld, I love you.

Now what shall I say about my wife on this single page of manuscript which she has not read, criticized, edited, rewritten, and typed—five or more times? There is no way of "acknowledging" her contribution to this book and the research on which it was based, any more than I can "acknowledge" her contributions to my life. For this book is but one small aspect of that life of which she is truly co-author—and indispensable collaborator.

Contents

In the Service of Their Country

1 «‹‹‹·

The Great Mandala

In the beginning all wars are popular. In the beginning they do not really exist. When war is only an idea it is a romantic idea. It restores to the adult that heroic proportion that leaves life with adolescence. All of us like the idea of standing up for the right, and it is the idea we are talking about, not the discommoding fact. If virtue comes free, virtue is common.

But even from the beginning the Vietnamese "engagement" seemed different. It was accepted, never embraced, and then only by that generation secured by age from intimate involvement. To the young it was, early, anathema, and even when the student was protected by draft deferment it dominated his existence. Like some enormous, expanding, obscene lump in the middle of his room, it could be walked around but not avoided. Always present, crowding everything else into the periphery, demanding more and more attention, distorting scale and value.

I am not a historian. I do not know if this war is unique, but as a psychoanalyst I know it is uniquely unsettling to the current generation of young men. It is remote and ill-defined for them. Its purpose is at best, obscure, at worst, humiliating. It is stripped of romance. (No songs are written to celebrate it.) It is unheroic. (The pictures of Vietcong prisoners always seem more touching than menacing.) It is dirty—worse, dull. It is unreal. It dominates their lives but doesn't exist for them.

It is hypocritical. The middle-class father defends the morality of the war while making sure his middle-class son is protected from its consequences; so school is converted into sanctuary, but in so doing school is destroyed, for sanctuary becomes prison. Only with the cashing in of middle-class IOUs has the "rightness" of the war been reconsidered.

It is corrupting. For those who cannot claim religious objection (the only kind acceptable in an essentially irreligious society), only dishonesty pays. Claim to be a homosexual: be one. Claim to be an addict: be one. Claim to be psychotic: become. For in the process pretense can become reality.

But be not afraid. For the most part only the poor and ignorant suffer loss of life. The privileged suffer only loss of pride, pleasure, dignity, youth, and innocence.

With time, of course, there are no privileged. In September 1967 I was approached by a friend who was concerned about his only son. He was a graduate student, and when the draft was revised to deny deferment for graduate study, he dropped out, his sole motivation for advanced study having been eliminated. He was now eligible for induction and unalterably opposed to the war. He was not a religious objector or a pacifist opposed to wars in general. He would not lie (he later did) and therefore realized that the only course open to him was to go to jail or flee the country.

The father approached me as both a friend and an "expert." He wanted facts, or at least a professional estimation as to the potential harmful effects of each of the two alternatives. He was not asking me what course his son should take (he was too sophisticated for that), but which would be better from a psychological standpoint.

It was a reasonable question, logically directed to precisely the person who should be expected to know the answer. I was a psychoanalyst and as such a presumed expert on human behavior and environmental influence. My special field of interest was in the application of psychoanalytic concepts to social problems. I had even written articles about psychiatry and the law. Yet I was totally unequipped to present any intelligent answer.

The question is not a simple one. Superficially it might seem that leaving the country would make more sense. Life in Canada cannot be that different from life in the United States. While Toronto is different from Boston, it is probably less different than Los Angeles is, and different does not mean worse. But even a cursory examination of the problem exposes the complexities. To choose to leave is different from having to leave. It is the difference between volition and duress; between reaching out and running from; between courage and cowardice (depending on that notoriously unreliable capacity to fix or trust one's own motives). There is also a finality about such cutting of ties, roots, loyalties, and associations that haunts the exile. The concept that you can't go home again, ever again, tends to romanticize the concept called "home." It now becomes a standard, and everything is judged in terms of its distance or deviation from that idealized norm.

Imprisonment could have psychological advantages. It is clearly an act of will, of assertion, and defiance. It can be seen as an act of heroism and independence, particularly to the age group involved, where belief in the former is still not abandoned and confidence in the latter is still not established. It is clearly "standing up," but at what price. The pivotal information necessary even to attempt an answer involves an understanding of the nature of imprisonment. Before one can know what imprisonment does, one must know what imprisonment is.

I had never spent one hour within the walls of any penal institution. My subjective impression of prison was formed by too much exposure, at too early an age, to too many Saturday matinées at the movies. Prison to me was a mélange of cons and screws (do they still use those words? did they ever?); of riots and "shivs"; of Pat O'Brien, clerical and calm; of Jimmy Cagney, defiant; and Frank McHugh, contrite; of tin spoons banging against tin cups; and of one solitary Negro crooning soft spirituals to an otherwise pure white population.

Balancing this was a limited intellectual conception based on those few articles on prison reform, rehabilitation, and so forth that I had chanced upon. While I knew prisons were unlikely to be as pictured by Warner Bros. (they had let me down badly on college life), my knowledge of the conditions in institutions in general indicated that prisons were likely to be a long way from the ideal. I began to read the available literature on prison life, the meaning and purpose of imprisonment, the intended and actual impact of imprisonment, and I began wondering on what facts those war resisters who had elected to go to prison based their decisions. For them it was no theoretical decision, but two to five years of life.

I could find no research on the imprisoned war resister in the literature and assumed that some studies must be in progress. I inquired of the Bureau of Prisons as to who was currently doing research in this area. To my amazement I found that no one was, at least not officially. Even such pertinent information as to the number of imprisoned objectors, what percentage of the total draftable population they were; their racial and religious backgrounds; their stated reasons for choosing prison—none of these had been tabulated. For historical reasons, let alone sociological ones, a statistical survey at least was indicated. Moreover, with the growing resistance to the war by the end of 1967, with the prospect of an increasing number of men choosing imprisonment over service in the armed forces, it would seem crucial for the future as well as for the present crisis to know more than just the statistics. Who were they in personality terms? What factors influenced their decisions? What were their motives? What were the determinants within and without each individual that shaped his course of action? This kind of material must be studied at the time of its happening to be at all fruitful. If it is studied after the fact and approached historically, the group is dissipated and no longer amenable to direct examination in a statistically or psychologically meaningful way.

With this in mind I decided that I was going to research the problem.

It is customary for research to start with a research proposal. Half promise, half puff, and all pitch, an elaborately constructed proposal is usually directed toward one of the hundreds of foundations that provide funds for, and therefore in great part determine the nature of, scientific and sociological research. I decided not to apply for a grant from a large fund primarily because of time and a sense of urgency. The preparation and processing of a proposal for the National Institutes of Health has been known to take longer than the performance of the proposed research.

There were other reasons. Psychoanalysts have traditionally financed their own research. In the early days research paid for itself since all research was a derivative of, and incidental to, psychoanalytic treatment. The patient in treatment was willy-nilly a research subject, educating the doctor at the same time he was re-educating himself. The very open-endedness of the procedure made it enormously productive. To look too closely and too single-mindedly in one direction in this kind of research would often serve to blind one from recognizing more rewarding, unpredicted information from unexpected sources in uncharted areas.

The psychoanalyst, however, was often guilty of ignoring design and structure in research areas where they were only too relevant. The major foundations, as a result, have never been very responsive to appeals from psychoanalysts, particularly since the psychoanalyst rarely shares their passion for the "scientificalness" that statistics and measurements are presumed to accord.

The decision to bypass foundations did not mean that I was on my own. While funds were a dispensable luxury, subjects were an absolute essential, and these particular subjects were literally locked away, in what I metaphorically visualized as impregnable vaults, the keys to which were in the recesses of some bureau in Washington.

The approval of the Bureau of Prisons was essential, and I anticipated some difficulties. This was a politically volatile subject, war resistance; in a sociologically vulnerable area, the prisons; conducted by a questionably respectable type of researcher, a psychoanalyst. The proposal was simple; the rationale more complex.

I proposed to interview for five to ten hours a representative sample of the imprisoned war resisters (perhaps twenty to twenty-five) over an extended period (perhaps the entire length of their imprisonment), utilizing psychoanalytic concepts and techniques of interviewing.

I used the term "war resister" because among the Selective Service violators in prison were markedly disparate groups. There were draft evaders, that is, men who through fraud attempted to avoid service but who had no more specific objection to service than to any other responsibility. There were religious objectors, such as Jehovah's Witnesses, who, individually, had no objection to the war as such but who I suspected (and later confirmed) refused service as a matter of allegiance, not conscience. And there were those who for political, moral, or individual religious belief were taking a stand—those who chose prison—the war resisters.

A statistical survey of the entire population at a given date might seem a more logical beginning, but a common deficiency of large population surveys has been that only after the completion of an expensive and expansive study, often after the dissipation of the group, does it become apparent what the critical information was that should have been sought. Part of the excitement of the psychoanalytic approach to interviewing on sociological problems is the unpredictable nature of the pertinent information that is elicited. What emerges from the intensively scrutinized sample can then serve as guidelines in designing an intelligent survey of the total population.

Since psychoanalysis is so predominantly perceived as a form

of treatment, it is often forgotten that it is also a potent explora-
tory device in determining a person's attitudes, conceptions, prejudices, expectations, fears, aspirations, frustrations, resentments.
While none of the prisoners would be placed "in analysis," some
of the same techniques for getting information could be adapted
for a diagnostic or evaluative set of interviews. What are some of
these techniques?

The psychoanalytic interview is essentially "non-directive"—
which is already a misnomer. What it really means is that the direction of the interview is primarily dictated by the person interviewed rather than by the interviewer. The very direction chosen
is the first step in self-exposure. It may seem a discursive and
uneconomic approach. Questions and answers always seem so
much more direct, so much more informational. But a questionnaire not only defines that which is included, but also that which
will be excluded. To think one knows the appropriate questions
to ask is to presume too much in a psychological survey. In addition, how should one value the answers?

It is over seventy-five years since Freud discovered that it is
only when you stop asking questions that the truth emerges.
When you question someone as to personal feelings, the answers
you get are most likely to be what he thinks he should feel, what
he would like to feel, or what he thinks is prestigious to feel—
and only accidentally what he really feels.

Sociologists are dependent on sampling population, but the sophisticated ones have long since been disillusioned by direct
question and answer, and, while not trained in psychoanalytic interviewing, they have other methods. Direct observation and
behavior correlation prove much more reliable. A measurement
of the number of trips a man makes from his desk to the bathroom, the water cooler, the coffee shop on the ground floor; of
the number of accidents he has; of the number of illnesses he
has; of the number of personal telephone calls he makes—all
would be far more reliable indicators of his interest in work than
his answer to the question, "Are you interested in your work?"

Ask any group of typical Americans in direct polling what is most important in his selection of an automobile—safety, styling, or power—and safety will win hands down. But the Detroit motor executive, in all his wisdom, becomes rich by producing unsafe, flashy, and powerful automobiles. In a recent poll published in the newspapers, the vast majority of people indicated that whether a candidate was a Negro or a Jew would affect his voting not at all. Party leaders know better. In the area of opinions and beliefs the reliability of question and answer is so poor that few social scientists still credit the specific answers given. (This makes it particularly distressing that pollsters have entered blithely into this area, and that politicians are accepting these "opinions" as valid determinants for public policy!)

With a non-directive approach and patience, the individual will eventually get around to telling you all the facts you might elicit via questions—his age, siblings, life history—and in the way of telling, the order of telling, the emotion of telling, he tells you more than the facts. If he omits a significant area, you are always free to question and have as a bonus the significance of the omission itself. Since everything is selected by the interviewee, everything exposes him.

The various sources of information available to the psychoanalyst in the course of an open-ended interview are so numerous that they warrant a book in themselves (a project that is begging to be done). For our purposes here, let me mention briefly the most significant and broadest informational sources—and allow more detailed points to be observed as they emerge in the actual interviews.

First, there is the verbalized material of the interview: the expressed facts and opinions. As has been indicated, verbalizations reveal more than this; by emphasis, associations, expressions, they also expose tacit feelings and opinions. Moreover, the various qualities of the verbalizations, independent of content, reveal the person. We all have a different image of the woman from whom words pour like water from a faucet and of the man who measures words like pennies pried from a change purse. The analyst utilizes all aspects of verbal communication: the voice quality; the nature of the speaking (hesitant, whining, seductive); the degree of fluency; the degree of spontaneity; the breadth of vocabulary; the nature of vocabulary (florid, sparse, pretentious); the purpose of speech (to intimidate, ingratiate); stammers; ticks; hesitations; slips of the tongue; and on and on and on. Even on the simplest level of content, however, the psychoanalyst will define facts in a special way with a special emphasis.

In addition to verbal communication, the emotions speak to an interviewer: the range of emotions; the quality; the degree and depth of emotionality; the capacity to expose emotion, to share it, to elicit it in the interviewer. (I always ask my students at the psychoanalytic clinic whether they "like" the patients they interview, and while students are often offended by the subjectivity of the word, their answers invariably say something about the nature of the patient—as well as themselves.) Does the interviewee see emotion as a strength to be used or as a weakness to be controlled? Is he aware of his own emotionality? How attuned is he to others (the interviewer)?

The defenses of the individual, so important in understanding the quality of ego and the nature of patterned behavior, are a principal focus in a psychoanalytic interview and ignored in most others. When threatened or challenged, does the individual use projection, rationalization, denial, isolation? Does he lie or confess? Ingratiate or attack? It is not just the nature of the defense but also the repertoire, the strength, and the limits of the defenses that count.

To test the defensive structure the interviewer will often place the subject under stress. At the crudest level this can be done by baiting him to see how much it takes to make him angry. How does he handle his anger? Will he expose it (to himself, to the interviewer)? Will he be frightened of it? guilty? ashamed? This approach has recently been publicized as the "stress interview." Usually a psychoanalyst will avoid a direct attack or provocation, which, in any case, is rarely necessary. More often than not, the patient with his transparent needs will advertise his anxieties, and stress will be produced merely by refusing to give the normally expected responses to tacit pleas for reassurance. For example, with a person who is particularly and obviously anxious to please, all that may be necessary to produce stress is to withhold the normal amount of head nodding, clucking, smiling, and yessing that we all routinely use to indicate "we understand."

Still another very special source of information that has been pre-eminently the property of the psychoanalysts is dream interpretation. Not much can be said about this that would be convincing to the unsophisticated and doubting short of a treatise. I am afraid that it will have to be here accepted on faith (or dismissed out of hand) that dreams have meanings and that these meanings are the truest, most objective indicators of the emotional state.

Part of the reason that a psychoanalyst prefers an interviewing schedule extended over time—that is, two hours a week for three weeks rather than six hours at a stretch—is to permit the recording and analysis of dreams. Equally important, however, is to encourage the development and observation of the transference, the final source of data-gathering that I will discuss here.

Transference is in many ways a summation of all the others. It is sometimes loosely used to mean any emotional responses the patient has to the analyst (as counter-transference is used to mean the emotional response elicited in the analyst). Its meaning is usually extended to encompass the nature of the total relationship that the patient enters into with the analyst. Its importance rests in part on the underlying assumption that the patient will impose on the essentially neutral interviewer the preconceived attitudes and sets formed by the patient in his early relations with parental figures. It is a tricky business, because the analyst does have to compensate for the fact that no interviewer is really a neutral figure and his input will affect the relationship too.

Nonetheless it is always a fresh amazement to observe the distortions that occur in the subjective appraisal of the analyst even in cold, hard, objective areas. I have had patients see me as twenty years older than I am and ten years younger, six inches taller and four inches shorter, a slob and a dandy. When it comes to personality appraisals, they will range from Charlie Brown to Adolf Hitler.

The transference has an additional value. It is the only area in which the analyst has firsthand knowledge. He experiences it rather than hears about it. Everything else is told by the patient as viewed through that astigmatic lens each man reserves for his own behavior, filtered through the selective medium of memory, and screened by the ever protective ego. Of course, in time, the analyst learns to compensate for the degree and nature of any particular person's distortion, so the hysteric's "unbearable" is translated as "annoying," while the stoic's "discomfort" means "pain," but the transference is the real mirror of truth. Moreover, it supplies a variety of other dividends. Take one example: if a patient sees himself as trusting and behaves consistently in a guarded manner, you have not only corrected your view of his openness but have learned in addition something of his insight.

These, then, are a few of the investigative devices used by an analyst to uncover an individual's history, feelings, perceptions, and behavior. How that information is to be interpreted is an altogether different matter, raising altogether different problems.

Psychoanalysis approaches all behavior in terms of the psychodynamic concept; that is, any piece of behavior is seen as a resultant of many forces and counterforces. The behavior can never be understood as a thing in itself but rather as a compromise among influences. Moreover, it is rooted in the past, and what one does at a particular moment is determined by all the previous experiences that have been programmed in. The given act is therefore merely the end point of a sequence of behavior preceding it. These determinants are never fully known by anyone, so that man's behavior is influenced by many thoughts and feelings and motives of which he is unaware (and obviously by some of which he is aware).

This concept of the unconscious offers a new source of information and a new perceptual model for understanding man. And here an unfortunate distortion has been introduced. There is a tendency (particularly elaborated by psychoanalytic biographers) to think of the "inner" man as the real man and the "outer" man as illusion or pretender. But the unconscious represents only *another* view, not a truer one. Though a man may not always be what he appears to be, what he appears to be is always a significant part of what he is. To probe for the unconscious determinants of his behavior and then define him in these terms exclusively, ignoring his overt behavior, distorts the view more grossly than does ignoring the unconscious altogether. The saint may in his unconscious behavior be compensating for and denying destructive unconscious impulses identical to those which we see the sinner acting out. But the similarity of unconscious constellation in the two men matters precious little since it will not distinguish Attila from St. Francis. In short, a knowledge of the unconscious life of a man is an invaluable adjunct to understanding his behavior. It is not a substitute for his behavior in understanding *him*.

This brings up another unfortunate distortion that inevitably fuddles reason when approaching psychoanalytic material. There is a tendency to think of "psychodynamic" and "psychopathologic" as identical terms. If we discover complex symbolic reasons rooted in infancy and childhood that have been determinants in a man's going to jail rather than into the Army, that does not *per se* make his going to jail a neurotic action, for we would find equally intricate unconscious factors that determined another man's decision to go into the Army. It is the psychoanalytic assumption, remember, that *all* behavior is psychodynamically determined. There is that infuriating and erroneous tendency of both psychoanalysts and lay people to see the unconscious determinants as somehow discrediting the conscious action. I suppose this is a residue of the fact that traditionally the exposure of the unconscious has been incidental to and in the service of psychotherapy. There we start with a neurotic symptom and work back to discover its origins. While I am utilizing a similar method, I do not in advance define going to jail as a neurotic symptom.

Psychoanalysis can be utilized in social research in at least two broad ways. Psychoanalytic interviewing techniques can be used to elicit data that can then be ordered or interpreted in many ways. Or data collected by any method (psychoanalytic or otherwise) can be used to make psychological interpretations of behavior. In this book I am using psychoanalytic methods primarily as investigative and explorative tools, to garner information from which essentially sociological conclusions will be drawn—conclusions that are social, political, moral, what have you.

I decided to take the calculated risk of taping the interviews. If this proved too threatening or too inhibiting it could be discontinued. (It was not.) My original purpose was to avoid the distortion that reconstructed notes might introduce when involved with a relatively few interviews over a long period of time. I wanted a fixed and detailed record—particularly since what was significant might not become apparent until after a considerable period had elapsed. It freed me from assuming the pretentious posture of the note-taker.

The value and impact of the tapes went well beyond the original intent. When I started the project I anticipated publishing my results (with emphasis on specific psychoanalytic conclusions) in technical journals. I had no idea of publishing a book for the general reader. My interest was purely intellectual, not emotional. But then I had not met these young men. I had not seen the walls of a prison. I had not measured the brevity of time in which youth can be lost and hope abandoned. I came as an observer and left as a participant. My involvement with these men has enriched me, and because of the tapes (with their words intact—often unliterary and always honest) I am able to offer the same privilege to others—to share the passion, the sacrifice, the witness of some men of principle.

So there was my plan, my rationale, and my method. It only remained for "The Bureau" (always described that way by my colleagues who had "served time" as prison psychiatrists—and visualized by me as something akin to Kafka's Castle) to open the door and let me in. That is precisely what they did.

There was some backing and filling, checking of credentials and seeking of reassurances ("No, I do not anticipate rushing off in a couple of weeks to *Ramparts* magazine"). In light of the volatility of the subject and the vulnerability of government employees, caution could be understood, and while it would have been difficult to give a flat no to a respectable researcher from a university, he could be bound and gagged in bureaucratic red tape until exhaustion overcame desire. Such was not the case. John Conrad, Research Chief for the Bureau of Prisons, turned out to be a man of uncommon intelligence and dedication, and I was at all times treated by his staff in Washington with courtesy, cooperation, and friendliness. At the prisons, the situation was different.

2 ⋘

Down the Rabbit Hole

For the purposes of the research it was necessary to
have a representative sample of those who were in prison. If Selective Service violators were assigned to particular prisons on
the basis of special conditions or types, it would be necessary to
arrange the research so that a sampling of each institution could
be made. Inquiry indicated that assignment to a prison is primarily dictated by geographical proximity to home. This simplified
my task.

The research was conducted in two separate institutions which
I shall call Crestwood and Oakdale. Since the total population of
war resisters in both institutions was less than thirty, I was relieved of the task of devising a sample population. I simply included all of them. Visiting two distinct prisons, while not contributing to the understanding of war resisters, certainly helped
me in understanding imprisonment.

I was directed to start my research at Crestwood. It was presumably selected for its convenience, but primarily, I suspect,
because it would be more receptive to this type of research than

the other institution and was seen as a relatively more congenial atmosphere for my initiation into prison life.

Federal prisons tend to be in relatively inaccessible locations. They are poorly advertised in the communities in which they are placed and tucked away from sight like some embarrassing relative who cannot be disowned but should not be displayed. I arrived in the town in which Crestwood is located expecting to find signs directing me to the U. S. Penitentiary, certainly one of the leading claims to recognition of this particular city. I saw many signs directing me to the business district, an area of no distinction, to the local hospital, of which I had never heard, and to the interstate bypass road, but nary a sign indicating the existence of a federal penitentiary. It became necessary to stop and inquire, and I was immediately given directions by the first passerby.

Though the directions were accurate, I passed by the entrance to the prison. The sign was so genteel and discreet—it merely said "Federal Correctional Institution" in small letters. The building itself was placed well off the road on the slope of a hill and, being colored a dull green, seemed to get lost on the horizon. As I drove up the entrance road I was impressed by the tidiness of the grounds.

Crestwood was built in 1940 as a prison for intermediate-security prisoners, who, because of the nature of their offenses, their personalities, their strong community ties, the shortness of their sentences, or the fact that they are near the end of their sentences, are considered to represent only moderate risk in terms of behavior and escape. Crestwood has a present population of 750 inmates although its optimum population in 650. The average length of a sentence at Crestwood is 40.2 months. Therefore it does not require the extreme caution of a maximum-security prison and is not expected to have the problems of control in terms of obedience or violence. There are no gun emplacements, no towers, and seemingly no walls. The entire building is a rectangle enclosing a large central court. On entering the building it becomes apparent that all prisoner activities open only on the center court and the buildings themselves constitute highly effective walls. It is necessary to enter the usual space between two sets of locked, barred gates.

When I entered the outer lobby there was some confusion. The man at the gate seemed not to have been apprised of my coming despite written notification to the prison, by both the Bureau and myself, of the time of my arrival. This was to be a chronic problem. I had always pictured prisons in terms of drills, marching men, and bells—that is, with an obsessive militaristic emphasis on regimentation—but while for the prisoner regimentation was the order of the day, it was not of a militaristic fashion and coexisted with a kind of sloppiness and discoordination. This situation extended into the administration and will be discussed in some detail later.

My identity having been established, I was admitted to the area between two sliding barred gates, greeted by a prison officer, and then admitted into the body of the prison. Again I was immediately confronted by an assault on my stereotype. The courtyard was occupied with small knots of men (in fatigues, not stripes) simply lounging around, doing nothing, walking or sitting on the grass. I was also surprised by an internal reaction—I began to feel anxious.

As a psychiatrist I had worked for years in closed institutions. During my training I had been considered particularly effective on closed wards, and I had never experienced any anxiety in relation to violent patients. I had "a way with them." I am physically large, six-foot-two, and size frequently has a quieting effect on violent patients who are often most terrified of their own impulses. It gives them the reassurance that someone is there who is capable of checking their hostility.

Since I had never been fearful during my earlier experiences, I was surprised to find myself feeling fear now at Crestwood, and the feeling recurred the first half-dozen times I entered the inner prison environment. Why there should have been more of the caged, trapped feeling in a closed prison than in a closed ward of a hospital, I am not sure. It may well have been that in a mental hospital I identified with the staff whereas in the prison my identity already was with the prisoners.

I was then taken to meet the warden. The warden is a key figure in any prison. He is not just the chief administrative officer in an equivalent sense to the president of a corporation. I was impressed by the fact that the wardens of both institutions were not referred to by name. They were never called Mr. Smith or Mr. Jones. They were always called "the Warden." It was an unusual means of referral, yet it struck a familiar chord, and I recognized that it was precisely the means of reference that existed in the Navy, where the captain was always referred to as "the Captain" or "the Skipper."

There is an analogy between the two positions of captain and warden. There is a quasi-military hierarchy in the prison, and the warden has an unusual degree of autonomy from the central control of the Bureau of Prisons in day-to-day functioning. It may be that in security situations this is inevitable, that historically, like a navy ship, the prison is in a somewhat isolated situation and immediate matters of security might arise that would not allow for the leisure of consultation, although in our day of communications it is obviously not so.

The warden at Crestwood was a large, somewhat heavy man in his mid-fifties. He enjoyed talking and was pleased by the idea of having a research program going on in his prison. He reminded me of a high-school principal in both manner and looks, and indeed, there was something pedantic about his speech. He was affable and cooperative and invited me to his staff meeting, introducing me to the key figures of his staff. He suggested that I spend a day or two merely getting the feel of the institution. It was a wise suggestion and one that I followed. He had a somewhat embarrassing way of referring to me as "the professor." It was not said tongue-in-cheek but rather with the air of a man who respects education. He transmitted to those with whom I would have contact the sense that he was receptive to my being there, and that in serving me they would also be serving his interests and desires. This made for an atmosphere which I was to appreciate fully only when I had my contact later with Oakdale. I was immediately assigned an office for my use. The prison literature and records I required were made available to me.

Oakdale was quite different. It, too, was tucked away out of sight on a thousand-acre government reservation with no sign off the main highway indicating where it could be found. The approach to the main building was through a community of beautifully tended and landscaped homes—housing for the staff I was later to find out—with one particular house that could only be described by any standards as a mansion. This, as one might expect, was the warden's home.

From a distance the main building looked like a peculiar hybrid of a large city high school and armory, with the tower of the Palazzo Vecchio thrown in for good measure. As I approached the broad drive I became aware of the wall that completely enclosed the prison and the twenty-six acres it encompassed. I also became aware of the gun turrets. A small, barred gate in the massive outer wall was opened on signal and then closed behind me. I found myself in a space between two walls. Perched on high in a glass-enclosed booth was an officer who established my identity, called the guard in the main building, and opened the inner gate. I was now in the main compound. I approached the main building where a guard, seated at the reception area, pressed a button permitting me to open the heavy door and enter.

Unlike the cramped main entrance to Crestwood with its candy-vending machines and posters, the massive entrance to Oakdale—all brick, stone, and concrete, with high vaulted ceilings and a view of a small garden—was in the grand manner, reflecting the Renaissance aspirations of the depression days. I was directed to the office of the warden's secretary and then ushered into the presence of the warden. He sat behind an enormous desk in an office that was larger than any private office I have been privileged to enter.

To exploit once more the movie stereotypes, if the warden at Crestwood can be thought of as Pat O'Brien, at Oakdale he was Jimmy Cagney. A small, tense, fidgeting man who never seemed to be able to rest his eyes anywhere, he made little attempt to conceal his disdain for research, researchers, and the whole area of psychological research in particular. I knew immediately that he would be cooperative because he was ordered to be so, but his cooperation would be confined to the precise letter of the order. He turned out to be a master of the small obstacle.

He was in his mid-forties and obviously had impressed his superiors, because he had risen in the Department of Prisons at an unusually rapid pace. His forte was considered to be discipline and order, as was evidenced by the fact that during the time that I was there an informer whose life had been threatened by the Mafia was transferred from another prison to Oakdale for safe-keeping. Despite its reputation, the prisoner was murdered not too long after his arrival.

A comparison of the subject matter of my interviews with the two wardens reveals a significant amount about their differences. With the warden at Crestwood the session was devoted to his explanation of his philosophy of prison and the history of its development. He suggested a bibliography, and he traced the history of the changing attitudes toward prison from its original concept as a place of detention, to the idea of its being a form of punishment, and then to the present emphasis on its being a center for rehabilitation. He discussed his philosophy of running a prison and indicated his interest in areas of experimentation by his pride in the work-release program, a program under which selected prisoners are permitted to leave the prison during the day and work under supervision in the neighboring community. Though he expressed a liberal philosophy he exuded an air of caution and conservatism.

The Oakdale warden had no time for philosophy or history. He immediately let me know his personal way of handling difficulties. He was a no-nonsense pragmatist with a basic theory that most difficulties were manufactured by people who enjoyed difficulties.

"I believe in simplicity," he said. "If a prisoner comes in who is uncooperative he is immediately isolated, put in solitary. My concept is no work, no services. If you don't want to move yourself around and contribute your share, don't expect anything from the rest of us. So he gets no use of the educational facilities, dining-room, library, or laundry. He has to wash his own cell, wash his own clothes, gets nothing clean from us. He can live in his own slop."

He then recounted two episodes to explain his simple, pragmatic approach to problems. "There was a boy who was giving the psychiatrist some talk about his being afraid to leave his bunk. A lot of this anxiety stuff. We were having a conference about it and my attitude was, 'Let's see what this smart Harvard boy really wants to prove.' The psychiatrist started getting all excited, telling me my business, saying he thought it would be dangerous for the boy. And I said, 'Wait a minute, Doc, all you have to answer—is he of sound mind, is he legally sane.' "

The other episode had evidently just happened and was fresh in his mind. "Just the other day one of these guys collared me in the hall and said, 'Warden, they're after me.' We get that all the time, and I have a way of handling it. I said, 'You just sit there on that bench, I'm busy now, and I'll get to you as soon as I can.' Well, it's a hard bench, and after a few hours you'd be surprised, nine out of ten times they'll go back. So it couldn't have been that serious to begin with."

The warden then notified me that, except for four war resisters who were at the farm directly attached to the penitentiary, as of the date of my arrival the rest were at a work camp some fifteen miles away. I interviewed all of them once, and on finding that there seemed to be no particular difference between those assigned to the Oakdale farm and those assigned to the work camp, and since I had more than enough population for my study, I chose to use only that group of twenty-four at the work camp as my ongoing population, to save myself the logistic problem of moving back and forth.

The work camp was yet an entirely different installation from the other two. While it was directly under the control of Oakdale, it was a minimum-security set-up, housing three hundred minimum-security prisoners, and there were no walls, no gates, no fences. It was set back no more than a mile from the main highway, and in theory all that a man had to do to escape was to walk down the road to the highway.

The men were free to roam within the prescribed area of prison grounds, where there were wild berries and apple trees. They were not allowed to pick the fruit. They did so, however, and the fermentation of the fruit into liquor was one of the hobbies and one of the chief causes of discipline. The camp itself consisted of a main administration building, three dormitories, an education building, and a building for prison industries. It all had the ramshackle temporary quality of so many buildings that were put up during World War II. The camp was founded later, in 1952, and my understanding was that some of the buildings were originally considered to be temporary but, as so often happens, temporary has a way of stretching out to permanent.

The titular head of the camp was an older man, ready for retirement and dreadfully intimidated by the much younger warden. His predecessor, I was told, had been released from his position of authority and humiliated by being brought back to the main prison in a lesser status after a conflict with the warden. The difference between the Oakdale penitentiary and the other two institutions was enormous, but the work camp, despite the absence of walls, differed from Crestwood essentially only in terms of style and facility. There is one major exception to this statement—the work camp existed in the shadow of "the Wall," the term used by the prisoners for the main Oakdale institution. It was all technically one installation and therefore required no prior approval of the central authorities in Washington to move someone from the camp to the Wall. The threat of this loomed constantly over the people at the camp, for the population at the Wall, with an average time of internment of 80.5 months, contained the kind of rough, irresponsible, aggressive con that was not a significant part of the population in either of the other two institutions.

There is almost a pugnacious determination among prisoners to prove their institution is the worst. While the warden of Crestwood might sound like a more benign man than the Oakdale warden, from the prisoners' standpoint, in terms of the fundamentals, of what he was either prepared or capable of granting them, he was no more a benefactor than his counterpart, and he was equally disliked. Only the reasons for the anger and contempt differed.

Despite the reverse chauvinism each institution did have distinct advantages and disadvantages. The facilities at the work camp were the most primitive because it depended and presumably could draw on the facilities of Oakdale. However, fifteen miles was a long way, particularly when the services of a doctor were needed. Neither at Crestwood nor at Oakdale work camp were there any reasonable inside facilities for exercising. So the winter months were long periods of stagnation with little opportunity for physical activity of any sort except the perennial prison occupation of weight-lifting.

Above all, the difference in the prison environment and its impact on the prisoners were primarily quantitative, not qualitative. While there was no question that the warden set the tone for his whole staff, and consequently the level of hostility at Oakdale was much higher than at Crestwood, the problems of prison were essentially the same in all the institutions and the process of prison life followed similar patterns.

When a man is brought to a federal penitentiary he is first entered into the admission-orientation unit. This is commonly referred to as "A and O." He is given a shower, an initial physical examination, and is issued his prison clothing—work fatigues, which may be brown chinos or blue denim. During his stay here he is acquainted with the institution rules and procedures, given educational and psychological tests, sometimes including aptitude tests and always an intelligence test. The results of these tests are grossly inadequate. One young prisoner who had completed three years at a major college was classified as having a 78 IQ with a borderline intelligence. His was not the only example of obvious mistesting.

All of this is a part of the staff's attempt to evaluate the prisoner and to compile a classification study, which becomes a part of the man's permanent record. In one of the publications about Oakdale penitentiary, issued by the Bureau of Prisons, it says: "It is an accepted axiom that an accurate diagnosis must precede a cure. It is true also that before a physician can treat effectively he must know and understand the patient as well as the disease. Similarly the prison staff can train, treat, and control the inmate intelligently only if he knows all that can be determined about him. This procedure is known as classification."

The classification procedure is generally weak, partly perhaps because of the uncooperative nature of prisoners, partly because the level of professional personnel in the prisons is not of the highest order. Crestwood, for example, does not have a psychiatrist or psychologist on its permanent staff. Any who are there are attached to a special research project in narcotics.

However, none of this has any significant meaning in terms of the war resisters. In their case no pretense at rehabilitation is offered (for the most part they don't require it), and no opportunities for education are available (because of their high level). They are there purely to be punished. All the double talk cannot disguise that fact. It is evident in such things as their exclusion from the work-release program.

At Crestwood they are utilized as clerks and teachers. But at the work camp there are a significant number of "white-collar" prisoners also capable of filling clerical jobs. The war resisters are therefore assigned jobs almost at random. I say almost at random because troublesome or even potentially troublesome prisoners are not rewarded with comfortable positions. By troublesome I do not necessarily mean the most aggressive or hostile but the most politically active. In a prison environment a certain amount of aggression generally pays off better than passivity. For it must constantly be kept in mind that the major objective of a prison director is neither to rehabilitate nor to punish but to maintain order. This being so, a man is not pushed beyond the point where he may become aggressive. A man is kept at a dirty job as long as he will take it quietly.

Bill (who will be discussed in detail in chapter 6) worked for months washing pots and pans in the scullery only because he is the sort who would do any job that was assigned to him and would not offer any resistance. Johnson, a psychotic prisoner who was in jail despite official knowledge that he was schizophrenic, was an ideal kitchen worker because the passivity of the schizophrenic offers little resistance, and his complaint would produce little credibility.

On the other hand there was Robby, that marvelous original, who said to me, "I consider all the time I spend in here as dues paid and I mark it all down in my dues book. Lately I've been paying less dues. All I do now is teach music and black history. When I first came in here the camp director sent me to the general farm, which is the usual policy—that or the kitchen. I told him I wouldn't like that. It wouldn't be good for the farm, you know, and it wouldn't be good for me. I told him the only thing I wanted to do was play my drums. He told me that everyone was obliged to work, and I told him that the judge hadn't mentioned work to me, you know, and it wasn't included as part of my sentence. I told him I didn't want to work on the farm because of my great appreciation and love for animals and nature. If I were sent there and I saw any kind of mismanagement or mishandling of the animals it would upset me terribly and I would feel it's my moral responsibility to defend those animals in any way I knew how, like getting word to ASPCA. He considered it for a moment and then thought it would be best in the long run for my future rehabilitation to place me in the educational department, so all I do now is teach music. I don't have to get up and go to work in the mornings, I just do this at night."

After the period of A and O the prisoners are assigned to one of the various dormitories. At the Oakdale work camp one dorm is difficult to distinguish from another; but with the importance that minor items attain in a prison milieu, there is an established order of desirability and generally a new prisoner is assigned to the least desirable and may work his way up. There is also the feeling that the administration attempts to keep "types" together.

At Crestwood the accommodations are more variable. There is a closed section for tough homosexuals and the potentially violent, and there are more substantial differences in the dormitories. Ironically, at the highest level of priority are the old cell blocks (not kept locked), for these afford prisoners a small measure of that most precious commodity in prison—privacy. These generally are reserved, however, for men on work-release who have irregular hours of coming and going.

The dormitories in Crestwood are ridiculously overcrowded (bunks are lined up almost next to each other) and clean. The dormitories at the work camp are ridiculously overcrowded and decrepit. Being out in the fields, they have an additional unofficial population of insects and rodents. Nonetheless, it is an enormous relief for any of the conscientious objectors (COs), particularly those at Oakdale, to get out of A and O and be assigned their permanent jobs and quarters, ending the constant threat of sexual assault and violence that exists in the general population of the maximum-security prison.

The routine of daily life varies with the job of the prisoner, but certain constant features can be described. Meal hours generally are: 6:30 breakfast, 10:30 lunch, 3:30 to 4:00 dinner. The dining-rooms in both camps are cafeteria style, with plastic tables for four. The food is plentiful but high in carbohydrates (one meal included a bean soup, a stew heavy with potatoes, rice, corn-bread, and an unidentifiable cornstarch "pudding"). The quality, even by institutional standards, is not good. There are no long tables and no tin cups.

Among the privileges of prisoners are those that involve contact with the outside, and these assume enormous importance. Only authorized visitors may come. The visiting hours are determined by each warden. In each institution only three and a half hours of visits are allowed per month. This is more rigidly enforced at Crestwood than at the work camp and is a constant source of bitterness among the inmates, who use it as an example of the "phoniness" of the liberal posture of the warden. When I asked the warden why the visits were so restricted, he said it was a matter of logistics, they simply couldn't handle more. I tend to doubt that. I think it is more likely a punitive measure.

The mail is also limited to a list of authorized correspondents. Unaware of the regulation, I wrote a letter to one of the prisoners, and it was returned, marked "Not an authorized correspondent." The mail is censored. The warden insisted on calling this "spot checking." He said it was a vestige of an earlier period when censorship was extreme, and its intention was to detect escape plans and to prevent criminal activity from being conducted within the prison. He still felt it served a worth-while purpose— to indicate when people were disturbed, agitated, and heading for trouble.

I have mentioned a work-release program that is a particular source of pride to the warden at Crestwood. This permits a prisoner to go out in the community during working hours and maintain a job there. When I first asked one of the correctional officers at the prison why COs were not permitted on work-release, I was told it was because work-release was for the purpose of rehabilitation to the normal community, and these were people who did not need rehabilitation. It seemed a nonsensical answer, and when I presented the warden with this he was honest enough to dismiss it as double talk and gave his own reason. He felt that the program was extremely important and still on trial, and that it required the cooperation of the community and was very vulnerable to community pressure. He did not feel that the town would respond well to the release of war resisters. I am not sure that the townspeople would have felt any more put off by the presence of war resisters in their midst than of rapists. I think he was suggesting, once again, that for purposes of deterrence it was necessary for prison to be sufficiently punitive, and that the hawkish elements of the society at large should not be offended.

One special feature of prison life that is an important part of the reward-and-punishment system is "good time." Good time, or "good days" as they are often referred to, are days earned off one's sentence. There are four ways of earning it.

First, there is statutory good time. Everyone gets this unless he has been in trouble. It operates on a sliding scale proportionate to length of sentence, ranging from five to ten days per month.

Industrial good time is an additional two days per month and up (again depending on length of sentence), earned by working for prison industries.

Camp good time is an added bonus, starting at three days per month, given to men assigned to work camps. This is because such minimum-security installations require the most in cooperation from prisoners—and they offer the minimum in facilities. Prisoners are compensated for both aspects with additional days off.

Finally, there is meritorious good time, which allows a man who is not in industry but who performs an outstanding job to earn the same number of "good days" he would have earned in industry.

While "good days" are accumulated over years, these are never really owned by the inmates for they are capable of being withdrawn anytime until the terminal phase of a sentence. Five years of steady work earning good time can be removed for one day's infraction.

One quality of prison life that I find most difficult to describe has been labeled by one inmate "prison blah." It is a combination of ineptitude, indifference, and insensitivity. While it is true that each prison has a "personality," determined in great part by the warden, they all seem to share this quality of "blah." Perhaps I can demonstrate it by recounting some of the difficulties in conducting my research there.

There is, for example, an obsessive fussiness about Oakdale that makes Crestwood seem sloppy; yet, ironically, the disorganization and inefficiency are no more at one than the other. Over a period of a year and a half, I never arrived at the reception room of either institution without confusion. Despite the fact that any visit was preceded by a detailed letter to the liaison official notifying him of the day of my arrival, the hour, and the people to be interviewed, the word never seemed to get adequately passed. Each time was a first time, where I had to establish credentials, where no one quite knew who I was, and where arrangements were not ready.

At the main reception desk at Oakdale, the abruptness, suspiciousness, condescension, and sullenness of the officers on duty were a constant source of amazement to me. At the work camp, which is run in a more informal manner, the officers were more receptive but there was a general lack of manners, form, courtesy —call it what you will—that must be the inevitable end product of treating men as properties.

As a psychoanalyst I was used to a rather strict punctuality. I assumed that among all the disadvantages of working in prison, one advantage would be in precise scheduling. In an advance letter I would list the names of the prisoners I wished to see, their numbers, and the interviewing schedule: 8:00—X, 9:00—Y, 10:00 Z, 15-minute lunch break, 11:15—A, 12:15—B. At Crestwood there was no problem since most of the time I was seeing only two prisoners. But at Oakdale and the work camp, a prisoner was rarely on time and often wouldn't show up at all. To maintain a schedule seemed beyond the capacity of the institution, yet every four hours (yes, four times a day during the waking hours) everything came to a halt while prisoners lined up to be counted. Knowing this, my having to wait for over an hour (as I did at Oakdale twice) because they couldn't "locate" a prisoner was most ironic.

My first day at the work camp I notified the authorities that all I needed was a small room where some privacy and quiet could be maintained. I was placed in the infirmary, a large room next to the scullery, with prisoners constantly walking in and out, where we had to shout above the noise of the dishwashing machines to be heard. Assuming that there were no available free rooms during the week, I started to come on weekends so I could use the office of the camp administrator or of a case worker. Later I was to find out that there were adequate places for interviewing in the educational building. I can only guess that these were not offered to me because they wanted me in the administration building where they could keep an eye on me.

On my very last visit to the work camp (before this writing), I re-introduced myself at the reception desk. They had my letter, forwarded from the warden's office, with the names of the prisoners I wanted to see, and they told me to go ahead with my interviewing in the visiting room—a big open room in which were seated a dozen other prisoners with visitors. I replied that I had been coming there for a year and a half and hadn't they yet been made aware of the fact that the nature of my work was such that I needed a room with privacy. They opened an unused storeroom about 8 by 10 feet, thick with dust, where the heat rose to well over 100 degrees during the course of the interviews. But I had what I needed, privacy.

At Crestwood I had the cooperation of a charming woman psychologist who (although involved in her own project on narcotics) did some of the testing for me. The psychologist at Oakdale was not charming and not a woman. He was openly antagonistic for reasons I never did understand, but he agreed that if he were paid adequately he would be willing to do some testing for me. I was not impressed with his attitude, let alone his general competence, and indicated that I would bring in a psychologist from the outside. This proved to be more difficult than I had anticipated. For one of the few testing psychologists (in an area not rich with them) who agreed to work with me was declared *persona non grata* by the warden—despite the fact that he had done research work in the institution, and indeed had once been requested by the warden to teach some courses. Moreover, he had been approved in advance by the Director of Research at the Bureau of Prisons. The warden let me know that the Director of Research cut no ice with him. Again the military analogy comes to mind, the role of a medical officer in relation to a line officer in the Navy. There is still a certain respect for rank but the medic is not really considered in the hierarchy of authority.

Perhaps nothing can indicate the difficulty of doing research with an uncooperative warden better than the following incident. A distinguished leader in the anti-war movement was imprisoned at Oakdale temporarily. I did not hear about it from the administration but from the other inmates. I requested the camp director for permission to see him and was told this would not be possible because Mr. X was not within the purview of my study. When I pressed the point the director said that the authority for my research covered only COs, not other categories of prisoners, and Mr. X was imprisoned because of destruction of government property. Since Mr. X was imprisoned for destroying Selective Service files I realized that technically they had me, but since Mr. X was not in isolation or segregation I could not understand why I should not be permitted to interview him anyway. I indicated that I didn't feel such technicalities were warranted, that it wasn't terribly important what the actual charge was, that my interest was in the war resisters, and that this man certainly could be defined as such and could help me in my research.

He insisted that it would be impossible. I insisted that he call the warden. He said that would not help. This surprised me because I know how generally intimidated he was by the warden. When I asked why, he sheepishly said that the warden had told him that very morning to make sure I did not talk with Mr. X. I was so infuriated, I drove the fifteen miles to the penitentiary— only to find that the warden was unavailable to me. He, too, could not be located.

When I got home I called the Director of Research, told him of my problems, and he agreed to try to make the necessary arrangements. Despite all his efforts, the authority of the warden was sufficient to make these efforts unavailing.

But by this time I was prison-wise. I told Washington that if I were not granted permission to interview this prisoner I would like an official letter stating that I had requested such permission and permission had been denied, with the reasons for such denial. I indicated this might prove more illuminating in the long run than information I might get from Mr. X. Shortly thereafter I was granted permission, but by that time the prisoner had been transferred to another institution.

In considering a prison and what it is like, one must always keep in mind the nature of the population. How did these primarily middle-class young men perceive, and how were they perceived by, the general inmates, the guards, and an institution established for different types? One of the best accounts of this was given to me by an inmate I will call Mike. Mike was not a war resister. He was in for assaulting a cop, violating his parole from a previous charge. I interviewed him at Crestwood at the suggestion of one of the war resisters.

Mike was a leader in the black community in prison, enormously respected, and influential in the general power structure of the prisoners. He had also spent considerable time at Oakdale. Mike said of the war resisters: "As far as prison life is concerned, there's a definite weakness in most of them. They are seen as meek pacifists, as not being aggressive. In an institution of this nature, because of their mannerisms, because of their more comfortable backgrounds, this is going to be interpreted as not being too masculine, even though I know there isn't anything wrong with them. I used to tell them that I respected their idealism and belief, that I didn't hate them, but I saw one thing wrong with them—that was the counsel they were getting. They didn't really know what jail was like, they had no ideas on how to defend themselves so people wouldn't take advantage of them.

"I would tell them to try to gain a little confidence in themselves as individuals rather than always looking for comfort in a group. I would explain to them, the first thing they've got to do in prison is just survive. They've got to be men first, and then protesters and objectors.

"When they come in here they're not heroes, just nobodies. As a matter of fact, just the opposite, because everybody in prison is a flag-waver. They compensate for being locked up by identifying with the power structure. They resent these boys. Here in Crestwood it's different, but in Oakdale they take a personal affront against these guys. There was an incident there—you heard about that—this guy who was raped by some fifteen men. He was a pacifist and refused to fight, but that changed him. There are prisons in this country like X, Y, Z, where they have a field day on the COs. They have them locked up for protection.

"The warden then can use that. The warden thinks a guy's a wise guy, he'll place him in the general population where the word gets around that he refused to go in service. The hillbillies will do anything to him if they get a chance. They figure if the guy gets a couple of knocks, possibly rape, it'll draw him in line.

"Also at Oakdale there's that big, high wall and that has an impact on anybody who's never been in before. I think the officers are different there too. Once when I was there I talked with Dr. B., the psychiatrist, who had told the warden about one boy who was sure to get in trouble. The warden said that if he takes a few slaps it'll straighten him out.

"You've got to remember these are very young guys, in addition to looking soft. The hacks call these guys communists and, while I don't think they would knowingly allow them to get sexually abused, they will let them take a punch in the mouth if necessary.

"It's not as bad as the receiving prison. I was in there once when a marshal brought in a young CO. He wouldn't walk so the marshal dragged him in, gave him a bump with his knee, threw him against the wall, kicked him in the groin, and then turned to the inmates, saying, 'Here's a real rat. I don't think you want him in the cell with you. He's a communist.' Then the marshal went. I told the guy to stand up, but he was afraid to. He was just lying there. I said, 'Stand up, damn it!' Finally I convinced him to stand up, and I said, 'This kid is man enough to stand up for his ideas' and that stopped things.

"Also with these COs, when they say they're not going to cooperate some of the hacks just love that. They dig the noncooperation like not working and eating. I think they get a sexual kick out of that, 'cause then they have to force-feed them. They get into a big thing, arguing among themselves about who's going to twist the arm, who the leg. Those kids take a lot of abuse that isn't in the record. When they don't cooperate they get roughed up—much more than a typical prisoner.

"You should have heard all the talk around here when all the hacks were volunteering to go to Washington for the big march. They were falling all over themselves to go—did they love it! They loved being deputies in a demonstration and they described how they hit out at these guys. You couldn't stop them— they all wanted to sign up to go—particularly that group at Oakdale.

"I've only been in the two places, and I prefer Oakdale. There you're more left alone. You can gain insight in yourself, and you can see America in all its meanness the way it really is. Here they really stress the programs and all that shit—treatment and rehabilitation stuff—it's all phony anyway. Since the real purpose is to serve time I prefer a place that lets you alone and just lets you serve it. The Oakdale warden, he doesn't crap around. He hates you and he's not interested in educating anybody and he lets you know it.

"Actually the COs have one great advantage that they don't seem to recognize or appreciate—they can talk. They're well educated. The level of education of the other prisoners is so low, but they look up to an educated man, they respond to smartness, they respect it. If only these boys would open up and let them know."

The COs, or war resisters as I have called them, can talk, and at this point it may well be best to let some of them talk for themselves. I have focused on six war resisters. The ones I have selected are not necessarily the most poignant or dramatic. They are not in anyway more important or meaningful than the others. They have been selected because they seem to be representative.

3 ««

C-42893: Matthew

It is impossible for me to think of the imprisoned war resister without first thinking of Matthew. In many ways he was unrepresentative: older than the average, twenty-eight; early involved in the resistance, 1960; toward the end of his sentence, eight months left on a three-year sentence. In all these ways atypical, to me he will always typify the group. Because he was so articulate? Because he was so intelligent? Because he introduced almost every major conflict that I was to meet in all? Because he quickly shattered so many of my preconceptions? Or merely, because he was the first I interviewed.

Matthew was fine-featured and slight of build (as were they all), and appeared even slighter because of the overly large prison blues, yet he managed in some unfathomable way to look fastidious. He always produced a scrubbed-from-the-shower effect. As a clerk in the parole offices he had one of the clean prison jobs, but I suspect he would have managed to look the same had he stepped out of the scullery.

He was courteous but cautious and controlled in his emotions. With his pipe, horn-rimmed glasses, and intense concentration he could serve as the model for a junior faculty member at an Ivy League college.

He informed me that he had "checked me out via the grapevine." I had been approved and would be accorded full cooperation. He then asked me what I wished to know. Since it is in the nature of psychoanalytic interviewing techniques to be non-directive and non-supporting, particularly in the opening phases, my response was the stingy (or greedy) single word "everything." He flushed slightly, then, after only momentary hesitation, began methodically to outline the history of his involvement with war resistance.

"My draft resistance is of much longer duration than most of the people here. It really began as an outgrowth of the culture I was in at school. I had entered Swarthmore College. The first few years I was caught up in a sort of communitarian philosophy —very idealistic. We were a small group with different political orientations but were very close and worked well together. We gave each other much support—the kind of thing that today is becoming a nucleus toward the building of small communities. I became involved with numerous organizations—NAACP and other civil rights movements. Particularly in the summer of 1960, my activity in the civil rights movement in the South became intense."

He then proceeded to give a detailed account of his activities. It became apparent that he had had a profound and early commitment and had been actively involved in founding many of the significant movements and organizations that exist today.

During this part of the opening hour his account was perfused with quotations from the political literature of the day, which revealed directly a great sophistication in this area and indirectly (and psychologically more significant) his urgent need to be taken seriously, to be respected by the interviewer.

"I came back from Atlanta, my first experience with the Deep South, deeply concerned with my own relationship to society as a whole. I'd had a couple of experiences in those little county jails, being shaken up and pushed around by people with clubs. In addition to my civil rights activity, I'd been interested, but not active, in the Left—or what there was of it in those days —but again primarily in a theoretical way.

"I began feeling that my exposure to the more brutal aspects of American society demanded not only participation in the civil rights movement but also some way of disaffiliating myself from the broader system of global violence—what I saw as a violent preoccupation in America with policing the world. So I returned my draft card about November of 1960. Nothing seemed to happen. I later returned a second card and kept up a heavy correspondence with them, although there were no personal meetings.

"In the spring of 1961 a couple of FBI agents came to see me on the campus. This time a friend and I had written a short pamphlet saying that the way one can express resistance is to return the draft cards. The FBI agents were very concerned about this. They took a statement from me and left, and again nothing happened, yet I would always imagine their coming. You can spot them a mile away—that's not just folklore. There's something about their demeanor, their bearing, their briefcases—it's a whole *gestalt*—the FBI agents. They're always in pairs like nuns. I've enjoyed being able to spot them here and there. You must believe me, it's not a paranoid thing—it's more a game. But meantime they were doing nothing. Later I was to find out that during this period they had no interest in indicting anyone, so my file was kept permanently in the back of the cabinet. Only after a new federal attorney had been appointed and the policy from Washington became that of indicting, did my case come up again.

"Meanwhile I had left school after three years because I had run out of money. My father had died just after I had started school. While the financial factor was certainly the significant one, there were also feelings of wanting to leave school for a while. For the next couple of years I was active in peace movements while supporting myself working for a newspaper. It was an excellent job. I enjoyed it. I had an opportunity to do some writing and to maintain political contacts.

"In 1964 I finally received my notice to appear for the physical. So I wrote that I would not come there and explained why. A couple of months later I got another notice to appear for induction. Again I answered, telling them why I would not be there. So they sent back a letter saying that I might be entitled to exemption as a conscientious objector. I had already told them that I felt the whole process of exempting people for religious beliefs was unconstitutional and discriminatory. Even though I might have qualified—I was born and raised a Quaker—I would not avail myself of that. The draft board said that since I was a declared Quaker they were willing to exempt me if I *merely* signed Form 150 requesting exemption as a CO—I would not have to fill out the form or answer any of the questions. They considered them already answered by my letters. But I said no I would not sign it. They then turned it over to the U.S. Attorney, and I was indicted several months later.

"Because of the complexity of the case and the constitutional issue it dragged on for several years. The newspaper, of course, knew about this, and it didn't bother *them* in the least. I was, I suppose, the young radical there, and all the old radicals looked upon me with avuncular interest. Some could not understand why I would not take the offered exemption. I felt that even though I qualified there were people whose feelings were as sincere as mine who could not. If I were to cop out and take the exemption I would be leaving them in the lurch. This would have been unethical.

"I always considered that my views were a combination of ethical and moral, religious, social and philosophical—that I was not distinguishable in categories. They all coalesce in my personality, who I am. But the draft law at that time was written in language that said you may be exempted by reason of religious training and belief, including the belief in a Supreme Being with duties involving those superior to any human relationship. They specifically excluded moral, political, sociological, or essentially philosophical objections. This seemed to me the worst kind of hair-splitting. The law now says only by reason of religious training and belief.

"There was also a political motivation. I knew perfectly well that the actions I was taking, what I was saying and doing, would have an impact on others, political and personal. That kind of political or moral stand inevitably involves and influences other people—a kind of exemplary influence—by making it clearer that acts do have consequences, do have reasons, and that there is a relatedness in what people do and what happens to them and how they feel. In college there was always a great deal of psychologizing about our behavior, and invariably any philosophical discussion ended up on the draft. I remember a roommate of mine who was always a staunch communist taking out his draft card and tearing it to shreds and saying, 'Well, that's it, I've had it with the draft.' Later on that night I found him piecing it back together again with Scotch tape. He said apologetically, 'Well, you know, I want to get into medical school and. . . .' I said I understood.

"I feel justified in what I've done but I've never felt a finality about any decision. I've always asked myself, with changing conditions, whether my position is still relevant. A lot of my friends were running to the hills, going to Canada, becoming perpetual graduate students. Most of the people I know who are close to the draft find various means of mitigating the conflict—of finding easier or different solutions—but I think a growing number are taking the position that I did. I've never been self-righteous about it. I've never been able to work up any anger toward the people who decided that I should be in prison. Some do. Nor do I think that there's anything wrong with those who find other solutions."

Precise, orderly, logical, and unemotional, this is the image with which Matthew typically confronted his environment, and consequently so confronted me. When I say "image" I do not imply artifice, for these qualities are a significant part of his personality—but only a part. The first interview was dominated by the obsessional defenses, but despite the newness of the relationship, by the end of this very long (two-hour) session he was prepared to relax his defenses and reveal his emotions. He had a strong emotionality and great warmth that were not easily exposed or recognized. They had to be probed for.

Not insignificantly, it was anger that first broke through. At the end of the first interview Matthew described a confrontation with a guard and a personal humiliation, which will be dealt with in detail later. At this point I mention it only because it was a significant exposure of fact and feeling for a man in as vulnerable a position as that of a prisoner to make to a total stranger. To have done so in the first interview indicated a major capacity for faith and trust, and impressed me with both his courage in making such potentially harmful exposures and my responsibility in receiving them.

Despite the emotional ending of the first session, the second interview began with the same formality as the first. I started by saying that this time I would like to hear a little bit more about who he was, as a person.

He paused, sucked on his unlit pipe, and said, "I'll try."

He paused again, obviously disturbed by the directive to talk about "himself as a person" and the non-directiveness as to what that meant, and then he said, "Are you sure there isn't something special that you'd like?"

I was silent.

"I'd be happy to start with whatever area you're most interested in."

Again I said nothing.

"Are you going to be totally non-directive?"

At this point I weakened and said, "Nothing in life is total." It was meant as a joke. He was not amused.

"Maybe you could narrow it down more precisely," he said.

When I again did not respond he resigned himself to the conditions and plunged in.

"Well, then why don't we start with the basics—me and my family. If what you're interested in is how I came to be me and what I am, there are a lot of factors that I don't understand myself, or at least haven't completely digested. Physically I'm a very rootless kind of person. My family has lived in fifteen or twenty different places in the last twenty-five to thirty years. Consequently I've never felt that any place was home except maybe in the last few years. I was the first of five children."

Matthew then began the discussion of his family by mentioning his father first. This characteristic predominates in the interviews with the war resisters but is not necessarily characteristic of the average interview. More typically an individual starts the story of his life and background with his mother. The father-son relationship in the majority of cases of the imprisoned war resister is overwhelmingly the dominant one. And, strikingly, the imprisoned war resister is almost to a man the eldest son.

"My father was a physicist and, ironically, for the greater part of his life worked on government projects involving nuclear development. It necessitated our moving around the country, and I was always in and out of a number of schools—maybe fifteen elementary schools—although I did go to one high school for four years. At a very young age I began to feel different—that I wasn't like a Brooklynite, or Southerner, or Midwesterner. I had an aloofness from that kind of rootedness, and rather than finding my roots in region or family I found it in terms of ideas and a relatedness to people. I feel this ambulatory existence was a positive thing. I can't remember at any time having felt uprooted or torn out of a place or very sad that I was leaving it."

I questioned him rather vigorously about negative feelings involved with the frequent moving. Was there no resentment, no anguish over loss of friends, disruption of life? Children generally cling to the familiar pattern and dread uncertainty and change. I pressed him for this more typical response. He persistently denied this.

"I know it's not what you would expect and I know it seems to strike you as strange. We all accepted that as a part of the way we lived. There were always new people where we were going. It was like one long adventure—the kind of thing that some kids have fantasies about but we actually went through—long train rides, moving across the country. It was really something. I remember enjoying it. . . . Like once moving from Washington State all the way to Delaware and taking the train across country. I remember so vividly that it was New Year's Eve of 1950 and I was on the train, and we were someplace like Iowa and I had a very specific feeling that we were in mid-century and in mid-country. I was ten at the time and felt somehow that this was all important.

"My father died about ten years ago. He was only forty-four. He died of cancer, which was presumably radiation-induced, and at the time he died I was in my second semester at school. I'd known for quite a while that he was terminally ill. . . . I've been thinking about this recently. I've become aware that I've never been grief-stricken at the death of anyone, including my father or any of the public figures that have been assassinated. I've naturally had few of my friends die and I've never been to a funeral."

"Including your father's?" I asked.

"Yes. They didn't have a funeral, just a memorial service. I was at that. I remember that I shed no tears. Not even when I was told of my father's death. I was at school and I was playing basketball in the gym, and my hall adviser—he was actually my age although he was two or three years ahead of me in school—came in. He had been called and told that my father died and someone was coming to pick me up. He was ill-at-ease. He didn't know what to do. He had never confronted a situation like this before and he was concerned about my reaction. Actually my reaction was to wonder how long it would be before my family would come for me. Perhaps this was due to the fact that we had known that his death was inevitable and that he had been dying a long time. It was true for the whole family, even the smallest children. There was never an overt demonstrativeness in situations like this, although in affectionate, happy situations we all can be demonstrative. We don't show these kinds of feelings. If we do express emotions it's apt to be the more joyful kind."

I asked him about his allusion to the death of public figures.

"I was at a restaurant at the time of John Kennedy's death. Someone came by and said the President had been shot, so we turned on the radio. A woman came in and she was crying, and then the radio said he was dead and the waiter started crying. My reaction was that I had to get back to my office, that I would be needed at the paper."

We discussed for some time the question of showing grief or exposing deep emotions in general. I said that I sensed he had a problem in exposing his emotions and asked him to recall for me the last time that he did cry. He replied that it was not as uncommon as I might think and that the most recent incident was a very vivid one when there had been an abrupt disruption of his personal life and then a reconciliation a few days later. He described a situation a few years prior to his imprisonment. He had been living with Jennifer, the girl to whom he was engaged at that time and still intended to marry. In a bizarre situation he allowed the fiancée of his best friend to seduce him. He made no attempt to hide this infidelity from Jennifer, as he felt almost fatalistically that what he had done committed him to break up his relationship with the girl he really loved. He went away with the other girl for a few days and then returned home to the following scene.

"I found that Jen had torn the place to shreds. She had tossed all of my books off the shelves and torn the bedding apart, busted my record-player and thrown my records around. She was nowhere in sight. The place was a shambles. I looked around in dismay. I didn't know what to do. I was disturbed by my behavior. It seemed so atypical of me. I loved Jen. I knew it, and I didn't know why I had done what I did. I felt perhaps it was a result of the tensions that had been built up over the past five or six years because of what was going to happen to me in terms of my legal situation. At any rate, faced with the chaos in the apartment, I felt that it wasn't worth fixing the place up, so I pulled the mattress back on the bed and went to sleep.

"When I awoke in the morning Jen was there. She was trying to tidy the place and put things back in order. I asked her what on earth she was doing. She said, 'Well, it's really my place as much as it is yours,' and then she said how bad she felt about having torn it apart, because after all it was the only place she really had.

"At that point I dissolved. For quite a while I just had wracking sobs. I couldn't control myself. Because—I don't know why—because she had come back, because she had been accepting. It was only a year after I had been so betrayed and hurt by Mary, and I never was able to express any anger with Mary."

Matthew then related the story of his earlier engagement to Mary. A week before the wedding he discovered her with his best friend. She revealed that they had been having an affair during the entire period of her engagement to Matthew. He remained calm and logically explained that marriage now would be "illogical." He expressed no anger, bitterness, or outrage. His betrayal of Jen may well have been a retaliation or a testing of his new love. The connection between the two episodes did not become apparent to him until he retold them to me.

This release of emotion in sudden bursts, as if a barrier has been removed, is characteristic of obsessive personalities.

Between my visits time was available for recomposing defenses. So each new visit began, despite his intellectually expressed pleasure and joy at seeing me, with a reserved and somewhat stiff manner. Each successive visit, however, required a progressively shorter period of time for the relaxation of the barriers. While this reserve was probably typical of all Matthew's relationships, it was obviously most prominent in relation to authority.

It was in the third interview that a series of small incidents conspired to expose the depth of Matthew's ambivalence about authority figures, and indicated its obvious link to his relationship with his father.

At the beginning of the third session Matthew, as usual, was waiting for me at the head of the hall leading to the small office in which the interviews were conducted. He was involved in conversation with Steve, a young intern in psychology with whom he had become friendly. I passed by him without his noticing. After a few minutes of getting settled in the office I came out and called his name. He was startled to see me in the office and said abruptly, "How did you get there? I've been waiting here and you couldn't have gone by me without my seeing." My offhand answer, "Didn't you know, we analysts are all magicians?" was seen by Matthew as a putdown, a reaction that was to come out as the interview progressed.

In the session Matthew reported a number of dreams. Most of them were sexual dreams (the predominant dreams of prison inmates whom I have interviewed). One of the dreams he reported, however, followed our previous interview and was an obvious reference to myself. I asked him about this.

He answered in a somewhat stilted manner: "Yes, it's possible. I'm not sure that the dream referred to our last interview. I was very interested in the fact that this is a very welcome break in an otherwise very dull routine. I also enjoy talking about some of the things that are still somewhat unresolved. Many things have not been explored fully in my own mind. I enjoy very much having the opportunity without any of the restrictions you find in here to talk to people. The only other person that I could talk to freely is Dr. L [the woman psychologist]. Yes, I can honestly say I enjoy the interviews very much."

"Did you have any personal reactions to me?"

"Yes, very positive. Very empathetic. I was thinking later that you reminded me of someone—I can't remember who it is—but someone. Perhaps it was Dr. X, he's a psychiatrist I met at college. I went through a long experimental procedure with him. As it turned out, it was sort of a fake—not really—what I mean is that I was led to believe that I was the subject of the experiment and actually I was merely a control, so that anything I was involved with or that was done to me was purely artificial. I was vaguely suspicious once in a while that I was being put on but I was not sure."

"Do you have any feeling that I'm putting you on?"

"No. I don't think so. There is a certain restraint—I'm aware of that. There's an element here that I have to get over. I've always had a block against the thought of my going into some kind of therapy, on the grounds that I was a very healthy person who didn't need it. My interest has always been intellectual only."

"Does that explain why you're terribly self-conscious? Are you aware that you are?"

"Yes, I am."

"When we walked in today, you were a little surprised to see me and I made a simple-minded joke, and you got all flustered and blushed. Why was that?"

"I don't know. . . . You said something about magic. It seemed to me this was a kind of flippant sort of thing to say," Matthew replied hesitantly. "It's hard to say. I think I had the feeling you were taking advantage of the fact that I was surprised to see you and that I couldn't figure out how you had gotten there without having passed me—being more or less certain you hadn't come in. It may also have been due to the fact that I was talking to Steve and there was sort of an audience to a deprecating remark to me. Maybe it wasn't deprecating. I did feel it that way, though. But maybe this is all conjecture—it was such an ambiguous situation. I felt embarrassed. I felt flustered."

"What about the general on-guardedness that I detect at the beginning of every session? Your first reaction always seems to be to hold yourself in," I remarked.

"Well, I don't know. . . . It's not holding myself in in terms of being open and frank. I think I'm always as honest as I can be. I suspect you mean in terms of my emotions. I think it relates to how situations are set up—the mechanics of it. The tape-recorder doesn't bother me, but being in an office on this side of the desk —that does. And then don't forget we're in the prison situation. I always get very nervous when I confront any of the authority figures around here in any kind of a situation. When I'm called in by the Captain, he's always sitting in the same position behind a desk. He wields immense authority over me—power. I have no real defenses. I'm in a very subordinate position. I sit down and then I'm lectured to on my shortcomings. This has happened very infrequently—about six times in eighteen months, but at each instance I've been nervous because I don't like this kind of subordinate position.

"Basically I feel I shouldn't really be here anyhow—I shouldn't be subject to their arbitrary authority. These are people whose only power over me is purely physical and legal, and I have some idea of their attitude toward me. They consider me a subversive and dangerous person. I represent to them what they would like to exterminate in this country. So considering the power they wield it makes the situation a very tense one."

"Do you think it would make a significant difference if you were sitting behind the desk and I were on the other side?"

"No. But I think it would make a difference if the desk were removed, if we were sitting face to face with each other with nothing in between."

"Well, that can easily be rectified," I assured him. "The only purpose of the desk is to hold the tape-recorder."

"I realize that, but a desk has a symbolic value also. I noticed it the other day when I was talking to Dr. B. [a psychiatrist on the narcotics project]—the only time I really talked to him. It started out with his sitting behind his desk and me in the chair next to it, and our conversation was stilted. I was sort of nervous because I didn't know him, and I think he sensed this because he moved his chair next to mine and it became very much more relaxed."

"Would you rather I moved over now?"

"No. I don't think it makes any difference. It's of little consequence. I really think I'm overexaggerating."

"Why? I thought you said the desk had a symbolic meaning."

"I don't think it's going to hamper communication for what I have to say," he insisted. "It's just not worth bothering about."

"Why not? Let's just try it," I said, leaving the desk.

I then moved my chair next to his. Since the room was not much larger than an oversized closet, we were literally knee to knee. When it became obvious that my proximity was making Matthew tense, I remarked, "You seem a little frightened."

"I would say anxious . . . I wouldn't say frightened."

"Don't you find it interesting that someone who is as anxious about authority figures has had a history of standing up to authority to the degree that you have?"

"It's not authority *per se* that I have difficulty with," he said. "There are different kinds. For example, I had a lot of contact with deans and never had any problem with these people. To me this was a legitimate authority. I had no animus against them. The only kinds of authority I really get anxious about are the kind represented by a great deal of power residing in a figure which to me is either illegitimate or not clearly defined. I don't know what they can do to me or what I can claim of them."

"Is that the category I fall into?"

"No, I wouldn't say so."

"But there's a certain amount of anxiety, irrational though it may be, that I have sensed every time you walk in here."

"That stems, I think, not from the fact that you represent an authority but that you are a psychiatrist. I think it is the situation, the prison situation, that is controlling a lot of the interaction. If you were in your office in New York I don't think it would be analogous to your being here."

"That's true. But I have a feeling you still would be anxious."

"That might be true," he admitted. "But I sometimes feel the same way when *I'm* in a position of authority, when I'm teaching and students come in to see *me*. I become sensitized to the authority kind of relationship. Maybe it's rooted in my relations with my family, with my father. It's hard to explain. It's hard to get at because I haven't really thought of this. I don't have any equation for it. I've never really thought it out."

"Fine. Then you could think it out now."

"Well, then I suppose I'd better start talking about my father. He probably had a great deal to do with it. You know, you remind me of my father, now that I think of it. He had a sort of dual nature, being warm and distant at the same time. There was always some kind of reserve but it wasn't expressed in any kind of pushing away. Part of this was due to his going away frequently on business trips and also partly due to the fact that we knew from very early ages that he did very mysterious things. We were not allowed to know what he did."

The confrontation about the placement of chairs revealed as much as any biographical data the ambivalence Matthew felt about male authority figures—a desire for closeness and an anxiety about it. The "insight" that I reminded him of his father (recall that previously he was groping to identify whom I resembled) seemed to shock him; it had the quality of revelation and ushered in a spontaneous flow of emotional reminiscence that was freer than anything that had preceded it. And not insignificantly the opening remarks he chose ("warm but distant . . . always going away . . . doing mysterious things") were a remarkable demonstration of the dual meaning of the transference, for they referred equally to the analyst and the father.

"I remember an incident in which I was playing—I was about ten. I pulled open the bottom drawer of the secretary, and there were all these blueprints rolled up, so I took them out and was looking at them. They were all drawings that had SECRET stamped on them. All of a sudden there was a looming shadow behind me and I was abruptly raised up, turned around, and informed that under no circumstances was I to have anything to do with those blueprints. They represented the mysterious aspect of what he was doing that I couldn't find out about. Actually they probably were very old at that time and no longer secret.

"Another incident that I remember, with my next youngest brother—a year younger than I am. At one point he and I went through an intense period of rivalry which frequently broke out into physical combat. I was about fourteen or fifteen. One day we got into a violent argument about something trivial and started fighting. My father, who rarely used corporal punishment, came in and said, 'What's the argument about?' When he found out it was extremely frivolous he said we just wanted an excuse to fight, so if that were the case why not fight with him? We said no, we didn't want to fight with him. He said we wanted to express our anger with something, so why not with him?

"We all went down to the basement, put on boxing gloves which we all had, and started sparring with my father, who was very tall and physically fit. He played tennis all the time. He wasn't playing around. As soon as we started taking swings at him he gave us a rap right in the head—so we forgot the idea of fighting anymore. This wasn't because he took any sadistic pleasure in doing this. But it was a very good object lesson at the time. If you're going to get into fights, you're going to get yourself hurt. And not only that, you'll annoy and disrupt other people."

"He was a very imposing figure, in all aspects, almost frightening," I tentatively suggested.

"I'm not sure fear is the right word. Respect seems more right —or apprehension. We used to take great advantage of our mother, because there were five kids and it was often quite a strain on her because my father would go away for weeks at a time to various testing places and we sort of ran her ragged. There was a sixteen-year difference between the oldest and youngest, and she had to take care of very young children and those of us who were constantly making demands for lunch money, school, et cetera. When he would come home he would usually give a very mild but pointed lecture about the need to stop the wear and tear on Mother's nerves."

"You hesitate to say fear," I pointed out. "Yet, if your mother would say, cut that out, you might ignore it. But if your father said it, there would be something felt inside."

"Right."

"Wouldn't you call that fear?"

"Right—right," he repeated.

"What were you afraid of, his disapproval?"

"No, I would say apprehensive over the uncertainty of whether he would take any notice. It wasn't the case of transgress rule X and punishment Y will follow. It was a conditional thing. He had a high tolerance level, and the normal exuberance of children didn't bother him. He wasn't the kind of guy who liked absolute peace and quiet except if he had an important visitor or was doing something important in work. We were generally noisier, probably more so, than most families. So you weren't exactly sure that if you threw a ball through the window anything would happen. But if it did, you knew that the kind of lecture you got would not be ranting or raving. It would be a reasonable, forceful, logical rendition of the consequences of this kind of behavior, with emphasis on the influence of your acts on other people —and the need for consideration."

"You almost make it sound like a reward."

"You felt relieved after it was over," Matthew agreed. "You realized that if you were someone else's kid you'd have been paddled or something like that. Relieved that you had been treated as an adult."

"Did you enjoy these lectures?"

"Yes and no. You didn't enjoy the actual lecture but after it was over you had the lingering sense of respect that you had been lectured in that manner."

"Was there a good deal of competition for his attention when he was home?"

"Yes, there was. I don't think it was as important to me as to some of the others to get his attention. I had a very adult relationship with him. I didn't make very many demands on his time, but when we were together by ourselves it was a very good relationship. For example, my father used to take me to the very sacrosanct tennis—he had a group of friends he played tennis with on weekends religiously—and being taken to that with him was quite a treat. You'd be allowed to play some tennis with him and mingle with these guys. It was a very nice kind of thing which I enjoyed very much. Each of the children had a sort of different kind of way in which they did things with him. My younger brother had no real interest in tennis, so they would do things like go down to a ball game or go out driving."

"The most intense competition was with your next younger brother?"

"Yes, because we were sort of isolated at the top."

"And generally rivals?"

"Very much so until just a few years ago."

"In what sense?"

"He represented to me lots of things I wished I had. He was very rugged, very combative, very sociable, lots of friends, always going out and doing things. He resented me, on the other hand, because he was a year behind me in school and every time he'd go into a new year the teacher said, 'I'm sure you're going to do very well, Jim, because Matthew did such a good job last year.' He was not a scholar at all. He resented the comparison. He used to make fun of me because of this. He has always been very attractive to women and had thousands flocking around. Much more so than I."

"Why?"

"I was not successful. I sort of tried to convince myself it wasn't really that important, that a few friends were as important as many, that quality was more important than quantity, but all the same, especially in high school, it was a bad period for me socially. We went to a very upper middle-class suburban high school—people who were only interested in cars, parties, et cetera. We had a sort of ambiguous position in town. A great many of the people who lived in the community worked for my father, so everybody sort of deferred to us, and yet on the other hand we were thought of as sort of weird people.

"It was well known in town that we were all atheists. My father had eccentricities like riding bicycles to work instead of driving. The car he did own was an ancient rattletrap instead of a new one, which didn't conform to his position in the company. We were thought of as slightly deviant. We didn't entertain as much as people thought we should, and when we had guests —like ladies for tea, which my mother hated doing but felt she had to—well, she would invite her maid to sit down to chat with them. This sort of scandalized the neighbors.

"The fact that my father resented very much the FBI conducting periodic security exams on him. He used to do things to annoy them, like getting a copy of the *Worker* and leaving it on the coffee table. He knew there was no suspicion of him but he didn't like it anyway. He was a Republican, a leftist in social values, very interested in racial equality, et cetera, but very conservative economically. He didn't like unions. He was like a great many upper middle-class Republicans who contribute to NAACP and belong to NAM. He came out of a very deprived background."

The "explanations" offered are transparent rationalizations for Matthew's social failure since the same conditions were obviously operative in the life of his successful brother. In someone as intelligent and logical as Matthew, the clumsiness of the ego-defense can only be a measure of his persistent sensitivity to the early competitive failures, and I spared him the humiliation of pointing out the obvious, indicating, however, that I was not content with the explanation by asking for more details about his social-sexual life.

"I dated only infrequently in high school," he started. "My first couple of years in college I went out but never had any sexual relations. I never got into any lasting relationships. I'd go out with a girl three or four times. I became very attracted to one girl in my second or third year. She was very beautiful. We had been working together closely in the peace movement and I became very, very fond of her. I went away to work at Harvard for three months and corresponded with her frequently. I came back, and she said after a couple of weeks that she didn't want to get attached to anyone permanently but that she was very fond of me. Our relationship would be that of friends. We worked together, but she made it clear that was all. There was very little necking, petting, et cetera.

"This was sort of back before the days of the new morality. A lot of people avoided the whole bit of going to the only drugstore and asking for contraceptives. Maybe in a big city it would have changed much sooner, but where I was was so small and everybody knew everything. So during the time I was in college or before, I didn't have any sexual relations.

"I was twenty-one when I left school. There had been petting, but no mutual masturbation. Partial undressing. The facilities were very bad for that sort of affair. It was very risky. The college had crackerbox dorms and lots of rules—no locks, et cetera. Lots of people went out in the woods, but that didn't appeal to me."

"In high school, did your brother have an active sexual life?"

"I'm sure he did. He talked but I didn't know if he was boasting."

"How did you respond?"

"I was envious but at the same time said, 'If you want to, go ahead.'"

"How do you explain, with this kind of avant-garde, independent, progressive family, your being so sexually inhibited—so sweaty palmed?"

"I don't know. It's hard to say. I can't think of any one factor.

Intellectually it was desirable. I didn't have any self-doubts. I was hoping that things would improve before long. And they did."

The rest of the session was devoted to Matthew's revealing much of his sexual and social life after leaving college. It was all told with an openness, a warmth, and a free range of emotions.

Following this interview, there was a long hiatus before I could return to Crestwood to visit Matthew. The meaningfulness of the relationship that had been established is I think best exemplified by the letter he wrote me (although I had never indicated that he should write) during that interval.

August 9, 1968.

Dear Dr. Gaylin,

I just scrapped three pages of very tedious autobiographical hoo-haw, most of which was merely addenda to what you already know. It was mostly Mea Culpa stuff of the most obvious variety. But I do have some sort of compulsion to say something, perhaps because a boring week is dragging to an end and I'm tired of staring at the wall.

Let's see if I can give you some sort of clue which might help in understanding what seems to be the most puzzling antinomy—my desire on the one hand to rebel, to lead a Thoreauvian life, to disaffiliate from a sick and violent society; and on the other hand my hesitance to confront those who wield the Big Stick, to say out loud with e. e. cumming's Olaf, the Conscientious Objector, that "There is some shit I will not eat." I have this chronic feeling of having copped out, especially when I think of those hardy few who have no fear of going to the hole. Who knows? Perhaps, having made a stand by choosing to go to prison, it is merely superfluous to carry non-cooperation to the extremes of refusing to shave and making loud noises about censorship.

I just finished reading a brilliant book (read: I agree with everything it says) by a young Scottish psychoanalyst, R. D. Laing, called *The Politics of Experience*. Laing's special interest is schizophrenia and family processes. His basic point was once stated by William Faulkner in these words: "Sometimes I think it ain't none of us pure crazy and none of us pure sane until the balance of us talks him that-a-way. It's like it ain't so much what a fellow does, but it's the way the majority of folks is looking at him when he does it." Here, for example, there are half-a-dozen inmates popularly thought to be "crazy"; their speech is disjointed, they exhibit paranoia and they are in and out of the hole with great regularity. But they seem to me to be in a desperate struggle to fight off massive attacks on their egos, and who wouldn't thrash around in a pool full of sharks. As Laing says: "The perfectly adjusted bomber pilot may be a greater threat to species survival than the hospitalized schizophrenic deluded that the Bomb is inside him." For the Bomb is inside us, and to muffle its ticking by wrapping it in conformity is not going to defuse it.

I am fairly confident that for the next six months I will come to work every day and do an adequate job, that I will accept the absurd limitations on what I can read and listen to, that I will not explode in the face of snide and crude comments and that I will keep kicking myself for doing so. Why should I jeopardize almost a year of good time; why should I risk being labeled a nut? This place is Catch-22 come to life, and even Yossarian knew that the war would eventually end. Why take it seriously, why pump myself full of adrenalin every time I see or hear something stupid?

What concerns me even more than stretching myself to adapt to this distorted reality is whether I will remain bent out of shape after I get out. Having been in an almost constant state of suppressed rage for two years, will I be able to relax, to regain some of the gentleness and tenderness which I was trying to nurture and which I want to be able to bring to Jennifer? I have always been apt to jump on people, to fight off "mushy" feelings with a cutting remark, but this is a trait which I have been able to control and master, at least after a series of traumatic encounters. I think that this experience has actually softened instead of toughened me. Outwardly I have adopted the persona of the inmate, to some extent, but this is very self-consciously a pose. What I really want is to be accepting and gentle, to stop being "loving" in the sense that Laing describes it, as a form of violence.

The doctor has been administering some of the tests you asked for. We haven't yet done the TAT and the Rorschach, which will take some effort to loosen up and edit my responses. She is very much aware of my pedantic approach to tests; I answered questions on the WAIS with exaggerated precision, sort of like over-kill. I can't get rid of this hyper-competitive attitude and this desire to excel and impress. This is the same antinomy; I won't grade students but I want to know my own grade; I am relaxed in the structured situation and tense in the unstructured situation; I tell Jen to be independent and send her lists of things to do. Emerson may have been right about consistency, but it would be nice to have a little better convergence between preachment and practice.

This letter has lost its original purpose, whatever that was, but it served a cathartic purpose and that's enough reason. I'm sure you've met enough COs now to realize that we're a pretty mixed bag. Personally, I sort of prefer the company of bank robbers and dope fiends; at least I am sick and tired of talk about the draft and pacifism.

Peace,
Matthew Smith

Despite the intimacy and warmth of the letter (or maybe because of it), or perhaps because of the long interruption, or more likely because Matthew will always approach close contact with another human being with wariness until reassurance comes, the opening of the next session was almost a caricature of stiltedness.

"I have 252 statutory good days plus 59 extra good days. I have to serve all that time under supervision less 180 good days. The last 180 days they forget about. They can't violate you during that time. Good time is really like a parole."

Long pause.

"There's nothing really in particular that I have to discuss. I'm

still somewhat unsure about what your over-all purpose is."
Long pause.

"You could approach this research in many different ways: what are my political and social needs, what are my attitudes about the draft, what are the personality factors involved. I wonder at which level you are most interested."
Long pause.

"It must be difficult. Prisoners are all different. Prisons are a microcosm of the larger society. Given the fact that you may have five, six, eight hours to spend with me, the question becomes, is the time going to be fruitful for you? How are we going to winnow the chaff from the wheat? I'd be interested in some sort of clue as to what I should talk to you about most."

"I'm always interested in your feelings," I told him. Then, since Matthew was begging for direction, I added that I wanted to hear less of his ideas and more of his feelings. Nothing better indicated the strength of his protective pose than the fact that, despite his urgent request that I give him some direction, he chose to ignore completely that which I gave him.

"I could recapitulate. In fact what Sykes* says is very close to what I think. From a personal point of view the impact of prison is very difficult to verbalize. The effects of experiences are cumulative, and they're not over yet. Things may change near the end —who knows? The way I feel at a particular moment, the mood I'm in, the responses I have to situations, change quite a bit depending on what I'm doing, whom I've been seeing, what's going on outside.

"I think the most difficult part of doing time is the realization that the people who are the ones responsible for locking you up are not very bright, not very perceptive. All the staff, from the warden to the hacks, they're used to dealing with people as inmates, not as individuals."

"How does that bother you," I asked, with emphasis on the "you."

---

* Gresham Sykes, *The Society of Captives.*

"I don't like being treated as if I were a 'thing.' I like to be treated as myself. It becomes obvious that these people know nothing about you. The file is very shallow. It's all on the surface. It will say something like, 'He's an SS violator. . . . He's known to be a difficult person to deal with. . . . He's known to associate with such and such kind of people.' They assume that we'd only associate with other SS violators—the so-called intellectual group. Yet I know that during the time in prison I've had only two close friends—one is in on a violence charge, and one is a bank robber."

"You mentioned moods. What about your mood today?"

"Well, I've been in different moods for the last two weeks. You tend to go through cycles in prison. It's very obvious. Everyone learns and experiences them, these cycles. You feel good or lethargic, sort of by months, say, three-month cycles. It also goes by how long your sentence is. If it's near the end or if you're in the middle of the sentence, you may feel, 'Well, at least I'm halfway through.' Then you get a little past the middle and you say, 'Well, it's still a long way to go.' It's like doing every day over again. Then you get closer and closer, and the last few weeks are really excruciating. I'm due out in February but I have seven months left. Right now it seems like a short time. In a couple of months it'll seem like a terribly long time; five whole months left. One of the reasons I've been feeling good is that we've gotten into this physical-fitness regime—Jim, Mike, I, and a couple of others. After a great deal of pressure they finally opened up a jogging track around the yard. We can all jog after a baseball game. We were never allowed to run before that, just walk. There's something about a running man that makes other men nervous. So since there were no facilities here we would walk and walk and walk."

At this point the interview was interrupted by an official who walked into the office for a few minutes. Matthew then mentioned that the officials were very suspicious of me since I was not part of the regime. Speaking of suspicion reminded him of a dream that he had. As was usual with him, he had a list of dreams for almost every night of the week, and among them was one he described as a "typical paranoid prison" dream.

"I was in the office at the end of the hall and was looking in my desk and found a microphone under it. So I started crawling on my hands and knees looking under all the desks, and under all the desks were little microphones hidden and lots of wire. There was a long row of desks set up in the hallway with inmates sitting at the desks, and they all had transcribers like the one I use for typing up tape. In the side of the transcriber was a piece of yellow paper—tape like one of those AP tickers—and the name of the person about whom the tape was being made was printed in very large black letters on the yellow paper. I went around, and there were a number of tapes and mine was in at least one of them. Probably more."

I asked him what he thought the dream was about. To me the allusion to our interviews was only too obvious. He, however, related it to the prison situation in general, avoiding the interview as such.

"I think it's a conflict between what I think, which is that there should be no confidential records in prison, and the fact that in the office there is an extreme emphasis on security. Inmates are not allowed in the file room although they do go in. You're not supposed to see any files, including your own. But we work with them. It's obvious I read other people's files whenever I can get my hands on them. I don't know why. Just to do something to disobey the rules. I don't see any point to the confidentiality. A lot of the files which are supposedly confidential contain information which is untrue. The parole board reads the pre-sentence on the man when he goes up for parole, and there may be the most outrageous lies in his file. A guy has no way of knowing what other people have said about him, no way of confronting them.

"I feel everyone should be entitled to read his own files. It wouldn't bother me if anyone read mine. What this stems from really is that working in the parole office you're under a lot of pressure to let people know what is in their files—from all sorts of people. They're always asking you. They're extremely interested. I type all the parole reports and each one wants to know what's in his, what do they say. Sometimes I tell them—mostly I don't. I say I haven't seen that report, I didn't type it. But if it's someone I know and the information comes across my desk, I look at it."

"Have you seen your own files?"

"No, I'm afraid to. I'd get into trouble if I was caught."

"Are you afraid there is misinformation about you?"

"I don't know. All I've seen of my file is an occasional peek at it when I'm looking through the file cabinets. I'm afraid to take it out and read it. I sort of riffle through the pages. I'm most interested in pre-sentence reports: is there anything substantial that they really know about me? Generally they aren't too bad. In the few paragraphs I've managed to see I've seen nothing but good reports about me—from the people who were questioned—my friends, that is.

"What annoys me is the superficial quality. For example, the social worker on the staff. He and I have had numerous conversations—see each other every day. Our conversations are about the most trivial things—mostly about his airplane or about his lawnmower. He's my case worker. So if someone asks if he knows me, he says, 'Sure I know him very well.' But he knows nothing about me, either factual or emotionally."

"Aren't you really trying to tell me, either through the dream or what you say now, that *I* may not know you very well?"

"I don't know."

"Well, let me ask you directly then—do you think I have a good picture of you now?"

After a strained pause he said, "No, I'd say you don't. Not because I've been holding back or been less than frank, but in order to gain a true idea of who I am would take a great deal of time, much more than seven or eight hours. It would take months. If I were seeing you on a professional basis and were seeing you every day for an hour, it would probably take at least two or three months. I'm not a psychoanalyst. I don't know how you judge how well you know people—after how much time."

I did not tell him that a psychoanalyst will often have a reasonably accurate sense of the total person within two to three hours. Instead I asked, "How do you feel my view of you may be distorted?"

"I think what hasn't been elicited, what you mustn't be aware of yet, is how I am during normal, non-inmate days. Just normal day to day. I know this may not make sense. We have gone over some of the most intimate details in my life. I've gone over some of the crises in my life. Sometimes I hesitated to go into them. I feel it isn't communicating the essence of them. While I've told you some of the most revealing episodes, it seemed almost like telling a story. Yet I feel there must be more details, still more detail, for you to completely understand me. Yes, it could be that you view me as having all these peak experiences and no valleys —not what it's like the rest of the time. I'm afraid you get too distorted or extreme a view of me."

"I don't feel that it takes as much time as you think to know someone," I countered. "I feel I have a rather good view of you. I see you in your everyday behavior in at least one relationship— that is, with me. And I hear about others."

"Generally I feel very good with you," he assured me. "I look forward to these interviews. I enjoy them very much. I know I seem to be sort of self-conscious and nervous, messing around with my pipe, but I'm very relaxed. You could say maybe by my movements and such things that I feel threatened. I don't feel that's so."

"No, I could sense that you like the interviews."

"I'm sorry they're drawing to an end. It's been nineteen months now since I've been able to sit down and talk to someone other than in the officer-and-inmate role. It's hard in prison to talk frankly with anyone, even with fellow inmates. You just don't, even if you want to. I don't know the reason why. I might think sometimes it would be nice to sit down and have a nice, frank talk with the social worker, but I've gotten to the point of knowing him so well that I know it would do absolutely no good. His comprehension would be so minimal that I would just as soon talk to the wall, so I don't. It's part of the situation. I couldn't even ask him to write to Washington to see if I could be paroled, even though I have worked so long for him. It's part of the system. Twenty-two thousand inmates come through here, and they come in and out, and he doesn't exert himself for one.

"Sometimes a staff member will reveal things to you. There's a secretary—very low level on the staff—who has lots of difficulties with the job and doesn't like it. So she identifies with the inmates and she will reveal a great deal. She told me the officers consider me a Communist. They read my mail and think anyone who writes this much is a Communist. So I started bugging them deliberately to see what would happen. I was writing to Jen yesterday and instead of the usual letter I threw some colorful descriptions in the center of the page and drew them red—the kind of posters they put out in Haight-Ashbury. I knew this would bother them and they'd think I'm some kind of hippy, but it's gotten to the point where I don't care anymore. It used to bother me what they thought because there was always the carrot at the end of the stick. Now there isn't the carrot anymore. The carrot was getting out earlier. Now it's hopeless. I've been denied parole, and while I'll come up again in November, it doesn't matter since I'll be getting out in February anyway. The carrot is so little that it's not worth reaching for anymore."

He then began to talk with animated resentment about the prison personnel and their lack of compassion. He was particularly resentful of the chaplain, who had refused him permission to go to a Friends' Meeting because it was beyond the geographical limit allowed.

"The chaplain had been begging me—he stops in every time he sees me—to please come down to services on Sunday. I say no, 'I don't want to go out with you. If you're not going to let me go to the Friends' Meeting, I'm not going to any.' He insists that the rules say he can't let me go to that. The rules don't say that, but he won't budge. So at least I get the gratification of being in the position where I can rub the chaplain's nose in it, and I enjoy it. I'm sort of getting worked up here. I can see the direction I'm going. I'm going to start denouncing everybody."

Indeed he was. A kind of automatic anger was rising in him, and his speech became more and more animated. He was almost jumping out of the chair.

"Sometimes, simple little things like going in and asking for a new pair of shoes—my old pair wore out. It takes me a long time, sometimes, to get the courage to go in and say, 'Look, my old shoes wore out, fell apart, and I need a new pair.' I don't know why it is. I don't like getting into these kinds of situations, hat in hand, where they can turn me and twist me and ask questions.

"Yesterday something happened which outraged me. If I were out in the street I would have slugged one of the officers. There's a young officer here who's an extremely arrogant, hoodlum type. He has long wavy hair which he combs back, and he has a tattoo on his arm which says 'Born to raise Hell.' He took a poke at an inmate by deliberately opening a door where an inmate was standing and slammed the inmate against the wall. The inmate pushed the door back at him, then realized that if the door hit him he'd be in a hell of a lot of trouble, so he quickly reached out and grabbed the door before it got to the officer. The officer looked at him and said, 'What the hell is your problem, bud?' Now if I had been on the street I'd probably have done something. At least I'd have made a snide comment. That's the kind of arrogance I just can't stand. . . . My voice is getting high-pitched."

He stopped, visibly composed himself, and continued. "I have a temper. I lose it so very rarely, but when I do I get furious."

This was not the first time that Matthew had talked about what created tension for him in prison. In every session he had discussed one aspect of the chronic agony of existence in prison. Almost always what emerged was some account of three central themes: the humiliation of being treated as a thing rather than as a man, the chronic anxiety generated by the environment, and the frustrated rage with the resultant impotence generated by the need to control all signs of anger. His discussion of prison life would usually occur after we were well into each session when he had begun to relax, and then generally his emotions would rise.

I have previously mentioned that at the end of even the first session he was ready to reveal his anger. In that session Matthew discussed how prison was both less painful and more painful than he had anticipated.

"I had an idea of prison, having been in a couple of county jails. But I didn't know what it would really be like over an extended period of time. It's something none of us knew in advance, and we often say maybe we should let others facing the decision know. But how do you describe it? The traumatic fears that I anticipated were not for the most part accurate. And what is accurate, because of its lack of drama, tends to sound petty on description. I get put off by all the crap they dish out . . . the petty bureaucracy . . . the way in which some of the hacks make life difficult. But then again it's nothing you don't find in any of the institutions of society. When they distribute your mail they make cracks about your mail . . . the hassles in the clothing room . . . the trying to get the right size . . . the indifference . . . the standing up, always in line, standing for count . . . the patronizing. It varies among institutions. The couple of weeks I spent in the penitentiary the regimentation was much greater. 'No talking in the halls! Button your shirt up! Get that haircut—I mean now!' The difficulties I had with my mail—the retaliation, the losing of letters, the throwing of mail on the floor—I'd made the mistake of referring to one of the officers as hacks in one of the letters. Actually I had written to my mother and said the hacks weren't too bad, but they objected to the term.

"There's a special tag on my mail because they spot-check the mail generally, and when they come across something they don't like they'll put a special tag and read all. And then the draft-dodger is a special case. There's this grapevine among officers, and certain inmates get reputations. There are all sorts of inmates—stool-pigeons, brown-noses. I got the rep of being a wise guy, not because of anything I said but because my relationships with the officers are very perfunctory and matter-of-fact. In addition, some simply don't like draft violators. They're a super-patriotic bunch. Some are even fascist types. A number of them are avid Wallace supporters and some of them even wore Wallace buttons. It's the arrogance and condescension and the stupidity. . . ."

At a later meeting he described his particular upset at the "official stupidity" in the records.

"I can't stand it when the social workers make superficial analyses of the inmates whom they barely know, and whom they probably couldn't recognize, and yet these descriptions will affect whether a guy gets out or stays in jail. For example, here is a direct quotation from one of the caseworkers: 'This man is a suitable man for adjustment in the community if he can circumvent his proclivity for devious means for remuneration.' *That's* the kind of thing that makes me angry. It's utterly meaningless, and what are they saying about me? All of the people that we associate on the street with compassion, sympathy, and warmth—social workers and the chaplain—treat us all as complete idiots. When I confronted the chaplain in the episode where he refused to allow me to go to the Friends' Meeting, his answer was that there were many reasons why I couldn't go but that he was under no obligation to tell me what they were. It was so gratuitous and condescending. It was so unpastoral. I just walked off. You can't get angry. It isn't safe to get angry.

"Two or three times I've had people walk over and hit me for no reason. More often than not this will be black inmates doing this to whites. The only safe response is to ignore it, because in any kind of physical combat both parties are judged equally guilty and locked up. It's unimportant who started it. The last time this happened to me, a guy had been talking very noisily during a TV program and I didn't say anything. All I did was shift my chair a little so that I could see around his head. He leaned back and said something like mother-fucker and slugged me very hard, knocking my glasses off and cutting my lip. I must have been close to passing out. My head was buzzing and I grew faint, but I just sat there. I didn't say a word. Everyone was talking, wondering if the guard saw it. That man has since been transferred to a penitentiary. He was a psychopath but I didn't get visibly angry or say anything. It would only add to the impression they already have of me—that I'm uncooperative or dangerous."

Matthew tended to trace this attitude of the prison officers back to a particular episode which in many ways epitomizes the kind of problems that are unique to a prison and the kind of punishment that can be enforced on a prisoner. He told me the following episode:

"My brother was traveling in Europe and sent me one of those airmail letters in which you fold up the envelope and write all over the inside. The officer in the mailroom was evidently saving stamps and tore the stamp off and half the letter with it. It made the letter meaningless. I mentioned this to the warden. I didn't mind the officer taking the stamp but I didn't want the letter to be destroyed. The warden went and chewed up the mailroom officer and told him not to do that any more, whereupon the mailroom officer spread the word around to the others that I had ratted him out."

Matthew then said that a prisoner's total visiting periods were restricted to three hours a month. Understandably, each visiting hour was anticipated and treasured. The kind of punishment meted out to Matthew by the guard in retaliation for reporting him was particularly malicious and psychologically very sophisticated. There were no beatings, no marks, no physical abuses. But the psychological abuse was great. It is the duty of a guard to search every prisoner after each visiting hour. This is usually a routine frisk. With Matthew every visiting hour was followed by his being taken into a room, where he was forced to strip, to have his mouth searched, to bend over so that his rectum could be probed. The knowledge that each visit would end with having the humiliation of being undressed and probed was a constant source of anguish, which succeeded in destroying the anticipations and pleasures of each visit. This procedure went on for months.

Matthew then discussed the fact that the level of abuse and violence differed according to the type of institution. The prison in which he was now serving his sentence contained mostly prisoners with "short time"—less than two years. This reduced the potential violence. In addition it was not a maximum-security prison, which also meant a more stable population. Nonetheless each week would bring some gratuitous form of unpredictable, random violence, but still, as Matthew said, less than he had anticipated.

"When I first came here it was merely the unknown. I didn't know what to expect. I was afraid of the guards, the other inmates, getting beaten up or stabbed. One thing I knew, I didn't want to come to jail and die. That was a very short-lived time.

"One of the most difficult experiences within the first weeks was getting used to the homosexual approaches. I had heard the usual stories about rapes and attacks. I had heard that the COs, being young, considered "pretty," and generally being small, were particularly set up for victims. Most of those who approached me were willing to take no for an answer. One was particularly persistent, almost demanding. I was very nervous. He was a big tough-looking guy. He kept remarking that I was shaking. I sat down on the bed. When he saw how frightened I was, somehow or other he changed. He was sort of bisexual, homosexual in jail but not on the outside, which is evidently true of a lot of them. After a while he decided I was terribly naïve and maybe he'd better tell me some of the facts of life, which he proceeded to do. He said, 'You're obviously not responding to homosexual overtures, so my advice to you is that if anybody comes up to you and does this to you in the future, don't just stand there shaking and listening, but break a chair over his head. That's the best way to stop it. Or else if you can't do that, let it be known that you have some very large friends who will beat the shit out of him.'

"It was very handy advice. It never happened again. I never had any run-ins with any of the tough, aggressive homosexuals. I know who they are. I've seen them. Maybe I've just been lucky in avoiding that kind of thing. A very good friend of mine had a very bad experience. Usually the worst experiences are in the jails or in the penitentiaries, not in the work camp. His was in jail. He was set upon by a group of ten or fifteen, beaten over the head and raped. The authorities can't protect you, they say, and there's nothing you can do about it if there are more of them than there are of you. But I don't think that happens here."

The last two interviews with Matthew were during the period when he was getting "short"—that is, preparatory to discharge. He demonstrated those wide mood swings which I have since discovered to be characteristic of an inmate before discharge. He began to be philosophical about his imprisonment, and one could see, alternating with the bitterness of the experience, the rationalizations that he was preparing to justify his years in prison. It is not easy to think of being deprived of two or three years of life, and I have found that it is typical of most prisoners (like most ex-soldiers) that after it is *fait accompli* they grope desperately for some explanations that will depict the years as having served a useful purpose. Matthew was not quite ready for this yet, so he would vacillate between his resentment, the feeling of having been cheated out of part of his life, and the desire to feel, somehow or other, there had been a value in terms of growth and maturity that accrued during the period of imprisonment.

His resentment of the institution was most apparent in his inability to accept any positive statements from me about the prison. After a few months of work at Crestwood (Matthew's prison), I began my investigations at Oakdale. This meant a long interval between visits with Matthew. He then asked me, since I had not seen him for a while, what my experience had been at Oakdale. I said merely that I found it more difficult than working here, which was evidently interpreted by Matthew as a compliment to Crestwood. It made him angry.

"It's funny. I don't know why everyone thinks this warden is a nice guy. He's nothing—a big, fat nothing. I guess he projects this image of being some sort of liberal character. It's all a public-relations front. His total concern is with public image. He sees me as dangerous to the institution in the sense that any publicity that might come from what I do could be harmful to that image. For example, there was a proposal a couple of weeks ago that I spend a couple of weeks downtown setting up research for a poverty program. They sent several people up here to ask if I could be released for two days a week on a volunteer basis. It was left up to the warden to decide. You know of course that his great pride is the work-release program. He came and told me that he couldn't do it because it would create controversy in the community if it were found out that a conscientious objector was going downtown. That of course is the last thing they want up here—any kind of controversy. He passes himself off as a vague humanitarian, an innovator. I don't see any of it. Apparently he's quite adept at snowing outside people and making them feel there is something vital going on up here—forging new trails in penology. As far as inmates are concerned, they don't believe a word of it because they know they don't see it."

I meekly suggested that if the warden were compared with the typical person who chooses to become one, he might still come out ahead.

Matthew responded: "That's the trouble with liberals. They make all kinds of apologetic statements about the struggle against bureaucracy and all that baloney. All these fine distinctions. In the long run it's all the same—whether a guy is an out-and-out Nazi type or merely playing it safe—the same kind of thing winds up being done, so who cares what the public image is? I have a very bad impression of the warden. He is a difficult person to communicate with. He never talks, he always lectures, and in a very condescending way. Anyway, I don't like him, but I'm not going to waste our time on him. I guess I'm just jumpy now."

He then told me that he had seventy-five days to go and that he was trying to wait out the time—not thinking, trying to keep himself in some kind of limbo. He talked about his hopes for the future and his confusions, the fact that he was going back to get a doctorate, that he didn't know if he wanted to teach or to work in some social-science field or in government. He also told me that he would be marrying Jennifer as soon as he got out. He felt that their relationship had been solidified by the prison experience and by her loyalty during that time.

He then mentioned that he had finally been allowed to go to the Friends' Meeting. I remarked that I sensed he hated admitting something nice had been done. He laughed and said that it *was* hard and that he tended to think of it as an oversight on their part.

"If they really knew how much I enjoyed it and how free it was, it wouldn't fit their definition of religious activity. It's part of the general confusion of the place anyhow. They operate under the assumption that they are following a set of rules, when in effect there are none. They make up rules as they go along and change them to suit themselves, and include exceptions whenever they feel like it. They can always come back, though, and say, 'This is the rule, and we can't let you do it.' It creates an enormous tension, a real feeling of frustration, because you never know when the rule will be applied and in what way. For example, when people apply for certain programs like work-release they never know if they will be approved or not. Or if refused, on what basis. That's how they operate."

He then, at last, described the culmination of the stripping episode.

"After repeated strip inspections for three or four months, I told the officer that technically stripping should be done no more than one out of four times and that I didn't like his doing it to me every time and that I thought it was a personal vendetta. Now I wasn't yelling or anything, but he wrote me up for insolence. I had to go before the adjustment committee and I was reprimanded. They said, 'You're too smart to do things like this. You should realize that some of these guys don't like you and you should put up with it.' A report like that could bring a number of punishments. They could lock you in the hole. They could take away your good time. They could do any of a number of things. Generally, the first time, you just get reprimanded. This was the only time for me."

He then went on to say that the officers thought of him as a "hard-nose." "I don't make any bones about telling them what I think is ridiculous. I insult the staff in a very subtle way, and they know it—just by my tone of voice and the attitude that I project. I've never said 'yes, sir' since I've been here. It's a very conscious thing on my part." (Actually the impression I had received was that he had been close to a model prisoner. I, of course, would not say this to him.)

He talked about the fact that occasionally, and only rarely, there was a friendly officer. But "most of them are very suspect of the COs and think of them as Communists."

The caseworkers he felt were no better. He had more contempt for them because of his greater expectations from them. "They discriminate among the inmates. If you're in here for bank robbery or embezzlement it's much easier for you to get things done than if you're from Harlem and black. It's a cultural discrimination. They're not really social workers—only paper workers. They deal only with reports, not people."

He then told of some personal experiences that upset him. One social worker was writing a paper for a graduate course, and for several months Matthew had been typing the paper from dictation. Matthew found that the social worker was plagiarizing from some material that Matthew had given him several months before, incorporating some of Matthew's work into his own paper. Matthew was angry but did not confront the man.

"I thought of it. But he's too simple-minded for it to have an effect on him, so I just let it go. I got annoyed at him but didn't feel vindictive."

"But isn't that your problem in general—direct confrontation?"

"Yes, it is."

"I suspect not just in here," I ventured.

"Well, that's hard to say—whether there will be any difference from before I came in to after I leave."

"Wasn't it true before you came in?"

"Yes, it's true. But then again, I didn't have as many situations in which I felt hostile. That's the irony. Before I came in here I wasn't a hostile person. Now I'm semi-seething all the time. It's the general dehumanizing aspect of the place. I do feel there have been changes. Here all my confrontations are colored by the fact that I'm an inmate and they can do practically anything to me. I think once that barrier is removed and I can confront people on the basis of equality, that I'd be able to assert myself better. Although I'm hoping the hostility will go too when there's less cause for it.

"I'm hoping, and have the feeling, that I've developed more self-confidence in here. Perhaps restriction brings about liberation by forcing one to confront the facts of oppression. A person then instinctively knows what freedom is. But people who never have to confront oppression face to face are nonetheless involved in it. Like being wound up in cotton—the liberals of the outside world adjust themselves to it and begin to believe they are free when in fact they are bound in by a vast number of restraining influences which they are unable to recognize and which they come to define as perimeters of freedom. It's hard to put in metaphorical terms. It's like having barbed-wire walls coated over with rubber and not seeing the barbed wire. Here you see it bare and aren't fooled anymore by the rubber coating when you go back out.

"I think the two years in here have been useful to me. More than the two years, I don't think so. A Yugoslavian writer who spent eleven years in prison for political offenses said: 'Two years is good for the mind. More than that is bad for the soul.' It's a good way of putting it. Like Cleaver spent nine years and he'd rather be killed than go back. That's why he took off."

"What if you had to face coming back?" I asked.

The response was immediate. "I wouldn't do it. I couldn't do it. I'd leave the country first!"

"Why didn't you the first time?"

"I don't know. I had enough opportunity. In fact, shortly before I came in I was in Canada, thinking about it, but there wasn't really any hesitation. I didn't think about it hard. It didn't scare me much then. In a way I was half looking forward to it. I don't know what the difference is now. I now feel there is no legitimate reason for me to be locked up. That wasn't really my feeling before. I was still accepting some of the liberal ground rules. I had forced a confrontation with the government, knowing the consequences, and I had an obligation to accept those consequences. In other words, we were operating within the rule of law on which society is based, and I accepted this. Now I don't believe this. I don't believe we're operating under the rule of law. I have very little regard for this rule. This for sure has changed since I came in. My basic feeling about the law is that it's merely an abstraction which has no reality outside of the way it's enforced. Law, *per se*, is nothing. It only has a meaning by the way it's administered by the people in society. That is its only legitimacy."

Toward the end of this session, which was our next to last, Matthew asked when I would be coming back. I asked him why, and with some embarrassment he said he was wondering if he would see me before his discharge. I indicated that I would try to, and he told me how much he looked forward to meeting with me and added with great embarrassment that he liked me.

In the next interval I received my second letter from Matthew. It is ultra-analytic. All of his actions are interpreted in traditional psychoanalytic terms. It represents a gift from him to me. He is offering me the kind of information he thinks I want. This does not mean that he is not often accurate. Much of what he says, while intellectualized, is true. But he is very hard on himself, and there is a danger to this kind of thinking. The psychoanalytic construct must always be seen as simply an alternative way of looking at material, not as a truer or more accurate assessment of behavior. Unconscious determinants in no way discredit the validity of conscious behavior. Matthew sensed this intuitively and, after explaining himself almost entirely in psychological terms, defends his position sociologically.

January 17.

Dear Dr. Gaylin,

Being so short—34 days to go—is a good feeling, but along with it comes a rush of emotions, sort of like those you feel when a long relation with someone is ending. My relation with the draft, and all of its consequences, has been sort of like an alter-ego I have been living with for eight years, and ending it is almost like leaving an old friend/foe, perhaps like a policeman who has tracked an elusive criminal for so long that catching him is as much a let-down as a relief. At any rate, I thought some of my thoughts this close to the end might be of interest to you.

Introspection is a very imprecise scalpel, since it is wielded on oneself and you tend to avoid cutting into the more sensitive sections of the body. But I think there are some insights about how I got into this and how I reacted to it that coming close to the end have uncovered. The major factor has to do with my relation to my father and the un-acknowledged trauma of his death. He is still a somewhat unreal and shadowy figure, and at the time of his death I felt no emotion about it. But I am sure I felt guilty about never having had a close relation with him. He had a great deal of status, and I was always aware that people respected him, and that his friends and the people he worked with felt a closeness to him that I never felt. I don't know whether his association with the government and the nature of his work (which I was always aware of) had any real effect on me, but it's possible that I resented the government's having preoccupied his time and attention, and that I transferred this resentment to authority in general and the government in particular.

At the time I first sent my draft card back, I was doing volunteer work and also living in the hospital, and I had last seen my father alive in the hospital. In fact, seeing him helpless and emaciated had made me faint. The conjunction of these factors, plus my experience in being arrested by some brutal cops, may have triggered my predisposition to deny my guilt feelings through an act of rejection. The draft card I sent back could have represented this denial. Or, on the other hand, it could have been an unconscious attempt to demand the attention from authority that I had failed to demand from my father. Probably, both motives, in a sort of dynamic tension, were involved.

The problem of status insecurity is also a major factor. This probably explains why I am so intent on getting my Ph.D. My father, although he didn't have a doctorate, had at least the status that went with one. Incidentally, I'm the only one of the three sons who seems status-conscious, perhaps because I was the first son and always self-consciously intellectual. On several occasions I remember feeling quite good when people have assumed that I have a doctorate and have treated me as if I had one, which once led to a job teaching which I enjoyed greatly. Even in prison, I have made almost a fetish of my academic achievements and plans. When I hear of an impending shake-down of the lockers, I speculate about the effect on the officers of the impressive library in my locker, as if to say "You may have power over me now, but I have potentially even more power, which I hope you can realize." When academic people visit the institution I sometimes try to arrange meeting them or at least making them aware of who I am.

This all has a sort of pathological tinge to it, and it obscures what I think is a very healthy basic motivation for why I am here, but it does represent a form of resolution of the stresses in the situation in which I first broke with the draft. Since that time, and especially in the last two years, I have been struggling to strike a balance between my obvious attachment to an academic career and the life-style of the rest of my family and most of my friends. In the long run, I feel confident that I can balance my drive for status and recognition with the more relaxed way the rest of my family lives.

Now that it's almost over, I think I've worked out a lot of the conflicts that precipitated this whole thing. The prison experience itself has been revelatory, and my relationship with Jennifer and my family has provided a sustaining love and concern that I never had before. In a sense, being forced to stay in one place for some time and being forced to face the responsibility of maintaining a relationship with Jen has been good for me. I'd never before, except for four rather unpleasant years in high school, had to or been able to stay in one place and relate to one person for more than a year or two. I think the continual uprooting in my first 14 years made me wary of settling down and all that implies. Perhaps (although this is just speculation) my confrontation with the draft may have been aimed at forcing a settling down in prison. In other words, if I couldn't do it myself, at least the government could bring me to a temporary stop.

As far as my prison experience itself, it will take a period of detachment to find out what it really meant. On the whole, it hasn't been bad at all (in fact, sometimes I wish it had been worse, just to be able to know how I would have reacted to the most severe oppression possible). I obviously identify with the victims of oppression, and my own list of heroes is largely composed of people who spent time in prison. Perhaps I felt the need for punishment for having lacked closeness to my father and grief at his death. If so, that need has been fulfilled, although the grief has not been openly expressed. At any rate, I now feel much more comfortable with myself and confident about the future than I have before. I have avoided talking about the "real" reasons I chose prison; that is, my feelings about the role of our nation and the wrongness of the draft, but they are real reasons in the sense of being an integral part of my view of the world, and I still defend my action in those terms. They are factors as much as any psychogenetic factors, and they are all bound up in the way I think and act.

This has been a very self-conscious act of putting things into the perspective we share as intellectual people and the relation we share, which I enjoy and value. But there is also an unverbalized communication here—the sense of wholeness I think I have begun to achieve, and the great feeling of going out to love and meaningful work and the freedom to be myself. I hope this isn't obscured behind the words.

I hope you can get up again before I leave.

Peace,

Matthew

I saw Matthew for the last time just before his discharge. He had gone through a rough period. I had heard from the prison psychologist that he had been in rather a depressed state for a while but in the last few days had been almost manic with excitement. Indeed he started the interview that way.

"Actually I'm in better spirits than I've been in quite a while. I thought that the closer I would get to coming out the more anxious I would be, that I'd be frightened by the transition. But actually it peaked about two weeks ago and then all of a sudden it seemed to evaporate. You see, about three weeks ago I was allowed out for a couple of days. They gave me a furlough so that I could go and register at school. They had turned me down three times for halfway house and gave me this as a sort of consolation prize. I think they thought, well, they might as well give me something.

"When I left I was in terrible shape. For one thing, I was sick. I had the flu. In addition, I was extremely paranoid during the whole trip. It was a bad trip. I traveled by bus and it was terrible. By the time I got to the university I was truly paranoid—I didn't actually think there were agents sitting around and watching me, but it was as close to that as could be. I felt uncomfortable, a generalized kind of feeling. I found myself looking at people and being suspicious. It was a real comedy of errors. The man I was supposed to see hadn't gotten the letter telling him I'd be there, and he was in Chicago. So I went to Jen's to see her, but she wasn't there. So back I went to the bus station. Jen was there waiting for me, to tell me that the man wasn't in town. I felt, to hell with it. And we both went back to her place. I didn't think there would be any surveillance of me but I wasn't sure. I was supposed to be staying with my sister and brother-in-law, who live around the corner from her, and I was uncomfortable during the whole thing.

"We did go to my sister's, and the first thing I did was to get drunk. Then we stayed there till late and went back to Jen's, but I was very uncomfortable. In the morning I threw up. I haven't done that in ten years. I think it was a combination of the fact that I had the flu, that I hadn't been eating very much food, and that I was anxious. A few weeks before going out I simply couldn't eat. I wasn't hungry. The food was getting worse, I felt.

"There was a nightmare's quality about the entire visit. I was supposed to call the probation officer at nine in the morning and tell him I was in town. I kept trying, but it turned out they had given me the wrong number. Finally I got in touch with him, and it turned out he had never heard of me. He didn't even know I was in town. Then I went to school, and having to go through the whole registration procedure made me extremely angry because the whole thing was so reminiscent of coming into prison.

They even stand you up and take a little picture of you, and you have to fill out all those cards and stand in line. I had to argue with the bursar as to why I wasn't going to be able to pay my tuition then. Finally after a day I unwound and I stopped feeling paranoid. I figured that no one was trailing me.

"Even with Jen I wasn't myself. I didn't like the apartment she had rented for us. I got picky. It was too small, right up against another building, no view, nothing romantic. I was somewhat disgruntled by her choice. But she was in good spirits and gentle about it. I don't know what it was all about. Since that time— perhaps it was a catharsis and drained off all the tension—I've been in increasingly better spirits. It wasn't the taste of freedom I had expected. It was only thirty-six hours, and a great deal of that was in a prisonlike atmosphere—both the impersonal bureaucracy at the college and the very small apartment. There was really no chance to relax. But I'm still very glad I had the experience. It was a period of decompression. I'm glad I got that feeling of suspiciousness out of the way. It's unbelievable. I would have said two years ago that I'd be immune to this kind of thing, although my reading had prepared me to expect this paranoia.

"I think perhaps having gone through this dissipated my anxiety about getting out. I only have two weeks now. I don't know if it's a false euphoria that I've been building up since then, but I don't think it is. I feel amazingly cheerful."

"Why shouldn't you be?"

"I don't know. I'm always suspicious of sudden changes in moods in myself. At the moment I'm terribly optimistic. I'm taking things as they come. I'll go to graduate school in the spring. I don't know what I'll do in the summer. I may attend classes or go to the country and do nothing. I'm very optimistic about Jen and myself. Not that it's going to be a happily-ever-after kind of thing —I'm aware that it can't be, that I will bring certain disruptive things to a mature relationship—like the fact that I'm demanding at times—expecting certain kinds of behavior. When I feel happy I want her to feel happy. When I'm depressed I want her to be.

I'm perfectly aware that there are things in myself that I'd like changed, but at least I feel that I'm able to face it and deal with it. Jen is good for me. She's free with her emotions. She doesn't hold back."

He talked about his future, and he thought he'd want to be a teacher at a university. He was unworried about financial problems. He said, "Fellowships aren't that difficult to get. I've always had to do it on my own and I never had any great problems. If I have to quit for while to work to get money, it won't bother me."

Finally I asked him if he thought prison had changed him.

"I wouldn't say it's been so much change as a clarification. I like to think that I'm leaving more self-assured. I wouldn't even say that I'll be leaving more hostile, but I'll be more knowledgeable about such feelings. I've always had a basic hostility towards arbitrary authority."

"How about non-arbitrary authority?"

"I don't think I've had any hostility toward that, but then, again, you don't run into legitimate authority that much. Most of it is based on the hierarchy, which is arbitrary in its basic conception—even if not in its application."

I then told him that I had seen less deterioration in him than in any of the other COs I had talked to, and asked him how he might explain that. He was curious as to what signs of deterioration I had noticed in the others. I told him low energy, diminished self-confidence, less capacity or desire to relate, less interest in people, more despair, a sense of impotence.

"I think it might be a factor that you're meeting them early in their prison experience and you didn't meet me until after I had been in over a year. In terms of time it was all downhill when you met me. I think, aside from a few depressed periods—very lethargic periods which never lasted more than a month or two—I have more energy than I did before. I now want to do things that interest me, not that which is expected of me. I think there's a great deal of energy waiting to be released. Maybe in a better way than it would have if I hadn't come to prison.

"Another thing that may have made it easier for me is that I had faced this for some time, six years, before I went to prison. For six years I knew what was coming. Then, again, a third factor is that I'm older. I was twenty-six when I came in. For example, we got four new draft-resisters since the last time you were here. They're a different group again. They're college graduates. They're all twenty-four years or older, and they seem much more stable than the typical resister that you've experienced."

Then for the last time Matthew tried to articulate what in the prison experience is so devastating. He described an episode in which he was sitting in the psychologist's office with Steve, the young intern who had been working there during the summer and had come back for a visit.

"We were sitting around in the office having a pleasant conversation about what Steve was doing. He said, 'It sure would be nice to have a drink right now.' I said, 'It sure would.' He said, 'I shouldn't have said that,' and I said, 'Well, you're going home tonight and I'm going to still be in here.' It's that kind of indefinable thing. You run into people on the outside who are like the people who work here—who treat you the same way—the regimentation is minor. There isn't any overt oppression. But there's something about being in here. Not the loss of status or the feeling of being inferior—at least for the draft people; it's such an intangible thing. All I can say is that being in prison is different from not being in prison. Partly it's the feeling that things shouldn't be this way. Things shouldn't come to this end. Somebody who's basically a decent person, who hasn't the desire to kill other people or become involved in organized violence, doesn't deserve this fate. Even as minor as it may be or as bearable as it can be, it isn't the kind of thing that should happen to you."

He then repeated that he enjoyed his relationship with me and noticed how much less tense he now was when talking to me than when we had started—much less tense since he had "gotten to know me." I asked him if he felt that he knew me well. He said he felt he did. I laughed and reminded him that at the beginning he said that no one could get to know anyone in so short a period of time. He took the teasing well and said that I was the kind of person he enjoyed being with, that he didn't sense any pretension, nor did he feel threatened. He recognized that he tended to be arbitrary and quick to form opinions.

"If I sense early in the relationship that I'm not going to be very friendly with the person, I ignore him. I liked you from the start."

Since he thought he knew me well I asked if he now thought I might know him well. He laughed and said, "Yes and no," that he'd still feel better if I could see him in a different kind of situation, outside of prison.

And indeed, indirectly, he did let me see a little bit of him from the outside. One month after discharge I received an announcement of his wedding and a long, personal, affectionate letter. Dutifully, considerately, and conscientiously, he concluded with an addenda reporting the dreams that he knew had special interest to me.

4 ⫷

C-42901: Hank

$\mathbf{W}$hile most of the war resisters were thin, Hank was painfully so; "fragile" would be a more descriptive word. His face had the bony configuration of a high-fashion model, and on this delicate face sat the heavy thick-lensed glasses that one associates with the near blind. Nor was this the only incongruity, for his voice, which was soft and measured, with educated and refined articulation, was the medium for transmitting whatever patois or jargon he may have been impressed with in any particular week. Hank was a black man.

He had some difficulty with my non-directive, "let-me-hear-about-you" approach, but after a number of false starts started off.

"My name is Hank. Twenty-one years old. Born and raised in New England. My father comes from the South but my mother is local. I was raised and 'educated' in my home town. In high school I had a peculiar major, agriculture. It was a special school with a farm attached. At that time I had thoughts about becoming a veterinarian. Then I went to college for two years, at night and during the summer, and completed thirty-five credits. What else is there?"

"What did you do in college?" I asked.

"If I could have afforded it full time, I would have majored in either anthropology or music. I tried the music but it wasn't exactly it."

Hank then indicated that he was not interested in musical theory but rather in performing. He was evidently a talented jazz musician who had even at his age achieved some modest reputation. He discussed the music for a while and then came to a hesitant stop, looking at me inquiringly.

"What else can you tell me?" I asked.

"Like how did I get here?" he asked. "It more or less started out in high school. Involved in what was then known as the civil rights movement. Started working with CORE in my junior year in high school. I was also going at that time with a girl from Cuba—she told me a lot about Fidel. It was funny, because in school we were discussing Cuba at the time and what she was telling me was in direct conflict with what I was being taught. But then again, I suppose that was pretty educational in itself.

"Then I started traveling around on my vacations—went to New York, down South in the winter of 1965 for the Mississippi voter registration. So you see, I didn't start off in anti-war things. Like then it was the civil rights movement which of course is dead now."

"Why do you say that?" I asked.

"Civil rights movement—three words—a lot of connotations to them—take one, the concept of non-violence. That's had it. It excludes nationalism, that is, black nationalism. Things move in stages. You talked to some of the Muslims—while I don't go all the way with them—I'm not a separatist, yet—they do have something. Integration is not a good goal—it's a delusion. At this time though, I don't think that should be the issue. There's a lot to it and I don't pretend to have all the answers, but nationalism is one. There has to be pride, knowing yourself before you're ready to be absorbed. I've been doing a lot of talking too, since I've been in here, and it shakes up the ideas.

"I know that black people must have the right to determine their own destiny—that goes for the Vietnamese people too. You know, 'group self-determination.' But I also believe in class struggle. I suppose you could say I'm more of a Marxist. My ideas are still loose."

"I'm still not sure why you're here," I said.

"I'm here because they put me here," he answered.

"Well, did they?" I asked.

"Sure they did," he answered.

"There were other options open to you," I said.

"Alternate service, going underground, none of that was really open to me, not really. In a sense I suppose you could say it was, but not if you knew my background.

"I registered for the draft nine months late. I still hadn't had my eyes opened in those days. I received a notice to report for the physical examination, and I wasn't sure I was going to get into that thing. I was just getting involved in the anti-war movement. Really, I should start earlier. . . .

"There were two incidents that took place in high school. In the whole high school I went to, there were only two brothers, myself and another guy. I remember the time of the Birmingham children, that bombing. That grabbed us both. We wore black to school for about two weeks and wouldn't take part in the guard assembly. No one else seemed interested or concerned—it just didn't happen for them. . . . The other thing that took place was a military assembly where they brought in this great Army band and there wasn't a black face showing. That sort of got to us. . . .

"At any rate, with the examination, I kept stalling a decision. Then, three days before I was due, there was a picture in the newspaper. If you saw it you will remember it—it was a picture of a tank dragging a Viet Cong. That was the camel-breaking straw. On the day I was supposed to report for a physical I wrote the board saying I wouldn't have anything to do with the draft. I told them not to even consider using me for the Army. I was pretty sure all along, you understand, that I probably wouldn't pass the physical. My eyes, as you may have noticed, are very bad.

"They sent me another notice for a physical. At this time I got in touch with a lawyer. They managed to call me down for a hearing the day I was having a test at college, so I couldn't stay the whole time, particularly since they had neglected to tell me in the letter it was my hearing. I left, asking them to schedule me for another day. The next thing I got was an induction notice.

"All during this period I was getting more and more involved with political groups. I remember once going down to New York to visit some friends. There was a rally taking place; there were a good number of people just from the neighborhood. The crowd was surrounded at intervals by guys wearing orange triangles, and I was curious as to what that was all about. After a few minutes I saw. Two hecklers who were obviously pro-war were trying to down someone who was listening to the rallies. These guys sort of converged and wiped them up. I liked that. It introduced me to self-defense.

"Meantime the board kept sending me induction notices and I just kept handing them on to my lawyer. Then, in the summer of '66, I was picked up and arraigned for willfully ignoring, et cetera. I was arraigned in that summer. Went to trial and sentenced in the summer of '67. The issue was a legal one, not a religious one."

"Are you a religious person?" I asked.

"Do I have a belief in a Supreme Being? I would say so. I used to be a Catholic, confirmed—my mother was—but now I have no orientation toward organized religion. I believe that there is something there, but it has nothing to do with what's going on. In other words, I'm not about to call on God to help me."

"What is your sentence?" I asked.

"Five years," he said.

He evidently saw a look of dismay in my eyes, shrugged, smiled for the first time, and said, "What can I tell you? I've been finding out in the last twenty-five days that, in the eastern courts at least, that's what all the brothers get. One of the brothers is deeply religious, a strong guy and quiet. He has no political orientation at all. With him it's true religious conviction. He was tried twice, and both times the trial ended in hung juries. Then he had the misfortune of being tried by the same judge who tried me. He was also sentenced to five years. While I was in the receiving jail three white guys came in who were also sentenced by the same judge. One was sentenced to four years and two to three, but this seems to be the pattern, especially for the brothers in the East."

"Do you think your sentence was higher because of going to this judge?"

"The sentences are higher with this judge because this judge is the one that's seeing most black people. One of the fellows did an informal check and found out that the average Muslim received one and a half more years than the JWs [Jehovah's Witnesses]."

"How was your hair then?" I asked.

"Afro."

"And what were you wearing?"

"A dashiki."

"Don't you think that might have affected your sentence?"

"Of course."

"Was it worth a year or two of your life?" I asked.

"That's all of my life," he said, looking at me with a combination of dismay and confusion. "Man, don't you know, that's what it's all about? Am I free to have my style, am I free to have my hair, am I free to have my skin?"

"Of course," I said. "You're right."

"On the other hand, once you're in here, it's easier. We're the majority here." (This was an impression held by many, but untrue.) "I'm still not settled in. I don't know how long it takes.

I'm worrying about what's going on outside—the people that I go for. Then—I don't know—there's the idea of being confined. Sometimes I wake up in the morning and wonder if I'll live through the day. But you talk to the brothers who are here and they say that's natural. They say you think about that in the beginning and later on you just . . . live through the day. It's not like when you're young and you think prison is somewhere where you wear chains and food is shoved under the door to you, where you never see daylight—although the receiving prison had some of that atmosphere. But it's its own kind of bad.

"You asked before how I made the decision to come here. I don't think I made the decision. It was just made. Put it this way: being involved on the outside in activities was important to me. Right now there's a tendency for a lot of guys to get up around the draft movement. They tell the brothers to refuse the Army, and I'm all for that, but it doesn't carry too much weight when the guy telling you has a 4F in his pocket. Not that I disrespect the 4F, you understand, but it's more or less telling someone else to do what you yourself wouldn't do.

"I got a little uptight when you said I had a choice, but I did have a choice, and now, sometimes, I think that if I were on the outside I just might have done something else, 'cause now I know what it is in here.

"I've been here twenty-six days and I don't know—let me tell you something, this is a cop-out too. I don't know how to explain it, I'm just thinking about it. I have a lot of time to think here. I'm just going through some changes that the brothers who have been here longer have already gone through.

"Like a lot of times when I'm sitting around I can't keep my mind off the outside. My girl and I had saved some money for a car. We could have used it to go to Canada. I had an offer to go to Sweden—I could have made it there with my music. If I could take that kind of life, picking up your roots and going somewhere else.

But then I couldn't go to Sweden. It wasn't a real choice. Person could always cut off a leg, could commit suicide, and those too could be called choices. It's just chance because of my music that I was free to go. What about those who don't have that and can't go? What would I say to them?

"A lot of small things get to me here. The regimentation, eating at a certain time, the getting up at a certain time, having to listen to the orientation—all those words, all that talk about what they expect of you. There's a sign up that says, 'If you treat a man the way he ought to be treated, he'll become what he's supposed to be.' Same old bullshit. Even the name of the place gets me—'Federal Correctional Institution,' right? Have the guts to call it what it is—jail. There's no correction here.

"Let me put it to you another way. There's a doctor here, the psychiatrist, Dr. B. A friend—Mike—was saying that Dr. B. was leaving, and I said, 'Oh, he's copping out, right? He could do a lot for the inmates, they all like him, and he's copping out.' Mike said, 'No, he's not copping out. It was a cop-out for him to be here in the first place. What's a doctor doing in jail? Doctors are supposed to ease suffering, and a jail is set up to make life miserable for you.' When he said it, it struck me that he's so right. It just turned me around. It's not often that you hear words anymore that immediately turn you around."

It was not easy for Hank to talk spontaneously, and certainly it became evident that he was not a person who ever found it easy to talk about himself. As a result the non-directional approach was a source of discomfort to him. He would get embarrassed, would self-consciously smile during prolonged interruptions. In addition, his speech is hard to capture and impossible to represent in the printed word because it consisted in great part of fragments—suggested intonations. Sentences were often left unfinished, like the phrases of a bop solo, with the implication that the point was made halfway through and there was no sense in killing it with obviousness.

There was always the question in my mind of how much my

being white was a factor in putting Hank off. He was not reluctant to discuss race as an issue, but he had not mentioned it specifically in reference to me. An opportunity presented itself, however, during the course of the second hour when he was talking about the kinds of women that attracted him. He described a girl that he thought particularly beautiful with a very dark skin, wearing her hair Afro. I asked him if that was important.

"Yes, it is. It's more than just a style. It's becoming a symbol. I look for that right off. It impresses me. It suggests a certain attitude—I guess what I would call a black attitude, political thinking, throwing off the standard of beauty that we've been taught. It means everything—being against the war and all. I don't know how else to explain it."

"Is this hard for you to talk about?" I asked.

"It is."

"Is it that you don't know if you can trust me?" I asked.

"No, I've thought about that. It's really just that I'm not the sort that talks about personal things with anybody. Or at least not to most people. I don't get close to too many people. I usually keep my emotions to myself unless it's with someone with whom I'm very close. Like with Sandra [the girl he had just described]. It's funny, because I thought about your coming for a few days and I tried to work it out so that I could say as much as possible that you might find useful. I know I try to be as frank as possible—otherwise what's the sense? It may be hard because of the surroundings. They tend to make a person guarded about things. But then again, it would be hard for me to talk about personal things to any stranger."

"Do you think it would be easier if I were black?"

"I doubt it. In fact I know it would be more difficult."

"Why is that?"

"To go back again. You have to ask yourself, 'What kind of a person, what kind of a black man, could become a psychiatrist?' He wouldn't be exactly what he's supposed to be, would he? He'd have to be a cop-out or he lost something along the way.

What would be left of him that hadn't been sold to get where he is? I'll tell you this, I'd have a hell of a lot more questions for him than I have for you.

"For instance, I asked you about Columbia and what was going on on campus and all, and we rapped for a long while. I wouldn't ask him questions like that. I wouldn't."

This was the common response from the black prisoners I interviewed and indicated the black militant's enormous resentment of the black middle class, and the black intellectual in particular. I would suspect that this hostility based on generalization would disappear with vis-à-vis confrontation and that it would be easier to open up with another black man regardless of how estranged from the black struggle he might have been.

After this brief discussion of black and white, Hank sat there self-consciously. Finally he said, "You're really going to have to tell me what to say. I'm not one of these good talker types."

I asked, "Why is it so important to you that I pick the subjects? You know I want to know everything about you, so anything you say is okay."

"The problem is I don't know much about myself."

"Okay," I said, "we can find out together."

"Well, I like music, I can always talk about music. It means a great deal to me. As far as I can remember, I wanted to play the horn, especially in high school. I'd go to dances with the other kids and I'd be the one more interested in the band than anything else. I picked up some alto on my own, picked up some flute, and when I came to prison that was the one concrete thing I had in my mind. I would try to get some more music together. It was the one positive thing I could think to do while I was in here. It was the one thing I could salvage out of it all. Maybe you would like to hear what I enjoy about music and playing?"

"That would be fine," I said.

"Well, I like playing nice hot music, and when you feel the thing—when you get inside it—it doesn't necessarily have to be you know where you're going. You move with it as it comes, and what comes is part of *you*. All the things you've done and all the things you know just come tumbling out, and stuff you didn't know was there, because . . . it's beautiful . . . you also surprise yourself.

"Then it's important to have an audience—that's a big part of it, having an audience. When I'm playing alone I always see myself with an audience. I like the way I look. I look nice—not in the conventional sense but more the feeling that comes out of me.

"The sweat means a lot to me. I don't think that I'm playing well or saying what I want to say unless I sweat. Don't ask me why. Then it's important to see other band members—to feel that thing, that together thing—together with the band and the audience and the stuff inside of you. That's the one thing I can do here. I can spend my evenings playing—after six. It seems all my life, even before I played, I loved music. The whole family does."

"Tell me about the whole family."

"In terms of music?" he asked.

"Not necessarily—in terms of anything and everything."

"Well, by all means then let me give you a proper introduction. My mother's name is Mary. Then I have a brother Tom, twenty-three, and a sister Susan, eighteen. My stepfather's name is Joe. I also have two stepbrothers and a stepsister. My stepfather and mother have separated so I didn't really know the stepchildren too much. There was a lot of turmoil around the house."

"What about your real father?" I asked.

"He and my mother split when I was six or seven. I remembered him as a nice guy. He had a beard, a stubble. He used to play with us a lot. I remember a bell he brought back from India. He used to sail on ships and things like that. My mother said he drank a lot and that was the reason the marriage broke up. My mother said he was a beautiful father but a lousy husband. That's all she really said about him. I do remember loving him. It bothered the hell out of us—my sister and me—when they broke up. I was never terribly close to my brother. I remember a time

when my mother and stepfather were being married. I don't remember ever being told. Somehow we sensed it was going to
happen. We didn't like him. He was more or less an intruder and
still is. He doesn't do much of anything except nit-pick. He
would beat us up, ropes, that kind of stuff. Then we've only seen
my father twice since the separation because my stepfather
wouldn't allow it. He can be a mean man."

"Tell me more about him," I persisted.

"He works ten hours a day, sometimes twelve. I think that's
beating him into the ground, the working. He's no fool—he's a
superintendent in a large building. He knows everything mechanical and electrical but he's never been able to get into a
union. He's a bitter man. He never loved me or my sister. I don't
think he's cold—I think he's all torn up and wrapped up inside of
himself. On the other hand, there was so much difference in the
way he treated us and his children. We would be involved in the
same thing—ages correspond roughly—and he wouldn't allow
my mother to discipline his children but he sure as hell would
take after us. I remember many times going to bed without dinner—she would send us off. In a funny way it was her way of defending us before my stepfather got to us with the ropes and
whips.

"When they split up we moved to a new section. I didn't think
any place could be worse than the first—we were living in this
ramshackle house, you couldn't believe it. It's funny, I was rem-
iniscing with my sister about this just before I came in. We lived
for one winter without gas or electricity or heat. That winter my
sister wore a green plaid dress to school every single day for the
whole session, and I had an orange shirt and one pair of pants.

"When you're that poor it's hard to fight, and even if you have
the spirit to fight, life seems to be against you. I remember one of
those winters my mother was going to make a turkey dinner for
Thanksgiving and have my stepbrothers and sister down. She
cooked the dinner on the stove of a lady who owned a candy
store on the corner and dragged the cooked turkey up into the

house. She made the table look as pretty as she could and had the food on it. Upstairs, right above the kitchen, was a bathroom, and someone had clogged the toilet, and all of a sudden it started pouring down on the table where all the Thanksgiving dinner was spread out. It's not a thing you forget. . . .

"My mother was on welfare then, and that was something that upset her a lot." He paused.

"What's she like as a person?" I asked.

There was a long pause.

"I don't know. She worries a lot. She's sweet. She works long hours—she's a practical nurse. I don't know. What else can you say about your mother? She's short, she has a beautiful speaking voice, especially over the telephone. She sings. It's tough to describe your mother. That's about all I can say."

"Can you tell me more about her emotional make-up?"

"She's very emotional. She's also very affectionate. She worries —like about smoking and drinking. If she gets mad, it's quick mad and over quick. She's reserved but she can enjoy herself at a party. She doesn't party very often."

"Is she as reserved as you are?" I asked.

"Am I reserved?" he asked ingenuously.

Hank started the next session by saying he'd had a different dream this time. His dreams, prior to this, had all been fairly frank and overt sexual dreams. This was a dream of a violent knife fight.

"Have you ever been in a knife fight?" I asked.

"No, but there were a couple of incidents that might have approached that. Walking in the park late at night, they have a lot of rolls in that park, and on two occasions I barely made it out without an accident. . . .

"I had a long talk last night with a friend just over from Oakdale." (He was referring to Mike.)

"Did he discuss anything violent?" I asked.

"No, but violence is always here. It's always the topic of the day, how the brothers are ready, ready to take care of things the way they're supposed to be taken care of."

"Like what?" I asked.

"Grooving together, taking care of things. Whether it means picketing a school or even taking out a cop. It's in the air. The brothers always talk about it."

"How do you use the word 'brothers'?" I asked.

"Brothers? It means a person who is black and who knows what's happening. Here they're mostly the Muslims."

"The Muslim religion doesn't appeal to me. I don't know that much about it, but I get the impression you're supposed to wait for some ship to come out of the sky, or something along that line. Same way with all religions—they're too passive. I don't mean their ideology is pacifist, but as long as Islam involves submitting to the will of Allah, and that is what it all is—there's going to be a fatalistic attitude. I'm not ready to subscribe to submitting to anything or anybody. I've done my submitting, I've waited long enough.

"Speaking of waiting, I've been anxious to see you. I've been doing a lot of thinking about the family for you. And my early days."

"Tell me about the early days," I said.

"One of the first things I remember is my hang-up with baseball. I used to love to watch the baseball games on TV. Most of the time my sister and I were very tight. My mother worked at night from four to eleven. We hated to see her go. The minute we were alone we missed her. Sometimes we were frightened.

"School—I started about five. From the first grade it was great. I never went to the second grade. They gave me two reading books to take home over the summer, which I did. That September I was put into the third grade. Then we moved away from the neighborhood . . . and school was horrible. It was what they called "integrated"—that means there were maybe seven black students in my grade. I remember going through a lot of changes there. We were never dressed right for some reason. It seemed that whatever we had on was always wrong, and always funny. There was always all this talk about our clothes. I remember a teacher asking if my mother couldn't afford to dress me better. That particular day I had an army shirt on, and I must admit it was pretty big. Couldn't my mother afford to dress me any better!

"We used to take lunch to school because my mother wouldn't be home. She used to wrap sandwiches in wax paper from a bread bag, and that too was always good for a laugh. You see, we couldn't afford wax paper either.

"I remember my brother always being referred to as the brown boy by one teacher, but I suppose that was all right because another schoolmate was called a nigger by the same teacher. It didn't strike me as funny. I must have said something because I was called into the assistant principal's office. In telling him about the conversation I referred to the teacher as 'her' and I was smacked across the face and told to use her name.

"When the neighborhood is black, and everyone is poor, you didn't feel different. After about two years we just moved back into the black community. It was better in terms of the school life, but that was the really low point. That was the period I described before—that old beat-up house.

"Then we moved again into a three-family house, and the people downstairs were great. It was a very important part of my growing up. I'm still close to them. I used to work around taking care of the house. They were the ones who brought me around to what was going on. I worked in the backyard, helped his wife when she went to the store, things like that, and they gave me spending money. We lived there four years, and they became a family to me. Let me try to describe them to you because they brought me around.

"There was the man and wife and then there was a sister in her late thirties, single. It was a close-knit family—people liked each other and would be good to each other and friends came over on weekends and spent a lot of time there. Then a brother came in from the coast. He had been in jail. His name was Jimmy and he was really the man who more or less raised me. We just hung around together. We'd go out together, hear music, jazz, the progressive sounds of jazz I dug from him. I was only twelve and he was twenty-five but I felt so close to him."

"What had he done time for?" I asked.

"I'm not sure. I think it may have been manslaughter. It didn't make any difference. I really looked up to him. He was a giant among men. He was short but extremely muscular, very quiet and deep—a lot to him. He became my godfather. He took me all over—to friends, bars, parties. I never really felt out of place. I remember his buying a car, a little red foreign car. We both used to just love to get in and ride around.

"I also used to get an allowance from him. Like he'd be working, so I used to take his clothes to the cleaners, take care of his room. He smoked reefers a lot, and I used to beat him for a smoke. I was about thirteen then. I got a big kick out of this. I don't smoke regularly now, only occasionally. I like to when it's late. I won't smoke though when I play. I know some musicians like to be high, but I don't feel I have to, to play or listen to music. I don't really understand this whole fuss anyway. All this belligerence about smoking pot. It's much nicer than alcohol. I never had a hangover. I don't know anyone who has. I've also used LSD on three occasions, summer before last."

"Tell me about that," I said.

"It's great. The first time was with my godfather, as a matter of fact. He was sitting in a bar and he got me a piece. It was a small piece of cardboard with a blue diamond inkblot. I took half of it and chewed it. For about a half-hour I was disappointed—nothing happened. I was supposed to be picking up a girl at a wedding shower, but I found then I just couldn't leave the bar. I finally left, but much later than I had planned. Everything seemed bright and attractive. The barmaids all looked beautiful. I remember everything in a cloud. I remember going home, getting in a cab, getting the girl. I remember going to bed with her. It was great. The walls were beautiful shades of purple. I heard the radio also; it was a Beatles record in concert with a crowd—I could hear everything, the audience, all of it. It was impossible to sleep."

"You talk about it with such excitement," I said. "Is it something you look forward to again?"

"No, I think I've had enough of it."

"Why is that?"

"It's too much. You can't take it all in at one time. You think of so many things. It's too wild. Everything around you gets crazy. We were taking a walk, it was a nice night, misty sort of, but not cold. The grass was really a deep green. The girl I was with could break me up over anything. She'd point and say, 'What's that?' and I'd say, 'That's a chair,' and she'd say, 'No, it's a wall.' She did it with a fire hydrant and a car. I thought it was all just very funny. We stopped at a corner, and I remember looking up at a street lamp and the color seemed to come down like in showers. I saw this word written about eight feet up—it said, *suck*—it broke me up. I thought that was the funniest thing I had ever seen. I remember my impression when I came out that I was a lover."

"How do you mean?" I asked.

"You know, a lover. Person who loves and is lovable. I think I really am. I am a lover."

"All love, no hate?"

"I don't think of myself as an angry person, although it's easy to get angry. But I don't think most people who know me think I'm angry. Maybe the judge does. I know that there are things I don't like, that I'm totally against. Prison, for instance. I suppose there has to be a prison for some people, but if I could break it down I don't think even five per cent of the people who are here should be here.

"I don't have a lot of the hatred for whites a lot of the guys have. Partly I've had a lot of contacts with whites in growing up.

Some of them were good to me, and then all my involvement with the Left. I think those who go around actually saying they're anti-white really have a lot of white within themselves. It's an envy thing. Also, it's the order of the day. With the Muslims it's political and religious. It's like being a part of the group, wearing certain clothes. It's what's expected of them, so this is the way they act. I've seen rallies where guys have gotten up and talked about how anti-white they are and then come down at night with two white chicks on their arms. Muslim serves as a progressive force with the black people now, but eventually, because of the religion, I know it will become reactionary. . . . There are certain aversions to whiteness that I have."

"Like what?" I asked.

"Well, certain physical features—thin lips. There's a certain sallowness about white. I don't like blue eyes. There are very few whites that I find physically attractive, men or women. Their complexions are horrible. Get blotchy very easily."

He then mentioned to me that he had been feeling down the last couple of days.

"There are a lot of things I miss. You asked me what I mean about being lovable. I think that a word I can use to describe myself is tactility. I like to be close to people. I like to touch. That's impossible here. I worked around children for quite a while. Held a number of jobs around children. Last permanent job I had, as a matter of fact, was in a day-care center, like Head Start. On visiting days on Saturdays I always love to see the children come in.

"But it's not just missing what's on the outside. It's everything about the place. For instance, we just moved today. I have the top bunk with two locker drawers, but I can't lock my things in because the locks are broken off. The mattress is all bumpy. Everything's roughshod."

"But you've had some hard times before," I said.

"Sure I have, but it's not necessary to go through these things here. I can go roughshod on the outside. Just look out that window! Just take a look. We walked out of the door yesterday and a couple of us said that the sky and the buildings just blend in the gloom. It's not right—it's not right to be closed in like this. It's not right that people should be locked up like animals. It's not the discomfort really, it's the whole thing. Everything that goes into making a prison. The food, getting up at a certain time in the morning, walking around the yard in a certain way—we always walk along the grass, counter-clockwise. I don't know why. We always do it. Yesterday I said we should walk around the other way. Everyone said, why not, and we did. You know, it doesn't make any difference."

"You say you miss closeness to people. Can't you get close to people here?"

"No. Absolutely not. It's out of context. You're not supposed to. For one thing, the rules forbid anyone going into any other house except his own. I think that's because of the homosexuality. Not that plenty doesn't go on anyway. There's not much for you to go through together, and then you never knew the person on the outside, so there's no common experience. The experience here is too cut off. The range of emotion and the things that you can talk about are so limited. I'm lucky though. I've got the music, and in the music you do get close to people. We know what we're doing. We feel each other. Otherwise nothing really happens here, even between people.

"Life is suspended. If you pick out any one thing it isn't going to make sense. If I complain about the cafeteria, I know it doesn't make any sense. I never cared about food anyway. Some guys do. On the outside I could eat a sandwich and go a day or two. But it's where you eat the sandwich, it's all those men just sitting around.

"For the first time yesterday I noticed that the secretaries came into the court with four or five hacks around them like somebody would want to jump on them. They must really feel good in this environment with all these men. I wonder if they really think it's that dangerous.

"Another thing that makes it hard is being away from my people. Something is missing. You keep hearing about things from
the outside but you're not a part of it."

"Do you think it might make a difference if you had work-
release?" I asked.

"No, I don't think it would. To some it might. They're making
money and they like being away from the institution for a certain
amount. But for me, no. I'd still be locked up whether I'm working outside or not.

"Maybe if I had a chance to work around children I might. I
was planning, if it hadn't been for this, to continue working with
children. I think I told you I worked for a community center. I
avoided Head Start because of its tie up with the administration.
That's the kind of thing I like to do. It's good not just for the children but with the parents too. I was thinking of getting a degree
in social work. I wish I could have finished, to get my degree at
school at least. I got my political education there."

I asked him to tell me more of that.

"It started in an organized way with CORE—in high school.
But my politics really started with some of my experiences there
that hardened me. I went to an agricultural high school, and part
of it was working on a farm during the summer for credit. I think
I told you there were only two black students in the class. Working
on the farm, that was something else itself. First off, they
had trouble placing us on a farm. Not too many people wanted
to take black students. First farm I went to, as soon as the county
agent dropped me off at the door, the man asked if I had a knife.
I didn't understand; I thought he wanted to borrow it or something. Then later on I knew, and I was hurt. They used to ask a
lot of questions as though they were talking to another kind of
species, and they'd all manage to tell me coon jokes.

"Then I remember going into town one morning, and this
mother was pushing a baby carriage with a pretty little girl, ten
or eleven years old with her. And the little girl yelled, 'Oh
mommy, look, a nigger!' Her mother pulled her away. It was

then that I met the girl from Cuba, and she started telling me what changes Fidel had made."

He talked about the various political groups he'd joined and what he thought the values were of all of them. When he mentioned one, I asked him how he happened to join a Trotskyite group. He was surprised that I knew of the organization. He said he wasn't actually sure what Trotskyite meant or even what fascism meant.

"It doesn't seem relevant, either word. But it's the action I like, the people and the action. It's predominantly a white group, but many of the black nationalists respect them because of the principles and knowing that they also put out when it's needed. I've seen them come when the coming was hard, and I've seen them run out with bayonet points. I'm not sure about SNCC * any more. I'm not sure how I feel about that. The Panthers would be great—it's an action group."

"Isn't it a terror group?" I asked.

"Not that I know of."

"What about the recent case in the paper about the assassination plots against Wilkins and the others?"

"That's incredible," he said. "I know those guys. Some of them are the quietest, gentlest people in the world. It's a put up, an absolute frame-up. The only thing that many of those people had in common was that they belonged to a rifle club. And that's absolutely legal. If it's legal for whites, it's legal for blacks. I don't know anything firsthand about the Panthers, just what I read about them and heard from some friends, but I'm attracted to them. I'm attracted to action, and that doesn't mean violence. None of these guys are violent. If there's anything violent, it's the nation we're living in. Everything is violent about it. You always hear all this talk, but the violence is practiced against the minorities, not the Establishment. I can't see myself doing anything violent, and yet, if someone was trying to do something to me, that might change it around a little bit. I might feel different."

* Student Non-violent Coordinating Committee.

"Yes, that might make a difference," I conceded.

"It sure would, and that's the point. I haven't heard of any political group going down to a police station and taking it, but it's
come that far. Let me try it this way and get you to understand.
Power makes no concessions unless there are demands made. I've
been reading Frederick Douglass. You can't win anything unless
you have some power behind you, and that does mean violence.
Not because you want violence, but because it's a part of the
power. But power isn't just physical strength—the coolest dudes
I can imagine work on Wall Street."

"You mentioned taking over a police station. Do you think
that's what should be happening?" I asked.

"No, I don't really. But that doesn't matter. There will be a
time when it'll happen anyway. It all depends, if it turns out that
way. The Panthers say for Bobby Hutton's death* ten Oakland
cops should get it. I like that."

"Could you do something like that?" I asked.

"I don't know. Knowing what I do about Oakland cops,
maybe, I don't know. I don't know if I could do it myself, but I
think it should be done. I'm still not clear on that. I remember
reading what Trotsky said when he escaped, 'The strength of the
masses lies not in their ability to kill, but in their willingness to
die.' But before that he had said while liberation doesn't lie
with guns alone, if the masses had them it would be a great
asset."

A considerable period of time passed before my seeing Hank
again. He looked different, and I realized that he had gained
some weight. I commented on this.

"I've been weight-lifting. I've had the opportunity to work out
but never before was I interested in it. On the outside, when I
heard about it, it seemed like putting on muscle instead of culti-
vating the mind, but I'm really getting to like it."

"Are you doing this for a purpose?" I asked.

* Bobby James Hutton, a seventeen-year-old Black Panther, was killed by
the Oakland police in April, 1968.

"No. The only purpose is gaining weight, and I've gained about ten pounds. I was always a very skinny kid. I never cared."

"Then why do you care now?" I asked.

"I'm not sure. I suppose to be ready for what takes place on the outside, to be physically fit."

"Why didn't you want to tell me that?" I asked.

"I don't know. It does have something to do with getting out. I had a dream the other night about taking off a cop. The brothers talk about that all the time. In fact, there are brothers here who have. I get a kick about hearing it."

"Can you imagine yourself doing it?" I asked.

"Yes, I can," he answered immediately. Hank was obviously not aware of it, but this exact conversation had come up once before. When I had asked him the same question then, he had said no, he didn't think he ever could unless it was in self-defense.

"You know, when I first came in here, I had a lot of anxiety about something that was over my head. I had some charges hanging over me for assaulting a federal officer, a marshal. I didn't want too many people to know about that—I didn't know what they were going to do—but the charges were dropped. That was a great relief. That could have been another five years, especially if they tried me in the same court. My sister was in for the same charge. I was going down about my draft case this one morning and I was feeling nasty. They had taken one really beautiful brother and sentenced him to three years. I guess it was my feeling for him that made me as angry as I was. We had played together. He played the flute—beautiful. When they sentenced him to three years he gave the judge a written letter—he was very quiet. He said in it, if they thought that in jailing him they were taking away his freedom, then they were fools, because he could remember when his father died and then his mother died and he was alone as a child sitting on a bare floor, eating cereal and water.

"He was saying to this judge that jail wasn't depriving him of anything that life hadn't already deprived him of. That jail was at least three square meals a day and that could be all right.

"Well, anyway, that wasn't what I was starting to tell you. That day we went to court and there were about a dozen of us in the lobby. We were giving a going-away party, drinking wine. The marshal tried to get everyone out. He came over to me and shoved me out since he knew me, and we scuffled. That really was the whole thing, but it could have been five years."

"What did you mean before when you said you enjoyed hearing about taking off a cop?" I asked, bringing him back to the earlier statement.

"Just that more and more I can see myself doing it. I think it's because of being in here. You hear people talking about it on the streets, just about anywhere. But that's talk, not actually doing anything, but then you come here and the people you meet have actually done something. The brothers in here are more or less ready. I don't know what to say. I just know it seems right under certain circumstances. Mostly, I've seen the other, say, a woman being thrown to the ground and a cop beating on her and everyone standing around not doing anything. In fact, stopping those who are attempting to do something."

"Your talk of enjoying the idea of violence doesn't fit in at all with the way I see you," I said.

"I don't like senseless violence. I don't like to see blood for any reason. In fact it's hard for me to work at the hospital because I don't like inflicting pain. It's hard for me to give someone an injection. Guys were all panning me about that last week."

"That's more of what I would have expected," I said. "You're such a gentle person."

"Well, it takes a lot to get me off, but cops, the marshals, those are the people I can go off on, because of what they are and the circumstances which bring us together."

"It's interesting how you tell me these things as soon as we're into the hour. But at the beginning of each hour I sense you're holding back. Your first impulse is not to tell me."

He answered, "I think you won't find too many people who would open up. Not just like that. I can tell you this—I was most interested that you were coming today. I've thought about it at least three or four times in the past week. I've been thinking about some of the things I've said about psychiatrists. I'm not so sure that I'm right. I can see how a little psychological boost can help a person, and if you're a pro and know how to use it. Maybe I shouldn't have put it down the way I did.

"There was the incident with the weights the other night. There is this short guy, he's a Ph.D.—professor type, very fragile. He was working out on the weights and he was doing something on an inclined plane, that is, pulling up something at the elbow. He was struggling, trying hard, and what I did was just touch the bottom of the weight, just the barest touch, and immediately he drew it up. There was no physical help. All psychological. I had heard about it and was surprised to see how it just came up."

"You seem talkative today and in good spirits," I commented.

"I had a visit from my girl the other day, and I feel good about that, and then I got my instruments, and when I played the horn I knew I hadn't really lost it, and that was good. Yes, I feel more confident about making it here and all that. Time just goes by.

"I have this thing about waking up in the morning. A lot of inmates do. Waking up means another day. It's a good way to look at it. I haven't had any dreams for you, so instead I brought you a copy of something I wrote."

He presented me with a poem, and continued. "I just sat down and wrote it and surprised myself. . . . I wanted to tell you, I've been thinking about some of the questions you've asked. About why I didn't leave the country. I really think it's because of the people I knew. I felt I had a responsibility, not to the people who were going through this already, but to the brothers who are just beginning to come around, getting involved, having cases pending in the court. I feel that if you're friends with people who are going through something you must offer them encouragement.

It's not right to do something they couldn't do. I could leave because of the music, but they couldn't. No jobs, no money, it's hard for blacks. It's funny, the question of Canada coming up here, because I got a letter from a very close friend of mine, maybe my closest. He said that he dreamed that I was in Canada —he's white, Jewish. I lived with him for a while. He came to visit me and that picked me up. I can't think of anyone who knows me as well as he does. He's been worried about me. He now feels I could make it here. Anyway I'm sort of moving on up. My first few weeks when I started seeing you I was really on a downhill course. Now I'm really picking up."

"Is it because you're feeling closer to people in here?"

"No, not really. I talk to a few people, but more or less it's what they call doing your own time. The hospital is seven days a week. I've been doing the music and writing.

"I really wanted to tell you about my talk with the chaplain. That was a real one. I guess it's his job to see everyone here—any religion. I remember his speech in orientation about how he liked to see the motto 'In God We Trust' on the coins. He was haranguing about the people who want that removed. Then at the personal interview he just seemed completely unaware. He had no idea of what people really think of him. I told him why I stopped going to church, and he was surprised that I didn't replace this with anything—this great privilege of going to church. He then asked me if I was married, and I hesitated and asked if he meant the relationship with a man and woman that was sanctioned by the laws of man and society. He said, 'Yes,' so I said, 'No.' He waited for me to say more and I didn't. Then he asked me if I was a homosexual—that really shocked me—and I said no. He asked me to attend services and I said I wouldn't. I said that if I went to a service it would have to be with someone who would practice what they did in church twenty-four hours a day. I heard he has been married four times and is also an alcoholic. Anyway, I sort of feel there may be truth in the fact that religion is what you feel when you're alone. I heard later that he wrote down that I was a narrow-minded individual that couldn't be talked to."

There was another long interval between my visits to Crestwood, and Hank commented on it.

"I think your presence disturbs these people. They know who you're interviewing but they don't know what you're going to do with it. Particularly when you talked to Mike. He's not a resister, but he has the reputation of being a disruptive dude. I hope when he gets out on the street he doesn't goof up again. He does a lot of good in here. You know, the brothers ease tension by jugging at one another, put downs, but all in sport. He's good for that—all hours of the night. He keeps people from getting down into a depression. He's got terrific leadership qualities, in fact, he's known as the General."

"How do you explain leadership quality?" I asked.

"He's bold, he's outspoken. He has ability to crack fires—to say anything at any time. It's terrific to see the way he comes down on the police here. Like for work-release—you can make a dude walk a chalk line for work-release. All that nonsense, but holidays it's even a little extra. Like on Thanksgiving they play a heavy game. They have bedsheets for tablecloths on the tables, and you're supposed to come in with shirts, and Mike would come in with anything, all cut up, a ragged old sweatshirt when even a brand-new sweatshirt wouldn't be right, and then, he'd have it sticking out of his pants. He'd run up to the police to their face and dare them to do something. He'll tell some incredible stories about what he did out in the streets. You could barely believe it, but he has dudes in here who will back him up. One is how he disarmed a cop and killed a police dog. But it does seem a waste socking a cop. That's why he's back now. I guess it just appealed to him. He's very strong. . . .

"I'm feeling better now because there's time in back of me, seven months now. It's been going very fast."

"Were the holidays hard for you?" I asked.

"It might get a dude down if he were used to that, but I never celebrated them anyhow. There was really never any family, we were all lit out, brother here, sister there. Say, did you notice that I've gained twenty pounds? I have to start preparing myself for getting out."

"Getting out?" I asked, remembering his five-year sentence.

"Yes, I think I'll be out in twenty-two months. I base that on parole figures. I go up in January '70."

"Do you think you're going to be approved?" I asked.

"Sure, why not? I think they only want to see us serve our two years. I'm planning on it anyway. It doesn't hurt to be optimistic."

He then discussed the books he liked and didn't like. He didn't like *Wretched of the Earth*.

"I read it twice. I didn't understand it. It just seemed too heavy for me. I couldn't hook it all up. I think I must have something against the book anyway because it didn't seem that deep. There's a lot of intellectual types who run off at the mouth all the time, and they carry it around as a sort of Bible. I tried to get into it to see what they were talking about. Maybe I had a block against it. *Black Rage* now, that was good. *Soul on Ice* I turn to often. I read it before I came to the joint, and after I came in I've read it again. It all came out beautiful. He was writing from the joint and you could really understand what he was talking about, keeping yourself together and the heavy games they play, something as simple as putting a little pencil mark on the wall. You know, saying that's mine—they can take everything else but not that—because nobody knows it's there. A beautiful book and a beautiful brother too. Then, too, I read the short heist books—"

"What does short heist mean?" I asked.

"Journals for voluptuous reading." He laughed. "It has to do with sex, but not the real thing, just getting your mind uptight. Like short heist is usually a small robbery job—small potatoes—but it smokes. Like short heist is a gaper. Like my sister might show and tell Nick or tease him by saying, no gaper today. Which means she's not going to pick up her dress to show her legs—a gaper. See, my language has changed since I came in here."

Indeed it had, but I had expected some changes after a conversation with Mike. Mike had said that the brothers were trying to "bring Hank home—with the blacks." I asked him what this meant. He explained that the blacks generally were Muslims or JWs and Hank's orientation was primarily political, so that even his language was of the Left. "It's not us, the political talk, it's the white bag. He's got to learn to communicate, to relate to the black. You have to be one of us, even in small things, like you can't say, 'Well good evening, fellows'—that kind of thing. You can't think or talk like the middle class. That means you're out of touch with the reality of yourself. So we have Hank up there, taking him through these changes. He'll be all right."

When Hank changes he goes all the way, and from then on I could have used a translator on many occasions.

"The sex business is hard anyhow. I guess it's because I have some smoking dreams—they really smoke. I just about slept with every woman I've ever come across by now."

"Are all of your dreams sexual?" I asked.

"No, some of them are violent. In fact last night I woke up a couple of times and went right back into that same dream. What can you do about sex, except maybe think about it and talk about it when your girl comes visiting. I feel I've changed a lot in the seven months I've been here. I don't know how, some ways good. I feel lots more open—looser with people, with everything going on around me, stronger mentally, physically, emotionally.

"I feel it. I know when I hit the street I'm going to be one hell of a dude. I don't think I'll have to take a drink to get high. I haven't changed about politics. They may have become more sophisticated, but not changed. I just feel I understand a lot more. Like when Sandra writes to the effect of what she can do to rush the revolution I just shout some Trotsky back to her. Where

Trotsky was being tried in front of the Czarist court and was told
he was inciting the masses to rebellion and he said to the prosecutor, 'If you have anything under your cap, you'd change the
charge to *preparing* the masses for the rebellion because rebellion is inevitable.' He was just preparing them.

"But despite all that, I still hold out with the family thing—
you know, getting out, getting married, all that. In some senses I
guess I'm just conventional. Sometimes I want to get real involved in political activist movements, maybe the Panthers, but I
don't know if I could become one.

"You said you didn't see me as capable of violence. I thought
about that and I don't know. You can't really judge, can you? I
think everyone is capable of violence. Like one dude I knew, a
short, fat guy in the school. He was picked on all the time. Like I
backed him up in the corner one day and got my hands wiped.
That was a good lesson for me—very humiliating. Like a guy in
Cleveland who finally broke out and tore the place apart. I could
never see him doing anything like that. I'd always taken him for
just a cultural nationalist—you know, run off at the mouth, open
a store, rap all day and all night about whitey. He'd never be
found with a picket sign or at a demonstration. As far as the
draft, he might tell you to go out and piss on the floor. His idea
of standing up was to tell you to wear black underwear. But
when that action broke out in Cleveland, there he was right in
the midst of it. I guess he was pushed into his corner. Look at
Matthew, he's changing."

"How do you mean?" I asked.

"Well, when I first ran into him he wasn't very vocal. But now
he really opens up at you if you disagree. Like I got into an argument about politics with him, and he really let me have it. And
that's good. It's tightened up our friendship so we can have a go
at each other. Not like that other guy."

Hank mentioned another white war resister who had been in
prison for only a few months and had struck him as a "phony."

"What is there about him that you object to so much?" I asked.

"He's a character. Just the way he presents himself. Like he'll roll down on you even when you're involved with someone else. No class. I can give you a specific conversation. Like when I first met him—he right off in five minutes told me about the colored child he took care of. Then right after that about this SNCC guy he knew who married a white woman and cut her loose. Like he's telling me—you've been kicking our ass but I'm still with you, fella. Yeah, and that was in our first conversation. Why, he made me want to take my cigarette back from him! Why do you keep looking at your watch that way?"

I had indeed been looking at my watch and I was embarrassed. I'd run overtime with Hank and was on a close schedule that required my leaving. I said I was sorry, it wasn't that I wasn't enjoying the conversation but that I just had to go.

"Wow," he said, "and I was looking forward to a nice long rap."

"Well," I said, "we had an hour and I'll try to make more time next visit."

I was pleased with his response to the time, for it was consistent with the whole tone of the hour. There was a great freedom that had developed, and he was open enough, secure enough, to tell me in that one sentence that he liked me and was annoyed with me—both difficult to admit.

The next session Hank walked in with a jug of tea. "I brought you some tea. You go for that?"

"I'd love some. You seem to be prospering in here. You're gaining weight," I said.

"I'm doing all right. But you look a little tired," he replied.

He was right. It had been the end of a very long day for me. Again I was amused at his freedom with me and enjoyed it.

"Well, it's over a year now. I can almost tell time by your coming. Time just goes. Otherwise what can I say? No real bad periods because it's all bad. If I feel it coming on, I can always do something. I've got the music."

"Do you have good and bad months, or are you saying it's all the same?"

"For me it's all the same. When I think of good or bad months, all the months that are behind me are good and all that I can look forward to are bad. Like I thought January would be a bad month. It usually is, even on the streets. It's a comedown from the partying season, but past months are all good, and January is in the past. So now that's a good month. When I look ahead I break up the time into smaller units. For example, I see the Parole Board in eleven months. I have a schedule set. The political climate seems to be changing. I was right to be optimistic. You see where Johnson [a Black Muslim] got out after twenty months and three days of a five-year sentence?"

"Are you more optimistic about the outside?"

"No, I'm not. I don't know. Certain things get me. Like I picked up the newspaper the other day and saw a picture of Secretary Laird. I've been reading comments on the new administration, trying to find out the truth between the lines. The whole thing seems creepy to me. They're not quite real, all those men. But something about the picture of Laird. I worked in Wall Street for a little while and I know that face, very thick. The picture just grabbed me. I knew that guy was a diddler."

"Some of my dreams are getting strange. I'm not sure I like them. A couple of nights ago I was dreaming about the daughter of a friend of mine. She's only thirteen, and he's very uptight about it because she's very well developed. And here I was dreaming that I was taking her off—a thirteen-year-old girl. But she really doesn't look like one. But then I'd just gotten a letter from him the night before and maybe that's what brought it to mind. I don't understand it with these dreams. They weren't all sexual when I was out on the street. Actually when I was out I rarely dreamed at all. But then I wouldn't go to sleep unless I was really done in."

"Are you a night person?" I asked.

"All day long, man. It's part of what gets me down in here.

What really gets me down is just being in here. It may not be so bad, it's not as bad as I expected, and then it's worse than I expected. I wish I could tell you because I know it's what you want to know. But then I'm not so good at telling. I don't believe there's a dude on the planet who could have sat down and dreamed up shit like this.

"And even when I get out—what happens then? What will I be into? What will I be doing? I've told you once before that getting out sometimes scares me. I walk out—and then what? What am I going to do to make a living? To take some of these dreams off? I know people with college educations working as newsboys. As far as the music is concerned, it isn't easy to make money that way—particularly since I'm changing. You can make money in rock 'n roll and I was rock before, but I never really felt quite right playing it. I think I knew I couldn't play it although others thought I could. I wasn't satisfied with what I was doing. Now I feel I'm on to something more like me. I feel I'm improving and I'm playing more jazz. I've been encouraged—there's another alto player who came in and he's a lot more experienced. He's taken me under his wing, and every so often I'll get into a solo that's really together. I've thrown a few things that he's never heard before, and he'll stand off and smile—proudly.

"But on the street it's entirely different. Although a penitentiary audience is the roughest audience in the world, critical. You have to really move out among these guys. I'll get it together. I'm sure I will."

The ambivalence, the self-contradiction, was unlike Hank and showed the strain of maintaining control.

"I'm sure you will too," I said. I then asked him what he thought about the new COs.

"I don't know them well. I tend to hang out with the brothers more."

"Why is that?" I asked.

"I feel there is a lot to learn from them. I understand them. I can see things in a different light. Like one of them described riding on the A train, coming down from Harlem, between 125th Street and 59th Street, and there was this dude standing in the middle of the floor not holding on to anything, and you just knew he wasn't going to fall over.

"I don't know, there are lots of hillbillies here. You walk in the mess hall and one line is white and one line is black. I really can't say why. When there's a white cat that's with it like Matthew, that's fine. For the most part it's with the brothers. These are just the people I move with. The dorms are also mostly separated. The brothers and the troublemakers are in my dorm. Matthew is in a mostly white one, the quiet ones. I probably got in mine by chance.

"I'm staying out of trouble myself. I know there are a couple of officers around here who have this personal thing with draft resisters, especially black ones. You can tell when they talk to you. Like one won't let me in the auditorium when he's on duty. He knows I go in daily to play the horns, but he won't let me in. He says he can't be responsible. And then those days are long.

"There's very little to do. I'm an orderly. After all the dudes leave, Mike and I can clean up the showers, toilets, mop the floor. If we stretch it, it can take an hour, then nothing all day. I was transferred from the hospital."

"So what do you do all day?"

"I lay up in my room and read, listen to the radio, from about twelve to four. Then I go up to the auditorium to play if I can."

During the course of the session, Hank had become progressively more somber and depressed. I mentioned it.

"It's thinking of the outside. I'm sort of cutting loose, drifting away. The visiting doesn't even matter anymore."

"Wouldn't you miss it?" I asked.

"I don't think so. It just doesn't change anything. The one person I'm closest to isn't allowed to visit me. For my family it's a real hardship. The cash is prohibitive. It doesn't make sense to come up for an hour visit. Besides we're very tight, my mom, sister, and myself. It doesn't matter if they come or not. We have this thing between us and it doesn't matter. Like my mom came up before Christmas. I hadn't written, but she didn't come down on me. She said, 'Don't you worry about it. It doesn't matter if you write or don't write. We still communicate.'

"I think of my stepbrother who was in the joint. He just got out. They'd see the way he wrote, demanding letters, like, 'I expect you to be here, I need this or that,' all kinds of stuff which beats them into the ground. I don't want that. They know I'm here and I know they're with me. And someday I'll be out.

"But meantime it's like you're constantly on edge. It's a different place. You have to adjust to things. Even the way you talk to people. You have to watch that. A dude is jugged at so much where he's on edge with fellow dudes around him."

.. "Why do they do that?" I asked.

"That's something different. That's tight, and it's altogether different, but you've got to have the timing right. You've got to know when it's right—when it gets tension off. Everything is changed by the closeness. Like on the street, if someone wants to be left alone, you leave him alone. Somehow you know it. But here a dude can go off for some small reason—like a guy who's snapping his fingers to music on the radio in the next room. I've seen it happen. The tension. I've never been slugged since I've been here, but I've had to dig myself in to prevent my doing it to someone else. And this isn't me.

"Over in the mess hall the other day I got up and took a tray to the table and this dude backed into me and I spilled my milk. I set it on the table, and he just stood there looking a little confused, and I said, 'You could say excuse me, you mother-fucker,' and I was just that close to going off at him. It not only shocked me, it shocked the people I was with. The violence, they hadn't seen me like that. I found myself getting tighter. The whole scene bugged me. The poor dude didn't do anything really. It was just that he happened to be there at the moment. I think a little of Mike is rubbing off on me. This business of talking down the hacks . . . But things are getting tighter everywhere. I think it's bad for blacks on the outside too—they're going to come down just a little bit harder, that's all."

.. "What can be done about it?" I asked.

.. "I don't know. If I had any ideas, maybe I wouldn't be so pessimistic."

"Is there any route you can go?" I asked.

"I don't know." There was a long pause. Then he asked, "Are you still so sure I'm not capable of violence?"

I thought of the enforced passivity with its increasing call for action; I thought of the exposure to the survival philosophy of prisons and the resultant cynicism engendered; I thought of the harassment by guards and the sense of impotence in the face of it; I thought of the deprivation of love and affectionate contact, and of the need to learn to live without them; I thought of the sharp black-white polarization of prison, which he had somehow managed to avoid before; I thought of the dreams of violence, increasing in frequency and intensity; I thought of his youth. And I wasn't sure.

I wanted to be sure, to comfort him, to reassure him, but our relationship was beyond lies, deeper than reassurance. I merely shrugged.

5 ⫷

O-71486: Tim

$\mathbf{F}$air-complexioned, reddish-blond hair, long-lashed blue eyes, handsome to a point just short of prettiness, Tim is a Hollywood version of the boy next door, but there is a sense of tension and turmoil incompatible with that image. These are qualities that in many ways are his undoing, for they suggest the unpredictable (true) and the violent (false), both of which are threatening to authority. He resists description. He is certainly not surly or volatile; in behavior his speech and manner, if anything, are cool. But almost immediately one senses a contained anger, a tautness, a defiance that cannot be defined, only felt. He manages somehow even when compliant and courteous to be able to seem defiant. I suppose one would have to say that he is the world's worst dissembler, with an almost transparent body through which inner emotions shine through—and inner strengths.

Perhaps it was this essential power (rarely tapped) that so threatened the authorities for, from the very first, Tim was seen as a potential troublemaker. And because he was seen that way he seemed destined for the role of fall guy.

If he could not hide his anger, neither could he hide his affection. A man of empathy, capable of feeling strongly, he managed to elicit strong feelings in return. Here was someone with real leadership potential who seemed totally incapable of exercising leadership. I suppose what I sensed was a man who would go through life "feeling" more than thinking; a man who would be incapable of hurting anyone but himself; a man with an enormous capacity for compassion and passion. A man of irresistible charm.

Of all the inmates he was the one most likely to generate counter-transference problems in an interviewer. Counter-transference, as I have mentioned, is a psychoanalytic term to describe the emotions generated in an analyst by the patient, which must be observed and controlled in order that they not be permitted to obstruct the flow of treatment. They may be expressed or utilized, but only when they serve the therapy, not the therapist.

Tim's emotionality made him seem particularly vulnerable. His looks made him seem particularly boyish. His readiness to give affection encouraged one to want to give affection to him. He was a difficult person not to paternalize (at least for this analyst). And it was equally difficult to avoid treating him as a patient. The gap between his potential and what he was going to achieve was so apparent to an analyst as to be painfully seductive. I had to keep reminding myself that I was not there to do psychotherapy. But the way a picture hanging askew beckons the correcting hand, the obviousness of his problems called for insight and direction.

There is a kind of psychoanalytic bias that presumes that a person's fate is always a matter of his own selection—that he who suffers does so, not accidentally, but by design. Of all the imprisoned war resisters Tim most fulfilled the stereotype of the self-destructive, unrealized goof-up that most analysts might have anticipated the imprisoned war resisters to be. In actuality no one could have anticipated the heterogeneity that this group really represents.

Tim is not very articulate, and as a result it may be hard to sense him in print as a person. So much of him is expressed in the openness of a grin, in a self-deprecating shrug when he is taking himself "too seriously." It is best illustrated in the way he allowed himself to form a relationship with me. In an attempt to illuminate his personality as well as his history, I will focus on that relationship and the way it developed during the course of the interviews.

I started the first interview with the usual "Tell me about yourself."

He told me the following: "I grew up in the city. I went to a college for a while—the city college. I dropped out of school. I sent my draft card back in September of 1966. I worked for a Catholic mission group for about a year, until last January. Then I was sentenced to three years in June of 1968." Long pause. Inquiring glance. Then, "That's about it."

When I remained silent, indicating that I obviously felt that was not "it," he went on to outline his war resistance, in detail, and with an animation quite in contrast to the way he related his family and personal history.

Without going into those details, I might say that the content was such that within ten minutes of the first hour I found myself making my first "interpretation." I asked him whether positions of authority were as scrupulously avoided all his life as they had been in that period. He wasn't "sure what I meant," and his unreadiness to deal with it being the surest sign of the prematurity of the statement, I dropped the subject.

He spent some fifteen minutes giving me some colorful impressions of prison life, stopped, then said, "What else is there?"

I said to him that I didn't quite feel that I knew him or his background as fully as I might and wouldn't he tell me a little more.

"I don't know what to tell you except what I already told you."

"What have you told me?" I asked.

"Well, let me see. I was brought up in the city. I went to paro-chial school. There are seven kids in the family. I am the oldest. My parents now live in the suburbs. I'm twenty years old now."

Again he settled back as though he had given me a definitive au-tobiography.

"Let me hear a little more about your parents," I said.

"My father is a salesman and my mother is a librarian. My fa-ther tends to gamble and has to be careful that he doesn't spend more than he earns. I don't know what that's related to or why. My mother takes it and generates a kind of long-suffering atti-tude. She's been threatening separation for years, and it looks like they might actually do it this time. They're held together by this religious thing. A separation would be a great scandal.

. "My father is more gregarious than my mother. I suppose he's a little uncertain of himself. I like him as a man, although I don't know him very well. He always wanted to do the best thing for his family that he was able to. He wanted them to have a nice vacation every year, to buy a house outside the city. His big ambition was finally realized when I was a senior and the family could move to the suburbs. He showed a dedication to his fam-ily, I think. He's really got some personal problems that he hasn't been able to work out."

The story of the family makes Tim sound much less communi-cative than he was. As I have previously suggested, it was pre-cisely in this area that he had his difficulty talking. For most of that first hour he was quite capable of giving me a full picture of his involvement with the draft resistance and some of his resent-ments of prison.

In the second interview I did not press him for further family background but permitted him to talk about whatever he pleased. He was much more spontaneous, and again his talk was primarily about prison adjustment with no mention at all of his family. Toward the end of the second hour he reported his first dream. In the fact that it was a sexual dream it followed the general pattern, but with its emphasis on frustration and incompleteness it had Tim's original mark.

"I don't remember many dreams. When I do they're very colorful. If I remember parts of dreams it's usually pleasant. The one that I do remember was the one time that I had the feeling that I was out of prison. It was a conscious thing in the dream. I had just gotten out and Patty and I were going to bed and I couldn't reach a climax. It was very frustrating. I tried and tried and I was very aroused but still I couldn't climax. Then I woke up and it was doubly frustrating, both sexually and being back in jail. That's all I remember about it. It was very short."

This was just before the end of our time, and since I was on a tight schedule I told him we would have to stop then, and I attempted no interpretation of the dream.

On his way out he turned and, half embarrassed, said, "I enjoy these talks. It's a funny thing to say but I do."

It became apparent that when Tim trusts, he trusts openly and completely. The statement at the end of the second session was a declaration of affection and faith, and with a directness that does not come easily to most. The third interview revealed the degree to which he will go once he offers his trust.

He started in immediately. "A kind of funny thing happened. The last time you were here you asked me to remember dreams. Well, the first night that you asked I had a long and complicated dream. I dreamed that when you drove back to New York you hid a whole group of us and took us back with you. We all just drove back to New York and stayed.

"We were standing at the gate, and as you were driving out in a big car—a convertible—you said, 'How about going for a ride? Come on in and we'll just ride around for a little while and then we'll come back.' And that seemed all right, so we got in the car and went for a ride. Then we got to the town, and Paul was standing by the road, hitchhiking. I think the other person with me was Bill. When we saw Paul it was obvious that he had escaped so we all decided, why not give it a try. You had the car and we could drive to New York with you.*

"You drove us back, and then I was in the city. I went to the apartment of Jeff, a friend of mine, to get a change of clothes and some money to get out of the city. I figured I had two hours to get out before they would start looking for me. Sure enough, when I got to Jeff's apartment, there was Patty waiting for me. I told them I'd escaped but I wouldn't tell them how, and I wouldn't tell them where I was going because I didn't want them implicated. I needed fifty dollars. Jeff just kind of turned around, faced the other way with his head bowed, and chuckled the way he always did. He was so obviously amused. He was shaking his head and chuckling and at the same time he said, 'That's too bad. There were a lot of people there who liked you and thought highly of you.' It was funny because it was something you [referring to me] had said to me the last time. So then I told them I had to be on the move. I only had two hours.

"There was a lot of tension in the dream. I had to get everything done. I wanted to change my clothes. But when I looked at my pants they were tan corduroy pants, not prison pants, so I didn't have to change. I just needed the fifty dollars to get a bus to Seattle. I was going alone—without Patty. It seemed crucial that if I left, it not be with anybody that was close to me on the outside because I could be traced through them. So I was going to have to break off all my ties—with Patty, my family, my friends. If Patty were to come with me she would have had to make the same sacrifices, and I wouldn't want her to. But I expected that she would give me the money, which of course she did. I woke a few minutes later."

I asked him (he had not made it clear) whether this was a happy, sad, or frightening dream.

"The overwhelming feeling was tension, a great deal of tension. Everything had to be done quickly. Getting out in two

---

* Paul and Bill, both also COs, will be discussed in the following chapters.

hours, knowing they would be looking for me in exactly two hours. That's unrealistic really. You have much more time."

"You talk about this as though you were seriously thinking about it," I said.

"Of course. I make plans all the time. Most of us do. Half seriously, but sometimes quite seriously. I don't know anyone coming to jail who doesn't seriously think of escape, at least in the beginning. As you're here longer you work out an adjustment, but in the beginning it's almost a necessary part of the reaction to being in jail.

"With me I think it was perhaps more serious than with many of the others. Bill and Paul and I discussed it in earnest. But if we haven't acted on it by now we probably won't. The more time you've got in, the less time you've got to do."

"Did you think of me as a real possibility?" I asked.

"That was pure fantasy. I would never expect you to do that, but I had been thinking of you. You had asked me to remember dreams, and this was the first one I had. You were obviously on my mind. I don't know. I enjoy talking to you. I thought, 'Well, he'll leave and in a short time be in New York!' I thought how nice it would be to get in the car and just start riding. The main drawback of course is cutting one's self off from family and friends. I don't think I could do it, unless things got intolerable here or deteriorate badly on the outside.

"Then, from another aspect, I'm not sure what purpose escaping would serve. I suppose I could escape and then turn myself in as an act of publicity. But I'm not one of the established leaders anyway, and I don't think it would have much impact."

I told him that while everyone might have these fantasies I sensed that they were stronger with him. I then let him know that I felt serving time was harder for him (and Paul) than for most of the others. He wasn't sure that was so but he allowed that it might be. I asked him what he thought the reasons might be.

. . "I feel like a failure. There must be some purpose in coming to jail, but I do nothing here. I feel like I should continue to make some kind of witness against oppression in society. I feel I have to do something, and I'm not even sure that feeling is genuine, whether I want to do something to impress other people in the peace movement or if I want to do it because it must be done."

.."Isn't your being here witness enough?" I asked.

"That's a beginning. There are those who feel you have to go further, though, than just resisting the draft, that if it's worth going to jail, it's worth going on.

"It seems so easy on the outside to resist—you refuse to cooperate with the draft. It's direct and clear-cut, but once you're in here, what can you do? In here there doesn't seem to be any defined position. It's up to the individual. I've thought of non-cooperation. I think logically it may be a good position."

He then described his non-cooperation when he was arrested and went to jail. "I told them I could not promise to appear in court, so they issued a warrant and arrested me. They said that I could be released without bail if I signed a paper saying that I'd appear when my trial came up. I said that I could not honestly say—that I hadn't made up my mind yet. Since I refused to sign, they put $5000 bail on me. This was beyond anything I could raise. I had to go to jail.

"In there I continued non-cooperation. I refused to work, to accept any jail jobs. They then put me in segregation. I was there the rest of the time, about three and a half weeks. It was a small cell, about seven feet by four feet, with a double bunk, a toilet, and a sink. It was while I was there that I realized that if I were going to prison I might just as well work to help support the community. I realized that in those jails where there was no work, the prisoners' conditions were a lot worse. Perhaps it was a rationalization to get out of segregation. I didn't dislike being in segregation but—I don't know—it was much the same way as when I decided to oppose the draft: it was only after the fact that I began to really study the question. The action itself was all intuitive.

"At this point it's hard for me to say where I stand. I'm not sure that pacifism is my bag any more. I'd like it to be, but I'm not sure it is. There's something about being in here that confuses all issues. I think, in addition, I have a great deal of uncertainty about my own strength and about my own values. But then again I always have. I think it must come from my family— I suppose from my childhood."

"Tell me about it," I said.

"I don't know where to start."

"Start anywhere," was all I said. And what came out, as you will see, was in dramatic contrast to that sparse history he had given me in the first hour.

"I went to school, got good marks as a kid. It never seemed very important. It was always easy. I don't remember much of what happened when I was a kid. I don't even remember my relations with my parents very clearly when I was terribly young. Not until I was thirteen or fourteen. I know we never talked much. There was never any conversation between us. My father didn't have much confidence in me. Maybe it's just that, since I didn't feel it in myself, I assumed that he didn't. But no, I'm pretty sure that he didn't."

"Why do you say that?" I asked.

"Well, I remember several times when he showed such contempt for me. There was one time in particular that I will never forget. He called me . . . he called me 'goon,' once. It hurt me for about two or three weeks after that. It was so much pain, and now I can't even remember what the incident was all about.

"Then when I wanted to go to college he didn't want me to. He wanted me to get a job to help support the family. I had always worked since the time I was about ten, selling newspapers, delivery boy, that kind of thing. I used to work on Saturdays and turn the money over to the family. There was a constant money crisis. Almost always we were in debt. Sometimes we didn't have enough money for supper. My mother had to borrow money from neighbors. That's because my father drinks and gambles a lot. He always—we're very similar in a lot of ways—he always feels very inadequate, but he wants everything for his family. He wants everything to be well. He wants them to have good things and be comfortable. He wants his sons to succeed, but the way he wants them to have good things is so erratic.

"He's totally incapable of making a steady income. Everything is done in fits and starts. He's the kind of salesman who won't produce for months on end and then will go on a binge of selling, setting all kinds of records and making a lot of money. Everything would be fine then and we'd live off the fat of the land.

"I remember one year when he was $5000 in debt to his boss alone. We were almost frantic about what we'd do. But then the following year he made so much money that we finally bought that house in the suburbs he'd wanted for so long.

"Every summer he would insist that we have a big vacation. One summer we went to the seashore, and he wound up having to borrow from relatives to pay for the summer house. He threw a great big party, had them all come down for the weekend, and then hit them all to pay the rent. It was poor one month and rich the next—always erratic.

"It was frenetic, I suppose. I never sensed any stability in him —or in the home. Then when he would drink he could get mean. I was afraid of him. I think he sometimes beat my mother. We would wake up and hear her crying, pleading with him to stop. We were afraid to do anything about it. He was a lot bigger than us most of the time. I guess I felt terribly impotent about that. When a man is beating your mother you hate him; at the same time you can't hate him if he's your father. You're not allowed to hate your father. You have to love him anyway and forgive him. There's all the demands made on you by the church, friends, and even by your mother. 'Understand him, He's sick, He needs help, Don't hate him.' So what are you left with—conflict, guilt, and ambivalence."

"Did he ever beat you?" I asked.

"No, he never did, nor my brothers either. It has only been in the past two years that he has tried to attack me, only after I started getting into this draft thing. He interpreted it as a personal attack against him. I don't know, maybe it had been, maybe at least partially it was. He thinks I'm misled, foolish, duped—and that of course is another thing. For the fact that he thinks I am foolish reflects his lack of confidence in my judgment and intelligence.

"He used to say to me that I could never get along on my own. I couldn't get a job, I couldn't do anything, I couldn't even get myself arrested. I hope," Tim said with a grin, "I haven't taken him literally. He didn't say it very often but then again . . ."

"Is his opinion still terribly important to you?" I asked.

"Oh sure. I know it shouldn't be, but it is. I think I may identify with him. I feel very much like him. I'm emotional in the same way. I work in bursts. I don't carry things through till the end. At least I've always felt that way about myself. But I'm not temperamentally like him. I hardly ever get into a rage. I used to be frightened that I'd become an alcoholic, but it was an unrealistic fear. It's really not conceivable.

"All that period, just before my arrest, the crises in the family kept mounting. I was so torn between my responsibilities to the peace movement and my responsibilities to the family. I was working with the poor. I'd taken vows of poverty, but shouldn't I be working to help my family? It all seemed so confusing and such a contradiction. It doesn't seem right to ignore the needs of your family, but at the same time if the 'needs' of the family were to have a car and a summer house and a TV and fancy clothes, did that make sense?

"I simply couldn't resolve the conflicts, particularly in the short time I had. I knew that I would be sent to jail in a short period. I finally 'resolved' it by going away with Patty and forgetting both my work and the family. Now that I have more time and some distance the conflict seems less real and less urgent. I simply don't feel my responsibility to my family as much as I once did. I feel that I've finally left the family."

He continued, talking about his brother, giving me a detailed account of his brother's problems, indicating his concern that his brother not follow the path of the father.

"I notice you didn't mention your mother at all," I said.

"No, I didn't," he replied, grinning.

"Why do you smile when I ask you about your mother?"

"Because there is one thing I feel embarrassed telling you—I purposely didn't mention her first. I've just been reading certain books that indicate that you can tell the kind of person by the way he talks about his family. The uncommitted youth talks about his mother first, and very little about his father. The young radicals talk about their fathers, and very little about their mothers. So I made sure that I mentioned my father first. I didn't want to be an 'uncommitted youth.'" He laughed. "In all honesty, I do think he's the bigger influence in my life. I think, though, I might have been inclined to talk about my mother first because it would have been less embarrassing, and she's an easier person to talk about."

I did not point out to him that in the first hour, before he had read the book,* he managed to talk first, and more, about his father than he did his mother. In addition, as one might expect, when he did begin to talk about his mother he had exhausted the subject in about five minutes.

Unlike many of the others, Tim had no clear-cut idea as to why he was in prison. There was a basic revulsion to the idea of war and killing in general, and specifically the Vietnam war. He was deeply religious, even though he had given up formal Catholicism, and he had constantly striven for a life that would involve service and giving. Whatever his original motive and intentions, they were being altered by his confinement.

Tim likes people, he needs them, and the isolation of prison

* Kenneth Keniston, *The Uncommitted: Alienated Youth in American Society.*

was changing him, hardening him. He indicated this in the first hour when he gropingly attempted to define his present position and how his prison experience was changing it.

"I don't know. I used to think that I was a pacifist, but I'm not sure any more. I'm not sure that position ever exists in reality. Lately I've been reading things that suggest aggression may be a beneficial drive, and I can't really answer that. At one time I thought to become a complete and total pacifist would be a fine way to develop yourself. I don't think so any more. As I go along I keep changing my motives for not being in the army, but my conviction remains just as strong. I don't believe in this war and I don't believe in the domination of the weak by the strong. I have yet to develop a philosophy of which I'm convinced. Nor can I say that I belong to any political or, for that matter, social group. I suppose many people would have thought of me as a hippy. I had long hair and a mustache and I wore old clothes, but I never considered myself one. Certain things in the hippy movement I like. The concept of communal living. The concept of cutting down on physical and material needs. But to me hippies are hard-core drug people, and the drug part I stay away from. I do like their tolerance of others and emphasis on love."

I asked him if he was saying that his position on the war was more moral than political.

"I suppose that's right. It is political too, of course, you can't really separate them, but more moral," he answered.

I then asked him if he had thought of the choices other than prison.

"I don't feel there were any other alternatives. I don't know why everyone who is opposed to the war is not here in prison. I believe your behavior better indicates what you are than what you say. They all should be here. At any rate I feel I had to make a stand. I don't see any other way. You can't change society very much by claiming to be a homosexual or any of the other dodges. But then again I suppose I'm not changing society very much anyway.

"What it comes down to is you have to be honest. Even if you're afraid. At one time I was quite a bit afraid of the draft board and later of jail. Then, after having known people who had been in jail, I got over it. The terrifying things I dreaded aren't as bad as I had anticipated—brutality, homosexuality, the possibility of attack. The really difficult things are those I hadn't appreciated in advance: not seeing your friends, the people you're close with, your family; all the pettiness, the little things—'keep your shirt tails in'; the constant announcements on the loudspeaker; having your mail censored; having to go through all kinds of rigmarole to write people; the arbitrariness with which requests are either filled or not.

"And friendships have such a tentative quality here. There's a hesitance to make a close friend because he may go home before you. You don't feel like getting tight with anybody. I'm not sure why."

He then talked about his decision to work and cooperate and questioned the correctness of that attitude, suggesting that noncooperation and striking might more effectively dramatize what prison is really like, to those on the outside.

"When I think of reforming prisons I'm totally ineffective because what I'd really like is their total elimination. They do such harm to people, and I don't think when I'm out in the streets the danger of having to go to prison again would stop me from doing something."

He then talked about the bitterness that was beginning to develop in him. "I don't know where it comes from. I'm just discovering it now, toward guards, personnel, caseworkers. Especially the caseworkers. They're still cops although they think they're doing something more elevated, but all they're doing is being a cop, making sure you follow the rules. Caseworkers are afraid to do anything for the prisoners. They're so uptight—what will Washington think? They have the power to grant small things, like extra visits, but they usually won't. For example, a friend of mine was going to visit another friend who was already in prison, on the sixth of July. Then he heard that I was here so he called to see if he could see us both. Since he wasn't on my list he was refused the right to visit me.

"Then there is that whole silly hypocrisy of talking about rehabilitation. In actuality it is quite clear that what they want to do is punish us. It's so obvious. You merely have to study the difference in the attitudes of the Parole Board toward the JWs and the rest of us. The JWs are granted paroles—some after twelve or fifteen months. None of us gets out then."

By the third interview Tim was considering whether he wouldn't have been wiser to have gone to Canada. There was still, however, a marked attachment to his home and city.

"I don't think I'd feel comfortable staying in Canada for a longer period of time than a year or so. But being here and being cut off from society in general is terribly difficult. I love living in a large city; the numbers of different people, the aliveness. Canada in its way would cut me off from the past that I liked.

"The hard thing in here is the sense of time—time wasting. It's so peculiar. There's such relative freedom here. There isn't much supervision; people aren't looking over your shoulder; they don't force you to work actually. They assume you'll loaf and seem almost to encourage it since there isn't enough work to be done. I suppose if we could find some way to feel we weren't wasting our time, we would feel all right and there wouldn't be this pressure to escape—to do something.

"You can always read, and I've gotten some good books from some of the other inmates. Recently, however, it's getting a little harder to read, and my ability to study has been impeded. I've heard from some of the others who have been in longer that it gets progressively more difficult. It's the sitting around, the stagnation, the feeling of being cut off that's so unpleasant.

"And then it's the whole feeling of having come to prison for a political effect, and who knows what effect, if any, it's having. Certainly just sitting here gives one the feeling of doing nothing. Bill and I are constantly talking about what we can do. I think we both, as different as we are in our backgrounds, seem to share that same temperament. Maybe the talk is a substitute for the action. At least it gives us something to think about. And then it relieves a certain amount of the guilt we have for not being totally non-cooperative.

"Did you ever here of Cordon Bishop? He was a CO in World War II who, when they picked him up, just refused to walk, or move, or take any positive action on his own part. He would lay there and soil the bed. If they picked him up and left him in the corridor, he would just stay there until they moved him. He had to be force-fed. He said that he wouldn't have anything to do with taking care of himself for he wouldn't contribute anything to the functioning of the prison. I don't remember how long he was in, but he did this for his full time. And even when they released him he wouldn't move until they took him physically and put him in a car. None of us is doing anything remotely approximating that. Nobody is taking any form of open resistance that I know of."

Between my third and fourth visits with Tim, in January of 1969, there was the only organized action by the war resisters to occur during the period of my research, some two and a half years. (This will be described in some detail in Chapter 9.) The compliance of these young men had been in many ways astounding, and, as Tim suggested, totally unlike the COs in World War II, but they paid a price for it in self-respect and self-confidence, as can be seen from the previous conversation. The story of the rebellion as it occurred is almost a parody of misunderstanding and ineptitude, for certainly the administration could not have engineered things more poorly if it had been their intention to provoke a strike. In many ways it was sheer good fortune that the incidents with the war resisters did not escalate to involve the entire camp.

For some of the war resisters, as one might anticipate, the action was almost a relief. During the period of institutionalization their guilt had been mounting over their cooperativeness and their lack of assertive political action, which was seen as "emasculating," "giving in," and in many ways the provocative, overreactive behavior of the administration forced the prisoners to indulge in a degree of healthy indignation, assertive action, and expiation of guilt.

When I came to the prison camp in January I found that my total population was dissipated. Three of them had been transferred earlier to other sections of the country for the convenience of the government, and this seemingly arbitrary transfer had been in part a precipitating cause of the rebellion. Twelve of the men who had participated in the protest had been transferred to the Wall. Eleven of them were now in segregation. One was in "the hole." As might have been predicted, the one in the hole was Tim. To my surprise, and relief, I was permitted to see him.

He walked in with a big, self-conscious grin on his face. No shoes, haggard looking, red-eyed, needing a shave, looking gaunt, yet with a somewhat manic air. He was obviously delighted to see me.

"Some changes since you were last here, huh?" he started.

"What are you up to?" I asked.

"I guess I'm up to fasting and refusing to work, at least for the time being anyhow. It's a protest against the injustice of the prison system and the total lack of respect for prisoners as simple human beings by the administration. It was really provoked by the sneaky way they transferred Jim back here last Wednesday. I was dragged across the sidewalk with Jim and Al."

He then went into the background of some of the tension that had been arising between the COs and the administration that led to the particular confrontation. "When Jim said he wasn't going to walk, that they would have to carry him, I agreed with him in that position and decided I would try to support him by getting in the way of anyone who grabbed him. Not by being violent, but by putting myself between them and Jim, and in that way make it more difficult for them to take him to the Wall. When they came in I was with Jim, and they evidently assumed I was planning to go to the Wall with him, for they started dragging us to the door. Al sat down on the floor and wouldn't move so he got dragged too. He was the only one that got badly hurt. We were dragged all the way from the dormitory up to the administration building across the gravel road. I wasn't hurt. I was kicked a couple of times while being dragged. Al was badly scraped. Jim and I fortunately still had our shirts on but Al didn't. Then, in addition, he was dragged by the heels, and Jim and I by the arms. I was dragged about two-thirds of the way and then carried the rest by four officers. I simply wanted to indicate by some gesture my resentment and opposition to the treatment they were giving inmates in general."

Tim and Al were released at this point, but a few days later twelve of them signed a petition and were transferred to the Wall, where Tim was separated from the others.

"But why are you treated differently from the others? Why are you in solitary while they're merely in segregation?"

"I guess I did it again. When they started to carry us out of the visiting room they first carried me and Bill and then put us down, planning later to put us on stretchers. So when they put Bill on the stretcher I got in front of the guys who were carrying him. That's honestly all that I did, but now they're talking about my interfering with an officer or assaulting an officer—all kinds of vague stuff. I didn't do anything but sit down in front of him, but he claimed I tried to trip him, so they put me down here in the hole. The administration has always been a little leery of me." He grinned. "Something must show."

"How long will you be here?" I asked.

"I don't know. They don't tell you much. They just keep me in here. I did ask one of the guards, but he said he didn't know. I imagine sometime this week I'll get to talk to one of the associate wardens, and if we can work out some deal I'll be sent up to segregation with the rest of the fellows or maybe even back to the camp. I really don't know. I've been fasting since Thursday. It's been about three days."

"Does it bother you much?"

"I'm a little weak. Fasting itself doesn't bother me. I think I'll probably make an offer to them if I talk to them on Monday. I'll probably offer to eat if they put me back with the rest of them. In solitary you can't have books. You can't have anything."

"What do you do to pass the time?"

"I haven't done much today. I did some calisthenics and so far I don't feel too weak. If I stand up after lying down for a while I get faint. I don't know—perhaps I'd be allowed the Bible, but then again I'm really not that interested in it any more." He smiled. "I might regain interest if I'm here long enough. All you can do is sit and twiddle your thumbs and do calisthenics. I don't think they'll keep me in the hole for more than a couple of weeks, because by that time, having been fasting, you would require hospitalization. If I faint even once they'll probably have to put me in the hospital. I'm taking water, which makes it a lot easier, so I should be able to hold out for a few weeks of not eating. I feel pretty good but I'm getting a little uptight with the solitude lately. I did some walking. The cell is ten feet long so I counted off and walked a mile."

I was concerned about him. As a doctor I was not convinced that he could last three weeks of fasting without risking significant harm to himself. He is a slight young man to begin with. I asked him if he would go back to the camp and agree to work if they said he could. He hesitated for a moment, considering the answer.

"I don't think I should. Not right now. It would be nice to get some sort of concession from them if we can. I do want to go back there, and I do want to work, and I will in a couple of weeks. I'm aiming for two weeks to see if I can get from them some statement—some honesty, any gesture that shows that they consider us as human beings. A little more care about transferring people out for no reason. Actually I didn't really want to sign the no-work petition. I wasn't one of the activists. Truth be known, only Phil was really militant. I didn't want to take a position now, but I felt I had to go with the group. For a time I had thought it was almost inevitable that I would get in trouble sometime while here and wind up in the hole. But I don't want to take a position where I have to spend my entire time in segregation. I'm afraid of too much solitude. I'm afraid it would mess me up, upset me psychologically."

"What is it you're worried about?" I asked.

"Well, I could become a recluse. I could become bitter. I don't want to. I don't know—the first night I was in the hole it just didn't seem like a place for me to be. It seemed like a place they put someone who is disturbed, a mental patient, or dangerous. I didn't belong in a cage. There's a flap on the window, and they kept it closed for the first twenty-four hours.

"I was a little worried then, but I'm not too worried now. It's given me some time to think out my position—it's easier to think down here for some reason. I really wonder what's going on. I try to decide at what point I will stop—how far I will go.

"The guards have been decent enough. They keep coming around and asking me if I'm all right. At least they did the first day—less today because it's Saturday. We don't get metal plates down here, just paper plates. At each mealtime when they ask me if I want anything, I say, 'No, thank you, just water,' and they give it to me.

"Actually when we first got here they had me up on the third floor in segregation with the rest and I thought I'd stay there, but about forty-five minutes later they took me downstairs in the hall and told me I was charged with attempting to hit an officer. I said it's not true but if that's the charge, okay. I never did see an official at that time. I was sort of surprised when they took me down here. There are twelve who refused to work—eleven upstairs and me in the hole."

He then recounted again some of the incidents directly preceding the confrontation, with all the resentments, the slights, the provocations. It seemed to me that chance events conspired with the insensitivity—more, the anxiety—of the administration to encourage a confrontation. I indicated this to him.

He responded, "Oh sure, but I have a feeling that at some point it had to happen anyway. It was chance that made it now. The administration just doesn't care about anything except to see that we don't cause problems. Perhaps they feel threatened. The ironic thing is that there had been no plan; no action was designed. We were more reacting than acting. Then, somehow a point was reached where there could be no turning back. They carried it to a point of obligation. We had to do something merely out of pride. We were pressed to a point where it would have been humiliating not to have made some response regardless of how small. There is a point where a protest is demanded and a resistance is required. When their lack of respect for you is public, then your self-respect must be shown. They will ignore, deceive, humiliate—yes, even bait you. As frightened and as passive as you may have become, a point is finally reached where pride and manhood assert themselves. It is only a chance as to when you reach that point where self-respect itself is on the line."

I was touched and concerned, and there was a shared and intimate moment of silence between us. I then asked him if he had any idea of what would happen next.

"No, I don't. I think I may have gotten in over my head. For some reason the administration sees me as a ringleader. I'm not sure why. Perhaps I get a little more angry than some of the other guys, a little more frustrated. It's funny because I wasn't really sure whether I was going to sign the petition refusing to work. Originally I felt that it didn't make sense. My position was only made up after a couple of them indicated that they would go it alone if necessary and drew it up. I then signed."

At this point I discussed with him some of the feelings I had about him: about the enormity of his potential; about my feeling

that, of all the people in the group, he had the greatest aptitude
for leadership; that many of the other men saw in him this potential and were ready to follow, but that his own self-doubts and
distrust of himself led him to abandon positions of authority; that
he evoked affection, which he accepted and reciprocated, trust,
which he honored and served, and admiration, which he ran
from. There was no embarrassment by the direct praise.

"When I get into a position where I know for sure what I'm
doing, people will follow me. But too often I just get to the intellectual position, then force myself to remain in the background.
It's a reflection of something other than the specific issue—something in me. What, I don't know."

I continued to press the point, revealing my doubts about his
present capacity to utilize his potential, and my concern about his
tendency to be self-destructive. I made it perfectly clear that I
was not referring to suicide but rather more subtle ways of de-
feating himself. He obviously was well aware of those aspects of
his personality and behavior.

"I have a feeling—a sense of the rightness of what you are saying. Many times I've felt I could succeed in many different areas,
perhaps any area I wanted. I know I have the intellectual ability.
I get along with people well enough to do it, but there does seem
to be something holding me back. I don't feel I've ever extended
or realized myself in any undertaking. I don't know what it is. I
can't concentrate my attention on any given area long enough to
really get into it deeply. I'll go to a certain point and do well,
much better than average to that point, and then I'll lose interest.
I'll withdraw. I don't know why. This has been all the way
through. After easy accomplishment and success in grammar
school, I found myself not doing the work, neglecting studies,
cutting classes. Then in the eleventh grade I transferred to
another school and was shocked, and insulted, when I was
placed in a slower section. That seemed to give me some impe-
tus, so I started to work and did extremely well."

Tim related in almost classical detail what has been described by one eminent psychoanalyst, Dr. Lionel Ovesey, as a "success phobia." He then went on to describe incidents in his life through high school and college where he would succeed up to a point and then withdraw.

Some of this conversation continued in the next visit. By that time he was back at the camp. I told him I was glad to see him back and that he looked much better to me. In truth he still showed the physical signs of his fast, was quite thin, but in extremely good spirits. He started right in telling me what had happened to him in the interval. Tim has always impressed me with his amazing capacity to remember days, dates, hours, and details of our last conversation. This was true of many of these young men, and I think it was not just a testament to their memory and' intelligence but the fact that the visits had become a break in the monotony, a change in routine, and had been endowed with special emotional significance for them.

"Let me see, I saw you on Saturday," he began. "I'd been in about three days. On Monday they had court. They asked me if I knew why I was in the hole. I said I thought it was because I had sat down before a guard. They said nothing, they merely nodded. They asked if I would be willing to go back to camp and work if they gave me permission. I said I didn't think I was ready to go back yet and asked if they couldn't give us some statement of faith that the administration would try to be more honest with us. Actually I think I would have found some reason under any circumstances. I had my own needs for continuing to stay there. They then asked if I was ready to go up to segregation with the rest of the guys, and I said indeed I was. They released me from the hole and gave me a cell on the third floor.

"In segregation, as distinguished from solitary, there are two sections. The second floor, where everybody is in double bunks and they get out of their cells periodically for exercise. They also get out to get their food and bring it back to the cells to eat and then get out again to return to the hall. Then there is the third floor, which is where we were. You get out of your cell only if they want to take you downstairs for interrogation; otherwise only twice a week for showers. There are forty-four cells up there. The last thirteen are separated—cut off from the rest by glass partitions and wire—and that's where we were. At first they had been in the big dormitory, sleeping on floors.

"They interviewed us individually after a week and asked us if we were ready to go back and work. They said something at that point about my kicking an officer. I was surprised at this, explained it wasn't so, and in detail described what had happened. When I was asked if I was ready to go back I said I couldn't make that decision as an individual but would have to consult with the others.

"We all discussed it when we went upstairs. It broke down to about six guys who didn't want to come back under any conditions and five who weren't ready just yet. I was ready to go back, but I didn't want to be the first, for I knew, having been in the hole, I had become a rallying point for the guys. I did tell them I would be ready to go back for a variety of reasons, which all added up to not seeing the purpose served by continuing.

"I was still on a fast. Bill started eating after four days. He was chagrined about being the first, but we all understood. Food is more important to him than for some of the others. After seven days a couple of the others took one meal and then alternately fasted and then didn't. I spent fourteen days without eating anything. I just drank water. Nothing happened. I suspected they wouldn't start force-feeding us until three weeks or maybe more. One of the men went on a water fast for five days. They took him to the hospital. Then Arlo Tatum* came to check up on us and

* Arlo Tatum is executive director of the Central Committee for Conscientious Objectors—a man who almost singlehandedly has done more to facilitate things for both the imprisoned conscientious objector and those boys who are either considering imprisonment or confused and unable to understand the laws in terms of their eligibility for legal exemption from service. His small office in Philadelphia is the center of an information network that serves the East Coast.

spoke to us. He wanted to know how we were being treated. He convinced the man on the water fast to stop fasting.

"As time went on I began to feel we should really go back even without obtaining a single concession. There simply were not enough of us to make ourselves felt. I had been ready to go back and I now felt the group was, but I didn't know how to let the administration know this. There was some word passed, and the response seemed to indicate that I would be treated differently, that I might not have the option of going back.

"I didn't know what to think of this. I thought of the various dispositions they might make and how I would adjust to each. I was most worried that they would put me in the general population. The associate warden had indicated that they weren't going to bother with segregation for us anymore, but they would put us in Dorm G. This is the one that's known as the jungle. It's filled with the hard-core homosexuals and violent ones. There had been rumors that this would be the new policy to keep us in line. The associate warden told me that there was a lot of opposition to my going back to the camp but that they hadn't come to a final decision yet."

Tim had legitimate reason for anxiety about the new policy being considered. To place them in the better dormitories in the general population would have been extremely hazardous; to place them in G would have been simply delivering the Christians to the lions.

Tim continued, "Immediately after returning from the interview the hack told us to pack our stuff. We were leaving right then because they needed the space. It is a good example of the confusion between statement and action. So on Monday, the seventeenth, back we came.

"We later got confirmation that they are indeed using the policy of putting people into G. There was a new man who came in and refused to walk when he was arrested. He didn't refuse to work, however—he refused to voluntarily walk into prison. They have been keeping him at the Wall to soften him up but presum-

ably keeping an eye on him. The first night he was there someone tried to rape him. He was evidently hurt, but he was able to
fight the guy off. Then they put him into G, the jungle dorm.
This, even after the guy tried to attack him. I don't know why,
perhaps he still didn't seem compliant enough. It was a constant
terror for him, and they knew what was going on. Finally someone took some sympathy with him, and they put him in the hole."

"Well, now that it's all over how do you feel about it?" I asked.

"As far as an organized action goes it was ridiculous. It never
even approximated a planned or defined political move. It was
always purely individual and emotional from the very start, and
I might say from that standpoint it felt good. I know it made me
feel a lot better. I had been feeling so frustrated and pent-up,
and for a change I had expressed myself. It helped. I'm doing
more comfortable time now.

"There's also been a major policy shift since you were last here.
Some of the guys went up for the routine parole hearing and
heard of the new eighteen-month policy. The word spread all
over, and sure enough it's true. Since the first of the year, with
the new administration, they have been granting us paroles at
eighteen months. It all dates from the Nixon administration—
imagine that!—or perhaps it's due to the spreading disenchant-
ment with the war.*

"I can't quite relate to it myself. It's still too remote. But it
would make a great difference. It already has tangentially, but
the idea that I might be out six months earlier is something so
exciting that I'm almost afraid to openly contemplate it."

I then asked him what he thought he might do when he got
out.

"I don't know. I have no ideas, only fantasies. When I was in
school I didn't have any goal most of the time. It was just to get

* This was a misconception shared by many of the prisoners. As I was
later to find out, the Nixon appointments to the Parole Board first took
office in May, 1969. The shift in policy at this time was a brief and
isolated phenomenon that may have represented the reconsideration, or
guilt, of men who sensed their imminent departure from the board.

through college, to stick out the four years. Then when I started to work in the inner city I was going to strive for personal understanding and openness toward all kinds of people. I started out using words like 'helping people,' 'pacifism,' 'non-violence,' 'Christianity.' Then I discarded these—helping people almost seemed to be condescension. I really hadn't found a way. There must be some way you can use yourself with people.

"I thought I began to see some kind of plan or concept of a way of living just before I was jailed. I began living in a store in the inner city the month before I came into prison. I had a small apartment, if you can call it that, in the back. I had my door open at all times. People just came in. Late at night people came in to talk. They would ask, 'What kind of store is this?' I would say, 'It's no kind of store at all.' I would have liked to have had more things to give away—I didn't have much. I had a few tools, and some of the neighborhood kids would come in and borrow them. I was teaching myself to make sandals. I had some leather there. Then I had a bunch of old printing blocks, eight different styles of alphabets. The younger kids would come in to play with that.

"I was working hard—painting it, wiring, spackling the walls. As far as money to pay the rent and all, I used to go in a couple of days a week and wash dishes. I spent a few dollars a week on food, maybe ten dollars. I ate dinner many nights at friends' houses. People came to my house too for dinner, but I used to serve mostly rice and fresh vegetables, whatever was cheapest. I enjoyed myself and my life. People would come in to the store, at first out of curiosity, I suppose. I began to be a part of the neighborhood. I wasn't some freaky hippy who was hanging out with other freaky hippies. And I wasn't a do-gooder who had come down to 'improve' the neighborhood. My feeling was that if I stayed there long enough I would begin to have an influence on that block—the way people thought. Already in a very short time I had some influence on the way the kids thought. The first couple of days they were contemptuous of me because of my appearance. I remember their comments behind my back about the funny pants I wore. They were old and baggy—I had gotten them from some hand-me-down place. They asked me why I didn't get a haircut. My hair was long but not down to my shoulders. Then after a few days the nature of the questions began to change. They were twelve to sixteen years old. We began to know each other and become good friends. They wanted to know why I was living here and how I was living. I said, 'Come in and see.' My door was always open because it was summer. Anyway, there was a plate-glass window so you could just look in and see. I never locked the door, whether I was home or away."

My middle-class and middle-age identity somewhat threatened, I inquired, with constraint, how one managed life with just a plate-glass window and an open door between him and the streets.

He laughed and said, "Well, I did tell you there was an apartment of sorts in the back. It was really one long room, the whole thing ten to fifteen feet wide and narrowing toward the back. Right where it got narrower was a seven-foot high bookcase extending from the wall on the left, and while there was no back to it, all the books and junk on it made it hard to see through, creating a screen. Behind it was a bed on the floor. Then there was another wall closing off a tiny kitchen. There was also a shower that had been put in and a toilet that was walled off like a separate room. It was quite comfortable—very nice. There was a curtain in the window that could be pulled open or closed, depending on whether you wanted more or less privacy.

"The kids came in; we sat around and talked. I kept a lot of magazines and books around—they borrowed them. Some of them wanted to learn how to make sandals. I promised to teach them as soon as I learned myself. I began to feel some hope; I thought if I stayed there long enough I would either get a steady job or work part-time—either mornings or nights, so I would always have the afternoons off. I could feel my influence on the kids. I thought, first the kids, and then perhaps eventually I might have some influence on the block itself. Not only the block but people passing by at night.

"The block was almost all white, Polish. They had a real thing about the blacks who had just taken over the adjacent area. A lot of the kids who were my friends in the neighborhood before—as a matter of fact all of them—were black. A friend had a store there—she used to open it in the afternoons and I would help. It was a tiny storefront. She had arts and crafts. It was a place to play records and to just hang out. All of these kids were between five and twelve. So then they started coming over to see me in the new store and would borrow my tools and play with the printing blocks. At first the Polish kids would get uptight, but then after a while they didn't. I wouldn't say they were good friends after a month—there was no magical transformation—but they didn't get uptight any more when they'd see black people in the store. Their mothers did, but the kids didn't any more, and that's a start.

"I thought that's a good thing to do—just move somewhere, get to be known. Not get to be known as someone who is going there to effect some change but just live there and perhaps by living there over a number of years, without trying to be a focal point or center, still serve as a catalyst for some kind of social change. It would be a form of political action while still working on other levels—on the very personal level."

He paused and smiled self-consciously. "Perhaps it was just a dream, but it was a gratifying two months and it's something I could look forward to doing again."

I left him feeling moved and touched. I had no great hopes for Tim unless his brief experience with me would stimulate him to seek some guidance or therapy, but I thought that his experiment was worth doing, and, then, I knew that shortly he would be up for parole. There was an exhilaration throughout the group, now that the opportunity for parole had apparently been opened to the war resisters. For Tim it meant that another six months of imprisonment was all that he had.

Tim did go for his parole hearing in March and discovered
that he could not be considered. During the time of the "strike"
he had been deprived of his good days—seventy-two in all—as
disciplinary action. This not only extended the time he must
serve but automatically made him ineligible for parole. No other
inmate had lost good days or had been disciplined at all. It effectively added one and one-half years to the time he had to serve,
no small punishment, yet when I last saw him he told me that he
had never been notified of the change in his status or the reasons
for the change, despite the fact that officially he was supposed to
be told. He presumed it must all have been a result of sitting
in front of the guard. He was hurt but not self-pitying. Despite
his inquiries he never did find out why he had never received notification from either the camp director or the caseworker.

In time, and with inquiry, I was able to piece together the sequence of events: all of the protest, all of the conferences with
the associate warden, the segregation, the isolation cells, the discussions of terms on readiness to work, all of the inquiries as to
motivations and exact details of behavior—all were after the fact.
On the day of the transfer to the Wall, the warden himself had
made the decision to discipline Tim. Since Jim, who had initiated
the conflict, was too public a figure, too prepared to serve as an
official martyr, he could not be touched. So, much-too-honest,
much-too-open, proud, and vulnerable Tim became the fall guy.
The warden has yet to meet him.

6 ⋘

O-71487: Bill

What prototype could one possibly use as a starting point in the description of Bill? Two contradictory and seemingly mutually exclusive images come to mind. For Bill, in manner, point of view, and appearance, is a Harvard farm boy. Short and with a relatively slight frame, he has the muscled forearms and heavy hands of a laborer; stiff, bristly, sandy-colored hair; the weathered, tanned, leathery face of a field worker into which are inappropriately set clear blue eyes framed by the steel-rimmed glasses of the intellectual.

While painfully slow of speech (the long pauses in this narrative seemed more discomforting to me than they did to him) he was not inarticulate. He was merely a bad articulator. Even in speech the dichotomy was manifest: the drawl, the plodding nature, the New England country twang were often inconsistent with the ideas expressed.

My first view of him was a shock. He had come off the job drenched from head to toe, with his hands raw, swollen, and peeling almost in sheets, as though he were suffering from some unspeakable disease. He offered no explanations for his appearance but simply stood there staring at me, eyes blinking. I invited him to sit down. He did so self-consciously, then averted his gaze, and throughout most of his interviews rarely looked at me.

After I indicated that I wanted him to tell me about himself, there was a long pause before he slowly started.

"Well . . . I'm from a farm in New England. I'm nineteen years old. I was a freshman at Harvard last year. I turned in my draft card in November of 1966 at a Vietnam anti-war rally. My student deferment therefore expired in December, because without a draft card I could not renew my application. I didn't want the 2S classification anyway.

"From the time I turned in my draft card I assumed that I would end up in jail. I got my induction notice in the early part of May. I withdrew from school in the early part of the second year—I had an understanding from them that I could return when my problems with the draft are over. After that I hitchhiked to Oregon to work for McCarthy and then continued working for McCarthy in New York. I was tried in July and then sentenced."

All of this was told in a dry, matter-of-fact manner.

"How did it happen so quickly?" I asked.

"Well, in my section there aren't too many who refuse induction, so the litigation period isn't long."

There was a long pause.

"So that's about all," he finally continued. "That's why I'm here. I think I mentioned it was more of a political act than a moral one, if you want to separate the two. I think if I had applied for CO status at the time I had registered and hadn't gone to school I'd be doing hospital work right now instead of being in jail. In high school I was more authentically a complete pacifist, in a moral-religious sense. More than I am now. I think this was a political act—hoping that if enough of us took this course it would create chaos in the draft. It obviously isn't working. If everyone who said he would go to jail rather than serve had gone the joint would be jammed. It should be at its peak. I'm afraid as a political effect it's a disappointment."

"Do you regret having taken the step?" I asked.

"Not especially, because although it may not help much in stopping the Vietnam war, I'm not too badly off. I have time to read, do the stuff I want to do. I have a lot of free time in my job. I wash pots every other day. That's my job."

I now realized the cause of his appearance.

"How did you get that job?" I asked with a touch of irony in my voice.

"Well, when I came here everyone was using a pair of beat-up old gloves and was getting a rash on his hands, so guys were working hard for about two days and then had to quit. I came right in the middle of that, so they put me on it. My hands get a little battered up, but since I have a lot of time off, I'm willing to stick with it. I don't know—if I wanted to change maybe I could, but I think it's better this way. I've put in seven to eight hours a day in the steam room—it's pretty hard work—that's all I do, but then I have that other day off."

"What do you do on your day off?"

"I read. Right now I'm studying some Italian and Greek grammar. Then there are some apple trees around here, and on bright days I wander around. There's a lot of freedom here. There's an old church about a half-mile down the road with some blackberry bushes behind it. I read, talk to the guys, play a lot of chess, play volleyball and basketball. Actually when I was at college I'd like to lie on the ground, reading books, and I'm doing the same thing here."

"Are you saying that putting in time here isn't terribly dissimilar to putting in time at Harvard?"

"Well, there's one difference. There are fewer distractions here in the way of feminine company."

"Then are you saying it's better here?"

"Well, in a way. There's no other place on earth where I could study Greek grammar in the summer but I'm doing it here. Of course the library here isn't as good as Weidener, but this absence of distraction is very important to me because I'm very good at wasting time, and I'm pretty apt to pursue any distraction rather than study some dry material."

The enthusiasm about free time and the expectation of useful use of it are not uncommon in the very early days of imprisonment. With increasing length of internment the free time is seen more and more as a burden and less and less as an opportunity.

I asked him how long he'd been in, and he told me less than a month.

"How long is your sentence?" I asked.

"I don't know. The judge said I'd have to do a year in prison and four on probation. The judge reassured me that if I 'behaved myself' I'd be out very early, but then when I got here I heard that I had a one- to five-year sentence and I'd be *eligible* for parole after one year, and that's a hell of a lot different from a one-year sentence. Since none of us are getting parole anyway, I might as well have a five-year sentence. So I seem to have gotten stuck even though the judge clearly told me I'd only have to serve a year. If what the judge had intended had been right, with good time I'd be out in about nine months; but if what they say here is so, I'll be getting out in 1971. It's funny, everyone at home, including my lawyer, thought I'd get a one-year bit. We were all pretty elated about it." *

He then returned to his earlier statement that things were not so bad in prison and indicated that it might not have adequately expressed his feelings; that is, when comparing the prison camp with his experience at the receiving jail and his week in the penitentiary, the camp seemed so free.

"I expected it to be a hell of a lot worse than it really is. I thought I might be locked in a cell and come out only for meals. I expected it to be much more dangerous. It was in the pen, but not here. I guess I was lucky—I was only there about six days. Some guys have a longer stay. The jail was exactly what I feared

* See discussion of Youth Corrections' Act, Chapter 13.

and thought it would be. Being in a little cage, filing out for breakfast, coming back with nothing to do, just sitting there.

"This is more like a CCC camp, although I hear it's worse in the winter when you're cooped up in the dorms. Most of the breakouts occur around Christmas time, but I have a tendency to stay out of doors even in the winter, so if a hostile atmosphere develops I'll just go out. I really don't need people much, so maybe I'm suited to doing time, although there are some people I already miss terribly—only about six though—some friends I've known for about five years, and my brother and sister.

"I have had doubts already. The other day when I was washing pots and it was unbearably hot, I didn't know whether I could make it through the day. I started considering whether to get paroled into the Army or not. Once the thought occurred, I couldn't shake it. I seemed obsessed with it. I haven't seen a river in months, and thinking about that seemed to create such a pressure in me—and I was on the verge of going to the camp director's office and asking for a parole into the Army. Then Jeff came along. He had done about a year and a half. He had this can of walnuts with him that he'd collected, shelled, and dried. He offered me some walnuts—it was a small thing—I don't know what it meant, but somehow or other it changed something in me. We were just talking, and he offered me the walnuts, and I figured if he could last that long and do the kind of stuff like with the walnuts, and if it could mean so much to me, then I should stick around so that in a year and a half I can offer some comfort to someone new, discouraged, and doubting—like myself now."

I then reminded him of an earlier statement indicating that he might have received a 1-O deferment if he had applied for it before he went to college.

"When I was eighteen, had I still been thinking the way I had in high school, I would have applied for CO status."

"What was the change?"

"I don't know. It's funny, in high school I was an absolutist. I would have been willing to let anyone beat me up for anything. I was totally and completely dedicated to non-violence. There wasn't anything that really changed my mind. My fervor for non-violence just died down.

"In my last two years at high school I started looking at what was happening in Vietnam. I'd never thought about anything political before. I was influenced a great deal by my brother-in-law. He had been in the Korean War and he came out a committed pacifist. He is a biologist and I am very close to him. I spent two summers in the country with him doing field work. I'm terribly fond of him even though we're very different. When I was closest to him—involved with him—I was a confirmed pacifist."

"What changed you from being a pacifist?" I asked.

"Well, it could be that I never was a pacifist and just thought I was."

"Do I understand then that you're now not opposed to killing?"

"Yes, I am. Isn't everyone? But I can now conceive it as necessary in the most extreme cases. Is there such a thing as a relative pacifism? If so, I would say that I am still more of a pacifist than the average person. But the one thing that has changed is that I'm no longer dedicated to non-violence."

Our time was up, and I thanked him, indicating that I would see him within a few months. He then gratuitously and unexpectedly did one of those incongruous things that are so characteristic of Bill. He got up and recited a section of a poem to me. He said that the poem had influenced him greatly, and he was convinced of its message that one must learn in life to approach everything with no anger, no fear, and no hope.

He stopped, paused, still not looking directly at me, and said, "The fear is the easiest for me. The anger is weakening. But the hope is deceiving—the hope is difficult." He wheeled and, walking out, added, "It's a good system if it works."

The second interview was a few months later. I had just come in from a cold November morning and was therefore unprepared for the incongruity of Bill's appearance. He was drenched in sweat, his hair plastered wet, and his prison blues clung to him as though he'd just been hosed down. I remembered his job in the steam room and asked him somewhat angrily why he continued in what was generally considered the worst job in prison.

He hesitated in his usual manner for what seemed an interminable time, obviously collecting his thoughts, and then began: "Well, I've asked the head man in the kitchen about a job like cooking or baking, something that would be useful on the outside, but he doesn't seem to think there are any openings. I haven't really tried to get out of the kitchen. I suppose I could if I wanted to."

"Why haven't you tried?" I asked.

Again a long pause.

"Well, there are certain practical advantages to working in the kitchen. You get a little better food than the others. You don't have to wait in this long line for meals, and you do have quite a few days off. Nonetheless I am thinking of trying to get out—the job gets worse as the weather gets colder. A man washing pots gets hot and sweaty, and then to go outside into that cold is uncomfortable."

He stopped as though the subject had been exhausted and he was waiting for the next.

I asked him how things had been going, now that he had served more time in prison.

"It's okay, I guess. I'm not institutionalized yet, and I'm trying not to be institutionalized," he offered.

"What do you mean by 'institutionalized'?" I asked.

"I manage to come and go pretty much as I please. I try to avoid eating at the same time that everyone does—working in the kitchen your hours are different and a little more flexible. I used to sleep in a bunk in the hall of the dorm—now I've got one of the beds in the dorm. It's slightly bigger and I have a locker.

"Then I must get up very early, because of the job, and I avoid the crowd getting up at the usual time. Everyone is piling out all at once, doing the same things, and it seems more like an ant colony than at other times. At night I try to avoid the routine activities. Also, I didn't learn my number for about a month—tried not to."

"So what you mean by 'institutionalized' is losing your sense of identity as an individual," I said.

"Yes," he agreed. "I've always read that if you stay in jail long enough this is what happens. I don't want it to. I never thought about it on the outside. Your individuality is one of those things that you think about only when it is threatened. I find myself struggling to be an individual, to be myself. So even though I never gave it a thought, it must have always been important to me to be an individual."

I used this opportunity to let him know that I didn't feel I knew much about him as an individual.

"Oh, I thought I gave you an outline the last time you were here. What did you have in mind specifically?"

"Your background might be helpful," I said.

"Let me see. The other night Tim and I were talking about that, trying to figure out whether we could see in our earlier life any traces of what we were to become. I remembered the impact of *Catcher in the Rye*. I read it when I was in the eighth grade. It articulated a lot of my inarticulate feelings about authority and things that are wrong with our society. The teachers, the headmaster, the successful grad, a funeral director, who comes back and gives his speech on how he succeeded. I reacted in much the same way as Holden Caulfield did to all of that stuff.

"But then I was in junior high school and it was a bad place. The worst school I had been to. Run by this little guy—typical education and a typical educator. We all marched through the halls in single file, one stair at a time, and of course only up the up staircase, et cetera, bells and buzzers ringing constantly, you couldn't step out of line, monitors posted all over the halls and stairs. It was disgusting.

"There was this compulsively detailed system of warnings. If you were caught with matches or cigarettes the student council would call you down for a meeting and have their little trial, and after three warnings you were in danger of suspension. It was a very bad place."

"Even then you objected to control and rigidity," I said.

"Arbitrary control or rigidity," he corrected. "I'm not against it at all times, but I'm particularly opposed to rigidity with little kids like that. The whole unfeeling manipulation—Jonathan Kozol describes it in *Death at an Early Age*. At our school the abuse wasn't nearly on that scale, but the administration and teachers relished their authority and played games with their power in exactly the same way.

"There were some teachers there who left permanent memories. We lived about eight miles away, and one teacher who knew this kept me after school because I had bought a Coke in the machine at the gas station—kept me just long enough to miss the school bus. I then had to walk the eight miles home. It gets bitter cold up there in the winter. Only someone who knows how cold those winters are knows how long eight miles is. The same thing happened at least twice again. All this with the full knowledge of the principal.

"But maybe I should tell you about my family in general. My mother is away for a year on a foundation grant. She's a sociologist. I'm not sure exactly what this specific project is, but she's going to be gone at least a year and part of it will be spent in Europe. This leaves my father home all alone. My father is now working in a small town near our farm, in a foundry. He's all alone, and there's this drudge job, eight hours a day. They're not separated—it's just that my mother had this opportunity."

"How does your father feel about this?" I asked.

"I never asked him. I suspect that he accepts it, but it is obviously lonely living out there all by himself."

"What makes you think he accepts it?" I asked.

"Well, by now, come to think of it, he may resent it. But he accepts it on the surface. He never openly or seriously objects."

"Is that his style?"

"Yes, it is, I guess—although he's a fairly strong person in a lot of ways. He's tolerant but he can act."

"You sound as though you were thinking of some specific action."

"Yes, I was. For a long time, before I was even born, my family raised turkeys. My mother worked on the farm too. All five of us lived on that farm and worked it. We had about two thousand turkeys, fifteen dairy cattle, and chickens, and young stock, and gardens—but I'm getting off the subject. The specific thing I was thinking about happened just before Christmas. Everything depended on those damn turkeys—whether we'd eat or not, or at least what we'd eat—everything depended on it. A lot of times guys would come up from one of the towns to steal a turkey, so my father would sleep in that bitter cold barn from early in the fall until Christmas. On an old couch on the barn floor in the cold—with a shotgun to drive out anyone who came up. He'd never shoot at anyone but merely shoot to scare them off.

"There was one particular incident where some guys came up to steal some turkeys, and my father shot his gun in the air. Then, unbelievably, someone with a rifle shot back at him. He leveled his shotgun and shot back at them. No one could see any-one—it was dark—but it was a big to-do. We all came out and they lit up the back roads. Next day some of the townspeople came up, came up in a group, threatening my father. He didn't back down at all."

"It is hard just keeping a family alive on only 170 acres. We've always lived on the farm even though my father works in the town now. He gave up the turkey business. We usually had enough to eat but often barely, and it would mean bouncing checks to get even that. Then there was the house—it was a big thing. It was always cold as hell—no central heating—one of those big New England eight-room wooden-frame houses. I have this memory of when I was about four years old, standing on a rocking chair next to the stove, having breakfast, trying to keep warm—how damn cold it was! We had three different wood stoves, and you would break your back just chopping wood to keep the stoves going. Occasionally when things were good we could buy coal, but it wasn't often we could afford it.

"We had to have a car, but they were always a lot of trouble, and when they needed repair the expense was agony. Then there were the cows who needed milking and the hens who needed care and then that awful job of killing off two thousand turkeys by hand and picking and cleaning them and peddling them house to house to house. You had to wait until the last minute, then work almost around the clock. I remember driving around endlessly delivering turkeys, and once my feet getting frozen. I can remember a few incidents when the discomfort of the life affected me."

This struck me as an astonishing degree of understatement.

"To go on with what the rest of my family is doing now: my brother is in medical school—he's three years older, twenty-two. His political thinking is like mine but he is a different sort of person from me. Maybe he is the same sort but puts the resources to different uses. He's very good at science. He's a good logician. I don't really know what to tell you about him."

"Is he different in temperament or personality?"

"Yes, comparatively. He's quieter. In a way I think he's more naïve, probably less sensitive in a social situation. Yes, he's less social, I'm the more social one."

"You don't see yourself as a quiet person?" I asked.

"No, I'm quiet when I'm alone but not when other people are around."

"Do you think of yourself as talkative?" I continued.

"Normally talkative."

"Do you find talking comes easy to you?" I asked, my incredulity rising with each question and answer and evidently at this point becoming apparent.

"I think it comes easier than you might get the impression. When you ask a specific question and I'm trying to think of a specific answer, I'll pause a lot before I say anything. It gives my audience more of an uncomfortable feeling than it does myself, because I'm used to it. In high-school days I was in the debating class, and lots of times when I wanted to make a point I'd stand there and think about it and embarrass others. It didn't embarrass me too much. I have sort of a jerky narrative speech in general, not just here, particularly if I'm on unfamiliar ground."

Then there was a long pause. Finally he said, "Well, I haven't told you about my sister yet. She's a housewife. She lives on a farm and her husband teaches at a local college. She went to Radcliffe for two years and the University of Colorado for two years."

"Why did she switch?" I asked.

"She got married. Her husband is a naturalist and he was going out to school there. She had the same major. Now she has two kids and is expecting another one. Her main interests now are her kids, cooking, and gardening, although in the last year when my brother-in-law had to take a field examination for his doctorate she took over his classes for two weeks."

"What's she like as a person?"

"She's short, brown hair, kind of a sense of irony. She's pretty intelligent. I'm close to her, probably a little closer to her than my brother. I've become more close in recent years because I did that summer work with my brother-in-law and stayed with them a couple of summers."

I was confused about the disparity between the farm background, the father doing menial jobs, and the intellectuality in the children. I asked him where all this intellectuality came from.

"I think I know the source. I think it comes from my father."

The answer was not at all what I was prepared for.

"He was a very good student as a boy," he continued. "He went to a one-room schoolhouse and then to high school. He was a good Latin and French scholar, and then he went to the university after first working for three years on a road crew to make the money.

"I don't know what his goals were. They were all mixed up. He would take courses in ornithology, Middle English, and lots of poetry. Whatever his aspirations were, I'm sure they were idealistic. The day he got married he quit school. He felt his responsibility to support a wife. He taught grade school for a while and then he bought his first farm. He writes a little poetry now and then. Once in a while he gets something published. He reads only poetry. I don't think he ever read a novel in his life."

(I think it worth noting here that while Bill started his family discussion with his mother, the emotional emphasis once again was drawn primarily from the relationship with his father.)

From the moment Bill walked in for our next appointment, it was obvious that one significant change had occurred; he had been transferred out of the kitchen. I commented on the fact that it was strange to see him dry.

He chuckled. "Yeah, I've been off the job for two days. I got a promotion. I'm now shoveling shit with the farm crew. I had to get out of the kitchen. It simply wasn't worth the time off. Anyway, I find that on the farm, too, I can find opportunities to be by myself. Tim works there too. Speaking of Tim, he told me that you'd asked him to remember his dreams so I've been trying to remember them as well. I've been having a lot of weird dreams. There are two that I can remember last night."

"Tell me about them," I said.

"Well, my brother and I were both in this joint [the prison], and we decided to escape so we walked out. We just started hitchhiking and we made it home. My mother was there and some friends. We sat around drinking beer and listening to country music albums, particularly one album by Johnny Pukka. This is not the sort of thing I would do if I did find myself home unexpectedly.

"Then, that same night, I had a second dream. I was riding on a motorcycle. There were a couple of people on a motorcycle in front of me, and we were tearing like hell all over this highway.

There was an exhilarating sense of freedom. We could do anything. We were going down staircases, up walls, all on motorcycles. Then, in the process of passing a horse, I got caught. Part of my motorcycle gear got caught on the horse's halter or some damn thing so I couldn't get out of the way. And there I was, up alongside this plodding work horse, stuck. There was no way out. I was forced to go at that slow, agonizing pace."

Certain aspects of these dreams are obvious. I have already commented on the frequency of escape dreams among the prisoners. The first dream is directly in that category; the second dream indirectly, for escape and confinement are two aspects of the same problem. The second dream is also an example of another common genre—the dream of frustration and impotence.

The exhilaration and freedom of the motorcycle may or may not have a sexual implication, but certainly the motorcycle suggests unrestricted power and movement. To have this instrument, to have the equipment for such freedom, and then to find oneself trapped, hung up, caught in a harness, reduced to the pace of a plodding horse, is a special kind of agony. While the image of a horse is not unusual for a farm boy, certainly for Bill it relates directly to his new employment in the prison. The contrast between the work horse and the free-wheeling cyclist is a dramatic representation of the frustration of a virile young man forced into the artificial constraints, constrictions, and inhibitions of a prison setting.

None of this was interpreted to Bill, but rather he was encouraged to associate to the elements of the dream. After associating to the more obvious elements he said, "One thing is particularly funny though—the Johnny Pukka business." He started laughing. "I don't know how much you know about country music, but there is nobody called Johnny Pukka. The name is made up, and I know just where it came from. Once a friend of mine and I were stopped by the cops. When they asked for our names, this friend, at the spur of the moment and without hesitation, made up the name Johnny Pukka. We laughed about it like hell several times afterward, and Johnny Pukka became a kind of password between us."

It is interesting, and typical, of dreams that obscure symbols which have no apparent or universal meaning, when associated to, are revealed as part of the private symbolism of the dreamer and as such are particularly relevant in interpreting the dream. In this case Johnny Pukka as a symbol of defiance and contempt for police authority is not a chance element occurring in a dream of escape from imprisonment. Confinement in an open prison camp is a double burden for these young men. There is not only the frustration and deprivation of being in the prison, but also their shame at conforming and being obedient while there. The open camp makes their failure to escape a particular burden. It is interpreted by them as a betrayal sometimes, as a humiliation often, and as a form of impotence almost always.

After a few more minutes of discussing the dream Bill stopped, then said, "I see you are letting me talk again." He laughed, embarrassed, and continued, "I just don't know what to say any more. I'm not that much of a talker and see . . . nothing much happens here."

"Things happen inside—feelings," I suggested.

"Yeah, uh . . . well, my friendships have remained very constant," he said, really avoiding the direct question of feelings.

"Most of my friends you know—Tim, Paul, a few other COs. It's funny how different we are, particularly in background. You couldn't find three people more different."

"How about in personality?" I asked, again attempting to shift him from facts to feelings.

"Paul and Tim aren't too different. Paul, I'd say, is a little more —how shall I put it?—fast to react to problems than Tim. Tim changes his ideas and attitudes more slowly. He'll follow a line of thought for months, with gradual changes in his attitude. Paul will change faster."

This was a surprising statement. Tim was always appraised as volatile and Paul as placid and gentle. Surface appearances

aside, there was no question in my mind that Paul was the potentially more explosive person. It was intriguing to me that Bill had
sensed this. I asked him to give me some examples of what he
meant.

"Well, take the escape thing. Last August and September we
were all very seriously contemplating it. Tim and I continue to
consider it. We'll have to wait until the spring for it to be practical, but we still have a lot of time to go and it's still a real consideration. Paul was the most hung up on it originally—really
wanted to—it was an obsession with him and we were restraining him. Then he turned it off and forgot about it completely. He's not interested in it any more and simply won't discuss it. I'm not sure how much of it with Tim and me is just talk,
but when you're in here talk can change to action very quickly.

"I've asked myself if I were guaranteed a successful escape on
the condition that I would never see anyone I knew on the street
again, would I take it or not? I think I might. On the other hand,
if it meant hiding for the rest of my life, no. The whole escape
business is complicated. It isn't that conditions are so bad, but it
seems one should do something—it seems that there is something
wrong in staying here when you could get out. If we went it
would be a political act."

"Only a political act?" I asked.

He grinned. "Well, there would be a lot of private satisfaction
to be gained from it. Just to cross them up, to lose them, could be
fun. I suppose it really wouldn't be serving any political purpose,
but it would make me feel good if I could outmaneuver all these
people that were after me—if I were resourceful enough to make
it.

"One thing about a five-year sentence that makes it so tough is
that I don't dare to refuse to work or anything because if I lose
the good days I could be here until somewhere in 1972. If I only
had two years I wouldn't mind losing some good days—I'd be
getting out early anyway."

"Does the time seem difficult now? When we first discussed it, you indicated it wasn't so bad, but obviously the preoccupation with escape means that it is bad in some way."

"Yes, it is, and I don't understand why. I know that I've done harder time on the outside than I've done in here, yet sometimes lately—sometimes it's unbearable. I suppose it's the absence of the positive experiences, the satisfactions that I've had on the outside. In here there are no rewards. Life on the outside for me was often very hard, but it was also rewarding."

"Why is it unrewarding here?" I persisted. "You study, you learn, that should bring rewards."

"Goddam, I don't know. I really don't know why. It just is. It might be that on the outside if you master something you gain, in addition, money, social status, prestige, security—all that bullshit that you don't get here. They didn't hold much appeal for me on the outside."

"So why should they here?" I questioned.

"It shouldn't. But it must have held some appeal for me on the outside or I wouldn't notice its absence here. All I know is that it becomes progressively harder to do anything worthwhile. I can see all the plans of study going down the drain. There seems to be no incentive.

"The other thing is that in here I can't really—I don't want to really—get close to anyone. There's no one to comfort you here. It's impossible to demand that of anyone—to comfort you. Besides, there are times that you want the kind of comfort that only a woman can give. You need the reassurance and peace that come with physical comfort.

"I thought of it one night—it was a hell of a cold day and I had been working hard. Then I came back to that dim and bleak dormitory with no warmth and no food and no woman, and these are the things that you'd have had waiting for you on the outside.

"It may not even be that specific. That's why it's so difficult to verbalize. I just needed at that moment a decent place to go to.

That really may summarize it—that really must be it—there isn't a decent place to go to. On the outside, if you're cold and tired, you go and get warmed up in all different ways—through friendships, through love."

He stopped himself then as though he was embarrassed by the sentimentality, shook his head a little, and said, "Are we ever going to see the results of this study? I'm curious."

"Sure," I said. "What do you want to know?"

He was taken aback, laughed. "I'd just like to know what the hell you think of the people you meet in this joint."

"What you mean is, you want to know what I think of you," I countered.

"Yeah, that's right."

"Well, in what sense would you like to know what I think of you?"

The directness of the response was too much for him, and he switched off into a safer area.

"Well, when I tell you about dreams, for example, do you have some system whereby you can deduce something from it?"

"Sometimes," I said, "but not always." I didn't amplify.

"Right," he said.

There was a long pause. I waited for him, and he became uncomfortable. He realized that I was not satisfied that he had told me what was really on his mind.

"Well, I was wondering whether you think the movement has any point to it. Is there any sense in our doing what we're doing? Do you think there's any purpose in our being in here?"

"Doesn't it have a meaning to you?" I asked.

"Oh, yes," he said and then was silent.

"I think you're beginning to worry about it," I suggested.

"I'm not really anxious about it, but I've become progressively more aware that the impact is limited, very limited. But that doesn't worry me a lot."

"Are you sure?" I asked, knowing very well that it did.

"There isn't a hell of a lot more I could do. Maybe I should refuse to work. I'm very helpless. We're all helpless in this damn joint."

"I think you're too hard on yourself," I said, responding to his need for reassurance. "You have had the courage to go to prison for principle. This in itself is an uncommon act. I don't think you can anticipate all the consequences of an act. Who knows, maybe even your talking with me will contribute something."

He grinned and said simply, "Yeah."

On my next visit, in January, Bill was part of the group that had been transferred to the penitentiary. He shuffled in with a sheepish smile on his face.

"What's a nice guy like you doing in a joint like this?" I asked.

"You know, I don't know," he answered and then immediately asked if I knew how Tim was doing.

I had just seen Tim and reassured him that Tim was managing all right. He mentioned how upset his mother had been to see him under the conditions here. Then, after giving me his version of the action quickly, he returned again to Tim.

"He doesn't have a mattress or blanket, does he? No clothes, no books, no shoes?"

I said that was true, but I assured him that Tim was managing well nonetheless, and once again asked him how *he* was making out.

"Well, actually I could see it coming on Wednesday afternoon when they removed Jim in that sneaky way, and I was regretful. I'd finally carved out a comfortable niche in the camp, a better job. I was getting subscriptions to magazines, time was going faster. Then, when they shipped Jim out in that way, I knew we had to do something. I didn't want to, you understand, but we had to do something.

"Right now I don't really feel desperate, although I've had brighter moments in my life. I'm plagued with all these second thoughts. So far I've resisted them. I haven't given in. I don't know when I'll give in, but I don't plan on giving in now, that's for damn sure. I wish to hell they hadn't done that to Jim—damn right I do. I'd have been content just serving time and not reforming anything or striking—the way I was feeling then. But they seemed to want us to do this—they changed my mind for me. I don't want to complain, things really aren't that bad. I'm just a little bit hungry."

"How long are you going to keep up the food strike?" I asked.

"I don't know. I guess the last time I ate was Thursday, lunch. I've heard that after three or four days you stop feeling hunger, and I did have periods yesterday and today when I wasn't so hungry. It's not that bad.

"Isn't it strange that when your future is most bleak and your luck has run out, you should choose to make more sacrifices, like not eating? When things are going smoothly, you don't think of making sacrifices. I mean, if I were comfortable and free I wouldn't be fasting, but even if I were back at the work camp I wouldn't be fasting.

"It's strange. The rougher they make it for you, the further you want to go. It seems to me that the way to keep people docile is to make it easy. That's the damn part about this thing. Of course we couldn't be much more docile than we were—we're all ashamed of that. There had been a one-day fast a few weeks ago, and I wasn't even a part of that.

"I could have lasted a long time the way things were at the camp, even though I disliked the way the joint was run. I was upset about it, but I still wasn't committed to doing anything, only they forced me into it, sending Jim back the way they did. Even if they had just sent him back directly we could have swallowed it. The way they did it—we had to do something. They were asking us, begging us to do something. I often wonder if they expected it, even planned it. I suppose that's paranoid. They could have just been too stupid to see where it was driving us. Can they be that stupid?

"The petition we signed was ridiculous. We knew it wouldn't

get us anywhere. We almost did that on purpose. We thought pretty seriously of including as one of our terms 'immediate, unconditional release.'"

He laughed. "What the hell, we had tried talking reasonably with them before and got nowhere, so we figured to hell with it. It was obvious they sent Jim up here because he suggested an inmates' council. What a harmless idea . . . I mean . . . oh shit!

"They suddenly get very uptight, even though nothing was happening and no one was agitating. So even when they are not confronted with a real problem they manage to manufacture one. We never could get anywhere with reasonable demands—like better visiting hours. Right here inside the penitentiary they have visiting five days a week. We couldn't get that at the camp.

"None of us ever gets work-release of course. They wouldn't do any of the many small things they could to make life more bearable. They lie like hell about every goddam thing they do whether it serves a purpose or not. They profess ignorance about events they know—that they themselves initiated. So we figured what the hell is the sense of trying to negotiate with people like that. We might as well just make complete demands, ridiculous or not, since nothing would avail.

"There's a kind of contempt they have—not just for us but for our visitors. My mother went out to the camp, thinking I was still there, and every one of those staff members said, 'He's at the pen —we don't have any idea why.' For Christ's sake! They were the ones who carried me out of the goddam bus to bring me here!

"Then when she came here nobody knew anything. They didn't know where I was. It was as though I had disappeared. No one knew. She finally got some kind of admission that I was locked up in this room—with eight other guys, with cockroaches all over, mattresses on the floor, a hole in the window. But none of them knew when I got here, how long I'd been here, or where specifically I was. They lie like hell about everything, so what the hell!

"What I really want is immediate, unconditional release anyway. I don't really give a damn about work-release, councils, or any of that shit. I want to get out of this joint! That's all. I might as well ask for what I really want."

This spontaneous outburst was so atypical and so authentic in its emotions that neither of us had much to say. We sat in silence and were not uncomfortable.

After a few minutes I asked Bill what he was planning to do.

"I don't have any plans. I'm going to hold out as long as I can and refuse to cooperate for as long as I can. Who knows how long that will be? If they make any concessions at all I'll grab them, but I don't expect them to, you know."

"Do you plan on holding out without eating?" I asked.

"No, I'll start eating sometime in the near future. I might hold out for about a week. My twentieth birthday is Wednesday. I might eat then. I'm not really much for this fast bit—it's never been my kind of action. I never would have suggested it."

"What would you have suggested?" I asked.

"I like refusing to work much better. I guess the main reason I'm fasting now is that I wouldn't feel right eating up here when the others are fasting—you just can't do that."

"What if they offered to let you go back to the camp if you're willing to work?" I asked.

"I wouldn't do it if they offered it today. I couldn't. After solitary for a while—two weeks, two months, I don't know—I might take them up on it. It's just too soon to give in."

He then asked me about Jim, the spokesman who had initiated all this. "Is he working now?"

I said, "Yes."

"Is he fasting?"

I said, "No."

He shook his head, smiling. I asked why he shook his head.

"I'm not shaking my head because Jim is working or anything. It's just that the whole situation is so damn funny."

"You don't consider that a betrayal?" I asked.

"Oh Christ, no."

"How about the guys who didn't go along? Do you feel angry or feel they've copped out?" I asked.

"No, of course not. Why should I be angry with them? They've done no harm. We each do what we have to. You've got to understand—with those guys it's just not their bag. Can you see someone like Paul being carried out of the visiting room, say? That's not his thing—not the sort of situation he'd ever get into. It's so public. He'd rather do his bit quietly and get it over with."

"Well, is this your bag?" I asked. "Any more than Paul's?"

"No, it's not really. That's the thing. In a way I'm so confused —I'd rather still be there. I'd rather be just serving time. They had a one-day fast a couple of weeks ago—Paul and I weren't with it. It seemed silly. It seemed so impotent, particularly since everyone who was participating in it was also working on that day. I was damned if I'd go out and chop trees in the cold and then not eat. See, everyone was so damn anxious that they not get busted for it. I admitted I didn't really feel like undergoing the discomfort—the one-day fast with work. But Christ, the whole thing seemed to have only one purpose, to serve the self-righteousness of those who had participated in it. Really you had more the feeling it was their way of justifying their presence and cooperation in the camp. I'm not a rationalizer [indeed he isn't!], and I will never be able to justify that, so I wasn't going to even bother trying. I felt I might as well do the whole bit and admit to myself that I was cooperating. Say, did you happen to talk to Paul this morning?"

"Yes, I did," I said.

"Well, what the hell did he have to say about this scene? I mean was he upset or depressed?"

It is typical of this entire group—perhaps of this entire generation—that they tend not to judge others by their own actions or direction. There is something very attractive in the "your own thing" concept, the tolerance of individuality, the respect for difference, which is an important part of the philosophy of idealistic young activists in this generation.

Bill's response showed that and more. His somewhat hesitant, ill-at-ease, rough-edged speech and manner covered a fine sensitivity and perceptivity. He was concerned, not just about Tim who was making a greater sacrifice, but also about Paul who was making a lesser, recognizing that Paul might be feeling upset or guilty.

I reassured him about both of his friends, and I asked him if he could summarize his feelings about the whole thing.

"Christ, I don't know. I wish it hadn't happened, but given the circumstances what choice was there? For that matter, I wish the circumstances had never arisen that led me to come to jail in the first place, but since they were there I don't feel too regretful about that either."

"Would you do it over again?" I asked.

"Well, if I were released, knowing exactly what it was like, I couldn't go through with it again. I'd probably go underground. The night before we made our list of demands we had a meeting to draw up our statement. Oh, what bullshit! By then it was pretty clear that we were going to do something. We were specifically discussing a strike and somebody said, 'What should our goals be?' I said, 'I don't have any goals, but I don't mind striking.' That's still the way I feel about the whole thing, I guess. The only purpose was the act itself. Not to accomplish anything, just the act. As an act of self-respect, as an act of defiance maybe. That's basically what it was for me."

"Why do you need an act of defiance?" I asked.

"I don't know. Just to see the expression on those hacks' faces —shake the place up a bit."

"Is that worth giving up good time?" I asked.

"Right now, it seems so. Later, it may not. Something did come out of it—a sense of unity among one's friends and inmates.

There is a satisfaction, just to make the people in the prison system worry a little and just to make ourselves feel we can maybe still do something."

The next meeting with Bill saw him once again back at the camp. He described the resolution of the conflict. He was quite chagrined but matter-of-fact about his being the first man to break his fast. He told me that he felt quite guilty for doing it.

I asked him why he broke it, and with the simplicity and directness which characterized him, he said, "I was hungry."

He, like most, had the feeling that they would have been permitted to come back at any time they wished, but that once having committed themselves, they wanted a decent period of time to satisfy their own sense of proportion and value, while yet aware that nothing else was being accomplished. He, like the others, assumed that no one had been punished for it. The only consequence seemed to be that they were now treated as newcomers and put in the most ramshackle of the dormitories.

"Actually I like it. It's a little quieter than the others and there's a good supply of hot water down there, so we decided that even if we get the opportunity to move up we'll stay. One irony—when I came back I was shifted to a better job. I'm now in the education department. My total duties are making up the TV guide. I copy it and run it out on the mimeograph machine. Since my boss down there doesn't really give a damn, and since he only shows up for a couple of hours a day, that constitutes my sole required activity."

I asked him if he sensed any change at all in the administration.

"If anything, they're being overly careful. They seem concerned not to rouse us. After a while it became interesting. It was obvious that they were merely concerned with re-establishing a balance. Punishment of us might cause waves. They want things merely to return to a stable environment."

I asked him what his impression of the entire experience had been.

"Well, I think I learned something about my own weaknesses. For example, copping out on the fast as early as I did. I guess that bothers me more than I am willing to say. On the other hand, I learned that I'm not afraid of prison any more. So that's good. And then in a peculiar way it was what we needed for our morale. It brought us together—at least the old group. It dispelled a lot of the tension that was building up before. As far as concrete gains, of course there weren't any.

"The new guys who are the most aggressive seem to have had a negative response from the experience. They've been toned down and somewhat sullen, and there's a falling out among some of them. Those who had been here longer, though, have been brought together."

Bill was in a somewhat quiet and relaxed mood. It was a beautiful spring day, and I was reminded of our conversation when he was so seriously intent on escape. He had said it would have to wait for spring. I was curious whether this fantasy still existed and still had some possible hold on him, so I inquired whether he was still having his escape fantasies or having serious considerations.

"No, I'm not really serious any more. I discovered something funny. The other day I got a letter from a girl that I knew. It was a hell of a nice letter and it made me feel marvelous, and then again it was one of those nights when things are pretty good. I'd gotten in a couple of books, and there was a good discussion with someone, and there was a bridge game that night, and I had a high feeling that whole evening. It was a lovely warm evening, and the thought took over with great force—goddam, I'd like to get out of here! Even though things were okay at that moment I realized that with me, it's crazy, the escape fantasies occur when I feel sort of good or high, not when I'm down."

"What makes you down?"

"One thing is the constant sense of people being at you. Not the staff just—prisoners too. A tendency to make big things out of little issues, for people to get picky and quibbling. I suppose it's the fact that there's never any privacy, you're always available to someone, you can never be to yourself.

"But then things are going smoothly now. Things are as good out here as they've ever been, at least for me. There isn't too much friction. There's the excitement—I'm sure you've heard about the new parole policy—which means I could get out this January.

"Of course there is always the one constant drag. The feeling of being closed off from the world. After you've been here a while you get a feeling of isolation. I don't mean isolation from people, I mean from society. I feel like an outcast, cut off, not involved with anything that's happening. When I think about it, it doesn't seem like there's anyplace out there where I'll fit in either. I know this for sure. I've lost damn near all the identification I once had with the movement, and I think a lot of us in here have."

"Why is that?"

"I guess the joint just wears you down. It's not so much that either, though; I really don't feel I've been broken by this prison thing. Maybe it's just being away from the politics for so long, maybe it's seeing how impotent the movement is, and how goddam scared everyone is. That makes for a certain amount of resentment. Then there is the sense that nobody is doing anything. The whole damn country seems so helpless, so frightened, so powerless. The people are powerless. I don't know . . . I'm so confused. I'm not sure I can see myself being a college student any more. I just don't know.

"I had this letter from a friend of mine yesterday. He's a student at Cornell," he explained, as he pulled a folded letter from his shirt. "He says, 'Boy, with every passing moment it becomes clearer that what you've done was not only right but necessary. If the situation a year ago was intolerable, it's worse now. We lie to ourselves, tolerate it in the vain stupid hope that it will work itself out or perhaps simply vanish. Reason, civility, law, and order are at the moment the dirtiest words I know. What kind of civilization is it that, year after year, blindly and barbarously, slaughters innocent aliens and its own unwitting citizens, not just in the name of peace and reason—but here's the real horror—actually does it peacefully and reasonably. All of it sanctioned by our law and our lawyers. All the once noble attributes have been pre-empted by the civilized barbarians and their legal yahoos.'

"It was shocking for me to have him say that, for reason and civility were everything in his life. He's a typical academician.

"Hell, I don't know. I haven't been out there, but what *is* it like? Everything seems so fucked up. I don't understand what's going on in colleges. You go to college to learn and then you find yourself fighting all the time. The whole thing is crazy. No one knows how to figure it out. How can you explain the fact that since the Nixon administration the COs are for the first time getting the same breaks and being treated, in terms of parole at least, in the same way as the JWs and the Amish? Evidently we are all going to be getting out in eighteen months if we've been on good behavior.

"When I get out, what will I do? I was a classics major, you know. I'd taken Latin all the way through high school, and I'd started Greek in college. I suppose I'd still like to do it. I don't know. Is that at all important? You know what I mean? Not just classics, but learning and all that shit—getting a degree, teaching. Does any of that make any sense? And if it doesn't, what alternative do I have? If I wasn't going to do that and make a respectable living, could I just be a bum, traveling around? That's not for me.

"I used to see myself teaching in a small college in a small town in New England. I don't see myself doing anything any more, and I don't think I'm alone. I think of all the younger people here—not just the COs, but the big group now in on marihuana charges—none of us seems to know what the hell we want to do."

7 ⋘

O-71488: Paul

Like the third point in an equilateral triangle, Paul is as distant from Bill and Tim as they are from each other. Bound together by the prison situation, they drew friendship from sources unlikely to have produced even recognition on the outside.

His soft, pale, blond, "English" looks seemed more appropriate to tennis whites than prison blues. At twenty-one, Paul was the eldest of the three but undoubtedly still the youngest. He looked a boy because he was a boy, coming from a background where one had the leisure to grow up slowly, for Paul was not merely WASP, but Establishment; and his formalism, manners, and accent bespoke his wealthy Southern background.

He spoke fluently, trustingly, and openly, so that it was not long before I had a feeling I knew Paul, knew him well—indeed, knew him better than he knew himself.

"I had left Princeton after the first semester of the sophomore year on a leave of absence," he told me. "I took the leave to travel and write. My basic motivations for going are really hazy. It seemed just a wanderlust. I nonetheless kept in touch with my draft board, and while abroad I received a notice of my reclassification. I responded with a letter which indicated that, after careful consideration, I had decided that I had no choice but to refuse. This I did.

"I don't pretend to understand this whole business in Vietnam, but it violated enough of my principles that I know I could never be a part of it. It's a pity that moral issues can never be appreciated by politicians. I knew what I was getting into. I'd had more than a year traveling, thinking about it. I knew that if I left school the chances were that I'd be drafted, and I had more or less decided that I couldn't go into the Army under the present circumstances. Would it strike you as strange if I said I felt patriotic in refusing to go into the Army?

"I just feel that the interests of this country are at stake and that change is coming eventually. I don't know how better to put it to you."

I indicated there were many who shared his convictions but very few who went to jail, and that there certainly must be something more to the story.

"That's true, but everyone gets to the point where you either put up or shut up, and I suppose this was my put-up point. I had a long time to think of it—it had been hanging over me for more than a year. Yet I don't think I really accepted the fact of it until that night before imprisonment. I didn't really feel afraid till then.

"The fear must have been there somewhere—I was making all these somewhat manic long-distance calls to friends all over the country to talk to them for the last time. You know, I'm only twenty-one and kind of young for this kind of thing. It is a frightening feeling—at least at my age—to know that you have to take a stand, that they are going to do things to you that are going to be unpleasant, and that the only thing that is available to sustain you is that which is inside of you. I've never been in a situation where the only tangible comforts were inside."

"Did you have any idea of what those unpleasant things were to be? What prison was really like?" I asked.

"There were a couple of weeks after I refused induction that I went scurrying all around trying to find anything in print that would tell me. I suppose the only real impression that I had were the prison movies, of which I've seen my share. There are some handbooks but they're not much help. I really had no idea and, up to the very last week, considered going to Canada. I checked airlines, thought about the timing of when I'd have to leave, but I just couldn't do it."

"Why not?" I asked.

"It's this country thing, I'd have to say. It's my country and I'm not going to run away from it. Then, in the next few years, after this is all over, if I meet someone who has lost his son in Vietnam, I don't want to have to say that I had run away. There is this thing in me. These guys are getting killed every day, and that's the constant factor of the whole issue. They're Americans, and America is as much a part of me as it is of them. They're being shot at—I don't feel I should run away.

"Anyway, I think life is constructed from one's experiences. I know there are all kinds of rationalizations that COs go through, and that one of them is that the experience of prison life by itself is a rare one and is a character-building thing, but I definitely think it will be. I feel a lot older than I did when I returned from abroad, and I felt a lot older after having been there on my own than I did when I left on my travels."

"Tell me about this experience thing," I said.

"I've only started my sixth month. My sentence is three years. The policy, as you know, is that straight COs don't make parole, so they do the maximum, which is in my case twenty-five months. How can I tell you this experience thing? It's one thing you really can't understand unless you go through it. It's involved with being denied your freedom for an extended period of time. I was curious about it—I was afraid of it, but still curious. I don't like being here, and there are too many times when I ask myself what *am* I doing here, what's the point. But there is a point, and I believe that when this thing is over, and I go home and look back, I'll feel it was worth while. I know I haven't been here long enough to have it make any effect on me.

"Experience for its own sake can be useful, and this isn't really like a prison, the work camp. There's no day-to-day fear as to whether you'll make it through to the next day. Some of these prisons are real jungles, and it's hard to stay alive if you're not physically endowed or something. That's what I was originally afraid of.

"I was at the penitentiary for about eight days. It was very frightening. The place is crawling with homosexuals, all kinds of unattractive people, and to any of them it's easily apparent that a CO is a CO. They size us up, and we look different. I was terrified of being in with the main population because I'm not much good with my fists. Those are the fears that absorb you at first. Going to bed at night, I would rationalize them away by saying, this is what you expected and you must put up with it. I'd heard stories of COs who had had a great deal of difficulty, but I was lucky and I didn't have any at all. Nevertheless the terror was there the whole time.

"It's an eerie feeling inside those walls. It's the one thing I appreciate here. If you really had to escape, or just wanted to escape, you'd simply walk over those hills after chow and go down the road. Not that the basic oppression isn't still here, because that's related somehow with being denied freedom, but at least if you mind your own business you're perfectly safe.

"The first couple of weeks here I didn't realize that of course, so I was still pretty much frightened of what might happen physically. Being beaten is a more natural thing and a danger that one runs into on the street, so that didn't loom as large. I was much more afraid of being grabbed in the shower sometime. You know, it does happen all the time. It represents to me, at least, the most grotesque experience a human being could involuntarily have. I'm not afraid any more. I know it could happen here but it's unlikely. The homosexuals are aware of you the first few weeks you come into the camp, and it's established, one way or another, if you're susceptible. Once they find that you're not they leave you alone. I only know personally of one boy who was brutally beaten and raped. That was at the penitentiary. There are plenty of homosexuals here, but people are too short here to start any trouble. They don't bring guys here until maybe a year or so prior to going home. I've heard stories of guys who have been taken off here, but it hasn't happened since I've personally been here.

"Before I came in the prosecuting attorney for the government pleaded with me to change my ideas. He said, 'You're not the sort of person who should be in a prison. You don't want to go there. It's a place crawling with homosexual deviates.' In those days when it was all vague and general I said naïvely, 'That's part of the thing and I'll just have to take care of myself.' I don't know how I would have felt if I could have visualized graphically what I have since learned can and does take place.

"The only tough thing about this place is just being here. It can be pleasant. I'm a clerk, do letters, have time off, read. You tell yourself a hundred times a day that it's just a relative thing. But there's nothing really to do. I've tried marking the days off in all sorts of ways—a month at a time, a week, a day—but there's nothing really to get involved with. The first couple of weeks I'd wake up in the morning totally exhausted and look around and not know where I was, especially after a night's dream—if it had been particularly vivid."

Paul was the first boy who spontaneously brought up dreams without my asking. I was curious as to whether this indicated some special concern or anxiety.

"What kind of dreams?" I asked.

"Oh, all sorts. More or less the kind I'd have on the street. Idyllic situations on a campus with a girl, but then I've also had some unbelievable ones. A few days ago I had this most peculiar dream: I was being suspended over this huge vat of something like jello and slowly being lowered into it. Then I realized that I was inside a refrigerator and the jello was beginning to congeal, and I was up to my neck, stuck in this congealing mass. I was slowly being lowered, and the feeling was that I would suffocate."

This was a most enlightening dream, particularly coming from Paul. He was the only one to claim that imprisonment was worth while at the time he was in the prison situation. After the fact, any of them will state that it had been so, for in retrospect we utilize the past in the service of the present, and memory is modified to make life meaningful. Paul was saying that he was finding it a good experience while he was in prison.

How does one approach a statement like that? If taken at face value, it would be reassuring; but psychoanalysts rarely take anything at face value, and there were a number of things that were distressing about this statement. The first was the singularity of it —that is, it was an atypical response—and while atypical is not necessarily abnormal, it can often be an indicator of such. Second, the fact that in the course of the first hour Paul repeated the idea at least four or five times was itself disconcerting. It raised the question of whether these statements weren't frantic efforts to convince himself.

There are certain defensive mechanisms which psychoanalysts recognize as more primitive than others. One of the more primitive mechanisms is denial—that is, when an individual chooses to handle a threatening or an offensive situation by simply denying its existence. If one interprets this repetitive statement of Paul's as a part of a denial mechanism, then, rather than being reassuring, it becomes quite the opposite, a disquieting sign. I had been alerted to this, and then when Paul spontaneously presented the dream I was more convinced than ever.

The dream is a rather transparent one, and certainly an intriguing symbol for the problems in a prison, particularly one like this work camp. The idea of being confined, locked up, in an icebox—the cold, mechanical quality of it—and then again, the indefiniteness of that which is oppressive in a prison society. There's nothing to bang your fist against. There's nothing to attack. There's nothing to feel dramatic about, merely the idea of being entombed in a large gelatinous mass. More than being entombed, being suffocated, drowned in it. There's a nightmarish quality of the dream inherent in the very symbol. Yet when I alluded to the dream as a nightmare, Paul denied there was any anxiety.

"No, it wasn't a nightmare. I thought it was kind of funny, a rather interesting dream," he said calmly.

Again there was a threatening situation and the absence of an appropriate anxiety. His need to repress and isolate anxiety began to disturb me, for expressed emotions could be handled, dealt with, dissipated. When they were repressed as completely as Paul's evidently were, they could lead to a breakdown of psychological functioning, and Paul was a very real candidate for a serious depression. I was more pessimistic about his handling imprisonment than anyone else I had seen. I said nothing of this to him at this point. It could have served no useful purpose. Rather I decided to try to liberate some of this emotion, to help him face his anxieties, and to find out why he had such a need to deny his fears so completely.

Paul continued, "I never really thought about dreams very much, and I certainly never remembered them on the street the way I do here. But then here I find myself daydreaming frequently, having conversations with people who just aren't there. Most usually it will be with a girl, sometimes a personal friend. Occasionally I will imagine myself a year from now, free again, and addressing a group of people who are contemplating refusing induction. I'll talk precisely the way I'm talking to you now, and the fact that no one is there doesn't seem to bother me at all."

"Did your daydreams always have such reality to them?" I asked.

"I didn't do it as much on the outside," he answered.

"Do you recall any other nightmare besides the one with the jello?" I asked.

"Those really aren't nightmares for me. I never woke up frightened to my knowledge. There's something in me that says, 'You're in prison, these are unusual circumstances, and nothing that happens here has any legitimacy.' I imagine I could dream of being shot or pulled apart by horses and it wouldn't bother me at all. These are obstacles that must be overcome, just being here. Life presents a whole series of obstacles and external obligations a young man faces on the way to maturity. This is just one of those that I'm facing.

"I have a freedom from responsibility which most people don't enjoy. I'm never going to have to worry about working or where I'll eat my next meal. I'm financially independent. Knowing this, I must find ways to fulfill myself, to use myself for set goals, before I can begin living a free life. This hasn't come yet. In my immaturity I had looked at college as something I had to climb over with great labors and difficulties. Now I know how stupid that was. I'd give anything to be back there, I want it so much. I want to learn, and I want to write poetry.

"It's funny, with all the time, it's difficult to write here. I think you have to write out of experience, and there's no experience here, not in the sense of touching you inside. At the beginning I wrote a lot of immature poems trying to analyze prison. It was all intellectuality and indignation. I think the six months has made a difference. I am trying to forget the outer world and its values and treat this as an experience from which I can profit if only I maintain the proper attitude. You must do it yourself here, without the support of good friends."

"You don't have friends here?" I asked.

"I'm not sure it's the real thing. Friendships on the street are based on common interests, but here it's different. There are certainly nice people here, but all the talk is about parole, how much time left, et cetera. And then if twelve go up for parole and eleven don't make it and one does, that one may wonder what right he has to leave when the others can't.

"There was one prisoner here who had to be freed against his will because of this. I don't know if I have that kind of courage. I'm afraid if I were the one out of twelve I would just go home. I don't really want to be here. Inside, I'm praying that I'll be paroled, but I know that a CO has no chance. Criminals yes, JWs certainly, but not COs. If I'm refused parole I'm afraid I may have a great deal of bitterness. I don't feel bitter now. Actually I'm surprised that I feel so little of anything. I don't believe that I've just kept it in check either."

It may be difficult, for a reader who is seeing Paul only through the limitations of print, and who is not a professional in the mental-health area, to understand my growing concern for Paul. This soft and gentle boy, so earnest and so young, is also remarkably fluent. As a result, any one hour with him has produced twice the amount of words as in a typical interview. Yet even with the extensive abridgment my account of the interview demands, one can see the massive need for denial, the refusal to recognize a healthy rage or indignation, the need to repress fear, the insistence on seeing prison as a beneficial procedure, with the inevitable conclusion that if it is not so it will represent a personal failure.

He had said he experienced few emotions, yet I could not imagine visiting periods in prison without some breakthrough of feeling. I asked him simply who his visitors were.

"I don't have any. At this point I don't want any. I don't want any. I won't have them seeing me like this. Not friends, not girls. I don't think my mother could stand it.

"As for my father, he's a retired diplomat, and his attitude is unbelievably irrational. Anyway, I hadn't seen him for a couple of years. I've heard he feels that I've disgraced the family, violated the white man's code and all that baloney. There's a strong military tradition in my family. Also a whole lot of Southern parochialism.

"My father is a brilliant man, unbelievably accomplished scholastically, a great authority on American history. His entire emotionality is still absorbed with the Southern cause. He's very irrational. His concepts of duty ignore the realities of the sixties. He's never voted in a general election because he feels it's beneath him to get involved in politics. He left us when I was about fifteen. Before that we moved every few years. I don't think there was anything stable in my life until after the separation. When my father left, my brothers, mother, and I moved to my mother's home town [in a border state] where the family continues to live.

"The whole set-up is crazy. The antagonisms are so enormous. It's like a huge chess game—with my mother the White Queen and my father the Red King, and all the bishops and pawns. One reason I left college is that my paternal grandfather was paying for it and, while I was most grateful, I couldn't stand the fact that he considered my mother to be the evil member of the family and would say so in his letters.

"My father is a most peculiar man. We knew he loved us, but he was very strict. We couldn't watch television, we couldn't go out on Halloween, we couldn't go to movies, we couldn't listen to records, we couldn't do any of the things that typical kids do. He felt that since he was different, his sons must be. As the oldest—I have one brother twenty and another fifteen—I was expected to be particularly responsible. He never punished us physically, but there was this unapproachable quality, this disdain, when he was in a bad mood.

"When we'd go to bed I'd hear my mother and father arguing, and invariably she would be defending the children and he would be attacking us. It was ridiculous. I hear he has started drinking. He lives in isolation off of a trust established by his father. I know he refused to take his retirement money. Again, on some principle. He's not to be believed in many ways. He absolutely believes in class structure, in a social elite, and all that nineteenth-century baloney."

With the hour approaching its end, I asked about the status of his twenty-year-old brother.

"Oh, he hates the war in Vietnam too, but he's more rational than I am. He says he's going to do the sensible thing and go in."

"How do you feel about that?" I asked.

"It's his choice. I don't feel one way or the other," he concluded.

These innocent words had more symbolic meaning to me than he could have realized.

The second interview with Paul was less than two months later. He looked much the same, somewhat thinner I thought, and greeted me amiably. True to form, he started right in reassuring me and himself that things were really going quite well.

"It's better now. I start eight months next week. Pretty soon I'll be in the double figures. It's been easy so far, quite fast. The last vestiges of real concrete memory of the outside have gone, I guess, and that helps. I'm used to it now, and that's the whole thing, getting used to it. I know what to expect every day. It makes it easier. It's just an adjustment like anything else, I guess. There are times like yesterday when for a few minutes I began to think I was almost glad to be here. There are periods of contentment. I feel there really isn't anywhere else to be right at this moment. I know I'll be glad to get home, and I don't allow myself to brood about all the time I have to go. It's curious about these moments that come when I feel content to be here. I just can't escape those periods when I feel just content to be here."

"Why should you want to escape them?" I asked.

"I don't," he denied. "It was merely a figure of speech. I was just wondering if there was a way to control moods. There are simply these times when I can feel good even being here. There is nothing I can do about it. I can't just say, 'Man, you've got to keep track of where you are.' I don't know how to explain all of this. There are times when I hit a balance for the times when I can't stand it—when it's absolute hell."

"Oh, you've never mentioned those feelings," I said.

"Fortunately they're not as often any more. They usually involve the feeling that nothing is happening, that you're not doing anything, that there is no purpose, that it's all a waste of time, that there is nothing you can do to help yourself or anyone else. When you've been involved with living for twenty-one years and then you come into a situation where there is nothing to do, nothing to do at all. I really can't put my finger on it—mostly it's missing people. It may happen when I get a good letter, like the one I got recently from this girl at college. I felt so close to her through the letters, yet how can I trust feelings in here? When I get out I may not even want to see her. I suppose I could get a visiting permit for her, but I don't want to yet. I still haven't reached the point where I can allow anyone to see me like this. I'd just rather have it two years when I wasn't around."

"Are you saying this because of shame or embarrassment?" I queried.

"No, nothing like that. I just don't know if I would be able to emotionally handle seeing them. There are times when I think I have the months and weeks completely and absolutely under control, even though there is a huge bit still coming up, and this makes me feel good—when I feel I've reached this more mature stage, this more mature attitude toward time. In those periods I know where I am, and I appreciate how much strength it takes to get through it. Nobody can anticipate that. Nobody can counsel you in advance. After serving my time, were I to meet a young boy who is just refusing induction, I could tell him very little. For every eight hundred guys in prison there are eight hundred different experiences."

"Do you think it's particularly hard for you to serve time?" I asked. This was, of course, my feeling, although I did not want to tell him so.

"I don't think so, not really. I used to think it depended on what you gave up to come to prison. I was very happy on the street, I was beautifully content and serene, and I really enjoyed just being a human being—and here there's no time for that. Now, I don't think your outside way of life is a significant factor, except for perhaps the first six or eight months. After that the time is a constant factor and works the same for everyone, as far as I can tell. I'd go crazy if this were a county-jail environment, although I don't even know about that. Tim and I were saying the other day that the problem here is that there is just enough sanity—you're just enough in touch with everything in the street to make the deprivation the more painful. If we were kept completely out of touch, completely isolated from everything, it might be much easier. We see the TV every night, and the news and everything that's going on, and once in a while we hear some good music. But if you hear a little of it you want more—and it's hard to get that under control.

"Music is important to my generation. It's such an ordinary thing out in the street—if I want a record on, I could play it as long and as loud as I wanted to without thinking. Here there is much competition for the use of the record-player, and everything is potentially violent or dangerous. The smallest things become important to prisoners. Anything can lead to a scuffle. It isn't worth it."

"What else besides the music do you find hard?"

"There's always the girls. I would just love to touch a pretty face, or even have it about a foot away from me and just look at it for about a week—not take my eyes off it. One CO would have his girl friend meet him occasionally about a mile from the dorms on the compound. I could never have a girl come up and see me that way. The business with the girls is always on our minds. It's of course the most obvious, the most notable deprivation, especially at night."

"Has that been difficult?" I asked.

"Not as much as I had anticipated. It's a hunger but it isn't a terribly sharp one—at least for me. Of course I haven't done even seven months yet, so if you ask me the question in a year's time— if I'm still here—it may be worse. There's a guy in my dormitory who's done fifteen years and externally at least he doesn't seem much different from the rest of us. I had always thought that sexual frustration for any extended period of time would create enormous tension, but obviously there's a limitation that people place on themselves."

"Were you ever anxious that, with the inhibition of sexual outlets, you might get involved with homosexual outlets?"

"Not a chance. That kind of thing doesn't interest me. I was afraid of it, afraid of meeting someone bigger and stronger who would force it on me—I know it happens at the penitentiary every week to somebody, but I certainly was never worried about any internal impulses. If I were in here for my entire life I still don't think I could do it. It's a whole alien dimension. You always have masturbation—even if it means staying awake until everyone is asleep. I don't know, there is always some way. Someone tried to tell me that he had just finished three years in the penitentiary and never masturbated the whole time he was there. I wouldn't believe him. I could never get through without at least having that, I know."

"Did you have an active sexual life on the outside?" I asked.

"I was young and I wasn't one who ordinarily managed to get it every week, but for the last four months abroad I was living with an English girl. It was almost like we were married and it was lovely.

"It's all a relative thing, I guess. All of the JWs who are single, no matter how old, are technically supposed to remain virgins. It's what you're used to that determines how difficult it would be, and I'm about average I guess. I miss it but not to the extent that it really gets to me. I don't know whether missing someone sexually is any worse or even as bad as missing people that you're just terribly close to. There are times I realize how much I love everybody I knew on the street and how much they mean to me.

"It's never dark in the dormitories, you know, even at night. There's a night light that hangs over my bed which is never off. Unless I fall asleep fairly quickly I can stare at it, pretending it's a bright moon, and fantasize.

"I told you that whenever I get outside and walk around by myself I talk to myself as though there were a second person with me, and it's always a girl. I try to make it as natural as possible. Sometimes it's love talk, and always it's realistic. I'll pretend that I've just gotten out of prison, telling her the experience that I've been through, telling her how my thoughts have been confused, that it's going to take time to analyze them before I can make any commitments. So I tell the girl that I love her very much but I'm not sure what's going to happen and I must not make any commitments now.

"I've been thinking a lot about personal commitments, and the longer I'm here the harder I think it will be for me to make commitments to anything once I get out—particularly people."

"Why should that be?" I asked.

"I don't know. I think prison is beginning to show me that there's some element in just being human that makes commitment very, very difficult. Maybe I hope for too much. I would want a girl to be everything to me, my whole life, yet I can't imagine telling her that. It's a conflict between the ideal, which I desperately want, and the reality that I might have to accept. I would want someone to be my whole purpose, to bring a value into what has been up to now an uncertain life.

"Maybe I will change again. The most intense periods are at both ends of your bit. When you're nearly out you must get incredibly homesick. With such a huge avalanche of time as I have, you just don't let yourself think about it.

"Sometimes when I think of my friends on the street, I'll remind myself that I have friends in prison except that's a whole different thing. I'm not sure these are real friendships, because I don't know what these people would be like on the street, but then I realize I have almost forgotten what I was like on the street.

"The first thing I'll do when I get out is ask my friends: 'Well, you saw me before and after—how much have I changed?' "

"Are you frightened that you're going to change?" I asked.

Again, his first response was denial. "I think that if there is any marked change it will be for the better. It's an experience from which anyone should be able to draw some good. There was an article in *Time* magazine just a few weeks ago by a guy who had just gotten out, and he said he would recommend a small bit in prison for anybody as a character builder.

"I think the absolute loss of freedom, which is only experienced in prison, makes you think about it and cherish it. I can speak about freedom with an experience and authority that I never had before. I feel I have more faith in myself now. It's like getting a degree, I'm a step higher."

I wanted to avoid the rationalizations and return him to the area of relatedness and commitment. "Tell me more about your friendships in here," I said.

"I don't know. As I said, I can't wait to see some of these people on the street and see what they're like. Of course my feelings vary from one to another. Some I don't even like. I will hardly say a word to them."

"Who are they?" I asked.

"I don't think I should say. I really don't know. I don't feel I have the right to judge people."

"The purpose of my asking is not to evaluate them but to help me in evaluating you."

He was extremely reluctant, but I persisted doggedly until he named a few of the people he didn't like.

"I respect them for coming into prison nonetheless, but there are conditions for friendship, if I could be so bold as to say; these conditions are real, and they just don't fulfill them."

"What are these conditions?" I asked.

"Oh, I don't know. I can't put my finger on it. That's why I'm so reluctant to say I don't like anybody."

"A feeling doesn't have to be right or wrong to be valid."

"Often it's just a mannerism, something in the personality. I might only be able to say that I don't find them attractive. They need not be hostile, or loud, or conceited. It's just not possible to list reasons for disliking a person. And feelings change so rapidly when you're in here. There's too much contact—you get too close and you get sick of anyone. It's so artificial it could never exist on the outside. You have no time to look over and decide. You contact the people who are COs—you make the relationships, then find out that they're not working. I feel I could get along with any of them if I had to—it's just that I choose not to sometimes. Maybe that's conceit on my part. There are certain ones I just don't feel I have much to say to. It's not patronizing, we just don't talk at all. We're on different levels, I think.

"Then there are those that I feel very close to—Richard, for example. We both do a lot of writing, talk about poetry, et cetera. And, of course, Bill—I really feel this guy is a tremendous person and not for the standard reasons of friendship. It's just that I have an overpowering respect for the guy as an individual. He seems to have such good control over himself, yet he's such an off-beat guy.

"Some have such courage and strength—like Dick—he's one of those guys who refused to even take the army physical, burned everything. Or the case of Ken. I would have been delighted to accept the physical, get a 4F, go back to school, and live my life without feeling that despite being physically unfit for the army I had an obligation to oppose the system. With Ken there wasn't a chance in the world that he could have passed the physical. He had polio, he still limps, but, *knowing in advance that he would have failed the physical,* he refused to take it and came to prison. This kind of thing I respect very much.

"At the same time I'm not sure I see the point in coming to prison when you don't have to. I suppose there would be a point where you would have to refuse to go along with the system, but I would take the attitude of Thomas More. If there were any way I could take the oath, I'd take it, and not feel compromised in any way. I'm just not as absolute as some of these people. Perhaps I'm too human to be absolutist, perhaps too selfish."

"The ones you seem to be attracted to are the least dogmatic and absolutist," I said.

"I think that may be it. I'm just not a flag-waver in either direction. This isn't a political action for me—it's a matter of my conscience and my way of life. I reject personally and morally the American government's stand in Vietnam.

"It's funny how much more opposed to the Establishment I feel lately. I'm beginning to think not just in terms of the war but the entire system. Before I never thought that way. I have the sense that democracy has failed. That the system has stopped working, at least in the way that it had been outlined to me, and I don't know why. It's simply become too big and too powerful for its own good. Many times I wish I'd been born in a fifth-rate power like Denmark. I'd much rather be Danish than American and free of this burden. People say because America is so powerful she has responsibilities, but responsibilities require an enlarged conscience, not a diminished one. I have lost my respect for the institutions of this country. At this point I don't even know if I would go to war if it were attacked."

Just before the hour ended I asked Paul if it bothered him to talk with me, since I was aware that contact with the outside was often painful to him.

"No, it hasn't. The only time it did was a few minutes ago when you asked me to name people I don't like. That's terribly painful for me to do. My reasons for disliking a person are so suspect even in my own eyes that I hate to judge people. I know that I often do it unconsciously, but I feel it isn't right. Normally it doesn't bother me at all. I look forward to talking to you.

"When my brother went into service I had the most horrible nightmare I've ever had. I found myself at the wheel of some automobile, some flashy, garish one, and for some reason or other I got out of the car and opened the trunk, and my brother was just lying in a mess in the back of the car, all shot up. It could just happen like that. I was shaking for a whole week. The whole idea that this could happen to him. Just before the dream he had written about his training in a letter to me and how he was learning to use a rifle."

What can be made of that last statement, gratuitous, made on the way out of the door, out of context? It seemed both an offering and a confession. It demonstrated a readiness to face some anxiety and to share it with me.

It was Thanksgiving when I next saw Paul. The transformation in his appearance was startling. He had lost perhaps twelve to fifteen pounds. He had not been heavy to begin with, and on a relatively slight young man the weight loss in itself would have made a significant change in appearance, but not that significant. With Paul the physical man was always consistent with the personality—soft, refined, boyish. Now he no longer looked like a boy. There was a gauntness to his features. The gentle smile which usually played about his lips was almost totally absent. His eyes seemed sunk into his face and had a dull staring quality. There seemed to be a general absence of facial expression. He needed a shave. Prior to this I wasn't aware that he yet had to shave.

I was particularly concerned about this deterioration because, while there was good psychological evidence to anticipate it, I had not expected it to occur so rapidly. At no time during the course of this research have I experienced the frustration of a psychoanalytic investigator to the degree I did at this moment. As an investigator one sees all the pathology that is available to the therapist, yet with none of the opportunities to reverse it, and with only minimal capacity to alleviate the suffering. It is particularly distressing with a group so innately attractive, and in terms of immediate appeal and charm Paul would certainly rank among the first. Needless to say, none of my impressions or thoughts were shared directly with Paul. I merely started with my usual "How have you been?"

"I've been very tired in the last month I think. Something is happening—an indifference is creeping in."

"How do you mean?" I asked.

"Oh, I guess it's a depressive indifference. I'm beginning to have the feeling I'm never going to get out of here. It seems it's been a long, long time, and yet I haven't really done much time at all, a little more than eight months, with sixteen or fifteen to go. I keep feeling it should be getting shorter, but I haven't even reached the halfway point, and it's depressing. I don't know. I don't feel comfortable. Perhaps it's just a bad cold and I'm tired."

"You've lost weight," I said.

"I guess so. I haven't been very hungry. I've sort of slipped into a lassitude. It's possible."

"It's more than possible. I would think you've lost a great deal of weight," I insisted.

"I don't know. I haven't really checked. Maybe it's just the short-sleeved shirts. Maybe it's that I'm feeling down, maybe it's the holiday.

"Thanksgiving was always so nice on the street. It was one of my favorites, and I guess I just miss being there. I suppose I'd say I feel sad—just a pure sadness. It may be related to something trivial which I've paid too much attention to. For the first time I'm having dreams which take place in here. It began to happen about a month ago. Prior to that they had always taken me outside of the camp. Maybe that's another sign that I'm getting used to it, more acclimated.

"The specific dream had no emotion and no conversation. I was just routinely passing through the lunch line, and I noticed the people who were serving me, instead of being the normal kitchen help, were a mixture of guys who had gone home or people that I knew on the street who had never been here. I spent the entire dream on the lunch line looking at all these people."

"And what did you feel?"

"I don't recall a specific emotion. I just had the feeling that there was no escape even in my dreams. It meant that I was in here twenty-four hours a day. Perhaps it's merely the result of being here more time. The inexorable time about which I can do nothing has now forced itself right into my dreams.

"I'm afraid I'm not used to it. The last time I talked to you, I had thought I had gotten used to it, but I can't. I can't get my mind off the street. I can't even settle into something. I've been trying to teach myself Hebrew and got a couple of grammar books from home."

"Why Hebrew?" I asked.

"Because it's difficult and takes concentration, and it's sort of mystical, and so many people I was close to were Jewish. You read it backwards, you know. It fascinates me and intrigues me. I have an old Hebrew-school grammar book sent to me by a rabbi from home. The only things I can concentrate on are those I know nothing about, and Hebrew is completely foreign, it's different. It requires brute memorization, it takes nothing but intellectual application. I want to get involved so deeply in something that I will get lost in it—and time will pass.

"All the reading I had planned, the writing I had hoped to do —nothing. I'm just incapable. I can't make myself express what I wish to. This is an environment in which one can't see true or feel true because it's distorted by depression—depression which is there even if you're not aware of it."

This statement was perhaps the clearest expression that Paul made of the breakdown of his denial mechanism. For indeed he has been depressed or potentially depressed from the moment of entering the prison. This anxiety, which prevented his facing his emotions of resentment, anger, and fear the way many of the others did, permitted these feelings to grow within him and enhanced his feeling of despair; and when denial mechanisms began to fail, a sense of hopelessness emerged.

He continued, "The calendar year is almost up. I want to get past December and into '69. I go up for parole in January. I know there's no chance but I can't stop thinking about it. I could be out in twelve months instead of twenty-five. I don't know how I'll react if I'm denied the parole. I'm curious. I'll either affect an 'Oh, well, I knew this was going to happen' approach, or I'll be bitter. I'm bound to be bitter for a while. But this is silly, it's just speculation.

"Then so many other things have changed. The respect for values I used to have isn't there any more. You know, I used to have such faith in the liberal tradition of law and justice. Perhaps it's just plain cynicism. The country, that nationalistic part, whatever it was that I attached myself to, just doesn't seem to be there any more. Not that when I get out I will do anything wrong or against the country. I'm sure I'll never break a law, except politically. But I don't think I'll ever be motivated again by what used to be a great respect and even love for the country, and that was a pillar of my existence. Perhaps it remained a pillar because I never had to face it, I never had to examine it. It was simply always there.

"My family, you know, has been tied up with the history of our country, and it was something that had always been a matter of family and personal pride. I'm just beginning to realize that our institutions even in their purest form are all political. It had never occurred to me that there were politics involved in the law. How stupid I was! I believed the law was above politics—because it should be. The whole parole system is outrageous. One would think that at least the parole system would be equitable, but the politicians have an armlock on the courts, and it doesn't make sense at all."

He continued for a long while to talk about the law, the draft, his feelings about it, the need for a volunteer army, and intellectual discussions of that sort. I was determined that the hour wouldn't go without my approaching the subject of his depression, and perhaps helping him with it. So after ten or fifteen minutes of this I said, "Let's get back to you. I'm concerned with this depression. I don't think it can just be the holidays."

"You're right. That's just a part. It's so psychological—we're coming to the end of the year and I realize I still have more than a year to go. As soon as I get under a year I'll be better off. The whole survival in prison involves intricate rationalizations in trying to handle time, since there is nothing else you can do with time. I seem incapable of doing what perhaps some of the others can. I can't so deeply involve myself that I can forget where I'm at."

"Is there anything you *can* do to make it easier for yourself?"

"Very little. When I'm reading I don't think about it, but now I can't concentrate. It's hard for me as a person; I can't delude myself as easily as I thought I'd be able to. It's ironic—you once asked me if I thought I'd have a harder time than some of the others, and I suspect it's so. I had a comfortable life on the outside and in a sense I was freer than the others. Having a private income meant that I had no obligations, even to earn a living. My responsibilities were solely limited to myself and keeping myself healthy, educated, et cetera.

"I should be able to use that to help me," he said with rising emotion. "I know as soon as I get out that good life will still be there. It's just a matter of time. All I have to do is sit back and say, 'Look, man, someday it's going to be over, and you won't have to worry about it any more, and it's doing something for you, it really is.' I still believe that in the long run it'll be a good thing. But here and now that makes no difference. It's hard. And despair won't be eradicated."

"Can your friends help?" I asked.

"It's hard to describe the level of friendships here. It seems that there are periods when Tim, Bill, and I have a good thing together for a few hours—really great conversations or doing something—just the three of us. It was great, and we'd think about doing it more often, but there's that common oppression of time.

"There are periods when I feel very close and others when I feel indifferent. Sometimes I'm so thankful for them, that there's some communication, but then later it will seem incidental and unimportant. And then, every time you get closer to a person, it increases the points of friction, and antagonism will arise over the pettiest, most irrelevant things—being fouled in basketball, playing hearts and getting stuck with the queen. I see Bill's competitiveness. He's got to win in everything, and the self-justification if he makes a mistake! But then I find myself doing the same thing. I suppose if you throw two guys in a cage the most incidental things will be enlarged in importance. I hate to see that in myself. That's why I recognize it in others."

He then described an involvement that he has at work with one of the JWs, which is perhaps the best description of the prototypic paranoia that develops in relationships in prison. After going into some detail about the nature of the antagonist, his contacts and conflicts, he began to get progressively more emotional.

"I can't even get in an argument with him over religion, which is the only thing he seems to know, because . . . it's a snobbish thing for me to say, but that son-of-a-bitch is as ignorant a person as I have ever met. Yet his attitudes constantly reflect an enormous, unwarranted conceit. Over and over he tells me that he is completely and totally normal. One of his affectations is the use of the word 'bag.' He's constantly saying that his 'bag' is that he's totally normal and that others are not. He refers to the other prisoners as dumb cons.

"It's a combination of his personal habits, his lumpishness, and his unwarranted conceit that simply repulses me. He never does anything. He sits like a log for hours on end, and I sense that in his mind he's knocking me and I can't stand it. This is the thing that gets me—when I feel that I'm a much better person than he is and yet there's this supercilious attitude of his. Granted, it may be entirely imagined on my part. I doubt that he has the intelligence to be supercilious, but I can't stand that attitude. It's totally unjustified and gratuitous in every aspect, and it's that which bugs me. I try never to talk to him, but I can't avoid him. His attitude that he's a Christian, in particular, drives me crazy, because I know he couldn't possibly be a Christian. I'm not a Christian but I like to think I know what a Christian should be, and there aren't that many of them around.

"When he doesn't have any work to do he will just sit there

and suck all the juices out of his gums—making a horrible noise. Over and over again he sucks and makes that noise, and it drives me crazy sometimes. I want to grab him and tell him to knock it off, but instead I sit there and grit my teeth. I find myself saying into my desk, 'You have to pity him, you have to pity him, you have to tolerate him'—and I'll be typing out 'tolerance, tolerance, tolerance,' over and over again. But I can't show it—I don't feel I have a right to show it.

"I was talking to Tim about a month ago about it, and we were debating whether it wouldn't be the more honest and rational thing for me to approach him directly, to go up to him and say, 'I can't stand you, and it would be better for you to know that. I don't want you deluding yourself into thinking I might ever find you less than obnoxious. Since we have to be in this office together we have to be completely honest, and I think it might be a good idea if you knew exactly where we stand. So that's it. Don't let it bother you because it's purely academic. I'll never do anything to you, and I'll never say anything to you. Just remember, I can't stand you.'

"I couldn't approach a guy and say that to him. In the first place he wouldn't appreciate it. He wouldn't possibly understand why I said it and I couldn't explain it to him. At times when he's got his back toward me and for a small second a huge compassionate feeling will seize me and I will say, 'He's just a human being. He isn't as fortunate as you are and he has as much right . . . he has to be what he is. He has no control over how he acts, and you object on grounds that would be impossible for him to appreciate or to cope with.' While there are these times, more often he literally disgusts me, but I can't show it. I sit there mute, trying to control that emotion."

"Do you get into more internal rages in general than you used to?" I asked.

"Oh yes, and at a higher level of intensity than on the street. But everything in here is so tense—so intense. It's as though I'm now a rough surface and anything that strikes on me will make a spark occur. It may not show much on the outside—of course that's characteristic of me—but under the surface I'm much more antagonistic."

The expression of anger had the effect of animating Paul, and, as it characteristically will, alleviated his depression, at least temporarily. I utilized the opportunity to inquire if he was ready yet to receive visitors.

"No, I still don't have any visitors. I still don't want them. There were a couple of guys I knew from prep school who were going to college nearby who tried to visit me one week when they found out I was here, but the guards threw them out. I suppose it was just as well. I don't want to be seen in this place."

"I don't understand that," I said.

"I don't either, except that it's a total feeling, a complete feeling. I mean, I just don't, period! There's no way I can understand it intellectually or justify it to myself, let alone to someone else. I don't know if it's pride. I don't think it's pride. I just don't want to be in this idiotic place looking—what? I don't know. The people I know care about me. It bothers them enough to know that I'm in prison. They don't have to see me too. And I don't want to see them for an hour and leave—that I don't think I could stand."

Paul did not get involved with the protest movement and as a result was still at the work camp when I arrived that bleak January day. He looked simply terrible. He had lost more weight, and the gaunt, haggard look that had begun to show the last time was now dominant. He had been to the Parole Board—had no idea of the results as yet—and he said he was looking forward to next month because then he would have served a year, a big demarcation point. He then went on to give me a detailed and rational account, the best that I had received, of all the events preceding the disruption. He could not support the idea of non-working. He felt it was an impotent gesture, that the battle would have to be fought outside of the prison. In addition, he was frightened of what the consequences might be for him.

"I went to work. I don't believe in confronting these people here. This is neither the time nor the place. I feel there is a possibility they could mess one up physically. I want to get out of here in one piece and start working against this thing on the outside where you have something to work with. I felt quite honestly that the potential price was too high for the results to be anticipated. There was a small debate but no one pressured anybody, nor did anyone attempt to make me feel guilty for my decision. For some the action was a relief. It assuaged the guilt they had for abandoning their principle of non-cooperation. It's a beautiful principle but I don't feel an effective one.

"I admire these guys and sympathize with them one hundred per cent. I don't like the idea that they are in trouble when I'm not, and I guess a certain amount of guilt comes along with that, but they said I had to act according to my heart and my mind and I did. I thought the cause was trivial. I'd much rather have gone after the institution for their horrible medical attention. Just this summer a man died of a heart attack on the grass because there was no one here capable of administering first aid and no oxygen.

"The irony is that it's hard to find some legitimate thing to protest that would have meaning to people on the street. I don't honestly feel that they're that harsh here. It's much easier than I expected. The major difficulties are all mental. It's the isolation, separation from people, and the time—the time which looms so large.

"I still don't want visitors, you know. I've gone pretty far without them. I've tried to think since our last talk why I'm so opposed to the idea. I can't stand the artificiality of it. I don't want to see them for three hours once a month. When I see them I want to see them as I want to. I'd rather not see them than see them like that. It's hard enough on me and hard enough on them as it is. Coming here, seeing me this way, would be worse in the long run.

"As a matter of fact I decided I don't want ever to go outside the camp till I leave it for good. I wouldn't take work-release if they offered it to me. I don't want to see the outside. My grandfather is very old and there may be the question of getting out when he dies. I don't think even then I could go to the funeral.

"I suppose there's another reason I didn't get involved with the movement. I realize there's quite a difference between Tim, some of the others, and myself. They were men who were physically active in the movement on the outside. I'm not. I'm not what you call a card-carrying member of the peace movement. I suppose you'd say I was never a joiner of any sort. Then, I don't share many of the ideas. I'm not a pacifist in that sense of the word. I'm here because I wouldn't go specifically to Vietnam because it's immoral and not in the interest of this country. I feel that I'm doing a patriotic thing.

"Then perhaps I didn't join because I am more of a loner than the others. Although I've always had good, close friends, I've never felt the need to act in concert with others. That may be why I find the lack of privacy so difficult. My bed is as close to the next one as I am right now to you. While I have good friends with whom I share confidences, I always have to feel there is a part of myself that I share with no one. I don't know what it is. I couldn't answer, but I know that I tend to feel that I always hold back a little in any relationship. Perhaps it's because I identify with my father in so many ways."

Paul had briefly and casually mentioned this idea in the previous hour, and it had not concerned me then. He had said it in such a casual way. His primary love, devotion, and loyalty were to his mother. His neurotic problems, however, centered in great part in his ambivalent relationship with his father. It was interesting that only when Paul began to get depressed and withdrawn did he begin to view himself as like his father. This readiness to identify with an emotionally disturbed recluse said a great deal about Paul's deteriorating sense of self and self-pride during these months.

"In what way do you identify with him?" I asked.

"Well, for one thing the physical resemblance is incredible. I have pictures of him on the football field, and since we went to the same school I've shown them to people and tell them it was I. Sometimes it's like looking in a mirror.

"I get angry the way my father gets angry. I don't like this. I'm thinking someday I'll be married and I don't want to be the kind of husband he was. I don't blame him. He couldn't avoid it. He had this enormous sense of personal discipline and an emotional isolation, which may be the same thing—it was so rejecting and icy. This made it almost impossible for anyone to live with him. I'm frightened that if I get married I might react to a woman the same way—be unable to give, to be loving. I don't think it's true. I think I can, but there are similarities there which are striking. I'm capable of retreating into a bad mood when I get one too. I'll be internally seething and malevolent, and on the outside I'll look cool and detached. If I choose not to open up, no one will know, but it does make me vulnerable, and if I'm touched I can react explosively. I've seen my father withdrawn this way."

He then went on to describe his father in the same terms that he had previously and the ambivalence was, as usual, enormous. The martinet, the aristocrat, the depriver of small pleasures of childhood would be described, and then quickly he would emphasize the enormous brilliance, the various degrees, the numerous honors.

"I was afraid of my father in childhood. I think only because he was bigger. It seemed so unfair not to be allowed all those things which other children came by naturally. I spent as much time as I could with other people in their homes. They'd never be in my home. He was capable of tongue-lashing to an incredible degree. To a point of humiliation. I would alternate between obedience and defiance. As I think of it, I never really defied him openly. I suppose I was too afraid to do it. Most times I was superficially a good boy but inside I didn't feel compliant. Then I was the oldest and any mistake I made was magnified. I always had to be an example to my younger brothers, no matter what happened.

"Getting his approval wasn't easy. He was a perfectionist. Even though I did very well in school, if I missed an A in one subject he'd become enraged. It was incredible as I look back upon it. Even in the summertime if I would want to go out and fool around he would say no, go upstairs, write a paper. Can you imagine, in the summertime! I never had his discipline. I was sort of lazy. I guess it carries right up to this point.

"I don't think he allowed us to have a childhood because I don't think he knew what it was, he never had one himself. I hope to God I'll never be that kind of a father. Two generations is enough. I'm determined not to be and I'm pretty sure I won't. But when my behavior is similar to his it brings me up short. It doesn't bother me nearly so much now, because coming to prison —the idea that I could do that—signifies a real break with him, with his position, his background, his principles of service to country. These are his whole life, and here I am rejecting the whole thing. I suppose psychologically that may be a bit of the reason why I am here."

"How has he reacted to it?" I asked.

"Well, we've lost touch. He's somewhere in the South. I don't know where. I know he knows I'm in prison. He claims to have written but as far as I know he hasn't; if he had written, the letters would have been filled with disagreeable invective. He's most disapproving—that I know. He's been living in a self-imposed physical exile. There's no divorce because they are both very proud people and don't like the idea."

"How did you respond to the break-up when you were still a boy in high school?"

"I felt relieved, to be perfectly honest—relieved that he was out of the picture. I felt free. Exactly that. I realized afterward what a strain there had been on my mother. We all felt free."

After continued reminiscence about his early experiences with his father, Paul returned to the subject of his friends in the penitentiary and his concern for them. He said that some continued to think in terms of escape, as they were somewhat frightened and disturbed by the election of Nixon and what this might mean in terms of the direction in which the country would go.

"I never really considered the possibility that things in the country would get bad enough to think of escape, and permanent exile. I'm not saying they are now, but when I came to prison I wasn't thinking about that at all. At least now the possibility exists. Now I could be prepared to become a total exile. My God, I had the opportunity before and wouldn't dream of it. I'm getting very fed up with the country—the hypocrisy is so oppressive. Then again, maybe it's just the depression that's come on."

My next visit was in April, and the countryside had that fresh, vital, awakened feeling that comes with spring. When Paul walked in, it was as though he too had been touched by spring. Once again he seemed the boy that I had first met. It is always with a renewed sense of bewilderment and awe that I become aware of how much inner feelings can transform physical appearance. Paul still showed the marked weight loss. But he was now a thin young boy, not a haggard man. I started with my perfunctory "How are you?"

"I'm just beautiful." He beamed. "I've got a date—September. It's the new policy. The government Parole Board started the first of this year granting us all paroles when we've served 18 months. I had my hearing, although the feeling was that it was just formality. He asked a few irrelevant questions; he then said it was difficult for him with people like us since they don't have any organized thing to go by. I said, 'Yes, I know it must be a little inconvenience for you.' At that point it meant nothing to me—I was unaware of the new parole policy. It was merely a day off of work. I saw the board at the end of January, and I heard around the fifteenth of February.

"What a change! It's just that feeling that the end is in sight—

as simple a thing as that. I now have a specific day when I know I'll be free. Also, I know I'll be back in school in September, which is a good feeling, a hell of a good feeling—a beautiful feeling. It's been three years since I've been in school. I can't wait to get back. For all practical purposes it's over. I really have just one more season to go, and the best season of all, the summer. When it's warm, things are a little more relaxed and you can go outside.

"Before January I was desperately keeping my mind off the street as much as I could, looking at the ground, not thinking. Now I can look up—I just have to go through the summer. In January I still had the parole facing me and I dreaded it. I also hadn't been able to eat in that period—I'd been thinking too much about things. Then there's the January-February syndrome in prison—they're bad months—it's cold and there's no color yet.

"It was really beginning to get to me. I didn't know if I could make it through the winter and I had the knowledge that there was yet another entire winter still ahead. Once or twice I had the feeling that I might not be able to make it, that I might break. I felt people pressing in. I couldn't stand the crowding, the constant pressure of people all around.

"Then I was beginning to get frightened. I was beginning to think, 'God, I'm behaving just like my father.' There are certain things in my character which worry me to the extent that they remind me of him. I realize that I'm not him, that I am different, but I would find myself getting irritated and short with people, ready to feel hurt and disappointed in them, feeling that they had failed somehow or other to meet certain standards that I had set for them. I'd be short-tempered, sensitive, unable to take a joke.

"It was hard for me when the other men were sent to the penitentiary. I wasn't sure I was doing the right thing. I thought I was right, but a little guilt kept creeping in. Actually nothing was accomplished that I could see. I was worried for Bill—it was wonderful seeing him back. I feel very close to him. We all sat together and just talked and talked and talked about what it was like. It was as if they had gone on one train and we had gone on another and both gotten to the same place."

"Was there any sense of alienation?" I asked.

"I don't think so. I think that we're all mature enough to realize that that which binds us together is what we did in the first place—coming to jail. They acted according to their convictions and I according to mine. Another thing that is encouraging is that we began to appreciate more that there are a lot of people on the street who know we are here. This is an enormous advantage that we have over the average guy in prison. The hacks sense it, the administration senses it, and in a peculiar way it's our protection. There are whole communities of concerned people watching what happens to us. I know it sounds exaggerated but it's close to that. If I don't write a letter to somebody in three or four weeks, I get a letter asking what the hell is going on, has anything happened, are you all right. It's the same thing with all of us. The administration is afraid of us.

"There is one thing that I've wanted to tell you that I feel I've learned. It seems to me that nothing turns to disgust or hatred faster than idealism which has exhausted itself. I think maybe this is happening to me a little bit. I'm getting fed up with the machinations of the peace movement. I read things, articles, about us and what goes on in here, on the outside, and they're often ridiculous with their claims of gross brutality. I've seen in certain publications where we were dragged nude, a thousand yards, down freezing, cold corridors and things like that. They may mean well, but the exaggerations turn me off.

"On the other hand, I'm not sure how you write an article which can adequately describe this place. If you don't exaggerate, it makes it sound like a CCC camp, but it isn't. There's something different here, something horrible and destructive, something that forces a deterioration, and it is not rubber hoses and beatings. How can anyone describe it? But if you can't, you can't, and I don't think that even for propagandistic purposes it should be exaggerated."

"Is that all that's turning you off with the peace movement?" I asked.

He laughed and said, "You always seem to find the thing I don't want to talk about and get me right to it. There are a few guys that I find myself getting impatient with. I hate to criticize them because I respect them as individuals."

I remained silent.

He said, "Here we go again. I suppose I do have to talk about it."

He then went on to mention a few of the men who annoyed him. He particularly resented those few who seemed eager for martyrdom or those who were the most polemic. These were characteristically the newer inmates. It was generally true that the men who had served a longer time had little patience with what they saw as the jingoism and pomposity of many newly arrived prisoners.

"Why do you have such difficulty with angry or critical feelings?"

"Do I? Well, I guess I do. I think maybe it's part of another thing that I try to suppress—a sensitivity which I suppose is ego. It may be related to the sense I have of an isolated, inviolate me —which nobody can mess with. How wise it is to think that way I don't know, because sometimes it requires twenty-four hours' sentry duty. I don't think a person should concentrate so much, so diligently on his own self.

"I also like to think there is a basic, uncompromised morality inside of me too. But I don't know—in here you see human beings treated and then acting like animals, and who knows what anyone can be reduced to. I do feel that on a one-to-one basis there is a moral code which I would never violate. It's not that which is in jeopardy, it's my idealism in a more political sense, I suppose—my identification with the rest of the COs—and when one of these guys goes around saying the COs have decided this or that—well, fuck, I'm a CO and I haven't decided anything like that. I don't think that way—just say *you* thought about it that way—don't tell me what I think. It would be easier to be here on dope charges."

"Yet your friends here are the COs?"

"Of course they are. But even with my friends, as much as I respect or like Tim, he can get me annoyed. If someone is put upon, regardless of how slight, he comes charging in. If he feels someone's been abused—it might just as well be that the President was shot or Pearl Harbor bombed. I'm confused about Tim. There are times when I can like him so much. We are so different though. He's a community liver, a hitchhiker. When you ask him what he is going to do with his life or future he'll say, 'What difference does it make? That's not the important thing.' It's hard to stay mad at Tim though. He is essentially such a good person."

He then reported a dream which, while essentially a sexual dream, was important because it expressed his newfound sense of freedom and strength. The dream started as follows:

"I'm prone on a cart, like garagemen use to get under cars. It's on a highway. Instead of a median strip dividing the road, there's a small miniature railroad track. It has what looks like a ladder with grooves on the end for wheels. This little cart is fitted onto the track, and I'm pulling myself along on the rungs. I'm doing this all day long. It's a beautiful, gorgeous, tropical-type day. It's vegetation like in Tahiti or in the deep South—totally verdant, beautiful, just terrific. I'm in shorts and a T-shirt, and I'm in good physical shape and I'm pulling myself along—all day long—past beautiful things. I do it without thinking or feeling tired. I'm aware that there's some kind of fatigue involved—it's an enormous amount of work but I don't feel it. I'm aware that time is passing but I don't feel that either. I know that physiologically there should be exhaustion, but instead there's a sense of power and exhilaration."

The dream then continued till he finally came to his destination, which involved a beach, a cove, a girl, and a sexual experience.

When he finished relating the dream he looked at me, smiled warmly, and said, "I don't think that dream needs much interpretation. I'm on my way, and I guess that's beautiful; the blond girl is the pot of gold at the end of the rainbow. I do feel that I'm on my way and that I have the strength to climb one rung after another. And it's not going to get me down."

The next time I visited Paul, he started right in.

"It's really springtime," he said, "and what a difference! Only 118 days to go, and I can really feel myself on the way out."

We then spent the session talking about his plans to get back to college; his feelings about some of the men; his hope, particularly with Bill, that friendships could be resumed on the outside. He reviewed the changing of his moods; the highs and lows of the prison experience. He was still not willing to receive personal visitors, and he mentioned his annoyance even with the general visitors from the peace groups.

"I feel so damn guilty. Often I look forward to seeing them and enjoy the visit, but there are times when I don't want to see them, and I feel like a rat. They do a wonderful job. Sometimes, though, they'll put an arm around you and attempt an intimacy and talk in a paternalistic way. I know their hearts are in the right place but it puts me off. It's the same old thing—that I don't like attention forced on me when I'm not in the mood. Sometimes I'm delighted to see them, but I have to be in the mood."

"Did you ever feel the same way about seeing me? That is, not in the mood?" I asked.

He laughed. "The minute I said that, I anticipated your question. I'm getting to know you, as well as you me. No, I never did. I really enjoy this. It intrigues me. I've never done anything like this before, but I like it. If I didn't want to see you I wouldn't come. You're right to be suspicious because it's not typical of me to talk to a stranger like this, or to want someone, or to share so much of my intimate thoughts with someone. It's been a lesson to me, because it has been such a good feeling."

"It's incredible in what better spirits you are, and how much better you look."

"It's having a date. Knowing when I'll be out is like a new organ in my body. Like a transplant of strength and energy. It's an amazing feeling. I just can't describe it. But prison has left its mark. I feel much more pessimistic. I'm going to be more suspicious of people—not hostile suspicious, just wary.

"It was fairly rough in the beginning. There was a lot of anxiety. A guy who looks like me and is built like me—sort of young and slight—you hear about stabbings at the Wall. There was a stabbing just recently; then another horrible incident filtered down to us. One of the guys was raped by about fifteen guys—he was quite badly hurt. A thing like that shakes me up a great deal. I guess it does all the COs.

"It's as though this whole thing were a big, huge computer with fatal defects in it, and when it malfunctions, the chance of who happens to be at the Wall will determine who will be hurt. We're all in for the same thing as far as the prison is concerned, and it could just as well have been me there. I suppose it's not so different in war, when some guy is shot up right next to you. The feeling—it could have been me.

"This camp is a powder puff compared with some other places, and I'm thankful that I served my time here. The homosexual thing is well controlled here. It was just bad at the beginning, and even then I had learned the right thing to say. The first guy who came to me was big and tough. I told him he was going to have to knock me out and he said, 'I don't believe in forcing,' and that was that. I guess the word gets around with them too. But even without that there is an atmosphere of degeneracy here. It will take me a while to regain confidence in human beings again."

"If you had known what prison was really like, would you have taken this course or would you have left the country?" I asked.

"I would still have taken this course."

This was not the answer he had given me to the same question a few months ago. He evidently did not remember that, so I decided to reword it in such a way as to make it a practical consideration rather than a theoretical one.

"Supposing you go out now and they decide to reinduct you, what would you do?"

"I don't know. I really don't know. I've thought about it. I can't help feeling that if I couldn't come back to jail again, then I really didn't believe what I was doing the first time."

"Do you think you could face jail again?" I asked.

There was a long pause. "I don't think I could. Not really."

"I'm sure it isn't going to happen," I reassured him.

"I feel the way you do, but you never know. The military has been acting so barbaric. It's incredible that those guys drew fifteen years for just sitting down and singing.* Even though they cut it down, it's incredible that they could even conceive giving someone fifteen years for that. I understand they even considered the death sentences, so who can know. When you think of that, anything could happen.

"No, now that I am thinking of it—the more I think of it, I wouldn't come back to jail. I would fight it as much as I could, but finally I would leave the country if I had to. But then I'm much less a political activist than many. I feel alienated from all that. One of the men here said that when he gets out of here he's going to join SDS and get a torch and burn the library and dean. It's totally absurd—I couldn't be a part of that."

"Were you ever?" I asked.

"No, I was never part of a movement. I suppose I'm even less now. It was always in personal terms. It was a matter of con-

* Twenty-seven Army prisoners, who protested against conditions at the Presidio stockade in San Francisco on October 14, 1968, were tried and sentenced for mutiny.

science which would not permit my participation in the war. If they wouldn't have tried to force me, I would have probably done nothing. This is the way things have always been in my life. Unless I've been personally affected I don't act—at least not aggressively. I care and I'm interested, but I will not be an assertive activist unless I have a sense of personal involvement. I would have still hated the war just as much even if I never got beyond just being in college.

"Now if my brother were sent over and got killed while I had a draft protection, I don't know what I'd do. I have a feeling that something like that would get to me. I have thought about this many times before. My brother was inducted ironically on the same day that I refused. It adds a somewhat symbolic note. So I have thought about this a lot. If anything happened to him in the Army I don't know what it would do to me, I don't know what I might do. And, of course, it could still happen."

8 ⫷

O-70296: John

John is another of that group of slight, fine-featured, physically attractive men who predominate in the group of war resisters. He has sandy hair, somewhat on the longish side for prisoners, and hazel eyes. (The high index of good looks is something for which I have no adequate explanation.) The chief contribution to his appearance is a product of his emotionality. Unlike the naked youthfulness of many of the others, John exudes a certain "middle-agedness"—part cynicism, part weariness, part wariness.

John was a good talker, and once he got started he could carry almost the entire hour. This was in sharp contrast with his near-paralysis in starting, particularly if given no direction. Any question, any sentence, any lead would be sufficient for him to work on, but there was an enormous reluctance to initiate. The intensity of his inability to initiate, in John's case, was an indicator of a psychodynamic function. There was a reluctance to put himself forward, to take center stage front. He was repelled by the idea of presumptuousness or arrogance.

I started the interview by saying, "I want to know all about you, so start in anywhere."

"Well, that's too general. I don't know what you mean," he answered.

"I want to get to know you as a person," I said.

"Well, I grew up in a middle-class, upstate, Republican family, went to prep school, went to Dartmouth from which I dropped out in 1961. That's how I started getting involved in politics."

There was a long pause, followed by, "Now, you know, you really must ask me what you want to hear," he said.

"Just feel free to talk about anything," I said.

"I can't unless you ask questions," he said.

"Just try."

"This is silly. I'm really quite willing to say anything. It's not like I'm self-conscious about myself. As long as I'm asked I'll tell you anything you want to know, but I feel stupid just going off about myself. It's so presumptuous to just say anything."

"All right. What I'm naturally most interested in are your feelings, particularly about yourself," I said.

"Well, if we could start with some particular thing we could maybe then go off to another thing."

"All right. Let's start with your background," I said, being quite willing to compromise.

"That's too general. I couldn't presume to analyze myself at all," he said.

"I don't want you to analyze yourself. I just want to know how you feel."

"Please," he said, "this is very uncomfortable. Why don't you just tell me what you'd like to hear first?"

I relented and said, "Supposing you describe your parents."

He started in right away. "My father is a successful industrialist. He has all the money he needs but he continues to go to the office because that's what he wants to do. My mother is very warm, to the point of being overly warm. Her relationship with my father has never been very good, but instead of doing something about it and preserving some dignity, she plays the role of the martyr.

"My mother's family has money. My father really didn't have much. He worked his way up. I was born in Pennsylvania, but my father was always moving as he worked his way up the ladder, so we lived in a lot of suburbs in various states. I have a brother who is in the Navy. He enlisted at the time he was to be drafted."

"How do you feel about each other's position?" I asked.

"I could never be where he is, but I don't think he has any bad feelings about my being here. He went through a personal crisis. I think he disagreed with the war. I know that when he was about to be drafted he went through a lot of problems, but he felt he couldn't object."

"Are you the oldest?" I asked.

"I am. There's my brother and then a younger sister."

"Tell me more about your parents."

"They've always had problems. I'm not really sure what the problems were about. My father is a difficult man. He was always a big shot in areas that really didn't satisfy him. He managed to get all the things that he never really enjoyed, social position, money, prestige. It's funny, in many ways he would have been happier doing physical things. He would have loved being a landscape architect.

"I used to think of him as strong. As I became older I started to see him more clearly. When I ultimately stopped rebelling against him, I recognized that he was a pathetic figure.

"When I was a child he was threatening. It wasn't so much that he was a stern disciplinarian—I didn't feel he knew how to love, I never felt affection from him. I felt I was looked at more in monetary terms. How do I mean that? If he wanted something from me, a task, affection even, it wasn't presented in such a way that I would do it because we were family and would enjoy doing things for each other—instead I was always bribed, paid to do it. It became distasteful."

"Were you frightened of him as a boy?" I asked.

"Yes, in the beginning I was frightened, particularly when my mother and he would fight. It would often threaten to become physical. Never really serious, but a quick slap or something. I remember lying awake when I was a little kid, trembling and listening to the fight. My mother, in a sense, shared responsibility for this. She would come running to me. I became an in-between. What a horrible position! She came to me looking for protection even though there was obviously no way for me to protect her."

"Was your father a drinking man?" I asked.

"Yes," he said.

Then there was a pause.

"Were these arguments mostly when he was drunk?" I asked.

"Right, mostly then," he said. "That's when I had fights with him also. I can't remember really any of the causes. I just remember being frightened. Being grabbed and pushed around a lot. So I started hitting back. The first time was just an impulsive gesture—I didn't realize it was happening. I'd come home late from something or other, and he got very violent and grabbed me. Instinctively, without thinking, I hit him, and he was terribly shocked. Where he had always acted so tough all the time, he showed such vulnerability with this. He was so obviously upset and said something like, 'Look what I've done to you.' Of course I was no match for him physically, but he never touched me after that."

"How did you feel?"

"I know I didn't feel guilty. In a sense I was angry with him. I don't remember the exact timing, but as a child I had always been placed in this role of the protector who was incapable of protecting. With time I found myself still in the role of protector, but then I protected. I'm still at it I guess, although I've been in prison eighteen months.

"When I first left college, however, I was disowned, and my father wouldn't see me for a few years."

"What about your mother?" I asked.

"My mother is a mother. I'm her boy. I suppose I always will be. She'd come to visit me. I'd moved to another city."

"Why were you disowned?"

"Because I left college against his wishes and because of my growing involvement in different political activities. I was never a hippy but was early a political activist: civil rights demonstrations, protesting the Cuban invasion, all that."

"How did you get into all of that?" I asked.

"Well, I usually shy away from thinking in terms of psychological reasons. I try to think in terms of its validity, in a practical or political way. I'm sure there is a psychological cause, but I don't think that way."

My question had been general and in actuality I had not been thinking of the psychological reasons. I was simply asking for the history or background of his political involvement, the manner of his induction into national politics. The fact that he felt the need to search out specifically psychological causes made it apparent to me that John, probably the most sophisticated young man that I interviewed, assumed that as a psychoanalyst my bias would be toward psychological explanations of behavior. He was conscientiously attempting to present me with the kind of data he assumed I wanted. This was an early indication of his need to do "the right thing," his willingness to expose himself, and his essential honesty. I decided to let him continue, to see where it would lead us.

"I suppose the process of rebellion really started in relation to my schooling. I went to a prep school in New England: I didn't want to go there—my father had gone there, but I didn't really want to. I wanted to stay in the public school. I had a feeling he was making me into something—a businessman, a professional, somehow or other an individual to 'carry on.' That's still the thing to do, to get onto the treadmill. I didn't like it.

"I was reacting at that time to his values and his life. I would see my father unhappy, commuting to the city, on the train all the time, to a job he couldn't stand, back to suburbia, drinking at night because he didn't like his job, then compensating by acting the big shot because of his position and income.

"I started reacting to all of this. I saw the phoniness of the guys at prep school, the false values that people hold, and the false relationships. I decided not to go to college at that time—I wanted time to think it all out, maybe work for a year. But I was pressured about college—at that time I was still giving in." He smiled. "Even there there was a conflict. I wanted to go to a small college, my parents wanted me to go to Harvard or Yale. I purposely didn't go to those two, but as you can see, I ended up at an Ivy League college—that was my 'compromise.'

"After the first semester I was determined to leave. When I got home I told my father of my decision but was talked into going back. I got reasonably good grades, B's—if I'd worked I suppose I could have gotten A's. I wasn't working very hard. School was a treadmill for me—it didn't mean anything. I was just sitting there behind a cigarette. Ironically, as long as it was maintained on the level of talk, my father would meet me on the same terms —he had left school when he was a kid. But when it came down to the actual decision of leaving, that was a different story. I just wasn't going to leave, according to him. My mother wasn't a great help—she insisted it would cause her death, she would have a heart attack if I left. I suppose that was the excuse I needed, so I went back, not wanting to harm her. If I didn't know then, I certainly do now, that it wasn't for her that I went back. It was because I was afraid of the break. Then evidently I unconsciously discovered my way out. I began to study so little and do so badly that I created a situation where they'd kick me out. This was hardly the way to assert my individuality, so finally I just left in mid-semester and I didn't go home.

"I wrote them that I was leaving and hitchhiked across the country. I felt I had to make a complete break so that when I reestablished things with my family it would be on new terms— where they would not feel the need to control me. It was a great feeling when I left. I had some money with me, and some money in the bank, but I was determined not to use that. I traveled around the country getting involved with peace politics. I was very active in some of the organizations that were just forming at that time. I was active particularly in one important peace demonstration which involved my being in jail for eighteen days. From jail I went to New York City, figuring that's where the center of activity was. I had run out of money, but I got my own apartment and a job. I worked in book stores."

"Was there any contact with your parents during this period?"

"Oh yes, my mother would come and visit me frequently, and in the last few years there has even been contact with my father. It's been a nervous contact. Even though I disagree with him in most things and blame him for the bad relationship with my mother, there's a growing sympathy for him. I see him in a trap, in a constant conflict with himself more than his environment. His whole life has been that."

"How did they react to your being in prison?" I asked.

"They don't understand this at all. My mother applies psychological terms to it all. She feels guilty and expresses it all in terms of their failure as parents."

"How do you feel about this?" I asked.

"I feel good. I don't see this at all as a failure. Being here obviously is a painful waste, but waste doesn't necessarily mean failure. Because the reason I'm here is right, I have a certain amount of self-respect for myself. Basically, as long as I retain that I can endure imprisonment."

"How much longer do you have?"

"Well"—he smiled sardonically—"I have five years. I go up for parole next month. It's unlikely I'll make it. My case is much different from the others. I'm not truly a pacifist or CO. For me it was less religious and moral objection, and more political. I was fighting the basic concept of the draft. I was insisting on the rights of individual conscience. I think because of the nature of my defense my sentence was so large. I was in a sense challenging something basic to the government. Because the issues were hot ones and often picked up by political groups, with consequent publicity, I got the big sentence."

"How do you feel about that now?"

"How can I say? I don't know what effect it will have. I'm incapable of judging that. I did what I thought was best to do, what I still think was best to do. I don't see any more effective way."

"How do you find serving time?"

"It's very frustrating. There's a growing sense of insecurity about myself that I haven't felt for years. There's no sense in being assertive, not in here. It's not really a sense of being alive, and there's no privacy. That may sound like a luxury, but when you're deprived of it you recognize it as an essential need.

"The insecurity shows itself in a number of ways. There's a feeling of not being an actor but of being acted upon. There's a sense of drifting, and then it's compromising just staying here, allowing them to keep you here."

"Are you saying you see this as a humiliation?"

"No—well, I don't know. I don't think I'd like to use that word. Not so much humiliation as frustration. You feel time is passing, and that's a waste. What I did to get here was not, but the result was, and I'm willing to accept that as a price for principle. I can endure jail."

"I know that," I said.

At the opening of the next session John told me that he'd been tense because he still hadn't gotten the results from the Parole Board and it was longer than the usual time. He did not interpret this with any hopefulness. He assumed that he would most likely be denied parole.

I continued where we had left off the previous hour and asked him if he had thought of other courses besides prison.

"Since I still feel that fighting it in the courts and going to prison is the most effective way to combat the war and the draft, then obviously going to Canada would be taking a less effective course, besides involving a personal sense of demoralization. It would be running away from the fight, and that would affect my whole life. I have always felt that one has to stay and fight for what one believes, and as long as I feel this is the most effective way, I have no regrets. Objectively I can't be sure how much my court battle and the publicity that ensued had an effect on the operation of the war—or indeed on anything. The only thing I *can* say is that it was the only thing that had the potential for it. Certainly I see no immediate concrete effect as yet, and that raises certain self-doubts."

"Would you say there's a lot of self-doubt among the men here?" I asked.

"It's hard to say. I'm somewhat separate from the rest of the COs here. For most of them it was a very personal thing. They were fighting for their own morality, their own conscience. That was not my case. I wanted to challenge the war itself on the basis of the legality. I simply don't believe in imposing one man's conscience on another. I think there should be no draft. Certainly World War II required a call to arms and I would have likely volunteered then, but anybody should have had a right to say they were opposed to it and refuse to serve. To me, these are civil liberty issues. But even the draft seems diminished as a legal issue when one thinks of the war as a whole. Our very presence in Vietnam is illegal. It's a violation of international law— the Nuremberg trials. This is a significant issue, and since this is my country I must fight for it—not in Vietnam where its survival as a democracy is not really threatened, but here, where it is. If I ever get to the point where I feel hopeless about changing this country, then I might go some place else. Sooner or later, knowing myself, I must see results. Right now I still feel there is hope and I'll stay and fight the battle.

"The thing that most makes me despair is the movement itself. It seems to be going off into impotent directions. There's no sense of planning to build power. They hold demonstrations and then everyone goes home. It's not enough to just confront the police.

That has no lasting effect. The same thing is true about civil rights. Black power as an end in itself is a dead end, if it involves segregation. This country is a political country, and it changes with political power. I think you start forming a political base and move that way. I get into a lot of arguments with the people here, even those I am closest to. We get into these arguments, and then it will deteriorate to a point where we feel we are attacking each other's integrity. Then it becomes hard to communicate. I don't know what it is."

He stopped, then said, "I seem to have made a speech."

I smiled. "It was hard for me to get you started. But once you do, you talk freely and openly."

"I have nothing to hide. But I think it's natural to not want to open up right away. Maybe I'm rationalizing."

"I think it's shyness," I said.

"It's an old-fashioned word, but I think you're right. Then I always wonder each time, should I really be talking to you?"

"Why do you feel that?"

"It's just a feeling that somehow or other it's a kind of game. The artificialness of the situation, the whole thing. Then I'll think, 'He seems like a nice enough guy so I'll talk to him.' The whole idea of talking to a psychiatrist bothers me some. I don't know what the other guys do when they come in here, but a lot of them claim they come in and con you, that they're not being real. I wonder about that though. Then it's clouded by the sessions being attached somehow to the whole authority structure here."

"Are you suggesting that I might be a representative of the authority?"

"I really can't tell," he said.

"Do you have any doubts that way?" I asked.

"It crosses my mind that you might be some agent for the government. There's that slight suspicion, even though there's no justification for it. A lot of us have talked about it. We're confused because you don't seem at all that way. But, then again, I suppose if they picked someone it would be someone who didn't seem at all that way.

"You know we all get paranoid in here after a while. Prison does things to the personality. I find myself closing up since I've gotten here. I thought I wouldn't—I've been disappointed in myself. I thought I would be a lot stronger. Even with my girl and my letters to her. I find myself being so self-indulgent. Then I feel regretful. I have weaknesses, and they're all coming out here. I presume they were always there but never manifested themselves. It is simply that the jail has brought them out. I just wish I didn't have them."

"I'm not sure I understand how you're using 'self-indulgent,'" I said.

"Well, I get self-centered here, too concerned about my own individual problems. This place has brought out a whole sense of time passing, of aging. I never had that before. It may be the lack of a sense of being involved with the process of life. I get hung up on that.

"You begin to doubt things that don't warrant it, feel insecure about things you took for granted. Like relationships—like with my girl. There's absolutely no justification—I have complete and basic faith in her, but I get frightened and insecure. I've always responded to that insecurity by saying to myself, It makes no sense, it should never bother you because if her love won't last, if she finds someone else—then, indeed, it is just as well to find that out. It becomes a legitimate testing of the intensity and value of a relationship. I won't let it show. I don't get possessive but I have this sense of jealousy and insecurity.

"That isn't particularly the predominant one, I just use it as an easy example. I know that's sort of human and I would expect to have some of it, but I'm surprised at the intensity.

"A lot of people have said that I have a tendency to be perfectionist about myself, that I overjudge myself, and perhaps that's what I'm doing now. But then I have this feeling that I'm not doing anything. Even in terms of my political action I'm paralyzed. And there's a feeling that somehow I could be doing more. Do you know what I mean?"

"I certainly know what you mean in terms of your perfectionism," I said.

"I felt that, once I came to jail, being in jail wouldn't mean much unless I made something of it. Yet what can I do? I thought perhaps I should write more in here."

"Perhaps some of your ideas will be able to get across through me," I said.

"I don't know. I'm not sure that would work anyway," he replied.

"You mentioned before that some of the guys joke about cutting up in here and putting me on. Do you feel that you put me on?"

"No, I don't. I feel you know me very well, and it's been a very short exposure."

"Do you feel that you try to put me on?" I asked.

"I don't know. For a session I might have—at least in one sense. I have a deep, ingrained prejudice against psychiatry. I still basically think people shouldn't go to psychiatrists. I don't mean psychotics, of course. I mean when it becomes a way of not coping, of abandoning responsibility for your problems.

"Anyway, I have a feeling that maybe in that first session I had said to myself, 'I'll give this guy what he wants to hear. He wants to hear about the middle-class rebel and the family background and so I'll tell him about that.' Not that everything I said wasn't true. It's an honest story. It is really what happened, but I had the sense that maybe I started talking in this area because I thought you would be interested in 'how I got off the track.' So I talked about the family problems as the thing that would have the most validity for you."

"I take it, then, that you're not part of the group that meets with Reverend E?" (The Protestant minister who conducted a group therapy session with some of the COs.)

"No, I'm not. I feel it's all artificial. I understand the feeling that motivates people to a group like this, but it's ridiculous. They talk about the most intimate things in the group, then they will walk out and not speak to each other until the next weekly meeting. I think I'm capable of communicating with people I get close to—wholly and really—without the artifice of a therapy session. To me it doesn't seem meaningful."

"Do you sense any polarization, in terms of who has joined and who has not?"

"Oh yes. I think the ones that I would put as the hippy types are in it. Don't misunderstand that word—I don't mean the drug scene, beatnik. I'm using the term more loosely. They're less coherent, they're less structured people. There's a rebellion in them. I rebelled way back. Some of them don't seem grounded at all. They believe things and react to them intuitively. There's too much emotion and not enough reason. Rebellion should be a stage in the process of becoming an individual, but I have the sense that some of them just go on rebelling, and the rebellion is the thing in itself."

I then told him that I thought he might be in great part describing the difference between a nineteen-year-old and a twenty-eight-year-old. I then asked him if he was aware that because of his maturity he stood as a symbol of stability and reassurance to many in the group. He was transparently embarrassed by this statement of direct praise.

"It seems strange. A lot of people have told me how difficult it was to talk to me at first, that I seemed unapproachable at the beginning—that they were afraid to come and talk. Some even came and told me they were in awe of me. Many had heard of me from the outside. But besides that there was the personal thing. I don't know what it is. I worry sometimes about being unapproachable. Some of the people I have been closest to later told me how hard it had been to get to me at first. I don't know what that can be."

"There is a shyness or self-consciousness in you that can be interpreted as aloofness," I said.

"It's very strange. I wouldn't have thought of that. I know that I was terribly shy as a kid. I thought I had outgrown it. I had assumed that I accepted myself by this time of life, but there must be remnants that I'm not aware of."

"Tell me about your childhood."

"It's not a very dramatic one. I think my early childhood was fairly happy, at least I don't remember being unhappy. I built treehouses, went off to the fields with my dog. I didn't get into any real trouble, just the usual kid stuff. We used to run around in gangs, do a little mischief. Then there were the Cub Scouts, Boy Scouts, church groups, the regular kind of thing. I always had many friends, very close friends. I was never terribly close to my father.

"Compared to my younger brother, I suppose I was always the good boy; he was always more troublesome. My mother worried a great deal about him. I was always very independent in the sense that I could take care of myself. They didn't worry about me if I was off—'responsible,' I suppose, would be the word. I was the one they described as good—sensitive but intense. Too intense my mother would say."

"What about your social life and girls?"

"Oh, girls!" He laughed. "Well, I was in love in the third grade. Then I had a couple of very serious girl friends, both at the same time. Then there came a period after grade school when there was a marked amount of shyness toward girls. That was perhaps in the eighth or ninth grade. Then the shyness disappeared and it was all right again. I was a terrible romantic as an adolescent. I suppose as a psychiatrist you want to know about my sexual development. I think I was somewhat late. Besides kissing and petting and that sort of stuff, I didn't have real intercourse until I was about eighteen. I didn't really like the girl, and because of that it was disappointing. I've always wanted sex as part of a bigger relationship."

"Has the sexual deprivation been difficult for you here?"

"Yes, it's hard. That's a very hard thing. You find yourself getting preoccupied with it. I find I'm thinking of it more and more. Thinking of it even with girls I had nothing to do with on the outside, girls that I had rejected. And then thinking in sexual terms exclusively more than in terms of a total relationship. That would bother me, not thinking of them as people. I don't like just thinking in terms of bodies, not people. I know that I react in here the way many others do—the cruder concept of sexuality comes to the surface. I don't feel that I ever went that far myself, but I sensed that I was susceptible to it. Pornography is a big bore. That kind of fantasy never satisfied me."

"Were you worried about the homosexuality here?"

"No, not really. I had friends on the outside who were homosexuals, and it's nothing I've ever had a problem with. Maybe that's why I wasn't disturbed here. I've gone through that bit with people making advances while at college or hitchhiking. At the time I thought that perhaps it was my fault—something latent in me—that made homosexuals make advances. But I saw that wasn't so. I realized there didn't have to be anything in me. If you're young and fairly decent-looking, homosexuals are going to make advances. I don't know how some of the others react. I suspect that there is surprising little homosexuality among the COs. At least I don't know of any."

At the next meeting I asked him, "How have you been?"

"Oh, pretty good," he answered.

"Is that just conversation or for real?"

"What do you mean?" he countered.

"Well, it's a kind of routine answer," I said. "And besides, I find it difficult to read your mood."

He laughed. "So do I. It's strange. I made parole for February, and it's causing an enormous amount of anxiety. I was eligible in the middle of October but didn't get a date until February, which is remarkable anyway, so there's this sense of excitement about making parole, combined with this tremendous let-down because of the long time interval. You can't quite grasp it— you're still doing the time and the time seems endless.

"Then there's that anxiety about myself functioning on the outside. It's a controlled anxiety, but I have a vague feeling that the place may have messed me up. As soon as I heard about parole I began thinking about this place and me in it, and I don't like 'me-in-this-place.' I don't like the way I'm reacting. I think I mentioned to you in an earlier session, there's an insecurity, and it manifests itself in a self-centered quality. You know, there's a great deal of shame."

"Shame about what?" I asked, surprised.

"About being aware of all the different changes that are going on inside of me and yet not feeling I can control it. Not being able to control my moods, for one thing. I know I'm not defining it well for you. It has something to do with the isolation, and the lack of capacity to be an effective person. It's an indefinable thing—you lose that sense of being, you lose the very sense of self. I find so many things in me I don't like. 'Self-centered' seems to sum it up best. There's this feeling I have—and I'm sure it's completely wrong—that as soon as I get out of here I will have to stop and sort myself out, discard some of the things developed in me. Then start living again."

"Have you been very moody?" I asked. I've learned over the years that "moody" is a common word used to deny depression, to describe the emotion while denying its severity.

"Yes, very often. It's a funny thing. Sometimes I feel great, feel more alive, and then it goes away."

"When it goes away, does it leave you depressed?" I asked.

"Yes, it does, but not severe. I've only been severely depressed once in my life."

"When was that?" I asked.

"When my marriage broke up," he said.

"I didn't know about that," I said. "Could you tell me about it?"

"I went into this crazy depression. I don't think I'd ever kill myself, but there were times when I was watching this 'other guy' who was ready to jump across a subway train or something. I couldn't do anything. I'd try to go to a movie and within minutes walk out.

"It was unbearable. We had been messing things up for a long while. I felt that perhaps we should separate temporarily, but during that separation she decided that it should be permanent. It was she who made the final decision. There were too many factors, and I'm not sure I can separate out what was important and what unimportant. There was something in both of us that wasn't ready for it; we really loved each other, but maybe we were too idealistic or just too unsophisticated.

"We couldn't tolerate small frictions. If something went wrong, even a minor argument, we didn't know how to deal with it. It seemed we both had an idea of a romantic, idealistic love where everything must be in total harmony. At that time there was no awareness that a relationship is something you have to work at, that it's a constant process. If you define love as something beautiful and perfect and unflawed, you're going to have trouble. We both probably were too young."

"Do you think you're more mature about relationships now?"

He laughed. "I hope so. But, then again, that may be what's bothering me most in jail, because life does become distorted here, and some of the things that I had assumed I'd outgrown began to re-emerge, particularly this jealousy and insecurity with my girl.

"I'm ashamed of those feelings. They're not a part of the way I'd like to be, or the way I was. In one sense I feel that I shouldn't worry, that when I get out of jail I'll shed them, but then I wonder if I'm not being naïve. These things are in me. Jail doesn't manufacture them, it only elicits them. And that's disturbing me."

At this point I felt it necessary to point out certain things that I hoped would be reassuring, reassuring because they were true. I said to him that I thought that was a particularly self-destructive way of looking at things. Of course those things were present in him, because they were present in everybody. The difference between a neurotic and a healthy person, to use psychiatric language, was not in the things that were in him but in the degree of stress necessary to elicit them. The prison situation was one of the greatest stress situations that I'd been exposed to. It eroded self-confidence and generated feelings of anxiety and dependency in all people.

"I can agree with what you say intellectually," he said, "but I feel that stress shouldn't work this way in me. I'm terribly self-critical, and I say if I understand these things I should be able to control them, and then of course I can't."

"You're very hard on yourself," I said.

"Yes, but isn't one always hard on himself when he has a sense of diminished self-confidence or self-esteem?" he countered.

"I believe you're always hard on yourself, and that's a real problem," I said. "Don't you have pride in your having taken a moral stand that few people have been able to?"

"That was all in the past. And it wasn't that much. And it has no relevance now. Why am I not doing something now? I feel this frustration about being what I consider unlawfully contained. I should be doing something about it. Let me give you a specific example. When I first came in I was going to take a writ of habeas corpus to the courts on the issues again. I hired a lawyer to do that, and he delayed and delayed, until an entire year passed. At any point along the line I could have said, 'I'm through with you. You keep promising and not performing. I'll do it myself. Just forget it.' But no, I didn't do that. There was a sense I couldn't do it myself. I didn't have the confidence to work it out, so I depended on the lawyer, and time just passed. Then my parole was coming up at the summer session so I thought I might as well wait till I go up for parole. It's not worth jeopardizing that with another legal issue!

"There's this feeling in me that I didn't have to wait for my lawyer, that I could have done it myself easily, and that I sold myself short. I shouldn't have counted on other people, and I shouldn't have tolerated the stalling. My enduring it was a sign of my own weakness.

"On the outside I had the feeling that I would never stop, that I'd be in here writing, filing writs, going on to the UN, the World Court. I haven't done anything like that. There's something in this environment that defused me, and I don't like it."

"Do you have any idea why that happened?" I asked.

"No. I only know that this place got to me. And that leads to something else. Now that I've experienced jail, I'm worried that I will be afraid of it in the future. Much more so than I was before. I never had any fear that was great enough to deter me from doing what I thought was right. I didn't care if they shot me, that kind of thing."

"So jail was harder than anticipated," I said.

"In a peculiar way," he said. "In most senses it was easier—it was worse only in terms of me. As far as jail is concerned, it was really nothing."

"Let me hear what you mean," I said.

"Well, for example, I was never aware of such things as good time and parole. I thought if you got a five-year sentence you did five years. But then I thought of it as an end point. It was the consequence of some action that had to be done. I did it, and then I thought, 'Now I'll go to jail'—as though it were a thing. But it isn't. It's a process. It's a getting up every morning and a going to bed every night and an enormous interval in between. And it goes on and on.

"I thought I'd be in a cell. I expected much more violence, assault from other prisoners. I'd heard what had happened to some of the political prisoners. At the penitentiary there were many threats, physical and homosexual, but nothing physical ever happened to me, and fortunately I got out of there fairly quickly.

"No, jail is better than I thought. It's me that's not as good, or at least I've not stood up as well as I thought I would. See, there's the difference. It's me that's frightening, not what happened to me. It was how I reacted. And I suppose that's the anxiety that I feel about getting out. If I couldn't predict how I would react to prison, can I now predict how I will react on the outside? I vacillate between the feeling that everything will be all right, and a certain anxiety."

"What are your plans?" I asked.

"I plan to go back to college, take some courses and work part-time till I feel things out. I'll see what I will do after that."

I then told him that our time was coming to an end and asked if there was anything special he'd like to say.

He laughed, then said, "It's too bad that it can't be longer."

This was not an uncommon statement. Almost inevitably, all of the men, despite their wariness, despite their original embarrassment, despite the joking among themselves, hungered for the communication represented by these interviews, and they came to anticipate and even depend on them.

"Do you still have any doubts about whether I'm a spy?" I teased.

"No, of course not. At least I don't think so. At least I don't think about it. My doubts were never that big. And anyway I didn't care that much. There is absolutely nothing I needed to hide. If I had known you were a spy I would have said exactly the same thing. I wouldn't have had, however, the sense of unburdening, or relief. The boys don't joke about it the way they did at the beginning. I think the joking was in great part their anxiety about you. I don't know if you appreciate the amount of anxiety about your being a head-shrinker. It's a mysterious thing to many of the boys, and they're a little frightened by it."

I didn't appreciate it—and I was glad he pointed it out to me.

I greeted John for the last time before his departure on the weekend of the protest action. He was scheduled for release three days later. I asked him what he thought it was all about.

"That's very hard to say. Basically it's simply the frustration of being here and taking things. Finally one small disciplinary action will be the one that breaks the camel's back and people will feel they have to do something. I think it was purely emotional. I didn't think the action was properly weighed. Some of us are more ideological, and we tried to talk to the group the night before, but they couldn't be reached. They couldn't even define what they hoped to get out of the undertaking. They had come to the point of despair where they were willing to do *anything*. If I weren't going home in five days I might well have joined in.

"It brought to a head all of the feelings that I've had in the two years of being here, all the humiliation that one feels for 'going along'—the sense of failure for not continuing the battle that brought us here in the first place. I know that others say that our presence here is in itself a continuation, but you feel something else is needed. I certainly did. I simply didn't think it was worth the price.

"I contemplated it. Okay, I said, they'll take away my parole and that will mean that I'll stay for three years, but then if I do that, I must do it the whole way, not just for a brief interval of time. If they were prepared to do that, that was the sort of thing I could agree with.

"I've often felt, over the last two years, that should have been my course, that or trying to escape. That's why there isn't one of us here who doesn't emotionally identify with the group, whether we see the point rationally or not.

"There's no question in my mind that the transfers were the real initiator of this. It was the arbitrariness of it, the recognition that ultimately, to them, you are a kind of property. You can get into a rut in a prison—where if they only leave you alone you will just 'do your time.' But then someone is transferred for no reason, and it starts working on your emotions and it brings everything to a boil.

"At least one purpose will be served by this. Some of the frustration will be relieved. But I felt a more constructive way of doing that could have been figured out. Some way the emotions should have been utilized in the service of some legitimate demands. Instead, the demands were incidental to the emotions. Really, it comes down to the fact that some had reached the point where they couldn't take another humiliation and the authorities were too stupid to sense that. I don't think Jim featured in this as much as some may indicate. He's too unpredictable and confusing. He switches around too much. I only wish he were capable of the kind of leadership the prison authorities endow him with."

In almost every account, this particular action tended to be dated from the non-cooperativeness of Jim. Only John saw it as a continuum, with the actual onset being a full month or two earlier in the arbitrary transfer. As I pursued the story further, the absolute accuracy of his evaluation impressed me enormously.

"If at the point of the transfer," he continued, "the men involved would have been willing to take a stand, I would have been ready to join them. It seemed to me exactly the kind of legitimate abuse that one could and had a right to oppose. And there were other legitimate issues worth fighting for, but each one merely brought more meetings, and discussions, and lots of emotion. Ultimately fear and docility won out. But the emotions were there, stored like dry tinder needing only one more spark to ignite them. Unfortunately the issue that serves to spark is often an unworthy one.

"Like my almost losing my parole when I went up to argue about the dragging incident of January 9. A hack grabbed me, and I pulled away and in a rage said, 'Keep your hands off me.' I'm not sure what would have happened if he had touched me again. I know that I'm in somewhat a privileged position because I'm known in the peace movement, as is Jim. As a result they don't like either one of us to be in trouble. It might become newsworthy.

"Then, of course, after all of us had stuck our necks out protesting, Jim comes marching back the next day deciding he will work.

"That was part of what I tried to say the night before the

strike when I tried to talk some sense into them. What's the purpose of one day not working and the next day coming to work? It doesn't make sense. I tried to tell them that if you se-duce some of your people into getting involved by playing on their emotions, you have a terrible responsibility. You may cause them great harm, and why let them be hurt if it's not going to effect a change? Some of the newer ones are terribly young. They're uptight as it is. They still have to prove something, and they'll move with anybody who is moving. You can sense that masculinity is on the line, and it's cruel to urge them to meaning-less actions."

"How has this affected you emotionally?" I asked.

"Well, I was a little down when you last saw me and I'm still down. I'm caught up in the stuff that happened, of course, and then I'm not going to feel great leaving in the middle of this. It just adds a little more to the confusion of being short."

"What are your plans when you leave?"

"Well, I've always wanted to be a lawyer, but I don't know if the time isn't too late for that, all the training and expense. Then again, I'm not sure I could make the bar with a prison record."

"Would your family help?" I asked.

"I won't take money from my family. I can't take the chance. I'll have to wait to see how things work out. Obviously they have plenty of money, but in the past money was tied to control. When I got out of college, traveled, then came back and started night school, they offered to help. I took it, partly because I could use the aid, and partly because I felt they had a right to help if they wanted to.

"But then the same kind of thing started. My father would go out of his mind when he'd hear what was going on in the schools, and he'd often drive all night long to get to see me just to find out the dope. Then he would lecture to me, and I had the sense that he thought, 'Now I've straightened him out,' and he'd con-tinue his plans for my entering his business. I had the sense that he was inadvertently using me, that through me he could make a second fortune, a second climb to success. Once again I felt grabbed up, and stopped it.

"There was a second time that I went through the cycle—just before I came into jail. It looked like imprisonment might be postponed, and I thought I might try studying and going back to school again. I wrote the family about my intention and said that I would like them to help me if they understood that the assistance could not be seen as payment for some future services, for conforming to his way of life. I didn't want him to feel cheated or betrayed. I never want my father to feel that he wasn't getting value received, so I wouldn't want to take money if it was tied to their expectations. To my surprise it was agreed, but there was never any chance to test it."

"Actually," I said, "your aspirations now are of the kind that he would be delighted to support."

"That's true. I never thought of that. But then he wouldn't like my being involved in anything political, any protest. In the past, as soon as I accepted his help, he felt he had the hook in and he would assume I wouldn't get involved in any political stuff. The one thing I'm sure of is that he simply doesn't now have the power to control me psychologically or emotionally. I'm not that boy in college any more.

"It's all theoretical though, because I don't think I will take any money from them. Even without strings. There's a whole other thing—an emotional thing within me. I know there is plenty of money there, I know it wouldn't harm them, I know it would help me enormously, but I really don't want it."

"Why is that?" I asked.

"I don't know. You're the psychiatrist," he joked. "It's a new feeling that evolved in jail. Perhaps it's the fear of being again remolded. I don't want to be molded to society or any individual. When I left home I felt I had to cut all the seams. I never felt that my home was dominating me—I felt that I was letting it dominate me. You know, there's a certain sense of security on a treadmill, even if it provides no satisfaction. There's safety, even some comfort, in a defined role. I think I was somewhat afraid to take that jump into an unknown, unchartered area."

I had the sense that, without realizing it, he was talking about the anxiety of returning to life outside the prison, and I addressed myself to that anxiety without ever alluding to it— merely by my optimism in discussing his future, my tacit assumption of future achievements and successes. And as our time ran out, I became aware that this time I was reluctant to see the meeting come to an end, for with John it was not just the end of the interview but in all probability the end of a relationship. Despite all the training and discipline, this comes hard to a psychiatrist too.

9 ⫷⫷⫷

The Comedy of Errors:
A Tragedy in One Act

During the eighteen-month time span I spent visiting the prisons, only one concerted action on the part of the war resisters took place, only one organized overt group position of defiance. I will call it an action because that is what the prisoners called it, and because no better word comes to mind. Individual acts of rebellion or resistance had, of course, taken place, but this was the closest thing to what might be called a strike—a political movement. It is worth going into in some detail, not just for what it indicates about the war resisters as a group, but also because of what it has to say about the nature of crisis in a prison setting, which is totally independent of the particular ideological problems involved.

The prison environment is such that one can safely say that not a day passes by without some act of violence, some "scuffle" among the prisoners. It is unlikely that too many days pass by without some minor acts of violence performed on a prisoner by a staff member, and it's not even rare for there to be concerted action of one group of prisoners against another group of prisoners, particularly in maximum-security prisons. During the time this research was conducted, there was a public report of a major clash between two groups of black prisoners over an ideological conflict which was a reflection of the same conflict in the community at large.

What *is* rare, however, is an action by a group of prisoners against the authorities. Regardless of how mild such action is, it is perceived as a threat to the very existence of the prison structure. For a prison is just one example of a classic sociological situation—the community where a large number of men must be controlled by a small number of men. This large number of men have no weapons except their number, no power except their potential unity. It is, therefore, in the interest of maintaining order that the prison population be fragmented and that a sense of community be discouraged.

Since the majority of prisoners are dissocial individuals, loners, it is not difficult to maintain the isolation and estrangement desired. But COs are different, and because of this the prison authorities expected an enormous amount of difficulty with the war resisters. They anticipated that since their crimes were political, these would indeed be political individuals. This anticipation was also based on history. Some of the most truculent, exhausting, and threatening prisoners were the political draft resisters of World War II. This turned out not to be the case with this group. The different nature of the conflict generated a different population of resister, different sociologically and psychologically.

The current resisters are not completely, not even preponderantly, political protesters. They are a heterogeneous group which, while containing some political protesters, is composed primarily of what would be considered moral or religious objectors. They are also, I suspect, a less eccentric or extremist group than those in World War II, for their attitude—if not behavior—is more typical, more representative of the general sentiments of their generation toward "their" war. They are also young; moreover, few, if any, possess the typical "leader" personality. They lack the narcissism, grandiosity, or exhibitionism, the desire for power or status. They are contemplative and tolerant people who are individual rather than group-oriented. They are more confident of the questions they raise than the answers they offer. This is the stuff which intellectuals are made of, not political leaders.

Many of them had been non-cooperative on the outside. To my knowledge, no one maintained a non-cooperative stance during the course of his entire imprisonment. Many started that way, but within a short time their resistance was broken, despite publicity to the contrary. There was one young man about whose refusal to cooperate I had read in at least three publications. I interviewed him on my first visit to Oakdale, though he was not a part of my sample population. The facts were that he had to be carried into the prison but once inside he became cooperative and has remained so. Still, articles on his non-cooperation have continued to be published.

If these war resisters ended up being cooperative, it was not without paying an enormous price, for not an interview went by without one of them expressing a feeling of impotence, of betrayal, of guilt over this cooperation. But since for the guilty reward is still the best punishment and for all an effective instrument of discipline, the prison authorities control them with the promise or potential of parole, and the fact of good time.

One factor which is obvious to anyone in the prison setting, and which may explain some of the ambivalence, foolishness, and inconsistency encountered in the prison staff during the action, is the recognition that there is indeed one thing that unifies all prisoners, and that is their individual sense of personal grievance and the common hatred for prison authorities this generates. This means that any rebellion, regardless of how specialized its source or how esoteric its goal, will find common ground and universal sympathy. Any rebellion can become mass rebellion, and the tension generated by even the mildest rumble can be felt for weeks after.

The account that I am giving about this small crisis is pieced together from some dozen accounts of the prisoners, both those involved and not involved, plus some informal statements from members of the staff. It is not possible to get an official accounting from the administration. I am not sure to this day that there was an official report sent in at the time of its happening. When I arrived in Washington to continue a part of the research that took place there, the people with whom I worked knew nothing about it. Later, with search, I found that an official version of the incident was formulated well after the fact, when a release was required in answer to citizen inquiries about the events.

The specific actions are usually dated as stemming from incidents occurring on January 9, although two of the inmates (John and Tim) with particularly good insight, saw the events as starting two months earlier.

In November of 1968 the Bureau of Prisons needed prisoners capable of filling minimum-security positions (clerks, teachers, etc.) in one of their youth institutions in the South. The prison functions in great part by the utilization of prisoner services. Minimum-security positions require people who are safe and people with a certain amount of maturity and responsibility, people who do not represent a great risk. Evidently these qualities are particularly rare in the youth reformatories.

The Selective Service violators, with their superior education, non-psychopathic personalities, and non-violent orientation, are admirably suited for these positions. So without any questions asked, three of the COs were summarily transferred. The three happened to be particularly gentle, generally compliant individuals—which may or may not have been a determinant. None of them wanted to go. One of them strongly expressed his opposition to going. This naturally had no effect on the local administration, which was itself not responsible for the transfer. On the other hand, it wasn't the transfer but the gratuitous manner of handling it which caused the resentment—and that the local authorities *were* responsible for. There were no explanations, no preparations, and no understanding. It was done in the requisition, bill-of-lading manner utilized in the transfer of equipment from one installation to another. But even in shipping goods, we respect the innate properties of the articles transferred, and special consideration is given to highly volatile, potentially explosive, particularly fragile, and innately perishable items.

The arbitrariness of the action was a particularly bitter pill to swallow, emphasizing as it must the consideration of them as property rather than people.

Besides, it was frightening. It raised unsettling questions. What for? Why now? Why them? Who next? Regardless of how bad a prison is, there is a certain safety in familiarity. It is threatening to move from one bunk to another, from one dorm to another, let alone from one prison to another. Relationships are established which have meaning. These may not always be deep friendships, but there is a sense of who can be trusted, who must be avoided. The defining of environment establishes lines of security.

Here was an issue that could have been the focal point for an action, but the men had been selected, I suspect, carefully, and while they were deeply upset they were unprepared to put up a fight. The rest of the war resisters were enough shaken up by this so that the entire group might have been mobilized had those most intimately involved been prepared to set the pattern. Faced with their compliance, however, the others made no aggressive moves but merely smoldered. An oppressive, hostile, resentful mood was making them ripe for even the slightest affront.

It should be mentioned that there are pragmatic reasons, besides psychological ones, involved in a transfer from one prison to another that are damaging. In the initial phases in prison a man establishes his identity among hostile as well as friendly forces. He has already gone through the homosexual confrontation, he has established his right to be let alone. In addition, he may pay for the unwanted transfer with an extension of his prison sentence. As I have already mentioned, every day in a minimum-security institution, such as the work camp, automatically earns a certain number of good days—days off of sentence. The rationale is that by living in such lightly guarded institutions you have automatically established a trustworthiness and demonstrated the kind of behavior that are entitled to a reward.

These men, selected because of their reliability, were being transferred to an institution occupied by wild, young, explosive kids with great potential for violence, who naturally require greater security precautions. As inmates of that kind of institution they would be ineligible for the special good days.

Finally, they had been assigned to the work camp in part because it was the prison closest to their homes; therefore the transfer could mean a hardship in terms of either diminished visitation or a greater financial burden for their visitors.

Not a single prisoner I interviewed failed to mention the transfer, and the way it was handled, with particular outrage.

Winter at the work camp is always a season of discontent. The weather imposes an added confinement to that supplied by the government. There is less legitimate farm work to do, so more busy work is supplied. The denial of the privileges of work-release and the disparity in parole accorded the Jehovah's Witnesses become particularly galling when time passes slowly. And the winter holidays force carefully repressed memories of home, of love, of warmth, to the surface.

The first direct confrontation started with Roger (not a member of my study group since he was not admitted until November 1968). Roger had been non-cooperating in his first few weeks in prison. This in itself is not uncommon. Nonetheless, while still refusing to work or shave and despite the fact that he had indicated he would continue to do so, they decided to send him to the camp. This is uncommon. He would go to the camp and as long as he didn't work he would be denied the services of the camp—no TV, no library, no educational program, no laundry. He would also not be allowed to eat in the mess hall. Roger was expected to get a tray, carry it out of the dining hall back to the dormitory, another building, eat his food there, and then return the tray. The food would, of course, be cold when he got there, and in addition this would make sure that he spent all of his meals in isolation.

Try as I may, I cannot conceive what purpose could have been served, what good could have been expected from this. It is obviously an extension of the prison "philosophy" expressed by the warden of Oakdale on my first visit. He described the technique as his effective way of dealing with non-cooperation, but then it was in the special environment of the isolation cell, *not* in an open camp where it would become a public demonstration. It should seem apparent to any man of reasonable intelligence that the two sets of conditions are so different that what might well be effective in one would be guaranteed to create trouble in the other.

On January 9 at 3:30 p.m. the dining-room, according to the peculiar schedule of prisons, was filled for dinner. Roger came in for his tray and decided on the spur of the moment to sit down and join some of his friends for dinner. The guard in the mess hall, knowing the instructions, without any undue violence, physically hustled him out of the room. Tim, a witness to this, said to the guard, 'Isn't this a little childish?' The guard pointed out that it was not his rule but the camp director's, and that if Tim didn't like it he should talk to the director about it. So Tim and Roger went to the office. As they approached the office Jim was walking out.

Jim had been having his problems too. Jim is a most difficult man to describe. He was the titular leader of the group of prisoners. By titular I mean that the administration thought of him as their leader, and in an offbeat way many of the prisoners would have concurred. The only problem was that Jim was not a leader. He could be an inspiration—but not a leader.

Jim is a quiet, self-possessed, and self-contained individual who has a cool, withdrawn, unrufflable attitude. He expresses very little of himself. While he is a kind and considerate person, there is no real sense of emotional involvement with others. It's as though the kindness and consideration were part of an intellectual code. One has the feeling he will go through life doing service to others and getting little joy from it.

He was older than most of the others and had been very active in the peace movement, during the course of which he had demonstrated the capacity for performing acts of extraordinary courage. Often, however, they were impulsively determined and quickly abandoned. He was doing that which he had to do, when he had to do it. It was perfectly legitimate. He would never impose his way on anyone. But what would never have been offered as an example was often accepted as one, and confusion often resulted. In great part it was that Jim made demands on himself beyond his capacity for fulfillment. Perhaps beyond the capacity of most—for Jim is a man of strength. But strength is not leadership, and that strength created a charisma, and for want of anything closer, that would have to substitute for leadership.

Jim had been reluctant to go to work. His solution usually was to comply with the letter of the law, and only the letter. He had been assigned to a farm unit, and when I questioned him about his not working he said, "It's mainly building fences where they are not needed and tearing down ones next to it."

I asked him if it had been meaningful work, would it have made a difference.

"I doubt it," was his answer.

I asked if he had made a specific decision not to cooperate. He said that he rarely makes decisions as such, that what he does is half-conscious non-cooperation.

"I don't allow myself to motivate myself to do things."

But Jim had been excited by Roger's overt and consistent refusal to work. Jim had not quite been able to bring himself to do this, and under this stimulus he began to increase his non-cooperation.

So as Tim and Roger were waiting to see the camp director

Jim came out of the office. He told them that he was being sent to the Wall. Jim then went to his locker and took out certain personal items that he wanted to leave with his friends.

Jim had previously made the decision that if he were sent back to the penitentiary he would not go voluntarily but would have to be carried there. The others had been apprised of this. Tim went and got Pete, and they sat down on Jim's bed, keeping him company. They agreed with him that he should not voluntarily return to the Wall, and Tim decided that he would support Jim —at least symbolically—by lying down in front of the guard to make carrying off Jim that much more difficult. Pete, who was shortly due out, decided not to get involved.

When the guard came to remove Jim at 4:00 p.m. and saw Tim sitting on the bed, he immediately told him to get back to his own bed. It was time for the 4 o'clock count. Tim, as we already know, refused, so when the other guards came in they evidently assumed that Tim intended or wished to go back to the pen with Jim. At this point they began to drag them both. Al (another young, new CO), seeing this, lay down in the doorway so that he too was dragged. It should be mentioned that the dragging occurred right at the time of the count while all the prisoners were assembled, and it was a strange, foolhardy, and unthinking thing to do. Past rows and rows of prisoners, some five hundred yards over ice and gravel, these three young men were dragged.

Things began to heat up. People began shouting. Tim was kicked in the groin by one of the guards (verified by three separate accounts). Curses and insults were shouted out.

One prisoner said, "It was crazy, they were performing this right in front of the dorms. People began letting off at the hacks. It began to look like a small riot shaping up, closer than I have ever seen it to a general attack."

At the administration building, Roger, seeing the other three dragged, announced that he wouldn't walk any farther either. At this point they dragged Roger and Jim off, taking them to the pen, and, to everybody's surprise, told Tim and Al that they should go back to their bunks for their count, which they did. Jim and Roger were taken to the Wall, and from 5:30 until 7:30 left in the open court with no outer clothing—the temperature was in the teens. This was done in the hope that it would soften them up so that they would walk in and not create a scene. This was another favored device, which the warden had once described to me as a particularly effective method of his for gaining cooperation. After two hours, when they refused to enter voluntarily, they brought them by car to the door and literally dragged them in.

Inside the prison they refused to remove their clothes voluntarily (camp browns had to be replaced by prison blues), so they were dragged into the supply room and their clothes were ripped off. When they were naked they were dragged down the halls on their backs to the hole. The hole is a series of separated small cells. The temperature is in the low 60s, but because it is underground, a bare concrete cube, with a steel bunk, heat loss by conduction is great. Without mattresses, blankets, or clothes, it is impossible to keep warm, and only standing up affords a possibility of comfort. During the middle of the night a cotton T-shirt and trousers were offered Jim. He refused them because they were not also offered to the other prisoners, not COs, who for unknown reasons had been in the hole for two or three days in the same condition.

Jim and Roger were then interrogated by an associate warden, with several guards standing around, in an atmosphere that was seen as menacing by both. Roger continued to refuse either to work or shave. Jim, as was his wont, immediately changed his mind and decided he was ready to work. What he actually said was that he "would be willing to report to work." This was important because "reporting to work" did not necessarily mean working to him, and he was a man who would always be honest. He was immediately sent back to the work camp, to his great surprise. Roger was continued in administrative segregation.

In the next couple of weeks Jim continued to "report to work" although often late and in a haphazard manner. He had decided vaguely to "see how much he could get away with." While all this was going on, yet another prisoner was transferred to the youth reformatory. The COs were now more than ready for concerted action on what was a sound and valid ground, but again, the inmate chosen, unwilling to risk what could be a very high price, accepted, with some protest, the transfer.

It was during this period, and because of this, that much thought was given to the idea of having an inmates' council. There was precedent for this, as such councils existed in other prisons. Jim became the spokesman for this idea, and on January 25, when the concept had been formulated, he presented a proposal for a prisoners' council to the camp director.

On January 26 Jim was called to the office and told that the warden and associate warden would like to see him to discuss the implementation of his ideas. He was driven over to the penitentiary, presumably to see the officers. As soon as he was driven off, some guards came, stripped his bed, cleaned out his locker, and the inmates knew immediately that they had been had. It was simply a device to get Jim back to the pen cooperatively without creating the kind of scene that had occurred before. The COs were sick with anger and humiliation. The rest of the day and evening was spent with groups forming and re-forming, arguing back and forth as to what to do. They were badly split. No one was sure what to do. Everyone was sure something had to be done. They were unified only by their common sense of humiliation and frustration. The last few months had been a series of successive provocations which they had ignored, and now this last seemed too much to bear. The argument went on all through the day and well into the evening, past eleven o'clock, the time they were presumably all isolated in their bunks.

The issues were far from clear. Why was Jim transferred? The administration itself was giving conflicting answers as to the cause of the transfer. Some of the guards said it was because, while still on probation, he was fomenting trouble with this inmates' council. On the other hand, the camp director and one of his assistants assured some of the inmates it was because he was not doing enough work.

Jim admitted that he had agreed to do "a reasonable amount of work." To the administration this meant that he would do what they wanted. To Jim it meant that he would determine what was a reasonable amount of work.

Adding to the confusion was an influx of newer prisoners who had not served sufficient time so that the end was nearer than the beginning—for that is the time of caution. They did not hunger for that chance at a parole for it was as yet too distant to be granted any validity. They were questioning of the older men, skeptical as to how they could have allowed themselves to be moved around so and gone along quietly.

A decision as to what should be done seemed painfully slow in emerging. It was not so much the heterogeneity of the group as the lack of any forceful leadership in it. Augmenting this was the fact that imposition of ideas was alien to a group such as this, and the pressures operating on each individual were modified by the special facts of his external conditions and his internal drives.

Tim, who was seen by the administration as a firebrand, was quite hesitant to take an action, but he was even more hesitant to discourage, or even to be unsupporting of, an action that the majority wanted. The militancy seemed to come from strange places. There was Pete, quiet, serious, pipe-smoking, from a poverty-stricken small town, with a coal-mining background, who had all his life, let alone his period in prison, been a hard-working, conscientious, and self-effacing person. Pete was due out in only *three weeks.* He was tense, as are all prisoners when they are short. He had become, he told me, "irritable, bitter, generally fouled up. I wanted to get out, just get out, but then I began to feel selfish because I was preoccupied with getting out. At the same time, there was this enormous desire to ex-

pose people, to expose the situation and the rising bitterness
which I had not allowed myself to experience during my time.
Along with this was the intense frustration, that I had been so
passive, that I had taken so much, that I had so little guts, that I
had let them shit all over me, that I had forgotten that I was a
man."

The ultimate action was the formulation of a petition. It was
signed by twelve exhausted, unsure, confused, and disorganized
young men. I had the feeling that no one in particular was enthu-
siastic about it. As Bill said, the whole thing seemed like nonsense and he really wanted to let them have it with both barrels.
The petition he wanted to sign was to say, "We want unconditional release." In a sense, it was the petitioning, not the petition,
that was important. It was rather mild. It said, specifically:

> We, the undersigned men, prisoners of Oakdale camp, faced
> with the injustices and hypocrisies of the prison system, re-
> fuse to work. At least until some independent inmate coun-
> cil is established to voice the grievances of the inmates and
> work for their redress; at least until the threat of involuntary
> and arbitrary transfers is removed; at least until labor is no
> longer forced; and at least until generally more humane
> conditions are established at Oakdale.

When I arrived that third day after the transfer, I was shocked
to find the eleven boys in isolation, one in the hole, and all on
hunger strikes. When I asked Pete, to whom this might very well
mean another agonizing eight months in prison, how he got involved with the protest, he said, "You know, I think I would have
been happy to go right along and serve my time and get out. I
might have felt upset afterward about my lack of activity, but
honest-to-God we were really forced at every turn. It was one
humiliation after another. I'm not a non-cooperator type at heart.
I think you know that. My main objection is just the way they
did this last thing. I don't think I can put up with it any longer.
Not that they've changed, but the tactics have. They're less subtle, all along they have been doing the same humiliating things

but now they don't even pretend to rationalize or hide it. They're making it apparent to us, flaunting it.

"You know, you can get into a routine and forget why the hell you're in here to begin with. All of us had been doing that—just serving our time. My only objective was to get out. We weren't doing anything but talking about doing something. I think the new guys coming in were hot, more radical, but that wasn't the whole thing. You know, I learned more about the way prison works, psychologically and emotionally, in the last few months than I did in my whole bit before. It really came down to this—if we broke down now and gave in to this, it would tell them that there was nothing that we wouldn't take. No shit we wouldn't eat. I realized that that night, and that's why I signed the petition."

The signing and the non-signing cut across ideological and political grounds and cut across friendships. It was one of the real tributes to the group that there was no animosity, no vindictiveness, no pressure, no recrimination, and no "holier-than-thou" judging of one's fellow men.

There was, however, a fairly large residue of self-inflicted guilt on the part of some of those who did not join. Among those who did not sign, besides John and Paul, were Richard and Robby. Richard, warm, a poet by profession, popular with all the boys, friend to all, felt particularly guilty.

"I simply wasn't ready to sign anything," he said, "to take the chance of going back to the penitentiary. I have all these things I have been working on for fourteen months, poems, books. If I would have been shipped out, they would have been confiscated —all of this, and I was frightened. I don't feel comfortable having all of this on me and then losing it, particularly when I have so many questions about the validity of the action. It didn't seem the proper time, the proper strategy. It seemed to me more of a reaction than an action. It seemed to me more because of personal humiliations as personified in the treatment of Jim than outrage at something essential in the prison system.

"I am so confused—I am not so sure this isn't all rationalization. That I really didn't act simply because I was unwilling to give up my time. I know I'm getting out in less than three months, and that's totally important to me.

"Yet I feel hopeless and helpless that I am here and that so many of my friends are there. And I feel humiliated since I'm not doing anything. Whether what they are doing is right or wrong, I'm not doing *anything* to change conditions, or to continue the cause for which I entered prison in the first place. But then I can't think of anything to do that will be productive, while anything I do will cause me harm. In that case it seems so futile, so worthless, so masochistic. They were treating me with callousness and carelessness, that's true, but should I then put myself in a position to be treated even more callously? The situation seemed absurd. But nonetheless Jim is there and I am here, and he has beliefs and feelings which I respect and share, and I'm unwilling to do the same kind of thing that he does.

"It raises very serious doubts in me about myself, about my own strengths, about my honesty. How much of what I say and how much of what I believe will I ever stand up for? I don't know if I'll completely trust myself any more. I know that there is a flaw in me. I usually wait to react to things. That's one of the reasons why I'm here. I waited till I was put in a position where I was up against the wall—either the army or here. I wasn't like some of the others who had calculated in advance, gone out and looked for the battle. I'm not sure I'd ever go out and look for battles. Now I wonder how much I shy away from them. I know I would have said before that when they come I'm willing to face them and I assumed I could have done so with a certain amount of calm and self-assurance. It does say something about a person, even if he meets the battle when it *comes* to him, that he's unprepared to go out and *find* the battle wherever it is.

"I'm concerned about that because it will affect my work too. How many problems do I tend to avoid trying to find easy routes where I won't have to engage in a real question? How many sidetracks and distractions do I find to relieve myself? Yet the last thing that I want to do is to act merely to prove to myself that I can, to establish some kind of masculinity in a symbolic sense.

"I know with some of them that they had to do something, to prove that they were alive, to prove that they were here. To me, that's a waste of time. Being able to choose when to fight is equally as important."

Robby was another one who sat this one out, and it was important because Robby has a certain position of leadership in the black community. Robby was a wise, wonderful, weird drummer. That he was a little bit "crazy" was apparent to everybody. Not "sick" crazy, just crazy crazy. But then drummers always are, I'm told.

He was the most perceptive analyst of human behavior, the keenest critic of his fellows that I came across in this research. He was a hard-nosed, practical, political thinker on the one hand, and a way-out dreamer of beautiful dreams on the other. He was also an absolute believer in astrology, which put me off, although I must admit the astrology chart that he mapped out for me was uncomfortably accurate. He was a believer in prophetic dreams and he had "visions" the nature of which I never completely understood. Nor was his degree of acceptance of them ever completely made clear. I'm sure that they were at least one-third put on, one-third conviction, and one-third up for grabs.

Robby made it perfectly clear why he didn't get involved.

"Why the hell go out on a work strike? I know damn well what would happen. We would all be taken to the hole or dispersed to a dozen different places. It's madness when you're dealing with these people to come down to their level, and then you're subject to their choice of weapons and their battlefields. You don't start a power play with the person who has all the power. There are other means. There are ways in which they are vulnerable. We have access to publicity that's not available to other cons, and we don't use that adequately.

"If we had started in a planned, unified way we could have done something.

"Look at the twelve they took to the Wall—there was a leader for every two or three men there. I've never seen so many chiefs and so few Indians. Most of them weren't really conscious of what they were doing. They were just talking because they felt they had to take a stand or they wouldn't be true COs.

"I certainly don't see any sense in being stuck in the hole. What use would I be to my people there? As it is, there are too many black people locked up in those places. If you want to protest, go the whole way, let's burn the damn place down. That might have made some sense. Sure they were pushed to it, they were made to feel like fools, they had their noses rubbed in shit. Well, maybe I've had a little more training in that than they have —that's been the story of my life. There is no sense adding to the total of black men locked in cells. I suppose the only thing they can do is lock us up until they find a solution in the street. It's a way of postponing things.

"I personally tried to keep all the blacks out of it, for the very fact that when a scapegoat is needed, they'll always pick a black man. And why should we put ourselves in an available position?

"Those are good people in there, the best. I know that, but they're not really a part of our struggle out in the street. They're in here specifically because of this war, not because of the basic rottenness of the country. And for a lot of them all will be forgiven—their mommies and daddies send them money every month—but when most of us get out of here we won't have a pot to piss in. So I just tried my best to keep all the brothers out.

"I couldn't do anything with Lloyd, he went along. I couldn't stand his going along. I know he's going up for parole Monday and this will kill any chance he had.

"When I couldn't talk them out of it I told them to postpone it for a couple of weeks, not to go on strike until they could build up some publicity so it wouldn't be a wasted action. The administration has been frightened. It's been showing in a lot of little ways, and that's not good, because a frightened man with a gun is a dangerous thing. And they've got all the guns. Some of the younger hacks are real scared. The COs don't realize that they're playing around with something that's serious. They don't even know the consequences of what they're doing. They're playing at revolution, and there's much too much rhetoric going around.

"Oh hell, it may be good in a way, all that talk. They're like some of the black people who were doing all the talking until very recently. It lets off the pressure, the psychological pressure—that's why Stokely [Carmichael] is out there instead of in here. The talk lets off the pressure and then he doesn't have to act.

"If they really wanted to accomplish something I think my first suggestion may have been a good one even though I was joking. They *ought* to burn the place down. That would at least bring attention to them. You'll never change things from within here—it has to be from the outside."

And what about Jim, the original focus for all this activity? In that unpredictable, irrational, topsy-turvy way of the world in prison, Jim was out of the action. Jim had been released from isolation; he was in the general population, eating, cooperating, and working. How and why had Jim taken that course? Why had the authorities permitted him to do this? Was this some devious, Through-the-Looking-Glass strategy? I thought it unlikely. In prisons, expedience, not malevolence, is still the cardinal rule of functioning.

I met with Jim, and he presented his story of the events starting with the day he was tricked into returning to the Wall.

"I waited around that afternoon expecting to see the warden. They told me he was unable to see me that day but I would be held over, stay the night, and see him the next day. I was given a bed in one of the dormitories. I still had my khaki outfit on from the camp. I stayed the night and spent the morning waiting to be called up. Then I was called to the control center and told to go down to the clothing center to pick up my blues and whites, that I'd be working in the kitchen and living where I was, and that was it.

"I said, 'Well, I suspected something like that.' There never was an interview. It was a trick and it worked. They had gotten me back. So now I'm in the kitchen doing general work, odd jobs. I'll be doing that for a while, at least a couple of weeks. I play basketball on one of the teams here, and it isn't too bad."

"I'm not quite sure why you are working here when you refused at the camp?"

"Well, first of all, in order to get to see my wife. If I didn't work I'd be in segregation. Then there's a lot to learn here."

"I'm still confused," I said. "If they offered to send you back to the camp, would you work, would you go?"

"I'd go back. Yes, I would. I would do some work out there, hopefully not in what I was doing. I would still try to ask for another job."

"But you had told me that even if they had given you a different job you might not have worked," I reminded him.

"No, I might not have. I'd have had to see how it felt. I wouldn't want to give in completely to the system, ever. I always reported regularly, I just often didn't feel like working. It depends on how the different pressures come. There are still things I want to do. I want to organize an inmates' council; there might be times when I'd like to fast, or picket, or strike. I'll even do it here after a while when I begin to feel it's right again."

He was saying in a sense that he had made his confrontation and now he was going to comply. In a peculiar way it was an effective device. It worked against the administration by keeping them constantly off balance. He would refuse to cooperate, then capitulate. As an individual, it made him extremely difficult to handle, and in that sense, I suppose, it was an effective way of confronting the administration. However, it was extremely deceptive to those who might have chosen to follow his course. In fairness to Jim, it must be remembered that never did he suggest, encourage, or solicit this kind of following from his friends. He was doing his own time.

There is not much to tell about the follow-up. The group was determined to hold out as long as possible, fasting and continuing to refuse to work, hoping that they might gain some concessions, knowing that at least they would salvage some pride. As time went by and it became apparent that no concessions would be made, they were mostly eager to return, were waiting only for some face-saving device.

The administration was also anxious for them to return. There is danger in the unusual and ill defined. They didn't want to risk any moves of desperation. They couldn't grasp that all they had to do was give them some hook on which to hang a little pride or self-respect and it would have been accepted.

There were meetings, individual conferences, with nothing accomplished because nothing was offered.

With time there was potential trouble, for the story might get out and the publicity could be harmful. In addition, there was possible damage to those who were on the hunger strike. But the administration seemed totally incapable of effecting any rapprochement. So in an institution where security is the god, a potentially explosive situation was maintained because the security-conscious administration was totally inept in that one area that could insure security—the area of human relationships.

Finally, not with a bang, not even with a whimper, with a nothing, with a non-explanation, the men were one day simply returned to the camp. The show was over.

As I have mentioned earlier, when I was continuing the research in Washington seven months later, I could find no report filed by the warden to the central authorities. The closest approximation to an official explanation was the following excerpt from letters sent by the Bureau of Prisons to two senators and a number of correspondents—with identical text—dated April 18, 1969.

> On January 6 Mr. X [Roger] and Mr. Y [Jim] were confined at the minimum-security camp at Oakdale. Mr. X refused

to comply with minimum regulations regarding his participation in the camp program and Mr. Y refused to perform the work assigned to him. They were instructed to gather together their personal properties for transfer to the parent institution, the U.S. Penitentiary at Oakdale. They refused to walk from the dormitory to the vehicle waiting to take them to the main institution and had to be carried. They arrived at Oakdale during the supper hour. Again, they refused to walk from the vehicle to the institution. Since help was not immediately available to carry them some 100 yards or more they were held in an uncovered area at the rear gate. They had adequate clothing including jackets, the hour or so they were held. Thereafter, they were carried to the receiving and discharging room. Here they were asked to remove their clothing to change to clothing issued at the main institution. They refused to do this and their clothing was removed. They were then taken a few feet and placed in a cell in the segregation unit. A complete set of clothing was given them. During the night Mr. X threw his clothing into the corridor. The cell was adequately ventilated and the temperature at normal levels. They were served regular meals which they refused to eat. Within a few days Mr. Y agreed to work and he was promptly returned to the work camp. He refused to work again on Jan. 29 and he's now back at Oakdale. He is living in an open dormitory and is assigned to work in the third service unit. He is eligible to participate in institutional activities for which he qualifies. Except for the fact that these men were not given mattresses or blankets during their first night at Oakdale our regulations concerning persons held in segregation were complied with in every regard. I am personally satisfied that they were not abused.

The warden at Oakdale has been made aware of our regulations about mattresses and blankets and I'm sure there will be no repetition of this in regard to the future. Since carrying full-grown men for any distance at all leaves the way open for complaints about jostling and even abuse we have instructed all institutions to use a stretcher whenever a person goes limp. We are also issuing instructions that whenever a person goes on a fast from food and or water, he be hospitalized immediately.

Throughout all the inquiries and the routine letters of response there is no real description of January 29—the date of the uprising involving thirteen men. Nor has anyone ever offered any rationale for the termination of the isolation and punishment. It was arbitrary and infuriatingly indecisive.

And, indeed, so was the ultimate punishment.

Roger was kept at the Wall and Jim was sent back to the work camp.

Pete was discharged right on time.

Lloyd was permitted to go to his parole hearing and was given an unexpected early 18-month parole.

Tim was served up his usual curved ball.

And Bill, most surprising of all, who had "gone along," who could never be conceived of as a troublemaker, who had been given a one-to-five-year sentence with the assurance from his judge that if he were a "good boy" he would be out in nine months, Bill who had planned on parole in eighteen months, who was indeed recommended for parole by his interviewer (as the scuttlebutt said, and I later confirmed), had been "set back," denied his parole, and assured at least of another six months in prison.

The logic of it all lies deep within the recesses of the minds of the men who administer the courts, the parole boards, and the prisons—our society's instruments of justice.

10 ⫷

Prisoners
of Conscience

I have introduced you to the war resisters as I was introduced to them, as individuals rather than statistics, so that when faced with the statistics you will not think in terms of numerals but in terms of multiples—of Hank, Tim, Bill, and others like them.

The total number of imprisoned violators of the Selective Service Law as of June 30, 1968, for any and all reasons, was 739 men (only a minority of whom are war resisters, as I have previously defined). In addition to those in prison there is a relatively large population of Selective Service violators who are known, located, and available for prosecution but are not in prison because: their cases are pending in court; there has not been time to process them; in their particular districts there is a policy to delay or withhold prosecution.

There is a feeling that the government, in certain sections of the country, is reluctant to prosecute these cases, and this is confirmed by the appreciable difference in the number of prosecutions from federal district to federal district. This further reduces the total prison population.

But even were they all included this would be a small group when compared with the estimated number of *unidentified* draft evaders, for whom there are no exact figures available. The figures are a function of the Selective Service office rather than the Bureau of Prisons, and the Selective Service office is notoriously weak on statistics.

In the spring of 1967 the Selective Service Director, Louis B. Hershey, listed 14,422 draft delinquents. By the spring of 1969 the figure was 23,280. Presumably these figures represent the total lost registrants, those who ignored their draft notices.

We do not know exactly how many of them are out of the country or how many are merely underground, but we do know that almost any estimate of draft evasion has to be on the small side because, in addition to those who ignore notices, there is that population, particularly among the poor, who never even receive notices, because they have no official existence. This is a part of the perpetual underground of people who do not have any official records (Social Security cards, tax records, etc.), who may be itinerant, and who for one reason or another simply are not identifiable. It has been the feeling of many demographers that the census reports err in the direction of minimizing black population for some of these very reasons.

For one class of people, delinquency is not the major, and certainly not the preferred method of avoiding the draft, for it has been made relatively easy for them to avoid service in the Army while still managing to avoid violation of the Selective Service Act. Despite the fact that in my social circle there exists a large population of young men of draft age, up until last year I did not personally know one who was serving in the armed forces. It has long been a feeling of many people that the reason that this war has been tolerated for so long is that it has not existed for those people who are influential in dictating public policy—the vast upper middle class of America. By becoming a perpetual college student, one could avoid the war legally. Any college boy who did end up in jail or in the Army was there by choice.

Even with the change in the draft laws, when deferment for graduate studies is no longer as automatic as it has been in the past, there are still the exempt professions: medical school, some physical science fields, the religious seminaries, teaching.

The priority seems peculiar at best. For example, I have never been convinced of the logic behind exempting seminarians. If it is said that a minister is a man of peace, so should it be said that he is a pastor, a leader. If it is against the teachings of God and church for man to kill, it is against the teachings for all men to kill. If a minister believes that his relationship with God will not permit him to bear arms, he should be required in the same manner that any man does to declare himself a conscientious objector and prove to a local draft board the sincerity of this conviction. He cannot merely state that it is against his religious belief, for if it is against his religious belief it should be against the religious belief of every member of his flock. Historically, at any rate, the churches have never found war the anathema that one theoretically would have assumed they would.

The awareness of this inequity is very strong on the part of many young seminarians, and indeed, among members of the faculty, at Union Theological Seminary, where I have heard these concepts expressed repeatedly. But, from all the evidence, the massive weight of the churches is on the side of the military, and this is generally true in any country, in any place, in any war. Archbishop Roberts of Farm Street Church, London, formerly Bishop of Bombay, is quoted as saying, "If America had dropped contraceptives on Hiroshima and Nagasaki there would have been a howl from all American Catholics—but they merely dropped a bomb." There is no better evidence of the exciting ferment in the Catholic Church than the fact of the leadership role of radical Catholic clergy in the present anti-war movement, which is unmatched by the other major religions.

With the change in the draft laws suspending automatic draft deferment for graduate studies, the Bureau expected a flood of draft violators. They were apprehensive about this prospect. The Bureau was not anxious to have these young men in prison. There were no facilities for them—existing institutions were already overcrowded. Also, the Bureau was unsure as to how to use these men effectively. The Bureau was concerned for their welfare—they did not want to put them into general prison populations. At the same time, if special camps were established, there was danger in increasing the volatility, and there would also be the stigma of having set up what could be viewed as concentration camps for political prisoners.

But the flood did not materialize, partly because prosecutions were being held up, and partly because, like the tax laws, there are always built-in loopholes for the educated and knowledgeable. In the January 7, 1969, issue of the *New York Times* there appeared a five-column spread under the headline: *Teachers' Ranks Swollen by Men Avoiding Draft*. The article stated that in the year that the law was changed, the New York City Board of Education received twenty thousand more applications for teacher's licenses than the year before. The vast majority were men under the age of twenty-six (then the cut-off age for the draft). In 1969, of the thousands of participants in short-term teacher-training programs, 85 per cent are male college graduates under the age of twenty-six. And as an adjustment to the changed law, preparing for their future, there are eight times as many men as formerly now taking teacher-education courses in one city college alone.

Who then went to jail? According to the statistics supplied to me by the research division of the Bureau of Prisons, fully 75 per cent were Jehovah's Witnesses. In the official classification, Selective Service violators were divided into three classes, Jehovah's Witnesses, other religious objectors, and all others. The Jehovah's Witnesses obviously were not a part of the population that I had intended to study. They had not chosen to go to prison—the choice was made for them. They were not defying authority; they were merely defining the authority in a different way. They were not even necessarily opposed to the war; their primary opposition was to serving a secular power. They were just as opposed to working in a hospital, working for Vista, or the Peace Corps (which explains why they are in prison while the Quakers as a group are not). I interviewed a sample of them to confirm the general impressions I had been given. Indeed, they tend to be compliant, orthodox, obedient, untroubled young men, firm in the sense that what they are doing is right, supported by their families and their community.

The actual figures given to me by the research division showed a total of 739 Selective Service violators of which 574 were JWs, 62 were classified "other religious," and 103 a miscellany of "all others." Moral, political, and "individual conscience" resisters were in the third group. The "other religious" included a number of Mennonites, Shakers, small sects, and also Black Muslims. In interviewing a sample population of the Muslims, it became apparent that they, too, were not a homogeneous group. For many of the Black Muslims their reasons for not fighting the war, while stated as religious, were essentially political and primarily related to the black nationalism—the feeling that this is not their war, that they have nothing to gain by it. This group could then be considered part of the anti-war group that I was studying. On the other hand, a significant number of them were following "the dictates of their church." They were devout believers that their religion forbade them to enter into this conflict. They were in their way in every sense the equivalent of the Quaker or the Jehovah's Witness. They were not, however, accorded the same courtesy of belief and trust.

With this group I chose then to follow the policy of accepting the statements of the prisoners themselves, so that those who indicated that they were in prison because their church did not permit their involvement in this war were excluded from my population and classified as religious objectors. Those Black Muslims who presented it on a personal basis of defiance of the war, country, or whatever, were included in my group population. Hence I recognize that the statistics in terms of the black population may be blurred.

There was, however, another major obstacle in the presentation of the statistical material. The Bureau of Prisons publishes a statistical report for each fiscal year. In terms of research on Selective Service violators it is unfortunately limited. It must be remembered that the Selective Service violators represent a very small percentage of the population (and problems) of the Bureau of Prisons, which has over twenty thousand prisoners in its custody. In addition, when I first ran a set of computer cards through for data processing to determine such simple questions as the relative length of sentence of the Jehovah's Witnesses and others, I was shocked to find that of the 739 population (June 30 population), 306 were listed as JWs, 14 "other religious," and 419 "all others." These were impossible figures, inconsistent with what the Department of Research had told me and what my personal experience in the prisons had been. To compare these three groups on the basis of compiled government statistics was useless if the grouping itself was inaccurate. Unfortunately it was. When I checked this out in Washington the reason was immediately apparent to them. The figures in the statistical reports were compiled in Washington rather than at the local level. The reporting institutions bothered to complete only a certain percentage of their forms. Whenever the forms came in without this specific line filled in, they were classified as "all others."

The local institution, however, does know from its records who is who, and so with the unfailing courtesy and cooperation beyond that which I had a right to expect, a member of the Department of Research personally contacted each prison to make a new tabulation for me. Being the eternally wary researcher, I checked the figures out by direct observation in the two institutions where I had access to the records. The accuracy was impressive.

Another set of statistics proved remarkably accurate. The Central Committee for Conscientious Objectors publishes regularly a list of war resisters. They too have an accurate count although they tend to include people who are above draft age, arrested for demonstrations, and the like.

In the process of checking on the statistics, but also because I thought it would be interesting (as well as feasible, since only a small number of people were involved), I decided to review the total population of Selective Service violators at Crestwood. I interviewed each individual in prison as an SS48 violator regardless of what the indications were as to his background or the reason for the violation.

The figures that I had been given were that there were two JWs, six classified as "other religious," and six classified as "all others." I was then told that the population of war resisters was only two. My figures corresponded impressively with the amended list supplied me.

While the classifications are often difficult in certain individual cases, there is a whole class of draft evaders who represent a different population from the war resister as defined in this study. The "you-can't-blame-a-man-for-trying" individual, who avoids the draft until detected and then is willing to enlist, may end up in prison with an SS48 conviction, but he is not a part of the population of resistance.

The population fluctuated from day to day, and best estimate of the total number of imprisoned war resisters on the day I began my visits was seventy-four. The total number in the two institutions that I was utilizing was twenty-six; two at Crestwood and twenty-four at Oakdale. This research population constituted thirty-five per cent of the total population.

It should be remembered when evaluating any of the statistics that the sample population was a relatively early population. These were men who were in jail at a time when the law still permitted deferment for graduate studies. These were men about whom it could be more aptly said that they chose prison than may be the case of a study performed later.

Of the twenty-six, twenty-two are white and four black. Of the four blacks, two were raised as Protestant and two were raised as Catholic. At the present time one is a Muslim; one feels he has no religious affiliation but is investigating Buddhism, and Muslim and the non-Christian churches in general; one has no religion; and one is a believer in Yuruba. Of the twenty-two whites, there are ten Catholics, a surprisingly large number, twelve Protestants, and no Jews. This is in startling contrast to the college activists, who are always described as having a disproportionate number of Jews and a relatively small number of Catholics, and immediately suggests that the imprisoned war resisters are a different population from the college radicals.

With small populations, percentage of statistics can change somewhat dramatically in a short time. A week after this study began, one Jewish war resister was admitted.

The six men described in the earlier chapters suggest the heterogeneity of this group. To appreciate the true heterogeneity all twenty-six would have to be presented in detail. Yet some generalizations can be cautiously offered. As I indicated above, the conventional stereotyped equation of imprisoned war resister with the college radical becomes suspect with the mere breakdown of religious backgrounds. Most of them come from a personal sense of moral outrage with the war and with a strong conscience, which would not permit them to participate in it or to avoid the confrontation. When they are political, they are still not politicians. They are not for the most part organizers, and when they attempt such activity often fail. They are activists who believe in action by example and witness.

Politically they subscribe to no clear-cut dogma. Only two of them are professed Marxists, and even that in the modern sense of the word. Two of them are conservative, Goldwater Republicans. Most do not even think in political terms. There is a high percentage of sympathy with the anarchist-pacifist writings, and many of them describe their political philosophy as essentially "Christian pacifist." There are only two who by any stretch of the imagination would be called "hippie" types, unless one wants to include the Catholic Worker group (four members) who in dress and manner of living might be misinterpreted as such, but who in intention and action are entirely different.

Two would not have been in prison at all if they had had the money to go to Canada. But this would have represented a hardship on their families, in one case because of the bond that the family had put up, and in the other case because job opportunities would have been limited for him, as he was black.

Some should not be there at all. One was an Amish boy who was raised in that religion but who in his late teens stopped attending the church, although he continued to subscribe to its principles. His draft board refused him CO status.

Another fulfilled totally the new ruling as to CO status but came from a small Southern town where his draft board shared his ignorance of his rights. There was no lawyer to consult or guide his appeal.

Three came in specifically to test the legal validity of certain aspects of the war and the draft—two felt that the peacetime draft was illegal, and one proposed the right of individual conscience on the basis of the Nuremberg trials.

Over half are true pacifists (or were at the time of admission) who subscribed to total non-violence.

At least a third had clear-cut advance indications that they would not be eligible for the draft if they chose to exercise their rights to deferment.

Whenever I have discussed this group in the psychoanalytic community I have encountered a bias that assumes in advance a high degree of psychopathology. For one thing, it is behavior that represents a marked deviation from the norm, which is automatically suspect. Second, the fact that they have chosen prison suggests masochism—on the assumption that to choose to be in a punishing situation is in itself an act of masochism.

Neither the interviews nor the psychological testing revealed a particularly high degree of overt or latent malignant pathology. There was one overt psychotic, one compensated psychotic, and perhaps four to six that might be called schizoid personalities—

in lay terms, "loners." I am not sure this would deviate from a "normal" sample of this age group—however one could define, or wherever one could construct, such a normal sample.

While there was an abundance of paranoid thinking, the presence of true paranoid personality was surprisingly low. Latent homosexuality, which again might have been anticipated, was minimal and certainly well within the normal range.

"To the pathologist all is pathology" is a favorite axiom of medicine—and the psychopathologist is no different. Therefore it would probably be more helpful and less confusing to discuss pathology in terms of "kinds" rather than "amounts," and this will be done later.

As to character structure, they demonstrated a high degree of ego strength (stability, sense of self), considering their age group, but this was combined with a disproportionately severe super-ego (conscience). As a result, they expected a great deal of themselves and tended to be grossly intolerant of their own failures. This punishing conscience, particularly when combined with a low capacity for expressed anger, is conducive to the development of depression—and depression was a factor of real concern with some of the men—particularly Paul and one other (Clifford, a thirty-year-old who will be introduced briefly later). Almost all of the men went cyclically into depressed phases, but fortunately none developed an acute depression.

In personality they tended toward the quiet, contemplative, and introspective. There was a relatively low level of aggressiveness and hostility, particularly when allowing for the elevation from norm that one would expect to see in a prison environment.

In sociological terms they were service-oriented individuals who believed that a man must be judged by his actions, not his statements, and that ideals and behavior were not separable phenomena.

And assuredly they were not the population at which the Selective Service Act was directed, for under the intention of the act most of these boys were indeed conscientious objectors.

When a government does not trust itself, its purposes, or its population, it dare not depend on a volunteer army. When it cannot assume either the responsibility of its citizenry or the worthiness of its cause, it must establish a draft system, with severe enough punishment for violators, to guarantee a sufficient number of men to conduct effectively the business of the war. It is almost a certainty that most of the men in the armed services, if given a free choice, would not be there. Faced, however, with the limited choice of Army or jail, the majority chose the Army.

To that extent the Selective Service Act is successful. But the threat of punishment is effective only if the threat is carried out in the face of defiance. We therefore manage to keep in the Army that large population which is assumed will go only under duress by imprisoning a small sample group for which the law was not intended in the first place. They are the innocent minority who must be sacrificed to insure the efficiency of the punishment system.

But the choices are not so narrowly limited. The Army needs only a small percentage of the eligible male population. Therefore, besides the preferential treatment of the educated (which may be defended on the basis of maintenance of the country's institutions), there are other escape mechanisms, still within the laws that are available. All that is necessary is sufficient education, sophistication, money, or influence to exploit them. Among these are: expensive medical help to legitimize borderline conditions for deferment; membership in the Reserves (for what they are being reserved is not quite clear); the privilege of commission, thereby seriously diminishing the possibility of risk, damage, or inconvenience; appointment in the relatively safe service of the Navy or Coast Guard; the institution of the National Guard, which has for the most part not been activated, indicating, I suppose, that, despite the rhetoric, this nation is not considered to be in a position that requires guarding.

With all these "opportunities" available, it must be said that, in his failure to exploit them, the war resister becomes victim not only to the nation's pride, but to his own conscience.

11 ⋘

Here I Stand—I
Cannot Do Otherwise

Repeatedly, throughout the interviews, I would ask the prisoners why they were in jail, why had they come. As is usual with most of the questions a psychiatrist asks, I knew that the individuals would not have completely articulated answers, but the repetitive asking of a question will often bring to the surface an answer of which even the individual was unaware.

In some cases, however, and with this particular question, ready answers were more available, for it was a question that was asked of themselves by themselves well before the fact. And it was a question that would constantly re-emerge during moments of self-doubt and anxiety while in prison.

Except for that minority who were specifically hoping to make a test case, there was a similarity to the expressed motivation, yet the expression differed from man to man depending on his environment and his particular sensitivities. The black population generally tended to tie their attitudes about the Vietnam war closely to their struggle for identity and survival as blacks. On the other hand, one black CO could express it this way:

"I believe in brotherhood and loving people. I suppose that on an individual basis it's a natural thing for a man to protect himself as a matter of self-defense, but it becomes a different thing, even for self-defense, when it's institutionalized. I think that military institutions have disunited and separated men, and that is contrary to a basic belief of mine. I couldn't take a life just for that. That other man might be my brother. I don't think any war is ever justified. While I do believe that I'm against war in general, this one, particularly, just doesn't have anything to do with anything I believe in. I think all war is an expression of the sickness of mankind, part of that sickness which he should try to overcome. I just don't look at it as being a natural thing—like some people do. I just don't understand people who can think of war as a part of the way of life. I feel this is not me, and I can't participate in something like a war which seems crazy merely because some agency says I should. Basically, I'm just not a violent person."

Compare this with a young Boston Irishman: "I believe that the draft denies the man his right to life. You take a man and put his life on the line and you control him, lock, stock, and barrel. You deprive him of his right to exist. They can push my body around the way they do in prison, but no one's going to force my mind. They're not going to teach me to repair rifles and teach me to shoot it at a person, unless I believe in it. If I enlist, fine. If I don't enlist, they have no right to draft me. The only reason to go to war is self-defense, so the only war I would enlist in is a self-defense one.

"I would have gone to Canada. I did go up there—it was beautiful—people were friendly. I even had a job, filled out the papers, and then when I went to the border to get the immigration status, the fellow wouldn't give it to me. He said my job wasn't good enough. They wouldn't accept it. Ridiculous—it was as good a job as I had here in the States.

"The idea of leaving the country would have bothered me a great deal, but even though this is the greatest country on earth

I would have left it so that I would have had freedom of choice. Also it might not be a bad idea to have my son be a Canadian citizen. I wouldn't want him to go through what I've had to go through. Once is enough.

"It's funny me being here. I'm not active politically. It's just conscription that I'm opposed to. The other COs have what I would call more of a Left-leaning tendency. I don't go much for politics."

"What group could you identify with politically?" I asked.

"The Ayn Rand group influenced me a great deal, and I might go part of the way with Mr. Buckley or Mr. Goldwater, but not fully so. I don't really belong to any group."

The statement of another young man represented an entirely different point of view: "I would have gotten out of the draft any way I could have. I don't see anything immoral in anything these people do. These guys who claim things, they have a perfect right to. I would have claimed one of the other things if I could have."

"What do you mean, 'claim things'?" I asked. "I don't understand."

"You know what I mean—go in and do something crazy. Claim my heart is killing me or something. Claim I'm a homosexual. I wouldn't know how to go about doing it. You have to understand. I think it's great for those who can. I just can't, and it's not that I feel it's degrading—it's just not my style—it's just not what I could do."

There are a few men whom I've mentioned earlier who would have taken CO status had they or their draft boards been better informed. They tended to be men from the Southern rural areas. One of them said:

"I was never granted a CO status. Perhaps it was my own fault. The first time I got the application I crossed off the reference to religious belief. I did not feel it was because of some dictate of my church but rather my personal belief. That action worked against me all the way. After the broader Supreme Court interpretation I felt that I was ethically and truly a CO, but I had evidently set a bad precedent for myself."

"Was there a political aspect to your opposition?" I asked.

"I've never really been involved in politics at all. I'm not sure I ever had an ideology. I know I'll never go back to being the same. Then I was involved in my own work and my own life. Right now I'm for McCarthy because of his peace stand. Also I get the feeling from him that he's not a regular politician like the others. He seems less manipulative, more personally honest. Politics just isn't my bag."

"Why would you say you're here then?" I asked.

"I guess I'd have to say personal, ethical reasons. I'm opposed to war in general."

"Do you think you'd have taken this stand if you were drafted in World War II?"

"I think I would have. I don't think that violence is a way of solving disagreements, especially in international affairs, and probably also on a personal level."

Jimmy, who was an artist, was a particular favorite of mine and one whose story I would have liked to have told in detail. He was small, even by the standards of the COs, and young even by their standards. Jimmy was constantly putting himself down and acting the joker. He was the youngest in his family (the only one in my entire study), and he was still a baby in his own eyes even though he was a man in the eyes of his colleagues and myself. He told me:

"All through high school I was upset and angry about the war. I planned on being a CO. I was always a pacifist and completely against violence in any form. I wouldn't eat meat and I wouldn't wear leather. I had always planned on being a CO. Then, by the time my eighteenth birthday came, I was so repelled by the war that I didn't want to cooperate with it even to the point of registering. I didn't want any part of it. I didn't want to make any contribution to the functioning of any law which in itself contributed to the war. Although in the truest sense I think I am a CO. Everyone knew my convictions for a long time, and I had been told by my next-door neighbor who was the head of our local draft board that I would have no trouble getting a CO status.

"My birthday was in July. I gave myself three months to think about it and decide what to do, and in the beginning of November I notified my draft board that I was three months delinquent and had no intention of registering. I wanted them to know that I was breaking the law. I didn't want them to feel I was trying to evade anything.

"Then things moved rapidly. In court, I made a statement that I thought fairly expressed what I felt. I thought it was a good statement—there wasn't lots of rhetoric—I know I can be silly and snotty and I thought I avoided that. I remember the prosecutor's closing remark to the effect: 'What right does this nineteen-year-old child have to presume to decide what is right and what is wrong?'

"The jury carefully deliberated for ten minutes, and after giving it all of this consideration, they decided that this child was guilty. The prosecutor said, 'Why don't we give him three years?' and the judge evidently thought that sounded nice. For that's what he gave me."

Pete, who has been referred to in relation to the "action" in Chapter 9, summarized in his position what was perhaps the most popular one. He said: "I never filled out the form for CO but probably fulfilled the requirements for it. But there are a lot of people in jail who are by the strictest standards objectors. They simply don't have the necessary tools to put it down on paper to convince their personal draft boards. Now they're serving three to five years. Also, there are a lot of people who are not religious objectors as currently defined, but whose religious or moral objections *should* be as legitimate as mine.

"Secondly, I feel that those who do not have a religious objection to killing or a moral objection but rather a political objection and repugnance to this war are as entitled as I am to avoid the draft.

"And thirdly, I didn't feel I should be required to defend my religious beliefs to the government. I simply didn't wish to go before the draft board."

I asked him about Canada.

"It simply wasn't a possible thought. I never for a moment considered going to Canada. It seemed to be a cop-out. In addition, it meant for the rest of my life, as far as I know—leaving people, friends and relatives. I have lots of close ties that I wouldn't want to break."

And just to confuse, just to inhibit the development of any stereotypes, we must consider the case of Clifford. Clifford was thirty-one by the time he entered prison. He'd started his draft resistance at twenty-six, when, as an aeronautical engineer working in research for an agency of the government, he was thoroughly and completely draft exempt. One day he was sent a deferment notice, a routine phenomenon. He felt, somehow, that the peacetime draft was an injustice and an illegality. He said:

"After careful consideration I sent a carefully written letter to the draft board explaining that I would not be sending in the papers and my reasons why. I wrote two pages of this—that was in January 1964. They of course had no alternative then but to induct me since I wouldn't send in the letter. I then notified them that for the same reasons I wouldn't sign the letter I wouldn't be there for the induction.

"At that point I notified my supervisor and told him that I would continue working until something happened. He was dismayed. I had just received a merit raise, he needed me on the job. He talked with his superiors to see what could be done, and much to my surprise, and his, they didn't want me to work there at all. They said I must resign immediately or be fired. I then got a lawyer and told him I was prepared to fight this in the courts, because I felt the draft was immoral and illegal. He felt that we could take it to the Supreme Court. He estimated that it would take about two years and $4000.

"I gave it a great deal of serious thought, talked it over with my friends, and felt it was the kind of thing that someone must test in the courts. It didn't seem important that I win the case, but what was important was that a crucial issue of this sort be heard and argued in the courts. So I went ahead.

"My first court procedure was in the district court, and my first disillusionment came immediately. The judge refused to listen to any arguments of mine or anyone else. He wouldn't rule on the draft, merely wanted to know whether or not I showed up for induction. He couldn't understand that we were trying to establish the constitutionality of the peacetime draft. He gave me a guilty verdict, and even on the day of sentencing I wasn't allowed to express my views. I told the judge that I thought I should be allowed to make a statement. He was testy about that and told my lawyer that he had originally intended to give me only four, but because of my attempt to make a speech he made it five years. I ended up with a five-year sentence and a $15,000 bond. I had hoped for a smaller one."

He then went on to detail the long struggle. Finally the case reached the Supreme Court, and they refused to hear it. Clifford was crushed.

"I had no expectation of winning the case, but the disillusionment at the injustice of the whole court thing—not to have your arguments even listened to—was too much to bear. We simply never got a chance.

"I didn't know at the time I started this that the Supreme Court takes only one per cent of the cases presented to them—worse, I don't think my lawyer did either. My feeling had always been that if you have the courage and conviction, the financial backing and the lawyers, you could go to the court; that we live in the kind of country where anyone could get that hearing. I was terribly upset and I suppose I still am. The whole fight accomplished nothing. It took me four and a half years and $20,000 in legal fees. I went through eight different jobs and had a total of nine months' unemployment and an intense amount of personal anguish. I lost my girl friend in the process."

Clifford, while not an intensely active political person, was interested in national politics and worked hard in support of Senator Goldwater in 1964.

These, then, are some of the stated reasons why these men ended up in prison, but a psychoanalyst always wants more. He assumes that parallel with any sociological explanation must be a psychodynamic one.

Again, let me repeat what I have previously emphasized. A psychodynamic explanation is an alternative explanation of behavior, not a better one, not a "truer" one, not a "deeper" one. It represents an alternative framework in which to order the facts, which for certain purposes can be most useful. It does not ever negate the validity of such behavior when viewed from a sociological, theological, ethical, or political point of view. Unfortunately, the psychodynamic explanations that have the most relevance are inextricably woven into the total fabric of a man's life. It is for precisely this reason that I presented six detailed profiles before I discussed the population in general. With an extended exposure to one of the resisters you "know without knowing" his reasons. It is the implicit understanding of motivation that comes from understanding character.

Psychoanalysts often have their most difficulty when they attempt to generalize from the individual to the group. But there is one area here that is so uniform, so startling statistically, that it allows for generalization. Of the population of twenty-six, twenty-one are first sons. The statistic becomes even more striking and improbable when broken down by race. Of the four blacks only one is a first son, but of the twenty-two whites, twenty are so. In addition, one of the two exceptions is a product of a divorced family wherein there was a remarriage, and in the newly constituted family this man became the eldest son.

This fact was so unexpected and so preponderant that it

emerged before I began any statistical evaluation. I mentioned it one day to a group of colleagues, as my first hard fact. It was greeted with the professional equivalent of "It figures." I asked them to explain their responses.

The general answer was in terms of the conflict to be expected between the eldest son and the father. The struggle for independence and the need to defy would be greatest here, and the conflict with the father who over-identifies with his first son would be maximal. The political actions were an extension of the continued defiance of the father, in the figure of the new authority—that is, the institutions of government. Their reactions were therefore interpreted as displaced rebellion against the father figure.

Less than a week later an article appeared in the newspaper stating that every single astronaut to that date was an eldest son. (I do not know if this statistic is still valid.) I intentionally raised this question with another group of psychiatrists and asked them how they would explain the fact. They were quick to supply answers. The eldest is earlier cast into the role of independence; he is more capable of making moves away from the family, of being explorative; he early is given positions of authority and responsibility; he has greater drives for achievement and power, coupled with a greater self-confidence.

I think the two answers in juxtaposition are interesting and illuminate one major difficulty in psychoanalytic interpretation. Both the answers have validity. Both express conditions that are relevant to the unique position and special problems of an eldest son in relationship with his father. Both point to the fact that in his life the father-son relationship will have a more dominant influence, and certainly the two sets of explanations are not mutually exclusive. But a kind of bias is introduced by the ordering of them. Again, this is a reflection of the impact of psychoanalytic therapy on psychoanalytic theorizing. In treatment we start with a symptom, a fact, and we search for all developmental material contributing to it, forgetting for the time being that that same material may be pertinent to other factors. We are not concerned. Our goal at that point is to understand the symptom.

In the explanation I have just offered the psychiatrists were reflecting certain *a priori* assumptions. They started with the "fact" (really a value judgment) of the prisoner's action being sick or disturbing and the astronaut's action as strong and courageous. They then found the same statistic in both, but with their unconscious bias as to the nature of the act selected those aspects (all of them being relevant) of the father-son relationship that confirmed their original value judgment.

The fact is that if one examines almost any major achievement or assertion area, one will find a disproportionate number of first sons (as I have many times told my two younger brothers).

In the six cases presented, all five of the white cases, despite dissimilarities, showed markedly similar patterning in the role of the father. (In the case of Hank, interestingly enough, despite the absent father, he managed to find an older man who fulfilled something of the same pattern.)

What predominates is a conflicting, contradictory figure, one who is loved, admired, and respected, who projects an image of power, of positive virtues, and then dramatically can switch to become a figure of neglect, abandonment, weakness, or rejection. This recurs repeatedly in the stories of the prisoners. It is not merely a matter of a weak, inadequate, or absent father—it is practically never that. Nor is it a matter of a dominant, overbearing, strong, brutalizing father. The father is above all an ambivalent figure. He will be giving, strong, successful, and then in a variety of ways—but always with sharp contrast—a change will occur. A Jekyll and Hyde, he shows two different surfaces to the child. He may be a figure of enormous stature who may disappear (from the child's life) for long periods of time—a ship's captain, an Army officer, a diplomat, a physicist traveling from one installation to another.

He may be an alcoholic—but within bounds—so that it is a double figure that is presented. He may be a scholar-laborer. He may be an individual who has cyclic depressions. All of the fathers described share in common the confusing presentation of two separate figures.

Often this takes a more subtle form—the father who does not change but whose character will be perceived as strong by the standards of a five-year-old and revealed as inadequate to the more perceptive eyes of a fifteen-year-old. While this is a universal dynamic of "growing up," it is the dramatic nature of the changed perception that is evident here.

Or he may be a man with sharply isolated areas of relating—who, for example, gives in many areas but withholds in the emotional area. Richard (who was quoted in relation to the "action") described his father in general terms as being Catholic, Irish, and politically conservative.

"He was a good man in general but he was difficult to react to as I grew older. There was nothing to get into. He made rebelling against him difficult. You could talk to him up to a point, but if you wanted a positive reaction there was nothing to bounce off of. I wanted to make him react. I wanted to get something positive from him.

"Also there was an intense longing to have him approve of me, to have some respect. He generally tended to disapprove. If grades were low he'd say something negative, but if they were high there was very little direct approval. He tended to make a joke of it as though he was embarrassed by approval. In retrospect I think that's so. I think he was embarrassed by his positive emotions, but at the time it bothered me greatly."

Another described his relationship with his father in the following way: "My father was always away at sea until I was about ten or twelve. He was a captain of a tanker. In that sense, in those early days we had a great relationship. Every time he came home everybody was happy. He would bring presents and make a big fuss, but then there would be long stretches when there would be no relationship at all. Then when he settled down at home he became somehow or other a different person in my mind. He was very authoritarian. It was as if he was still on shipboard and everybody around had to listen. He liked to deal out punishment whenever he thought it was due. I didn't agree with his judgment on that, and there were times when I hated him thoroughly. Of course I never got any support in this area from my mother. And my younger brother would never get blamed because of the old story—he was younger. My father was always saying I should have known better, I was the oldest, that he expected more of me. Punishments were often physical. He would take the strap out. The worst thing is that they were never spontaneous, they were always controlled.

"When I was twelve or thirteen I left home and stayed away for seven days. That was my only way of fighting back. In a way it worked. There was a very dramatic change after that. I was left on my own a lot more and was much freer. I got a paper route and began to make my own money, and my father didn't seem as strong or threatening."

He then went on to a related area, which I think is nonetheless of some interest.

"I also grew up disliking my younger brother. I know now it's natural for a small brother to try to get the best of a big brother, and then he would do the traditional thing—run to Mommy. And Mommy would say it's all my fault because I was older. It was so incessant, her siding with him.

"It's strange how it's changed. He went into the Army at seventeen and was in Vietnam on his last tour of duty. He came back from Vietnam terribly shaken up and convinced that the war was terrible—we shouldn't be there. Because of that, and my position at the time, we developed a friendship that we never had. He had a hard time when he first came home. For about a week's time he would cry every night. This is a twenty-year-old guy I'm talking about. I guess it was a time when he needed me and I was there, and we were close."

I mention this particularly poignant scene with a younger brother because another extension of the father-son relationship so dominant in this group is a strong sense of paternalism. This, of course, is characteristic of eldest sons in general, and in psychoanalytic terms it is an extension of their identification with their fathers; that is, their readiness to assume his (a paternal) role. But not necessarily in the same way that their fathers did. It will often be in an idealized version.

In any event, these are people who are ready to father others. This can be seen not just in their family relationships, but in their activities. They tend to be "doers-for" rather than "stimulators of" people. They are ready to take the lead. They are ready to sacrifice for others. They are ready to become examples. They are protective and generally tolerant and understanding of the weak and inferior. They reserve their hostility and resentment for the strong. It is only because these dramatically split fathers have presented during their sons' growing up at least one image, one ideal, worth identifying with, that the sons are capable of so firmly taking this role.

Interesting, also, is that sibling discussion is minimal. This is often so in the case of eldest children and rarely so with youngest. The younger child will have a large proportion of his rivalry channeled through his relationships with his older brother. In addition, much of his ideal image, his concept of a man, will be formed in the relationship with an older brother—that is, both identification and competition with the father can be displaced and shared.

The eldest child confronts the father directly as a competitor with no intermediates. He handles the competitive thrust of the younger group by patronizing or paternalizing them. Nonetheless, he has difficulties in accepting the position of authority with confidence, and is particularly reluctant to be an aggressive leader.

The insecurities of these men in the role of leader and their readiness to doubt its validity, their readiness to distrust the enduring aspects of their courage, may also be related to the history of "seeing the mighty fall." The family patterning (again almost unanimously uniform in this study) is of a father who is the head of the house—the dominant figure often intimidating the mother, and always in the authoritarian position. Yet in a more profound sense he is often a weak man. Peculiarly, it is, as previously indicated, the kind of weakness that is identifiable only to the child with increasing maturity. The alcoholism which is a relatively high feature in the backgrounds of these men (about a third having fathers with serious alcohol problems) is a particularly good example of this kind of flaw.

Nowhere is the dominance of the father-son relationship better demonstrated than in the form (as distinguished from the substance) of parental discussion. With an incredible regularity, when they are told to discuss their "parents" or "background" (not specifically "mother" or "father"), or when they are not even told anything but merely allowed in non-directive fashion to choose their own subjects, the father will be introduced first and the portion of time spent on him will be three or four times greater than that which is devoted to the mother.

Because of the smallness of the black population, only four members, I'm extremely reluctant to generalize about them. Obviously the patterns of their lives were different. From this small sample a different patterning in terms of father-son relationships seems to exist.

In all of them the mother was early seen as the stronger figure in the household, a figure of respect and stability—but also hostility. The relationship among the blacks with their fathers tended to be a more affectionate and sympathetic one. They identified with him in terms of his being taken advantage of—not just by society but by the mother. In addition, it too had its ambivalence. There was the anger for his not being more aggressive, more assertive.

There is a tendency in sociological research, when confronted with the black family, often fragmented and restructured, to interpret this as downgrading the role and impact of "family," of seeing the family unit as a less meaningful one. While this is out-

side my area of expertise, I tend to think this is in error.
Certainly in this group, to say this would be in error. Two of the
blacks came from extremely stable families, albeit mother dominated. In the two families that were fragmented, they were very
early reconstituted with father substitutes, surrogate brothers,
etc., so that at any given time there was a strong group identification and a strong "holding together." It may not have followed
the white middle-class model, but at least in the case of these
members of the study they managed to establish their equivalent
of a supporting family group.

12 ≪

The Passion
of Peaceful Men

Whenever I am questioned about what is happening to these young men in prison, the direction of interest usually lies first in their exposure to either physical abuse or homosexuality, since these are the most dramatic components of the stereotypes middle-class people hold about prison and its dangers. To my mind, these are less significant threats than some of the other consequences of imprisonment—less significant in terms of the long-range impact on the majority of these men. Of course to those specifically involved these can be traumatic, and while not nearly in the proportion anticipated by the men themselves or the general population concerned with them, they are not insignificant. The horror stories do exist.

Only one CO was raped during the time of my research, at least in the prisons in which I was involved. He was attacked at Oakdale by fifteen men and rather badly hurt, as has been mentioned previously. Many others were approached, coerced, and threatened. The most extreme incident was the following:

"A few weeks ago I was approached and got into a very tight situation—a homosexual attack actually—and I had to fight, really swing away, and got hit—you know, a real fight."

I asked, "How did that happen—so late in the game for you?"

"This should be kept cool—not get back to the general population, or else I'm in trouble, and definitely so if the administration found out. I'd be in a mess."

"Don't worry," I said.

"Well, on this night a couple of guys I sort of knew—not too well—had some wine in here and we went out drinking on a hill. We were all pretty well drunk. I've always been inclined to accept someone's hospitality. But . . . after we were pretty well stoned they attacked me. First they put me on the spot and said, 'If we take you off, will you tell the administration?' I said, 'No.'"

"Why would you say no?" I asked.

"Because I wouldn't."

"But then in a sense you were giving them a hunting license," I said. "Even if you wouldn't tell, you could have told them you would."

"Well, not really. If you admit that you would, you're a rat in the eyes of the population. And also that's a sign of weakness, and any sign of weakness that you give them, any sign of being yellow, might act even more as a hunting license—if they think you don't have any 'heart,' as the expression goes. One of the romantic criminal codes.

"Well, anyway, I said, 'No, but you're not getting anything either.' They proceeded to try to take it, and I started swinging. You know, when you're very scared, physically you're apt to fight very hard or run very fast. So I started hitting, fighting, boxing, like a son-of-a-bitch, and they hit back. Both were bigger than me. So we went at it—I don't know for how long, five or ten minutes—and then they simply changed their minds and let me go—because I had fought so."

"Were you hurt?"

"Not physically much. They worked on my stomach."

"From all the stories I've heard, I assumed that you didn't have to worry about that sort of violence at the work camp," I said.

"Yeah, right, I heard that story too, but it evidently isn't absolutely correct," he said.

It should be emphasized, however, that this is not the typical experience. More often, in the minimal-security institutions, there are harassment, proposition, and seduction short of violence.

One man described his experience as follows: "Materially, prison is a lot better than I had expected: psychologically, a lot worse. At the Wall it was pretty scary. There was always that sexual thing. One guy would tell you, 'Watch out for him,' and another one would say, 'Watch out for that guy you just talked to.' You couldn't trust anybody. You began to get paranoid. I was there for about two weeks, and they were hounding the hell out of me. I think I let myself in for it. I had decided before I came in I was going to contribute a lot—be friendly, open, helpful. You can't be that way in prison. They get the wrong idea. They then assume you'd be easy to force into something. Once it came close to being physical. I was working in the kitchen with them —two guys that I thought were my friends. We'd been joking around, then it started getting progressively more physical. Then they started hitting me and groping for me and feeling at me. I just pushed them away. I got mad and started talking real loud so that they'd get scared that the guards might come in, and that's what happened—it worked. They went away. I think that ended it, but I was good and scared."

Another description is not too dissimilar but indicates an alternate method of dealing with the homosexuality: "The first month was very difficult, particularly in the Wall. People were convinced I was a homosexual and they were after me all the time."

"Why were they convinced?" I asked.

"I had long hair and I had let my fingernails grow. I guess that was enough for them. They wouldn't take no for an answer. In the Wall though, at A and O, there were cell blocks, and that in itself became the protection. They had only one or two people in the cell. Through a stroke of great luck I had this guy with me who was a bank robber, a big, tough, strong guy and not a homosexual. He agreed that if anybody tried to come in he would take care of them.

"Then when I got in the dormitories it was more open so it was difficult to force their way around. They would make comments but no direct confrontations. When I came here to the camp there were one or two incidents. I again met a few who wouldn't take no for an answer. It was a constant harassment, although I was never taken off, anything like that. One guy who was most persistent kept telling every new guy who came in that I was queer, so they would come over and proposition me and I'd say no, and this guy would figure I was just playing it cute or something. So finally I went up to one of the men who was in the 'in' group and wields a lot of power here. I had done him a favor by typing something up for him about his parole, and I said to him, 'Would you mind straightening this guy out?' He evidently did because I never heard from him or any of the others again."

Another aspect of the problem of homosexuality: "I was small and somewhat attractive and I was frightened that I might be attacked homosexually, but there hasn't been any real problem keeping them off. I was also concerned that somehow or other I might have unconscious desires for homosexuality. I know I'm a sensualist. I enjoy physical contact. I knew I would be in a situation deprived of all sexual outlet. I was afraid that I might find any physical contact attractive, even with a man.

"With the sexual deprivation, I find myself preoccupied and fantasying about sex all the time, and the worst part is that it has to be mental, because even masturbation is difficult here. It's hard to find the privacy. It's simply not acceptable to lie on top of your bunk and publicly jerk off. You have to find a way to hide it. You don't want anyone to know, even though everyone jokes about it and knows that we're all doing it, but being caught in the act, being seen, is simply a taboo in me—in all of us I guess. It's ridiculous. We admit it takes place, we purport not to see it as a weakness, we realize completely that there simply is no alternative, but there's this gnawing little thing that bugs you —this shame or humiliation.

"At any rate, I was afraid that I might find as time went on some latent homosexuality coming to the surface. Actually it has never come around to that. I seem to have no impulses in that way. I've seen guys going off together and it hasn't interested me."

The level of homosexuality among the COs by any standard of measurement that I have is extremely small. There is very little evidence of latent homosexuality reported by the psychologist. When I asked each member of the group to estimate the number of prisoners involved in homosexuality, the estimates ran from 10 to 20 per cent. When I asked them to estimate the number among the COs, they usually replied that there was probably none. Some made the possible exception of one specific member. This was the psychotic inmate who was referred to previously.

Prison hardships of a physical nature tend to occur more in local jails and state prisons than in the federal penitentiaries, although in the receiving prisons of the federal system physical abuse is certainly not uncommon. In the case of some of the COs this was often related to their non-cooperativeness, but this also varied with the institutions. Non-cooperativeness was maintained longest where the conditions were harshest or where, for any reason, the war resister felt abused.

One nineteen-year-old prisoner was admitted under the Youth Corrections Act with what the prisoners call the "zip 6" sentence. It is an indeterminate sentence up to six years that allows for parole at any time. Many of the sentencing judges, because of the traditional respect for their wishes in non-CO cases, made assumptions about the length of imprisonment of COs and shared these assumptions with them. One of the tragic things, which will be discussed in detail later, has been the disparity between the judge's intentions and the actions of the Parole Board in terms of the COs. This could lead to trouble. For example:

"When I first got in they told me I could be out in sixty days. The judge told me that if I had a good record in the institution the Parole Board would approve an application at most in six months. I behaved, was cooperative; then, when six or eight months passed and I found out I wasn't going to get any parole, and simply because I was a CO, I refused to work, I refused to do anything they told me to do. I'd gotten sore. I refused to shave, to take a haircut. So then they put me in segregation. So when they did that I told them I wouldn't do anything, and for one year and one month I didn't.

"This was all at another prison. Segregation quarters were actually a torture chamber. I would be in a week and out a week. There are no beds. You have to sleep on the stone floor. There's no water to wash with. Once they left me there for an entire month. I thought I would go crazy then, but at least they'd left a mattress on the floor. I was nineteen then. Now I don't care about anything. I'm getting out in September and I'll be leaving immediately for Canada."

"If you're leaving for Canada now, why didn't you take that option before?" I asked.

"I was just too damn young. I thought that it would be a great loss to lose my country and my citizenship. I thought it would matter a great deal. Now I really want to get a new life for myself, a new home, and, above all, a new country."

Another prisoner's story: "When I was sentenced in court I didn't cooperate except to walk to the judge and go through the trial. But then, when they wanted to take me to prison, I told them I wasn't going to voluntarily place myself in prison by walking in. It was the traditional position of the non-violent resister. They had to carry me out of the courtroom, and for ten days I didn't walk, change my clothes, or anything. The marshal carried me from one county jail to another. When I got to the

Youth Reformatory they put me in the hole for three days. Then they kept me in a cell in isolation. I was there for about two and a half months. I was like an animal in a zoo. We were only allowed extremely limited reading and allowed to write two letters a week. But there was literally nothing else to do. No way to occupy the time. Some had been there for more than a year. They killed the time by throwing things at the window, screaming at each other. It was getting very bad. I was getting restless, worried, sitting in a cell for twenty-four hours a day. It reawakened tendencies in me for nihilism, cynicism—tendencies to withdraw and not be involved. The only contact with humankind was through the printed word, and that was terribly restricted. After two and a half months the education supervisor asked if I would accept a job and promised me that I would be given no tasks that would violate my conscience. I accepted."

Another experience: "The only part of imprisonment that was really hard was the first ten days in a county jail. There the officers beat me up really. They tried to get me to do what they wanted by keeping the windows open and taking away my clothes. They were enraged with me because I wouldn't cooperate and walk into the jail. They thought if they exposed me to violence, roughed me up, it would scare me into cooperating. They put wrist clamps and twisted them on my arms and dragged me around the floor, threw me against the wall a couple of times. Then they finally dragged me down to the isolation cell in the basement, which was far from the rest of the population. For three days they had me wearing only underwear. They left the windows open and the heat off. Then they began putting soap in my food. The third day one of the guards came in and said, 'You're nothing but a Communist and a Minuteman.' He was really confused, linking those two groups. He told me to get up or he'd 'kick the shit out of me.' He began kicking hard, and when I could catch my breath, I would talk, asking him if he always treated people he didn't like this way. I generally tried to reach him through verbal communication. He stopped because he was called by one of his colleagues who had been watching the door for him—technically he wasn't supposed to be in the cell unless he was with a senior official.

"With him, it was obviously a personal thing. At any rate, he never repeated the beatings. He continued to put the soap in my food occasionally. But after that, on occasion he even showed certain acts of kindness. One of the guards even gave me a blanket and one a copy of the Bible to read since I kept asking for something to pass the time with. During the week all I could find to keep me busy was to unshred the blanket and then to weave the threads back together again."

Jimmy, the young artist mentioned earlier, described this experience: "I sort of expected it would be like your life was ending. Like a form of death. I had no concept of living every day inside of a jail. I thought, 'Well, I'll just be dead for a while.'

"The most terrible place was the youth institution. They're all young kids and they're too young to be afraid, and they don't think of any future so they all act stupid. Two kids were standing in a corner while I was there. One said to the other, just like that, 'I bet you wouldn't dare stab the next person who comes along.' And the second said, 'I would so,' and that's exactly what happened.

"I think the hacks are worse there than almost anyplace else. One day a group of us lay down in front of the control center and sang 'We Shall Overcome.' We got sent down to the hole. We went on a hunger strike and refused to eat for five days. They decided they would try to freeze us out so they opened the windows—it was February. They took away the blankets and all we had left was the coveralls. We told them that if they were going to freeze us out they might as well do a good job, so we took off our coveralls and gave them to them. The hacks then got into a fury when we did this, and one of them came in and almost fractured my friend's skull. I refused to stand up for him. I was naked and lying on my stomach. He walked in and started cursing and saying, 'I'll make you crawl!' Then he started kicking. I don't know how long he kept it up. It seemed endless, but afterward it turned out that he hadn't caused any injury."

The violent aspects, as I have indicated, were not as common as had been anticipated, but the potential violence is always there. Its operation on the prisoner's mind can be demonstrated by a dream whose symbols are easily translatable.

"I'm in water and the water is perfectly calm. All of a sudden I see these sharks, and these things come around me but don't grab me. They simply circle round and round, and the circling creates a whirlpool and the suction of the water begins to pull me down. The sharks never touch me—there's no pain or anything. But all that motion around me is creating a suction around me, and I'm going down and I realize I'm drowning, and just before the water covers me I call out, 'Shark.' Not loud or screaming, just 'Shark,' like that's my last effort. I actually said it, and it woke me up."

Pete offers a good introduction to the balance between the expected physical difficulties and the actual psychological ones: "The one thing that scared the hell out of me was the homosexual bit. I'd been in the jail for a couple of days for a demonstration, and one of the guys there scared the shit out of me by the way he talked about it. But generally I found that if you don't lose your head, if you keep your cool, if you absolutely don't appear to be frightened but talk firmly and rationally and let them know they won't get away with it, it worked. The only serious incident, and even that was mild, was when a man whom I rejected said that he would get me if I didn't. I had a few sleepless nights, but then, peculiarly, three days later he apologized and went about his business.

"The irony is that what you fear most is often the opposite of what causes you trouble. I had a vision of bars everywhere, of being cooped up, of being isolated. Instead, here I am sleeping in a room with fifty-six other men, with all that noise and friction. And no privacy. The crowding of people together in one space creates a paranoia and tension. Then, despite this, there is still the feeling of isolation. With all the closeness there is no one with whom you feel close. And you feel separated from those on the outside. And this leads, too, to a kind of paranoia, because there's a readiness to feel that those on the outside are taking you for granted. Whenever I miss a letter I feel awful. I feel the relationships are deteriorating, that the people don't care any more.

"In the dorm the problems take a different form. The paranoia is something different. It becomes urgent that you have a certain amount of dignity and that you protect that—in all sorts of silly stuff you somehow or other see your dignity involved."

Here are some examples of what happens to these men in terms of the estrangement phenomena mentioned by Pete.

Dream: "There was a fire on the hill. All of the inmates began to fight it. Then there was this image of cordons of policemen coming in on horseback, beating the inmates back into the compound, brutally beating. It seemed ridiculous. I couldn't believe it. They were more concerned with getting us back in than they were in fighting the fire. They seemed oblivious of the enormous danger out there.

"My mother and father were in the dream too. I tried to tell them what was going on—that there were people in here getting beaten up, but, in addition, the fire outside had to be put out. They simply went to bed. They didn't pay any attention. Then another strange figure appeared. It was Don Knotts. He leaned up on his bed, yawned, and pulled the covers over his head." (Don Knotts is a popular TV performer whom this prisoner associates with the "typical American attitude.")

Another example combines the estrangement from the outside and a sense of more personal isolation: "I no longer am looking forward to visits. I feel I've settled into a rut here. In a strange way I feel I could serve a life sentence if I had to. Just going through the motions, unfeeling. My girl friend said in a letter she'd probably be coming next weekend. I wrote, I don't know if I meant it or not, that I wished she wouldn't come.

"I'm all settled down in my jello existence [this is not a statement of Paul's, but it's interesting that he chose the same symbol], and when visitors come they break things up. I feel I'm sort of surrounded with jello and nothing can really get to me much. It all gets absorbed in jello—whatever blows, whatever stimuli are not going to have an impact. It will simply be absorbed in the mass. I guess it's my way of looking at things, my device for survival."

And perhaps the ultimate solution has been expressed by one young prisoner who was beginning to become mildly depressed and withdrawn: "I had a strange dream last night. I was walking down the main street in a little village where my friend lives. It's a very pretty place and I've always enjoyed it there, and all of a sudden I realized that I had amnesia and that I couldn't remember the last eighteen months of my life. It was all a blank, and I thought what a beautiful thing to have happen. If you can only make yourself go to sleep and let the eighteen months [the length of his expected prison sentence] go by."

The paranoia mentioned by some of these men has been discussed so extensively in books about prison that I'm not sure it warrants belaboring here. It is a common feature, described as existing in every prisoner. It is described as affecting guards. A psychiatrist with whom I talked at Crestwood said that the administration was more paranoid than the prison population in general, and he included himself in the administration. And, indeed, there is no question that I began to find myself getting paranoid. The atmosphere generates it.

One of the particularly noticeable changes that prison works on these people is an increasing hostility to the environment.

Jeff had described himself as a "Jack Armstrong" in high school —middle class, middle America, varsity letters, president of the student council, the works. Enormously respected by his colleagues in prison and having a reputation for never losing his cool, he had, needless to say, come a long way from the "All-American Boy." I told him during the course of an hour that he was patronizing toward me and I wondered if he had been aware of it.

He responded, "No, I had not been aware of it and I'm sorry— I don't like condescension. It's certainly not intentional. I suppose if I am going to condescend it would be toward someone who is in a position of authority or power. There's a force operating in here of which I'm so aware but nonetheless have difficulty controlling. No matter how much I accept your credentials—and I do now—I hope you believe that—you're still an alien to my last two years of existence. The last two years of my life have to be stacked up against the three hours that we have been together. It's simply not enough for me to come out of my bag, as the saying goes in here. It's almost as if, by instinct, blinders come up a bit in the presence of a person from the outside, no matter how acceptable that individual might be.

"For instance, take what just happened before. I was discussing the camp manager. I told you how much contempt I had for him. I sensed that you had a certain sympathy with this weak, inept old man. I can understand that. As a psychoanalyst you can see even the oppressor as a victim of the system, but our reactions in that particular situation were absolutely the opposite." His voice began to rise. "I have no sympathy for him—he's useless. If he's incompetent he's a menace. He treats human beings as if they were shit. I understand your point of view, but you simply have to understand mine. Your point of view automatically identifies you as a stranger to this environment. That kind of attitude, that tolerance, could never exist if you were a prisoner here. And this is only one small example of hundreds that separate me, with my experiences here, from the people on the outside—and maybe always will."

One of the areas that generated the most anger, because it was fed by fear, were the conditions of physical neglect existing in the prison. It was at its most crucial when the prisoner felt sick.

"The things that bother me the most," one prisoner said, "is the general response from the guards indicating the way they consider us. I could tell you that the guards and administration hate us, but I don't think they do. I don't sense, except for some individuals with their own axes to grind, that they have any grudges against us. In fact, if there are any grudges it's the other way around—it's us against them.

"But they seem to have an attitude of indifference—as though we weren't human beings to them, just sort of cattle. You don't worry about a cow's feelings, his sore foot. The important thing is to keep the herd moving around with as little fuss as possible. Make sure there are no mavericks. Everything becomes a matter of logistics."

Another prisoner had been particularly adamant that he was neither going to apply for parole nor accept it—that when he was free he wanted to be totally free, not responsible to "them." I was amazed, therefore, to have him tell me on my last visit that he was going up for parole when he had in the past refused even to fill out the forms. I asked him why.

"The biggest thing is this back trouble I've had since I was a kid. It was more or less straightened out, and then about five weeks ago it hit me terribly hard. In my job I have to stand all day, and this day I could barely walk."

He then went on to describe the classic symptoms of a herniated vertebral disk, that is, the pain was felt primarily in the buttocks, severe radiation down one leg, marked scoliosis demonstrated by the traditional feeling of walking with one foot on a curb and one in the gutter.

"It was agonies. I crawled to the bed and lay down. The medical technician from the Wall was here that day and he looked at me and said, 'Well, you're obviously in pain so you can take the day off, but don't start making a habit of it.' Here I am, crawling back and forth, and this guy thinks I'm faking. So I went back to bed, and the next day I tried to get up but simply couldn't. I was still crawling. I got another day off grudgingly, not from him but the guy who is here, who acts like a nurse. By night it was slightly better but it scared me—really. Because if I'm here and something happens to my back, these people are going to dismiss it and say it's nothing. I don't want to have to leave here a cripple. That's too much of a price to pay.

"A guy in my bunk had a fractured knee. These people said it was nothing, just a strain. It didn't look like any strain to any of us, but he walked on it for ten days. Finally they decided maybe he should have an X-ray, and it turned out to be a fracture. They put his leg in a cast. Another guy was playing baseball and hurt his ankle, it swelled up, and again they said it was just a strain. Three days later he had to go to the hospital at the Wall, and it turned out to be a break in two bones—that happened just three months ago. And I'm sure you must have heard from everybody about the guy who died of a heart attack, just lying on the grass, waiting for some help to come, because they don't have anything here. No oxygen, nothing."

One of the most disturbing factors was the presence in the midst of the COs of an obviously disturbed, schizophrenic young man. It was amazing to see the consideration he was given by the group—the tendency to include him and treat him as an equal and to ignore his obvious disability. The outrage of having someone so obviously sick punished by imprisonment offended the morality of these young men. But, of course, by the usual prison standards his sickness made him an ideal prisoner for unpleasant work chores. He would never cause a fuss. So for two years he worked as a kitchen orderly.

A small sample of my interview with him may give the feeling of this man.

"What do you do here?" I asked.

"I scrape spots off the floor and clean around the base."

"How did you get the job?" I asked.

"When I came down here there was a definite attempt to give me the worst job possible. My first supervisor was very much opposed to draft dodgers. But then they found out that I like this job. We get along now even though he doesn't like me."

Throughout all of this, his hands were in a filthy ash tray constantly playing with the ashes.

"Why are you playing around with those ashes?" I asked.

"I have to," he said.

"What if I move the ash tray away?" I asked.

"Don't do that," he said. "I don't know. But don't do that."

I reassured him that I wouldn't. I asked him how long he had been in.

"Three years in November. It's possible I could get out then. I don't know what I'll do if I get out. I can't postpone it indefinitely."

"Do you want to postpone it?" I asked, incredulous.

"Not really I don't think, but it is a lot safer in here than out in the street."

"What happens in the street?"

"I'm not sure. I've been in quite a few communities and the same thing happens. Eventually I have to leave because of pressure. I'm too colorful, especially for small towns."

"Why don't you live in larger cities?" I asked.

"I hate large communities, I hate cities. I'm repulsed by them."

"What are you going to do if you don't like large communities and small ones don't like you?"

"I don't know. So far I've solved the problem by deliberately ruining my chances for parole. I mess it up with all sorts of funny statements."

"Now you're up again for parole—what do you hope will happen?"

"I wouldn't mind leaving, but I've adjusted well here. First it was very, very bad in prison. They did things at the Wall."

"What things?" I asked.

"I'd rather not go into it. But the caseworker wouldn't let me be transferred to the camp. He thought I would take off as soon as I got out here. But it was bad up there at the Wall. Finally the psychiatrist recommended it."

What in the world was a man like this doing in prison? How

was he even convicted? I checked his psychiatric report, which read:

> At the time of his initial commitment to this institution the man was found to be overtly psychotic and was admitted to the psychiatric ward. While there his psychosis was resolved and he was subsequently discharged. His diagnosis at that time was schizophrenic reaction of a chronic undifferentiated type. Since that time this man has been working in the hospital and has been free of any overt psychotic episodes and has been able to function. Observation on an outpatient basis and most recent evaluation suggest no contraindications to transfer to the work camp. Generally speaking he is a mild, passive individual who does not present any danger to himself or for others even when psychotic. In addition, it will be easy to identify the onset of a psychosis since he tends to become completely incoherent.

His psychotic condition was well known to all areas of the administration. During the course of his imprisonment he wrote a letter to the Surgeon General's office, which said:

> Dear Sir,
> Perhaps you can use me for experiments in which it is difficult to find volunteers, for I am willing to make my body available to you for anything, anytime.

He received a letter of reply from the Surgeon General's office "thanking him for his kind offer," etc.

He was refused parole at first because of the fact that he was schizophrenic, irrational, had no home or ties, and was a wanderer. A year later, in the inscrutable ways of the Parole Board, this schizophrenic, irrational, homeless wanderer was granted parole.

Psychiatrists in prison are generally young men avoiding *their* draft (the doctor draft) by serving two years in the prison. They are almost uniformly superior people—and not a part of the prison establishment. One psychiatrist, then at Oakdale and no favorite of the warden, examined in detail the records in this case and concluded that the man must have been overtly psychotic during his pre-induction period, including the time of his examination. The 1A classification had to be an error. The psychiatrist wrote the medical director of the Bureau of Prisons indicating this, but evidently no rectification was possible then.

The clearest manifestation of the rising hostility that the prisons generate in what has been essentially a non-hostile population is in the almost unanimous conversion from the concept of non-violence. I realize that the conversion from non-violence to violence is a process that is going on among the young in or out of the prisons, but the switch seems particularly dramatic with the imprisoned group because of the intensity of their original dedication to non-violent positions. All of the quotations that follow are from those who were committed to the concept of non-violence at one time or another.

From one: "I felt that all along violence was not an intelligent response to a problem. It was an insane or irrelevant kind of response. I still see it as insane or irrelevant, but perhaps the times call for irrationality. The longer I'm in here, the more doubt I have about the effectiveness of write-ins, literature, marches, or any of those things. Perhaps the only effective things in terms of the blacks, the poor whites, even the young—perhaps the only thing—is violence. Perhaps we have to let the people in power know that when you introduce a weapon of violence you invite its use by the other side.

"When I first came in here my ideas were quite different. Actually, before coming in I was prepared to do alternate service. It seemed an honorable position. Since then I've changed. They wouldn't let me then—they told me I was a liar. Now I'll have nothing to do with alternate service, nothing to do with the draft, nothing to do with the entire system. Before I believed in dialogue—that you could speak to the system and speak to the people, and it could make a difference. Since then I've learned they don't pay any attention to your arguments. If they try again to put me back in jail I'll simply leave the country. It doesn't mean that much to me anymore."

Another one said: "When ideals die there is nothing that can set in but disillusionment, despair. I've changed my attitude toward order, toward the state. I no longer have any respect for the state or the structural order of society. The way I see law and order being implemented, it is more destructive than creative. I think the balance is no longer there between the just and the unjust. We have passed over into the area of the unjust. I'm not sure how I'm going to deal with this when I get out. I know I've lost my respect for our society and I will be much less likely to cooperate with it in the future. I had never been drawn to the more destructive kinds of social action. But now I'm feeling helpless. I don't know where to turn. Emotionally I'm ready to begin destroying, even though intellectually I feel protest must be creative or it's useless."

And another: "I think we all made a serious mistake. I think our government is too insensitive to respond to anything except violence and destruction. I mean literally. I mean the kind of destruction—like lighting a fire. It's all valid when the government is oppressive and tyrannical. Intellectually I can now even justify murder and assassination. Yet when I think of members of the Establishment whom I have known, they're not the grotesque figures of power that they appear at other moments of my perception. They're people, and I say to myself, how can you justify this action when dealing with a human being or, indeed, with the structure itself? But then how else do you deal with a structure that has no conscience, that is beyond the normal control of men? How do you deal with these men who are imprisoned by that structure? I'm worn out with dialogue and with trying to talk with people who lie to you because they lie to themselves."

And from a black who had been deeply religious at one time: "This business of religion in an organized sense is out to lunch. It's used *on* you, not *for* you. It's a psychological mechanism to keep you cool, to keep you in bounds as far as any action is concerned. It says, 'Everything will be all right. Have Faith, go along, just wait.' Personally I can't wait any longer. It's got to be now. My brothers, my sisters, my mother, my father, my great-grandfather, my ancestors all the way back—did all the waiting for me. They all worked in the system. I don't believe now that the powers that be are going to give anything up, and if they do, and when they do, you just know it won't be worth a damn to anybody."

From another black: "As far as violence is concerned, at one time I didn't buy it. But I'm beginning to see the advantages of what the brothers mean when they talk about going out and taking off a cop. Don't underestimate those advantages. It shows the powers that be that they have to tread a little more carefully on you or you're going to destroy those things they hold so dearly. You have to be careful not to do it on a large scale or in riots, because there you leave yourself open for direct backlash. Then they have a built-in excuse to retaliate with armored cars and all that. I do believe there's a place for a small group of terrorists who should take care of these special factors. We shouldn't expose our women and children to hoses and dogs. Particularly now, we have to be careful. It's getting down to the wall."

And finally a statement from a former Catholic seminarian: "When I came in here I knew precisely where I stood. I would have called myself a Christian pacifist. Now all that has changed."

"What has changed," I asked, "the Christian or the pacifist?"

"Both, I'm afraid. The pacifist as an act of reason, the Christian as an act of despair."

In every direction, therefore, what one sees as the result of imprisonment is a hardening of position, an increasing hostility toward the environment, combined, unfortunately, with an increasing distrust of one's self. This latter may be the most destructive impact of imprisonment. Contributing in no small measure to their self-doubts are both their inability to work in the prison environment and the low value set on work in that environment.

"I think the place is finally getting to me here. There's an attitude in prison which I just call 'blah,' a who-cares-about-anything attitude. I find myself getting that way now. The basic principle is that if it doesn't work the first time, don't try again, give up. If a movie flickers, you just accept it and everyone sits watching the flicker. If it doesn't work completely, you accept that. You teach a class without a book you need. A thing is broken, that's all right too. Things are dirty, incomplete, you accept it—even when they're readily rectifiable. Because that's the way things are—that's prison life. You get so, that the inactivity and the uselessness of your existence makes you turn things off. The loudspeaker is blaring constantly but you just turn it off in your mind. You get very good at it. You really don't hear it at all, and the amazing thing is that nothing happens if you don't hear it. They'll call you and call you, and if you don't hear your name it doesn't seem to make any difference at all. You know whatever it is that they want doesn't matter anyhow."

Another: "My boss in the industry told me that in filling out a report for the Parole Board he put down that my attitude is improving. 'Improving?' I said. 'What was wrong with it to begin with?' It turns out that what he meant was that in the past I had been a fast worker. I was always a hard worker—I enjoy the feeling of putting out a great deal. Then when I'd finish the work I'd have nothing to do, so I'd ask him for more work. It seemed all day long, according to him, I was running to him, nagging him for things to do. I eventually gave up on it. Now I just float through the time. I stall. I slow myself down. So I don't run out of work, and of course I don't 'bother' him for more. Therefore he feels my attitude has improved. He said, 'You're great now. You don't bother me all the time the way you used to.'"

Self-doubts are reflected in diminished self-confidence: "I had a dream last night. I was walking in the woods around the camp.

I came to a stream. There was a bridge over the stream which was broken as I came to it. I tried to reset the bridge by putting the wood back together but it didn't work. Then I waded through the stream and made it without difficulty to the other side. But then again I found myself back on the original side, looking again at the stream. This time it was very slushy, as though it were a thick, gelatinous material [third reference from third man to this mushy quality], and I was afraid to walk on it or through it because I didn't know what was underneath the surface. I was afraid even though I had just crossed the same damn stream. I thought the surface might break and I'd fall through. I should have remembered that I'd just accomplished this thing, that if I did it once before I certainly could do it again. If I had only remembered that, I wouldn't have been frightened, because the stream was not deep enough to worry about, but I simply couldn't remember the fact that I'd done it in the past."

His associations, as might be expected, led to the fact that he is a little less willing to take chances than he was before he came into prison. He feels he is losing his courage and capacity for action.

He continued his associations: "This whole business of proving yourself—proving your manhood, I suppose you'd say. When I was a kid I wanted to be a part of the group and be recognized, so I had to do well at sports. But I wasn't all that good, and I didn't resolve this business of proving myself through grammar school and high school. I felt I couldn't conform to the way that would have gained me recognition and make me stand out.

"Then when I got to college I realized that there were things I was interested in—books, thinking, feeling—and these started to grow and the problem of identity began to focus in this area. 'Could I be a writer?' became the means of proving myself. Even my early political actions seemed to be ones where social and political recognition—and recognition from my parents—were important.

"Then all the need for recognition began to disappear. I was beginning to reject all of the standard models. I remember feeling that it's absurd, it's unnecessary—it's worse than that. It is only when I unconsciously follow the very models I have rejected that I get caught up in competition, proving, and success.

"I began to feel like a man, I started getting confidence in myself as a writer, and I simply stopped thinking in terms of proving myself. But I can't write here in jail, and the self-doubts are rising. I don't understand that at all. I thought it would be an enormous comfort for me—my way of handling time."

The self-doubt expresses itself also in terms of acceptance and friendship: "I'm a little depressed. Things have been cold between Jimmy and me. You know, he's my closest friend here. I feel it's really my fault. I haven't acted right with him. We haven't even spoken too much for the last few months. Jimmy has had short-time blues too. He's been acting rather independent and domineering. I usually just say, 'Fuck it,' and walk off. But then I start making an asshole out of myself."

"In what way?" I asked.

"Oh, just bullshitting, I guess. It's a bad habit I used to have but I thought I had it licked. I can't relate on a serious level without attempting too much to impress. I realize that with Jimmy—a lot of times I'll make sour remarks about others and Jimmy doesn't approve of this. And then I tend to get sarcastic and argumentative when there's no reason for it—over petty stuff. I know what I'm doing is trying to establish my respectability and authority when I really don't have any. Nobody does in prison.

"I'm more on guard in here. I won't allow myself to expose anger—I just remember when someone offends me. Then I will later attack him in a subtle way without letting him know I've been angry. When you get angry you expose what you feel, and in doing that you expose your vulnerable spot."

"I'm not sure I understand why you're so upset with Jimmy now," I said.

"I've been having some doubts about myself and him. I know I'm very fond of him. One of these doubts is that Jimmy's just playing like we're friends simply because we're tossed in a situation where we have to depend on each other till we get free. But I like Jimmy as a person. I like him to the extent that I would want it to carry over into the street. He says the same things about me, but whether that will in fact happen when he hits his people I'm not sure. And I'm a mixture on the outside. I don't know whether Jimmy would find me that acceptable. I'm a very complex mixture of progressivism and reaction."

"What's reactionary about you?" I asked.

"Oh, I'm old-fashioned in the sense that I'm conventional. Jimmy thinks that such social customs as a shirt and tie are ridiculous. I'm a confirmed suit-and-tie man. I'm only hip in terms of attitudes, political and others."

The self-doubts are seen in terms of the decision to go to jail: "I'm getting just a wee bit dubious as to whether I selected the best way of doing things. Because all it means is that all the talent you have is being locked up. If I were advising someone right now, I would still tell them not to leave the country, that's no answer, but at the same time I would tell them to avoid this whole court process because not until the other political structures have been broken down is the court going to be the answer. Only now do I realize how much the courts are an instrument of power politics. I think we forgot that.

"That doesn't mean I think we should fake out. We should make our resistance known and open. But we should actually go into the Army, step over that line, while at the same time making sure that our position is clear. We'd get much more into the public eye if we did that, but, more important, what good are we doing in here? Who are we convincing? Ourselves? It's in the Army that we should be working. That's where the action really is. We should be getting to the brothers in the Army. That's why many of the blacks are asking for transfers now into the Army. If you state your beliefs and the draft board refuses to believe you,

then it's up to the Army—if they want to take a chance on accepting you with those beliefs they won't be able to say that they
weren't forewarned. I think actually the Army would be afraid to
take too many of us. There's too much risk. They don't want to
put you in a hot spot where at any moment you could open your
mouth and bring everything down on them. At least that way we
would be attacking the military complex instead of everyone
being so damned isolated.

"This all has to be thought out on a larger scale, and we're
sorely lacking in leaders. When I first came here I thought we
blacks were the most disorganized group, but now I've come to
see that this peace thing is really the most. Everyone in the peace
thing seems to be doing his own private thing—every cause
needs some martyrs—but if we're all martyrs there's no cause."

Or the self-doubts can be seen in the searching for simpler solutions to life, as in the case of a brilliant National Scholar from
Yale. Raised in a Unitarian family, he had all his life considered
himself an atheist. He had been separated from contact with all
of the COs during the largest part of his internment. During this
period he had associated exclusively with Jehovah's Witnesses
and had finally been converted.

"Do you think the conversion is a lasting one?" I asked.

"There's no doubt in my mind at all. I'm already changing my
life plans. I'll be out soon and I never plan to go back to Yale.
The education there seems irrelevant to the world at large. Once
I had a tendency to be involved in academic activities, but since
I've left college, and since talking to the Witnesses, I see that
there's more to the world than that. I went through the cata-
logues recently and there didn't seem to be anything that I'd
want to spend my life doing. I find that I prefer to just live out in
the country—do some kind of manual labor and be out in nature
rather than sit in an office in the city reading a book, or even
writing a book."

Perhaps the greatest area in which self-doubts are demonstrated is in the re-entry anxiety—the short-time blues that each

and every one goes through just prior to his discharge. One of the most poignant expressions of it was in the following long dream. The dreamer, Clifford, was an engineer, which explains the importance of the physical concepts of tension and the play on the double meaning of the word.

"I dreamed that I was in a hotel, in an upper story—somewhere around the thirty-first floor. But the hotel was a prison and I was being held prisoner. The peculiar part was that I had a cable attached around my waist. It ran to the doorway, out the corridor, and disappeared around a corner. The door wasn't locked—the understanding was that I was supposed to stay in the room. The guards would come in to bring me my meals and make periodic check-ups to make sure I was there. [Conditions essentially as existed in the work camp at Oakdale.] There were no restrictions on my activity except for the fact that I knew the guard was always there somewhere—plus the fact that I couldn't see out.

"I lived with this for a while but it was extremely difficult, because whatever you wanted to do had always to be done against the resistance of this cable. There was always just enough tension on it to make any activity uncomfortable. Even when you were sitting you could feel it pulling—even when you were lying in bed you couldn't sleep well because of the pull at you. There was a window in the room but you were tethered so that you couldn't quite reach it to see out. I finally got to a point where I couldn't stand it. I had to find out what the cable was, so I waited until the guard left, opened the door, and walked down the hallway.

"It was an average hotel hallway, and the cable was leading me down to another doorway at the other end of the hall. So I went there and noticed that the pull on the cable was getting stronger. The tension was mounting. When I got to the doorway it opened on one of those typical stairwells they have in hotels. You know, the kind you go down a few stairs and then there's a landing, a turn, and a few more stairs.

"I continued walking down the stairs, and because of the decrease of friction due to the shortening of the cable, the tension became ever stronger as I kept going down and down. I then figured I was coming down to the twenty-sixth floor since I started from the thirty-first and subtracted five." (While the figures are confusing, they all have relevance in multiple ways. He was thirty-one when he was admitted to prison, and he has a five-year sentence. That he sees it as a subtraction rather than an addition may possibly be related to the way he views the prison years. In addition, it of course relates to the five-year struggle in the courts before admission, which started when he was twenty-six. And finally, the passage of time is described in prison language as going downhill.)

"When I hit that fifth floor down, instead of there being a little flight of stairs there was a long flight, and instead of the cable running off to one corner like it had, it went straight down, and the last step was not like the rest. It was one of those orange I-beams. By this time the tension was getting real strong. I said to myself, 'You must be coming to some place where they're pulling this cable in.'

"I finally approached the bottom step. Just as I got there, with horror I realized what was going on—I never saw it but I figured it out in my dream. The cable was not attached to a winch—it was merely hanging out over the side of the hotel. And an enormous weight was hanging from it. Had I taken that last step to the edge I would have been pulled over by the strength of that loose hanging weight.

"Of course, when the cable was stretched out, winding up the stairs made enough friction so the tension wasn't so great in the room, but the further down the line I came the more the tension of the weight I had on me. I began to get panicky. I began to get worried about the guard because it was taking me longer than I had thought. He'd find out that I was not in my room, and I seemed to have some crazy idea that he'd shoot me if he found me out, so I was worried about both.

"I was trapped. I tried to fight against the pull, to get back up the stairs to my room. But when I was at the point of being nearer the orange I-beam I wanted desperately to look over and see but I knew that if I looked over that would be it—it would just pull me down. So I started instead to drag my way back upstairs. I could just barely make my way. Of course, trying to go up wore me out a lot more than coming down. All that night it seemed I spent going back up and being pulled down, going up and pulled down. It was one of those dreams where when I suddenly woke up I was still going up and down and sweating profusely."

This, then, is what prisons seem to be doing to the imprisoned war resisters (and probably all prisoners). I recalled what Robby, my wise drummer friend, had once said: "The whole rehabilitation bit is a joke. They claim they rehabilitate you, so I looked the word up in the dictionary and it means 'return to your former self.' And it's just what we're going to return to, baby. And that's just what the rest of the convicts return to."

In the case of the war resisters, I can only hope that it is so.

13 ⤎

With Liberty and Justice for All

When I originally set out on the research from which this book is drawn my goals seemed simple. I wanted to find out who the war resisters were, why they went to prison, and what happened to them in prison. As I began to answer my original questions I found that, in answering them, I was raising more important, more disquieting questions that could not be answered in the course of this research—questions of a legal and moral nature.

The prisons and the prison system were to be merely a means —a vehicle—for exploring the war resister and the concept of resistance. Instead, some of the most provocative information has been that which the prisoners reveal about the prison. For the war resister, special though he may be, is still a prisoner and as such a representative of that broader population. He shares a common fate with this general group whose importance far outweighs that of the resisters, because it is a larger population and a permanent one. The draft laws will be changed, and this war, too, will pass away. But there is no anticipation of a crimeless society in any foreseeable future.

The questions that are raised, both moral and legal, are not about the draft laws, the draft resister, or the war, *per se*, but in the way these epitomize the general problem of administering the processes of justice in our country. The problem seems to divide itself into three broad areas, prior to prison, the period of imprisonment, and release from prison.

PRIOR TO PRISON

Through the course of this book there has been much discussion by the prisoners of the legality of the draft law, and by myself of the equity of the draft law. Both those questions have validity. But even granting legality and equity, the questions of justice would not be resolved.

Despite the small sampling here, it is apparent that each draft board interprets the law with a kind of freedom and subjectivity that are somewhat frightening. There is no question that a few of the men imprisoned as Selective Service violators would never have been, had they been considered by a draft board other than the one that classified them. Unfortunately the naïveté or the sophistication of the prisoner is generally compounded by the same qualities in the draft board in his area.

It is, of course, just one more dimension of the tired, but so troubling, problem of inequities in the law between the rich and the poor, between the uneducated and the educated. And, once again, the chance of birth, of geographical location, of background, will in great part determine whether a man is to be classified a felon or not—whether he will spend three to five years of his life in jail or not. In its interpretation of the law, in its use of a broad or narrow standard in defining a conscientious objector, the draft board makes its bias felt.

The draft board will further express its bias in terms of the credibility it will grant an individual claiming to be a conscientious objector, independent of how this is defined. This credibility can be influenced in great part by an individual's ability to understand the law well enough to present an intelligent case, or by his capacity (financial and otherwise) to hire a lawyer competent to marshal his evidence, or by his personality. An individual's "likableness," which after all has nothing to do with culpability, has an enormous influence on his credibility, as many psychological researches have testified.

In one area, rich and poor, educated and ignorant, share equally the inequity of the law. No one may be represented by counsel in arguing his case before the draft board. This is only one of that excessively large list of quasi-judicial procedures (which may indeed be a matter of life and death) where an individual is deprived of a basic right guaranteed in the more formal (but often less important) judicial hearings.

Another factor is the specific composition of the community, in terms of the nature of the population and the relative sufficiency of men to fulfill the draft quota. This will affect the leniency and readiness of the draft board to allow legal alternatives to service. It is amazing to see the diversity among draft boards in terms of what they are prepared to define as essential service to the country.

I am well aware that many of the questions raised about draft board hearings can equally be raised about jury trial and trial before a judge in other kinds of violations of the law. And precisely because I am aware, I am concerned.

After the draft board has decided that an individual is in violation of the law, chance still continues to operate in determining his fate, for whether you have violated the law has no importance independent of the government's attitude about the law. What is of real importance is the readiness of the government to prosecute such violation. Some laws are encouraged to be broken because they are obsolete. Some laws are allowed to be broken because they are unenforceable. And some laws are allowed, by some prosecutors only, to be broken because the enforcement of them would be unpopular or inconvenient.

In general, there are national policies that influence all who deal in this area. There are times of toughening and of easing up, times when prosecutions are encouraged and other times when they are discouraged. Criminal cases filed in the courts vary markedly from one year to the next. Often this is due to the number of violations occurring in that year. But when the variations are extreme it can only indicate a matter of policy of prosecution, in addition to incidence of violations. In 1968 prosecutions for violations of the Civil Rights Act declined 36 per cent to a four-year low of 74 (1203 in 1965). Prosecutions for violations of the Selective Service Act increased 37 per cent in 1968 to 1876 (up from 380 in 1965, and the largest figure since World War II). It is ironic that these two areas, so closely associated, particularly in the minds of the young, represent the two greatest statistical swings in the course of a few years.

Beyond national policy there is marked individual variation. An individual's fate may depend upon a jurisdictional matter—the identity of the United States Attorney in his particular district.

I quote in part from an article in the January 17, 1969, *New York Times*:

> The New York Civil Liberties Union charged yesterday that the United States Attorney's Office in Manhattan has displayed unparalleled harshness and vindictiveness in its prosecution of alleged violators of the draft law.
>
> In a scathing attack following the two-year sentence given to a divinity student in Federal Court yesterday, Aryeh Neier, Executive Director of the Civil Liberties Union, told a news conference that federal prosecutors were "apparently unable to distinguish crimes of violence with acts of conscience."
>
> Mr. Neier said further that the "vindictiveness" was apparently not dictated by the Justice Department since "other United States Attorneys' Offices around the nation do not handle these cases in the same way."

This particular seminarian had been convicted of failure to report for a physical examination, failure to fill out a Selective

Service questionnaire, failure to possess a draft card, and failure to submit to induction. Added to this were two separate charges, each for the destruction of a draft card. The article continued:

> "This piling on of charges can only be likened to a vendetta," Mr. Neier said. "The United States Attorney's Office has chosen to prosecute for each and every violation of the Selective Service regulations as though it were a separate crime."
>
> Other practices called "unparalleled" by the Civil Liberties Union included these: "The immediate arrest of the young men who report for induction but refuse to take the symbolic step forward. A general practice of demanding bail in draft cases. The interrogation of young men in Selective Service cases about their political associations."

From conversations I had with a number of judges I gathered that the judiciary was aware that over a period of years Selective Service Act violators were rarely prosecuted in certain districts, whereas during that same period they were prosecuted with zeal in others. In fiscal year 1968, the variations within one state dramatize the difference: in Southern California there were only 12 defendants as distinguished from 155 in central California.

The readiness to prosecute is only the first step. Next is the readiness of a judge or jury to find guilt, and this of course has its unavoidable variability. In the First Circuit, only 16 out of 39 were convicted—60 per cent being dismissed or acquitted; in the Fifth Circuit, 105 out of 132 were convicted—only 20 per cent being dismissed or acquitted.

It is with the establishment of guilt or innocence that most of us stop thinking about the processes of justice, but the establishment of guilt or innocence is really almost incidental unless it is considered with what we do to the guilty, which cannot be separated from the process of sentencing. Unlike the individual emotion of guilt, the official pronouncement of guilt is not disturbing to an individual if no expiation is required for it.

I quote from the introduction to a pamphlet called *Standards*

Relating to Appellate Review of Sentences—a report of an advisory committee of the American Bar Association project on minimum standards for criminal justice:

> Among the ironies of the law, there are many surrounding the manner in which sentences are imposed in the majority of our jurisdictions. One of the most striking involves the methods for determining guilt and the methods for determining sentences. The guilt-determination process is hedged in with many rules of evidence, with many tight procedural rules, and, most importantly for present purposes, with the carefully structured system of appellate review designed to find out the slightest error. Yet in the vast majority of criminal convictions in this country—90 per cent in some jurisdictions; 70 per cent in others—the issue of guilt is not disputed.
>
> What is disputed and, in many more than the guilty-plea cases alone, what is the only real issue at stake, is the question of the appropriate punishment. But by comparison to the care with which the less-frequent problem of guilt is resolved, the protections in most jurisdictions surrounding the determination of sentence are indeed miniscule. As has been observed,* "the whole intricate network of protection and safeguards which were [the defendant's at the trial] . . . vanishes and gives way to the widest latitude of judicial discretion . . . nine out of ten plead guilty without trial. For them the punishment is the only issue, and yet we repose in a single judge the sole possibility for his vital function."
>
> It is not an overstatement to say of these jurisdictions that in no other area of our law does one man exercise such unrestricted power. No other country in the free world permits this condition to exist.

This appalling defect in our judicial process, the lack of a right to appeal sentences, becomes particularly urgent when one is aware of the fact that the federal judiciary has become progressively harsher in the sentencing process. The average sen-

* Remarks of Judge Simon E. Soboloff.

tence length for all court commitments to federal prisons has gone up for the eleventh straight year so that now the average sentence is forty-five months as compared with twenty-eight months in 1957.

A distinguished legal scholar who reviewed this chapter for me was so astounded by this figure that he was sure it must have been a recording error. It was not. Its source is the *Statistical Report of the Bureau of Prisons. Fiscal Years, 1967 and 1968,* page 10, Chart 5.

Psychiatrists know that in the review of any population above a certain minimum, a number of psychotics will be encountered —only the incidence varies. The population of judges in this country is well above that minimum, so that one can say, with complete assurance, that somewhere, in some city, state, or federal court, there are psychotic individuals sitting in judgment on their fellow men. The only thing that is debatable is the incidence. No laws concerning psychological or physical incompetence will mitigate this problem, for anyone who has had dealings with the idea of psychological incompetence knows how difficult it is to prove. Most school boards, for example, rather than bring incompetence proceedings against senile teachers, will prefer to retire them with full pay or to put them in nonvulnerable positions. I do not know if that power or that capacity is available at the level of a judge. But the problem of mental incompetence, while dramatic, is hopefully a small problem—a minority issue. When we enter into the area of personal value judgment and bias, however, we are involving the majority.

The biological and social sciences have avoided the consideration of ethics and values like some vestigial, medieval plague. When I say "avoid" I mean only that they have refused to admit the influence of their morality on their judgment. They refuse to recognize it while continuing to utilize it.

In my field one constantly hears that psychiatrists and psychoanalysts are not concerned with value judgments. This is patent nonsense. Every day, in every hour, with every patient, in each interpretation—by defining an act as healthy or sick, as desirable or undesirable, as to be retained or abandoned—they are exercising their personal value judgments. Unwillingness to admit this merely means that they exercise it on an unconscious level rather than a conscious level. The problems have become so urgent that at last a group of biologists, psychiatrists, ethicists, demographers, and others are establishing a center for the study of ethics and values in the sciences of man. This is the new Institute of Society, Ethics, and the Life Sciences.

Hopefully a judge will reflect in his values those of the society he represents. Certainly, it would be expected that where his values differ from those defined by law he would, as a judge, serve the interests of the law over his personal interests—although the history of the civil rights movement demonstrates there is no guarantee of this.

At any rate, he is expected to reflect the defined (whether objectively "true" or "right" is unimportant) values of his society. He is not, however, expected to reflect the prejudice and bias of that society. These are the emotional components of functioning, which fair men may recognize within themselves, but which, out of fairness, they intellectually reject—such rejection being reinforced by law. A judge, like all of us, is expected to act above and beyond his prejudices, and while I respect the attempts of judges to overcome their bias, the expectation can, alas, be realized no more fully by them than by any other group. *And there is no review of sentence.*

The cruelty of chance (in this case, geography) can create inequities that should be unthinkable in a reasonable society. In Oregon, of thirty-three *convicted* Selective Service violators, eighteen were put on probation. In Southern Texas, of sixteen violators, *none* was put on probation. In Oregon, not one single man was given a sentence of over three years. In Southern Texas, fifteen out of sixteen were given over three-year sentences (fourteen were given the five-year maximum allowable by law). In southern Mississippi every defendant (six) was convicted and every one given the maximum sentence. Such examples are end-less.

Statistically, the average black man gets a larger sentence than the average white man, and the average political war resister is given an inordinately longer sentence than the Jehovah's Witness, even though the same violation of the law has been committed. This in a country that claims scrupulously to exclude religious and racial considerations from the processes of government and the areas of public domain! An examination of the records shows that this disparity of sentencing is maintained even when one eliminates all possible other extenuating conditions, that is, previous offenses, stability of background, history of other anti-social behavior. When all of these are stripped away, there still remains a naked and ugly disparity between the treatment of the "religious" and non-religious objector, between the treatment of the black and the white.

The absence of any mechanism for review of sentence has disturbed legal scholars for years, and much has been written of interest in this area. The American Bar Association, certainly no radical organization, has been urging the introduction of legislation that would permit such a review. Public ignorance and public apathy have been the enemies since only an aroused public can arouse the legislature. There are some encouraging signs that we may be ready at last to correct at least this one deficiency in our system of justice. If so, it will be, in no small part, due to the efforts and dedication of such senators as Joseph Tydings of Maryland, who has consistently championed the cause of intelligent judicial reform.

IN PRISON

What is a prison all about anyway? What is its purpose? Who needs it? There is not a person I met in Washington in the upper echelons of our prison system who felt that the system was anything but a total and abysmal flop. This is the judgment, mind you, of an intelligent and concerned group (and I was enormously impressed by both attributes in the administration in Washington) made up of people who have devoted the major part of their adult professional lives to this system.

Prison, today, with all of its injustices, is still a more humane environment than the prison of the past. We have improved the facilities, decreased the brutality (at least on the federal level), modernized the methods, elevated the goals—and improved the effectiveness not one measurable whit in terms of rehabilitation of men or deterrents to crime. This is not my judgment alone—this is the judgment of the professionals involved. Over and over again, I have heard with a kind of despair that if the whole system could be scrapped and started from scratch, any old scratch, you could not end up with a worse system in terms of results—maybe not better, but not worse.

And whatever the goal of the Director of the Bureau of Prisons and his staff, it has nothing to do with reality, for reality abides at the local level. And there you are in the province of the director of the prison, and his goals are something else again.

As I have indicated, there is a great deal of autonomy officially granted the warden of a prison. Beyond that which is officially granted, there is a great deal of unofficial license, since there is no way of knowing precisely what goes on. The only effective way of judging an installation such as a prison is to be involved with it on a day-to-day basis or to hire a research organization independent of the government to evaluate it on a day-to-day basis. The typical judgment, however, is on the basis of spot visits and records. The dependence on records is enormous, as it is in any large administration. If I am aware of this, you may rest assured that the warden is too, for his future career depends on it. Records, therefore, are not designed as historic, or even research, documents, but, like annual reports, they are designed to snow the stockholders.

The "action" described in Chapter 9 did not even warrant an official report until, weeks after the fact, an inquiry by a senator (always a vital matter in Washington) necessitated the production of some official statement. This, despite the fact that everyone in the prison system is sensitive to the publicity potential in this group! One can imagine what must remain unreported when it involves the blacks, the poor, the disenfranchised—the unnewsworthy.

I have commented before on the similarity between the prison system and the military (perhaps because both are presumed to involve national security). This correspondence seems to extend into record-keeping also—for the prisons seem dominated by the rule that I called "negative perfection" when I encountered it in the Navy.

In those days all officers were given efficiency reports at regular intervals. When the time came for your efficiency report, your senior officer looked at your record, and if there were no black marks against it you were automatically given a 4.0—this was the perfect score. It is important to understand, therefore, that perfection was defined in terms of the absence of comment. In other words, if you did nothing to get into trouble you were perfect. On the other hand, nothing you could do of a positive nature could increase this, since there is no higher grade than 4.0. The only thing that any mark on your record, meritorious or deleterious, could do was cause trouble, depreciate you. Perfection was represented by the blank report. There is a tendency to operate the prison, at the local level, in the same manner.

The central group in Washington that determines the policy of the prisons, if it is judged at all, is judged by its effectiveness on a national level in achieving its stated goals of rehabilitation and deterrence of crime. No one can statistically judge a warden this way in his isolated parish. Therefore these are not his goals. His goal is to have a good—that is, clean—record, to have no trouble. It matters very little what the goal any central administration has if it is implemented by a group of different men with different goals.

Previously I have described the prisons as a sociological

330/ IN THE SERVICE OF THEIR COUNTRY

community in which a large number of men must be controlled by a small number—the large number having only the potential power of their number. If ever unified, they could threaten the authority of the minority. For purposes of security it is essential that the population remain divided. To that end it is necessary that a sense of community be discouraged, that communication among prisoners be made difficult; that leaders, natural or potential, be isolated; that passivity be encouraged and assertiveness, which is too close to aggressiveness, be restricted even if it might be applied to positive ends; that self-confidence be eroded and self-doubts be engendered; that prejudices and biases which divide the community be encouraged or at least tolerated; that sources that feed pride be restricted, because pride is potential power; that lethargy be rewarded; that individuality be obliterated; that the spirit of man be broken in the service of obedience.

All of these make sense, are psychologically sound, if the purpose is to keep a large group of men under the control of a small group of men. The fact that most of this is antithetical to the concept of building strength of character or rehabilitation, which is the purported goal of imprisonment, is aside from the point, because the purported goal is not the real goal. A warden's job is not the rehabilitation of prisoners: it is the maintenance of order. The entire prison system is built from the bottom on the concept of not making waves. Few wardens will risk that. Even the two wardens with whom I dealt, as different as they were, showed this in common, their dedication to the principle of homeostasis. If prisons are ever to improve, the power of the warden will have to be channeled more effectively to the higher purposes of the Bureau of Prisons.

I have mentioned the *de facto* discrimination against Selective Service violators because of the fact that prisons are not designed for men like them and therefore they are not afforded the opportunities—those limited opportunities—that other prisoners are offered. However, in addition to the *de facto* discrimination there is actual discrimination. They are not permitted involvement in work-release programs. They are not given jobs commensurate with their abilities even when these are available. Their mail is generally more heavily censored. And, most important, they are excluded from the normal standards for parole consideration.

Generally, the most disturbing conditions are not those specially directed at the war resisters, but those they share in common with all the prisoners. Again, to take one example, there is little one can do about the personal prejudices of any one individual, but when prejudice becomes institutionalized it would seem that it could be controlled. Constantly, throughout the prison records, there is evidence of the prejudice against the non-religious—the pressure placed on the prisoner to attend religious services. At Crestwood every classification study I went through had the same routine recommendation: "Encourage to attend religious services." Presumably the classification study produces an individually tailored program, designed, after the extensive study of the A and O period, to fit each prisoner's rehabilitation needs. It is conceivable to me that religion can be a force in the resocialization of an occasional person. When it is prescribed for all, it indicates more about the preconceptions of the institution than the needs of the individual. Throughout the period of his imprisonment there will be a judgment bias expressed which equates a prisoner's failure to attend religious services with defiance of authority or resistance to socialization. The culmination of all of this occurs when the crucial parole report lists under "Liabilities" failure to be a member of an organized religious group or failure to attend religious services.

The Parole Board after all, despite its incredible lack of supervision or review, is still an institution of the same government whose Supreme Court has deemed even opening prayers in schools a violation of its Constitution. Any agency concerned with First Amendment guarantees need only examine prison files to have abundant evidence of the coercive imposition of religious instruction in prison—coercive in the sense that religious involvement is considered a testament to the adaptability and cooperativeness of the individual.

Ironically, the enthusiasm for religion does not seem to extend to the reaches of Islam—yet, of all the religious groups, the Black Muslims have most effectively demonstrated their capacity to renew and redeem in a prison setting.

Finally, I must admit to a certain uneasiness about another proud prison institution—the prison industries. There is something morally offensive about bribing men, with extra good time, to work in industry; and then exploiting this labor by paying for it at the rate of seventeen to twenty-five cents per hour, thereby reducing the dignity of the work; and thus producing a profit of $20,000,000, which is in great part returned to the federal treasury rather than being used for the improvement of the penitentiaries.

I would suspect this is the most profitable enterprise of the United States Government, and I do not like the fact that men are rewarded with critical days off their sentence for turning a profit for the government.

Dissatisfaction with the results of imprisonment is the universal feeling carried away by all researchers entering this field —only the priority of disillusionment varies. Yet with all of this we seem to be not at all disenchanted. We remain a prison-happy community. We continue to send greater numbers of our citizens to prison than other equivalent countries. England has 65 prisoners per 100,000. The United States has 178 prisoners per 100,000 population.

RELEASE FROM PRISON

A man is released from prison when he has served the time prescribed by sentence minus the number of good days he has earned (as described previously), or he may be released earlier on recommendation of the Federal Parole Board. This agency, which wields as much power as the entire federal judiciary in terms of determining punishment, since it is entitled in most cases to reduce the judge's sentence by two-thirds, is one of the least understood agencies of the United States Government. My own ignorance in any particular area no longer surprises me; but, while I was reassured on a personal level, I was appalled by the implications of the general ignorance I discovered in all of my friends from diverse professions—psychiatrists, lawyers, historians, sociologists, and teachers.

In 1930 a central parole board located in Washington was created by Congress. At that time it was part of the Bureau of Prisons. In 1945 the Parole Board was ordered to report directly to the Attorney General for administrative purposes, thus taking it out of the Bureau of Prisons. The board is both a policymaking and an administrative body. It consists of eight full-time members appointed by the President, by and with the advice and consent of the Senate, for six-year overlapping terms. The board serves essentially a non-partisan function, but as is the case with any presidential appointments, political factors are always a consideration. This can be seen in tracing the reappointment patterns of certain members who come to have an identity as either a Republican or Democratic member.

Three of these members serve exclusively on the board's Youth Correction Division. That leaves five members whose function it is to rule on every single parole consideration of every single adult prisoner under federal jurisdiction. The board was called upon to make 19,815 separate decisions in 1968. Since decisions require concurrence of two, three, or more, one can see why this amounted to over 40,000 individual "member-judgments."

I could not conceive that five men, regardless of how prodigious their talents, could handle adequately or give fair hearings to so large a number of cases, particularly since much of their time is spent in traveling. I consulted with some members of the parole system, both at the level of the prison and in Washington, to obtain some picture of how the system actually functions.

A man becomes eligible for parole, for the most part, when a third of his sentence is up. There are variations on this, such as special allowances for life sentences and special rulings for the various indeterminate sentences. He is visited by a member of the Parole Board or an examiner appointed by them. (There are two examiners.) I asked whether any brief was presented, knowing how difficult and time-consuming it is to appraise and evaluate a man accurately from a record. No brief is drawn. They simply draw on the prisoner's file as presented, with the major attention going to the pre-sentence report and the classification report.

This was disturbing since I had not been terribly impressed by the accuracy of either of these reports (although the pre-sentence reports were far more detailed, far more carefully constructed documents). In the group that I had an opportunity to examine closely, successful students at Howard and Harvard were classified as having borderline intelligence, and one man was listed as a Negro in one form and white in another.

Nor was it reassuring to learn the length of time devoted to the records. I was told that for the most part they could be covered in five minutes. I then asked how long an interview was accorded. I had already heard from various prisoners that the length of time varied, but was usually from two to five minutes. Generally less than ten minutes, I was told. It turned out to be generally considerably less, as evidenced by the length of the recording of each session.

Again, my standard of comparison proved my undoing. I am on the admission committee of the Columbia Psychoanalytic School. When an applicant comes to us for admission he is interviewed by four psychoanalysts independently for one hour each. We then meet as committee, spending about half an hour per applicant, discussing the pros and cons of our various interviews. This is then submitted to the Executive Committee of the Analytic School, where the reports are reconsidered and a decision is made about whether an applicant will be admitted.

These interviews are done by men who have spent up to twelve years in graduate study learning to master interviewing techniques, whose professional lives are devoted to the refinement of the art of interviewing, and *we* make mistakes. Our mistakes merely mean that someone will be admitted to a school who shouldn't be, and someone who should, won't. If the Parole Board member makes a mistake he will effectively double or treble the punishment imposed upon an offender—an awesome responsibility, a frightening power.

The interviewing member may then call Washington, where a colleague has reviewed the records, and if the two of them concur a parole is either granted or denied. If there is a disagreement a third member will be consulted—it is necessary for two members to agree on the decision. When the decision is reached no justification or rationale is made, no argument presented. It is by fiat—and it is final, binding, and arbitrary—subject only to suit by the prisoner, which, for obvious reasons, is rarely undertaken.

If, as I have indicated, there are errors in the general prison records, it is also true that one can sense the time and energy (particularly in terms of the pre-sentence report) that have gone into them. They are serious efforts, limited and varying (like all records) according to the complexities of the situation and the skills of the examiner. But parole records, in general, are of such cursory nature, of such an obvious sloppiness in both form and thinking, that this in great part explains the oppressive air of wariness and defensiveness that hangs over the Parole Board offices.

Since no justifications of parole decisions are ever offered, I inquired as to the general guidelines for granting a parole. The answer offered was that the decisions were made in such a way that they: (1) protect the public; (2) conform to the law; and (3) provide fair treatment for the offenders. These are the official and published guidelines. In other words, that the prisoner is a good risk, that he is legally and technically eligible for parole, and that he has demonstrated by his behavior in confinement that he is worthy or entitled to parole.

At the time I began this research all Jehovah's Witnesses were routinely granted parole at fifteen to seventeen months. This was certainly reasonable and understandable since they adequately satisfied the conditions for parole. What was not understandable was why the other Selective Service violators were routinely denied parole.

The facts were conceded to be true. It was stated that it was the "policy of the board" to grant parole only to JWs because they alone were considered to be "true" COs. The others were given no parole, although recently it had become board policy to consider them for parole at twenty-two months. However, if they were "troublemakers" they still would not be considered.

I asked what statutory justification would be used to deny parole to the "well-behaved" war resister. The answer, which was immediately available, was contained in the section of the statute that stated parole may be granted if, "In the opinion of the board such release is not incompatible with the welfare of society." The implications were that national security required a severe enough punishment to guarantee a deterrent effect, that to allow people to defy the draft law and then release them in too short a time would not satisfy that purpose. National security required punishment severe enough to force people into the Army.

I was disturbed by this distinction between true COs and war resisters, because while generalizations about JWs could certainly be made, it had been in my experience almost impossible to generalize about the war resisters. By lumping them together you were denying them their right to be considered as individuals.

I was also disturbed, as I have been disturbed throughout this study, by the readiness to classify people by religious sect and, worse, to establish priorities according to sect. Certainly the same consideration that is given the JWs is not given the Muslims. This seems patently a decision based on race or religious preference. Stripping off all rhetoric and rationalization, you have two men, both first offenders, both violators of the same law, both justifying such violation, both having the same sentence, both behaving themselves in prison, and by policy and practice allowing one to be out on parole because he is a member of the Jehovah's Witnesses and denying that privilege to the other because he is not.

I then inquired of the parole office how they legally justified distinguishing among groups of prisoners on the basis of religious affiliation. Since being a JW seemed the only means for any of the group of offenders to satisfy their criteria for parole, were they not concerned about violation of constitutional rights? I was informed that they "didn't have to parole anybody" and was to hear for the first time the startling statement that parole is a "privilege not a right."

I asked how much weight the judge's intention in sentencing had with the Parole Board. I was told it had a great deal—except in the cases of the war resisters. This, again, is a clear-cut example of discrimination against the group, even to the point of defying the intentions of the sentencing judge. This is particularly crucial to those who are sentenced under the Youth Corrections Act where, it has been admitted, real and serious injustices are experienced.

As so often happens, exceptions to the law that are established to protect youth end by harming them. The long indeterminate sentence to six years, which is applied so frequently under the Youth Corrections Act, is intended specifically to allow for a short term of imprisonment and a long term of probation. It also grants the privilege of expunging the imprisonment from the record of the individual. This way the young offender may be spared the potential destructiveness of a long imprisonment but still be maintained on supervised good behavior, under threat of return to prison, for a long period. Hopefully he will enter adulthood with a sounder adjustment to his environment (by being maintained in it) and with no stigma from his youthful indiscretion.

It has generally operated in this way, and many judges, seeing no reason to assume the general procedure would be changed, have assigned these indeterminate sentences with recommendation for early parole consideration, assuring the boys that with proper behavior they would be home within a year. But the Parole Board is not bound by the intentions of the judges, and these young men end up serving *more* time in jail than if they have been given a conventional sentence, and on release they still face a long probation.

During my final stay in Washington in relation to this research I requested of the Parole Board profiles of its current members. I was interested in what background was considered to make a person eligible for such great responsibility. There was some reluctance to release these to me. This was surprising in light of the fact that the appointments are a matter of public record and would be attainable from the files of any major newspaper—or on request to my congressman. Knowing Washington by now, I indicated that the latter would be my course, and shortly after I was invited to meet with Mr. George J. Reed, the new (May 1969) director of the Parole Board.

While the meeting was presented as a condition (for obtaining the information) rather than an opportunity, I chose to view it as the latter. I was pleased to be able to raise with the chairman many of the questions about parole and parole procedure that had arisen. My hour with him was the most informative I had spent in the entire period of this research. It did nothing to assuage my mounting doubts about the operation of this vital bureau.

He started by informing me that I had been granted no authority to study or discuss "parole matters" in my research. I respectfully pointed out that while the research was now completed, well in advance of commencing the research, I had requested permission of the Bureau of Prisons, according to protocol, to do precisely that which I had done—visit prisons, interview prisoners, inspect prison files, and so on, and that "parole matters" would inevitably arise in the course of any research involving prisoners. I did not point out that while his power is great it is not unlimited, and that to my knowledge we live in a country where anyone is free to discuss any matters—within clearly defined limits set by law.

After a considerable length of time I was able to introduce more substantive matters. My first question, as might be anticipated, was directed toward board policy in relation to Selective Service violators. He informed me that there is no such thing as board policy on any matter, that members function as individuals. I was astounded. I pointed out that any statistical breakdown would indicate that JWs were granted paroles while others were not—independent of what individual members heard the case. I also pointed out that one could fix the time at which war resisters began to be given parole (albeit after a longer period of internment). He readily agreed to the facts but insisted it was not a matter of policy.

I then pointed out the constant reference in records and conversation to the "policy of the board"; referred him to direct quotations—for example, "X is making a good community adjustment. However, whether he is paroled should be in keeping with the Board's current policy governing this type of offense"; referred him to the *Rules of the United States Board of Parole,* which discussed methods of settling "general questions of policy"; and finally I mentioned to him a letter from a federal judge asking for clarification of the "discriminatory policy" related to Selective Service violators.

His answer to the last was totally beside the point but nonetheless revealing of another pertinent attitude. He informed me that judges lose all jurisdiction over cases after 120 days. He went on to remind me that none of this had any relevance anyhow, since it had all been tested adequately in the courts, and that in the words of those courts parole was a matter of "grace rather than right."

I had, of course, been presented with this argument before, and I replied that, while no expert, I did know that no court ruling was an absolute end point and that in this era I would suspect that the law demands of government at least the same equity in the distribution of gifts as it does in rights. I said, "It is certainly not my right to demand of my village government that it supply me with a swimming pool. On the other hand, if my village were to build a swimming pool and present it as a gift to the Presbyterians of my community, I do not think the courts would approve. The law of the land will not allow gifts to a favored group of the population. At least I hope it won't."

He then went on to say that he felt fairness was guaranteed in parole hearings by the multidisciplinary background of the board. He gave an example from some years back (he had served two terms under Republican appointment, which was not renewed under a Democratic President). He stated that one Parole Board member was convinced that no women were essentially harmed by rape, while a woman member (not the current one) naturally felt quite different, thus giving balance.

It seemed to me that rather than guaranteeing equity, this assured a gratuitous decision, since the poor rapist who was faced with the woman member obviously didn't have the chance that he would have had with the man. Mr. Reed pointed out to me that I was mistaken, because, after all, every parole decision is made by a three out of five majority.

I found that surprising, I indicated, because I never had seen more than two signatures.

Oh yes, that was quite true at this time, but it was, he assured me, a purely temporary arrangement.

The temporary arrangement has gone on for the past three years. While I did not discuss it with him, the statement that it is now reduced to two out of three is also a misrepresentation. That suggests consideration by three people who then vote, decision being by a majority. What actually happens is that one man decides; he then submits his decision to a second member. If that member concurs, it ends right there. If he does not, a third tie-breaking vote is sought. This is an entirely different procedure. Also the word "hearing" tends to suggest group discussion. Whether this is to be the case in the future, or was in the past, it rarely is so now.

During the course of the interview I had occasion to ask about certain simple statistical data that were unavailable, for instance, the degree of concurrence on decision to parole. In the course of this discussion it emerged that the Parole Board does not have a research department. Their budget does not allow for it. Their quarters are quite posh, by Bureau of Prison standards, and while I was there they were installing new carpeting, draperies, covered valances, and so on—but this is evidently an indication of priority rather than affluence.

It would seem to me that with power so great, with objectivity so limited, with method so subjective, with review so unavailable, with responsibility so awesome, were I a member of the Parole Board I would demand for my own peace of mind constant check on my methods and results.

I was then given by Mr. Reed a series of mimeographed profiles on the current members of the board. I was not impressed with the multidisciplinary background. They seemed to come heavily from the correctional field. The profiles were obviously made out by the individuals themselves because they varied greatly in the amount of information offered. Because we live in an age where issues of color dare not be ignored, where the volatility of our society and the sensitivity of our people demand its constant consideration, I asked Mr. Reed how many members of the Parole Board were black. He indicated that traditionally there always has been one Negro member of the Parole Board, but that the Negro member's term of office had expired; and he personally had decided not to recommend reappointment (why, he did not say); and in his review of the men under consideration he had not been able to find a Negro qualified for the opening. "Reluctantly" he had to recommend a white man, and a white man was appointed. I am not sure at all what requirements a man must have for a job such as this. *My* first requirement would be that he be black. And I would start there. And I would end there. And since the board is "multidisciplinary" I would scour the fields of literature, sociology, medicine, law, psychology, anthropology, history, economics, classics, finance, social work, teaching, and, yes, penology, and I would find a qualified black man, somewhere in this vast land.

I therefore agreed with Mr. Reed that it was "unfortunate" that we now had a Parole Board which does not have one black member.

If the American Bar Association finds the power of sentencing without review worthy of research and investigation, I humbly submit that the operations of the Parole Board seem equally worthy of such review.

WHY PRISON

When we talk about the length of sentence and the right to parole, we are talking about the equity in the distribution of the punishment. We are not talking about the nature of the punishment. In this country, imprisonment for a lesser or greater degree of time is, by and large, the exclusive punishment for criminal offense. We so accept the concept of imprisonment as punishment that we never question the nature of it.

It is a relatively new concept. Up until three hundred years ago imprisonment was not so considered: it was merely a method of detaining a man until his punishment was determined. It was a means, not an end. Punishment involved flogging, mutilation, banishment, execution. Our Constitution, being a humanistic document, forbids cruel and unusual punishment. As I have questioned earlier, what is cruel and what is unusual? More important, it is imperative to realize that we redefine cruel when we make it usual; that the commonplace will not be viewed or experienced as cruel; that almost anything that becomes institutionalized will not offend us. The kind of scarification that certain primitive tribes did routinely for cosmetic purposes would sicken and disgust our general population. On the other hand, we routinely do circumcisions on infants for no clear-cut medical reasons, which might equally offend and disgust members of those primitive tribes.

Driving home one day from one of the prisons, deeply touched by the experiences recounted by some of the war resisters, I began to think of their being locked away for these years of their youth. Being at an age where youth is a historic fact rather than a current reality, I am aware of both its value and the shortness of time we are privileged to possess it. I began to compare imprisonment with some of the former punishments, and I wondered if I would give up a year of my youth, indeed a year of my life now, as an alternative to giving up one finger. Without a moment's hesitation I decided that I would not.

I then played the string out—how many fingers *versus* how many years. Two fingers? Certainly! Three fingers? I began to have doubts—could I spread them over two hands? Could I retain the opposing action of thumb and index finger? Ultimately I reached the decision that personally I would go so far as to give up an entire hand rather than five years of my youth. I did not extend it any further.

I was haunted by this idea. The more I thought of it, the more monstrous it seemed that anyone should have the power to deprive another human being of five years of life—merely as punishment. By my standards, what we were doing to these boys was more cruel than chopping off a hand. (We are more than ready to do that in surgery to save a few years of life.) And I was disturbed that I had never seen it that way before. I recognized that, again, it was part of the problem of institutionalization of a word until it no longer has emotional meaning.

When I arrived home some hours later, still preoccupied by this, I mentioned my finger-year comparisons to my wife and two daughters. They were horrified and suggested that the analogy was a disgusting one that could only have been conceived by a warped mind. I countered by suggesting that their disgust with lost fingers, and acceptance of lost years, were evidence of brain-washed minds, and I offered them a second analogy. I described a civilization in which conflict over religion, territory, principle, was resolved by each side's selecting fifty young girls, making sure they had only the prettiest and fittest, and then throwing the hundred into a crocodile pit. The victor in the conflict would be decided by whose girl would be the last to be destroyed. I called this process of arbitration "gonk" and asked my daughters what they thought of it. They thought that "gonk" was further evidence of Father's perversity.

"You don't like that method of arbitration," I said. "Then let me offer you an alternative. Instead of fifty young girls, let's take five hundred thousand young men, making sure that only the healthy and strong are included. Let us line them up and equip them with adequate instruments of destruction. That side which most effectively destroys the youth of the other side will be declared the winner." We call that method of arbitration "war," and yet even while we oppose it, and even for those who most violently oppose it, the word has become a part of our daily lives and in so becoming has ceased to be an offense to our gut. It has become institutionalized.

Imprisonment is another institutionalized word.